In this collection of all-new, darkly imaginative tales, terror takes on many new faces. . . .

From the Borderlands

"Stationary Bike"
by Stephen King

You know how all those Stephen King stories end, don't you? Think again . . .

"Father Bob and Bobby"
by Whitley Strieber

A decaying city neighborhood . . . a crumbling church . . . a dark night . . . and an aging priest who is about to encounter a most unholy sacrament . . .

"The Thing Too Hideous to Describe . . ."
by David J. Schow

It's tired; It's cranky; It's not as young as it used to be. In fact, every night has become a struggle to maintain Its *joie de mourir* and find anew Its reason for killing . . .

"Story Time with the Bluefield Strangler"
by John Farris

A six-year-old girl learns that when darkness falls sometimes make-believe monsters are even scarier than real ones . . .

FROM THE BORDERLANDS

STORIES OF TERROR AND MADNESS

EDITED BY
ELIZABETH E. MONTELEONE AND
THOMAS F. MONTELEONE

WARNER BOOKS

NEW YORK   BOSTON

Compilation Copyright © 2003 by Elizabeth E. & Thomas F. Monteleone. All rights reserved. No part of this book may be reproduced in any form or by any electronic or mechanical means, including information storage and retrieval systems, without permission in writing from the publisher, except by a reviewer who may quote brief passages in a review.

Published in arrangement with Borderlands Press

Previously published as *Borderlands 5*

General introduction, acknowledgments and author/story introductions copyright © 2003 by Elizabeth E. & Thomas F. Monteleone.
"Rami Temporalis" copyright © 2003 by Gary A. Braunbeck
"All Hands" copyright © 2003 by John R. Platt
"Faith Will Make You Free" copyright © 2003 by Holly Newstein
"N0072-JK1" copyright © 2003 by Adam Corbin Fusco
"Time For Me" copyright © 2003 by Barry Hoffman
"The Growth of Alan Ashley" copyright © 2003 by Bill Gauthier
"The Goat" copyright © 2003 by Whitt Pond
"Prisoner 392" copyright © 2003 by Jon F. Merz
"The Food Processor" copyright © 2003 by Michael Canfield
"Story Time with the Bluefield Strangler" copyright © 2003 by John Farris
"Answering the Call" copyright © 2003 by Brian Freeman

Copyright credits continued on page 429

Printed in the United States of America

First Paperback Printing: September 2004

10 9 8 7 6 5 4 3 2 1

This one is for
OLIVIA,
our daughter,
who just happens to be
the most intelligent,
the most beautiful,
the most athletic,
and most all-around talented
girl we've ever known.

ACKNOWLEDGMENTS

A project of this magnitude cannot happen without the belief, support, patience, and plain old American hard work of many people. In that spirit, then, we would like to shine an appreciative light on those who have helped to make this book not only a reality, but the success we believe it is.

And so, in no particular order: James A. Mellow, Uncle Frank, Matt Schwartz, Keith Schaffner, Matt Bialer, Rich Chizmar, Michael Wilby, Jaime Levine, Kathy Ptacek, Kelly Laymon, Judy Rohrig, Jann Eckler, Tamara Keurejian, and finally, the more than six hundred determined and talented writers who submitted their stories to us, and who reinforced our belief this anthology is indeed a good place in which to be published.

CONTENTS

Introduction

TIME DOESN'T FLY ... IT RED-SHIFTS.

Hard to believe it, but the time between the publication of *From the Borderlands* and the previous volume is *nine years*.

Lots of changes in just about *everything* during that span. To name but a few: bricks finally weigh more than cell phones; cigarettes cost as much as a six-pack; dot.commers no longer name football stadiums; and eighty-year-old grandmas get checked for shoe-bombs when they want to fly to Cedar Rapids.

But there is at least one constant: the stories you find in a *Borderlands* anthology will be the best imaginative fiction being written.

Period.

We say that with confidence because we've worked hard to find the absolute best dark fantasy, suspense, and even a few real horror stories. For those of you who've never read earlier volumes of this series, we should hip you to some of the "ground rules": (1) *Borderlands* is a non-themed anthology, which means writers are free to explore any topic they choose; however (2) we are usually not very excited to see stories which are basically re-treads of familiar genre symbols, staples, and icons. (We're not looking for stories about vampires or ghosts or serial killers or witches or were-creatures or anything else you've already read somewhere else.) (3) This anthology is not restricted or "invitation-only," which means you'll always find plenty of *new* writers right alongside some of the most familiar and popular "names" in the business.

Okay, onward: we'd been planning to get back to the editing business for a while now, and when we announced we were reading for *From the Borderlands,* we didn't realize what that would *really* mean.

For one thing, we'd been told there was a whole new generation of readers out there who'd been chewing through *Goosebumps* when last we published an anthology, and we'd be as foreign and unknown to them as The Alan Parsons Project. We honestly wondered what kind of response we'd get to our initial calls for submissions.

What kind indeed . . .

The last time we were reading, we may have received a handful of stories in digital format (i.e. on a floppy disk), but *none* by e-mail. However, earlier this year, within a week of our first announcement, we received more than *two hundred* stories to the borderlandspress.com e-mail-box. Now, that was impressive on one level, but disappointing on another—one, we were surprised how many people wanted to be part of this project, but two, we were fairly certain all those stories hadn't been written especially for *Borderlands* in just a week's time.

We were right.

A large majority of the earliest stories we received

proved to be inferior work that had been making the rounds, or worse, had been retired to a sub-directory for stories-rejected-by-just-about-everybody. Many of these submissions were from writers who most likely had never read any previous *Borderlands* anthologies, or hadn't bothered to read the guidelines closely enough to discern what we were *not* looking for. It's mind-numbing to see so many writers stuck in such a creative rut that they can think of nothing more challenging than *another* serial killer, or (even worse) a low-life who goes around hurting people just so the writer can describe all the victims' gaping wounds.

We also received far too many stories that were obvious rejects from other "theme" anthologies looking for material around the same time as we. Hence the preponderance of stories where cockroaches made odd and sometimes totally nonsensical appearances. But our personal favorites were all the stories featuring that ethereal libation, absinthe—these tales usually followed a relentless plot that went something like this: *drank some absinthe, had some sex, killed somebody.* Can you say stunted imagination? We thought you could.

But as the weeks became months, and we worked our way through all the hastily-sent "trunk" stories, we began to see better fiction. Most of it arrived by e-mail, with a very small percentage through regular mail, and practically *no one* requiring the entire manuscript be returned. It seemed like we would sit down every evening to read ten or twelve stories, and every morning, there would be twenty *new* ones taking their place. It was incredible. We believed we were keeping up by reading submissions *every day,* but in reality, we began to get buried.

When we were approaching seven hundred submissions, we still had more than two hundred to read, and we had maybe room for five more stories. We had to push up the submission deadline . . . or we would *never* finish close to our original schedule. The plain fact was we'd been overwhelmed by the response. We were reading *nothing* in our lives other than stories for *From the Borderlands,* and we were holding up as well as a thatched roof in a monsoon.

The major reason this became an increasingly more challenging problem? We'd made a commitment to give every submission a fair reading, and make an attempt to provide honest criticism and real reasons why we were rejecting or accepting the story. In case you didn't realize it, that takes a lot more time than just saying: "sorry, not quite right for us." (Actually, we *did* say that in a very small percentage of the cases—only when a story was so completely not right, and we had *nothing* constructive to say.) Most of the time, we provided our writers with personalized responses, which is more feedback than they usually get.

Most writers seemed to recognize and appreciate our effort; we received lots of e-mails telling us our rejection notes were some of the most informative and helpful they'd ever received. Of course, we also got some snide responses (usually from veteran writers who assumed all they needed to do was send us *anything* and we'd accept it [we didn't]), expressing their disagreement with our editorial opinion. Hey, that's why America's a great country . . .

And while we're doing such a bang-up job of complimenting ourselves, we should also tell you we made it a policy to not read when we were too tired or too distracted; every story deserved our best because we believed every writer had sent us *their* best. The quality of the writing was, in general, very high. It was the content which usually sank them. We had no idea how many writers would insist on sending us ghost stories . . . so many we could have easily gathered together a great anthology of nothing but apparitional tales. Maybe we will someday (no, just kidding about that one).

That's about it. Its almost time for the enclosed stories to start speaking for themselves. The essence of all this is pretty simple: the stories in this volume are stories *we* liked—for whatever reason. We'd like to think we've picked up and ran with the rallying cry of earlier volumes that *Borderlands* is pushing the boundaries of imaginative fiction.

It's glad to be back. We hope you feel the same way.

—*Elizabeth Monteleone*
—*Tom Monteleone*
 Grantham, New Hampshire
 October 31, 2003

Rami Temporalis

GARY A. BRAUNBECK

During the Nineties, Gary A. Braunbeck had quietly become one of the field's finest writers. His previous appearance in the Borderlands *series, "Union Dues," was a showcase for his talent—especially his ability to capture the range of human emotions so perfectly. In the story which follows, he offers us a gentle tale of wonder and originality.*

"When I face myself I'm surprised to see
That the man I knew don't look nothing like me . . ."

—*John Nitzinger,* "Motherlode"

It started with the woman in the restaurant and her hysterectomy story.

I was alone in my favorite booth at the Sparta, enjoying the last of my cheeseburger, when I happened to glance up.

". . . and like I said before, she never listens to me—hell, she never listens to *anyone* when they try to tell her something for her own good. She's been that way all her life and look what it's got her."

She was at a booth toward the back of the restaurant, while mine was up front on the same side; I sat facing the rear, she facing the front, so she was looking right at me and there was no place to hide.

"I kept telling her, 'Sandy, your frame is too small to chance having another baby. You almost didn't squeeze out little Tyler the first time, there's no way you can have another one.' I think she knew I was right but she wasn't about to have an abortion, not with her Ronnie being the way he is—you know, all manly and pro-life: 'No wife of mine is going to kill our baby. I'll not have people gossiping about me like that.'"

Her tone suggested that the two of us had just resumed a previously-interrupted conversation. For a moment I thought she might be talking to someone seated across from her in the booth, a short person, or even a child—though why anyone would want to speak to a child about abortion was beyond me. I then thought she might be wearing one of those new cell phones, the type which you hang off your ear and have a small fiber-optic microphone, but, no: she was looking at and talking to me.

"I know she thinks I'm a nib-shit, but that girl has no idea how *terrible* he treats her. Or maybe she does and figures she ain't gonna find a better man so she puts up with it for the kids." She was on the verge of tears. "I mean, Ronnie *forced* her to have that second baby, even though he knew there was a chance it was going to . . .

y'know, *mess up* her insides. She almost *died.* They had to do an emergency Caesarean, and by then she was so tore up there wasn't no choice but to do a hysterectomy. She's only twenty-three and now she'll never be able to have more children—and Sandy *loves* children. She spoils that Tyler rotten, and she'll do the same for little Katherine. But she . . ." The woman leaned forward; secret time. I found myself leaning toward her, as well.

". . . she *bleeds* a lot sometimes," she whispered. "Not her period—she don't have those no more. It's on account of her still being raw in there from everything. And *sex*— forget that. She don't even want to *look* at Ronnie, let alone share her bed and body with him. But that doesn't stop him, no sir. If *he* wants it, he takes it, and who cares if she's doubled over with cramps and bleeding for two days after. She ain't a wife to him, she's just a possession, so to him it ain't rape. Them kids don't hardly exist for him at home—oh, if there's an office party or picnic or something like that, he's Robert Young on *Father Knows Best,* but the rest of the time . . ." She shook her head. "You know, I seen him just today. Walking into the Natoma restaurant with a woman from his office. Had his hand on her ass. 'Working late on the new contract proposals' my ass! And after all he's done to her."

"He . . ." I couldn't believe I was asking this. ". . . *forces* her to . . . ?"

"All the time."

"My God." The whole of Sandy's life suddenly played out in my mind and I felt soul-sick and ineffectual as I witnessed it; Sandy: under- to uneducated (as so many young women in this city are), no dreams left, working nine hours a day in some bakery or laundry or grocery store, then coming home to a husband who didn't much like her and children who—though she might love them and spoil them rotten now—would grow up following Daddy's example to not much respect her, and before twenty-five she'd be wearing a scarf around her head to cover the prematurely gray hair, read only the saddest stories in the newspaper, and spend any free time she might have watching prime-time soap operas and getting twelve pounds heavier with each passing year. I think I'd've known her on-sight, no introductions necessary.

"That poor girl," I said.

"Sometimes," the woman said, "I got half a nerve to just go over there with my truck and tell her to pack herself and the kids up and come stay with me. Maybe I should."

"That sounds like a splendid idea."

"*Does* it?" Look at how alive her eyes became when she heard this; goodness me, somebody actually thinks *I* had a splendid idea.

She finished her coffee, took the last bite of her apple pie, then gathered up her purse and resolve and walked up to me, her hand extended. "Thank you for listening to me."

"You're welcome."

Still there were tears trying to sneak up on her. "I just feel so *bad* for her, y'know?"

"But she isn't alone. She has you."

Her grip tightened. "That's the nicest thing anybody's said to me in a while—and you're right. She *does* have me. And I got a truck and she's got the day off."

"Ronnie's working late, I take it?"

"Bastard's *always* working late." She smiled at me, then released my hand, leaned down, and kissed my cheek. "Thanks, mister. I really appreciate you lettin' me go on about this. I hope it wasn't no bother, it's just, well . . . you just got one of those faces, y'know?"

One of those faces.

How many times in my life have I heard that?

I don't avoid contact with strangers. It would do no good. They always come up to me. *Always.* Take any street in this city at a busy hour, fill it with people rushing to or from work or shopping or a doctor's appointment, add the fumes and noises of traffic, make it as hectic and confusing as you wish—I am inevitably the one people will stop and ask for directions, or for the time, or if I know a good restaurant. "You got one of those faces," they'll say. I have had homeless people politely make their way through dozens of other potential benefactors to get to me and ask for change. I always give what I can spare, and they always tell me they knew I'd help them out because—say it with me . . .

This is why I'm thought of as a friendly person. Ask anyone who thinks they know me: "You want to know about Joel? Oh, he's a *great* guy, friendly as they come, the best listener in the world, sincerely."

Truth is, human contact scares the holy hell out of me. I'm always worried that I'll say the wrong thing or misinterpret a gesture or infer an attraction that's not there. So I listen, even though most of the time I want to slink off into the woodwork, especially when the stories are troubling.

But ask anyone what they know about me; you could groom your hair in the reflection from the glassy look. Just once I would like to have been asked something about myself. Just once, that's all.

"I'll bet you hate having your picture taken."

I blinked, looking around. Sandy's friend was long

gone and as far as I could see, I was the only customer on this side of the—

—scratch that. Across the aisle, one booth down and facing the front, sat a gaunt old man who looked so much like the late actor Peter Cushing it was eerie; thinning silver hair formed into a widow's peak on his forehead, aristocratic nose, sharp jaw-line, small but intense bluish-gray eyes under patrician brows; when he swallowed, his too-large Adam's apple threatened to burst through his slender neck and bounce away.

"Yes," he said—more to himself than me, "I don't imagine you enjoy it at all."

I gawked at him for a few more moments—he even *sounded* like Cushing—then said: "I beg your pardon?"

"That was marvelous of you, listening to that woman. You probably made her day."

"It seemed discourteous to do otherwise."

"'Discourteous.' Good word. So tell me: *do* you hate being photographed?"

"I don't know. I never thought much about it." Which was a lie, albeit a harmless one. I *despise* having my picture taken; forget the rudeness of it (*I got the camera so I'm going to get in your face and take this snapshot whether you like it or not*), which I object to on moral grounds—most people never ask, they just click away—it's that every time I see a picture of myself, I don't recognize me. I always look like someone just stuck a gun in my back and told me to act natural.

I continued staring at the man.

"There's a reason I look and sound this way, Joel—by the way, were you named after anyone in particular?"

"Joel McCrea. Mom's favorite movie was *Ride the High Country* and Dad's was *Sullivan's Travels*."

He smiled his approval. "Good films, and a fine actor after which to be named. I'm sorry, I seem to have forgotten—who was *your* favorite actor?"

"Peter Cush—oh, hang on!"

He winked. "I told you there was a reason. By the way, hello. My name's Listen, and it's not that I don't find shouting across the aisle like some sort of simpleton amusing, but wouldn't it be better to continue this in a more civilized manner? So if you would join me here, please, we can get to the heart of the matter."

"The heart of what matter?"

"Your face and why I need you to give it to me."

Everything inside was whispering *Get the hell away from this loony.* Okay, he knew my first name, no real mystery there—I was a regular and all the staff called me by name, he probably heard the waitress talking to me, case closed. How he knew Peter Cushing was my favorite actor was another matter; I have no real friends with whom I would have shared that. And as to how he was an exact double of Cushing . . .

I prefer my weirdness in small, bite-sized doses, preferably in movies or books. I was still rattled by Sandy's story and in no mood for games. *Your face and why I need you to give it to me.* Uh-huh. I suddenly didn't care how he knew what he knew and why he looked as he did; it was time to go.

I grabbed the check and started to make a clean getaway when he said: "Please tell me you're *not* going to make me have to follow you."

I turned. "Is that a threat?"

"Not at all. But I cannot emphasize enough how important it is to you and the health of your loved ones that you sit down and talk to me."

My chest went cold with anger. "What the fuck do you mean, the health of my loved ones?"

He sighed, then pulled a gold pocket watch from his vest and looked at the time. "In about ninety seconds your cell phone is going to beep. The number displayed will be that of a pay phone in the lobby of Cedar Hill Memorial Hospital. It will be your sister, Amy. Look up at the television over the front counter."

I did. It showed a viewing room inside Criss Brothers Funeral Home. Several people were gathered around a small casket. From the back, one of them looked like Dad—why would anyone else wear *that* jacket? He stood there until Mom—who I clearly recognized—came over, put her arm around him, and pulled him away. As they stepped to the right of the casket I saw who was lying inside and it slammed closed every window in my soul.

"She'll be calling," said Listen, "to tell you that your eight-year-old nephew Tommy has just been diagnosed with a malignant brain tumor. What she doesn't know yet is that it's been found too late. Tommy will be dead before his birthday in October."

No one—I mean *no one*—else in the family but me knew about the follow-up EKG Tommy was having done today. For the last couple of years, my nephew—who I love dearly—has been plagued by severe headaches. At first it was thought he was suffering from allergies, but the medications prescribed made him sick and irritable and unhappy. Another doctor's visit revealed he needed adenoid surgery, so that was done and for a little while the headaches stopped. But about two months ago they returned with a vengeance—nausea, crying, wild moodswings, fear. Tommy wants to draw comic books when he grows up. He's a small kid and gets picked on a lot at school because he's not into sports and thinks girls are *cool*. This morning his mother had taken him to the hospital for more tests because the first set came back inconclusive. The thought of him dying broke me in half. Though there's a lot in life I enjoy, I don't genuinely love much in this world but my sister and my nephew.

But for the moment I was staring at a videotape of him lying in his casket while Mom tried to look strong as Amy, shuddering, collapsed into a nearby chair while her lout of an ex-husband stood off to the side flirting with one of her friends from high school.

"The medical expenses will all but bankrupt her and she'll plunge into a black depression that will end with her suicide the following February—and right now there's nothing you can do about it."

Turning away from the suffering on the screen, I balled my hand into a fist and felt a tear slip from my eye. "I don't know how you—"

—and my cell phone went off.

"You can always depend on your sister to be prompt," said Listen, snapping closed his watch and slipping it back into his vest pocket.

I checked the display on the phone: beneath the number—which I did not recognize—were the words: unknown caller.

"You have only to sit down and I can make it all go away," said Listen. "This offer expires in thirty seconds. That isn't my choice, those are the rules."

Panic and desperation are curious things. Enough of either impairs your judgment; a gut full of both turns you into a marionette.

I sat down. My phone stopped beeping. The display was now blank, and when I pressed the recall button, the number listed was that of *The Ally,* Cedar Hill's only newspaper, where I am employed as manager of the paste-up department.

Listen smiled. "It's not showing the pay phone number because your sister never made the call. The tests came back negative. Right now she's sitting in a Ladies' Room stall crying from relief while your nephew is bothering the nurses about how much he wants to see the new Spider-Man movie."

"What rules?"

"Beg pardon?"

"You said 'those are the rules.' What were you—"

"—you might want to look at the television again."

This time it was some sort of convention. A large room filled with throngs of fans. The camera moved in on a table where a particularly long line of them stood with stacks of things to be autographed. There were three people seated at the table and it was the young man in the middle who seemed the focus of attention. As the camera came closer I saw my sister, her hair shorter and grayer, seated to the left of the young man—who I now recognized as an older Tommy. I sat on the other side of him, thinner, my slouch a bit more pronounced, hair and beard (I would finally grow a beard?) filled with streaks of white. A fan came to the table and held out a hardcover book. Tommy, smiling, took it and began talking to the fan, introducing his mother and then myself and launching into some story in which I seemed to play a major role. He then signed the book and had the fan step behind the table so someone could take a picture of the four of us, the fan beaming as he held his autographed copy of . . . of . . .

"I can't make out what's on the cover," I said.

"Well, no. *That* would fall under the category of 'Too Much Information.' Tommy's been diagnosed with migraine headaches and will be put on medication that will keep them more or less under control for the rest of his life." He nodded toward the television. "That scene will take place in sixteen years. Tommy will be a very successful writer/illustrator of graphic novels, and he'll have you to thank for the idea which leads to the creation of his most famous character. So it wouldn't be playing fair to let you see the title of the book, now, would it?"

I looked at Amy's face and saw the peace there, the happiness. "What about—"

"She'll re-marry in about five years. He'll be divorced and a recovering alcoholic who's been on the wagon for ten years. He'll never take another drink. He'll be a laborer, and not nearly as smart as she is, but that won't matter. He'll love her and Tommy with all his heart and be, after your nephew, the best and most decent thing to ever happen in her life. She'll be happy, and she'll be loved. That's all you need to know."

The television blinked and the image was replaced by the sitcom re-run that usually ran at this hour.

"H-how did you . . . do this?"

Listen arched his brows. "Do you really need to know the how and why of it? Isn't it enough that I did it and *will not* reverse things regardless of your decision?"

I nodded. "My face and why you need—"

He waved it away. "Yes, yes, yes, I already know why I'm here, thank you."

"Then how about you explain it to me?"

He folded his hands. "Fine. But first I *must* have a refill on my coffee and a slice of their coconut cream pie. Would you like some, as well? My treat."

"Sure." I remembered the parking meter outside. *The Ally* used to be right across the street from the Sparta, but had moved a year ago to a larger building on the other side of the square, so these days I had to drive over here for dinner after work. The meter would be expiring in a few minutes. I hoped that Listen wouldn't think—

"Not at all, dear boy," he said. "Go feed your quarters into the bloody thing, I understand completely."

"Be right back."

Outside, I was digging into my pocket for change and trying not to shriek with joy. I know how melodramatic that sounds, but it's how I felt. Elated. I knew somehow that all of it was true, that this weird little man had just saved the lives of my sister and nephew.

Like most people, I don't believe in miracles but often depend on them in the same wishful-thinking way that gets most of us through our days: Maybe I'll win the lottery, maybe I'll get that raise, maybe she'll say she will go out with me. But here, now, in this most unlikely of places, I had been witness to something genuinely miraculous and wanted to sing and dance until the Twinkie Mobile came to haul me off.

"I didn't mean to do it!"

He was in his early thirties, dressed in clean khaki pants and work boots, with a denim shirt and baseball cap. His face sported a vague five-o'-clock shadow that told you he *had,* indeed, shaved that morning. His blond hair was neatly combed and there was nothing about him to suggest that he was either homeless or insane.

Except his eyes. To look in them as he spoke you would have thought he'd swallowed a leathery chunk of pain.

There were perhaps half-a-dozen other people out there, but I knew at once he would head toward me.

"I swear to God I didn't want to do it, *I swear to God!*" His gaze locked on me. I found my change, pulled it with a shaking hand from my pocket, and immediately dropped most of it on the sidewalk.

"I didn't mean to hurt her," he said, stopping right in front of me and jamming his hands deep into his pockets. "They *made* me do it! They *always make me do it!* I don't want to. She's so *little*. And she *loves* all of us. She looks at me with those sweet eyes so full of trust and then I have to . . . to—I swear to God I don't want to do it, they *make* me, you understand? *They make me do it!*"

Every inch of his body trembled with helpless rage. I stepped behind the meter in case he exploded and got his crazy all over the street.

Tears formed in his eyes. "I don't want to do it anymore." His voice broke on the last three words.

All I could think to say was: "How bad is she hurt now?"

"Not too bad this time. She was doing pretty well when I left. They won't do anything to her, they never do. They—"

"—make you do it for them."

"Yes."

I wanted to run away but I couldn't. Listen might take offense and that was the last thing I wanted.

"Can you take her places?" I asked.

He stopped trembling and looked in my eyes. "Uh-*huh*. I'm the only one who ever does."

I tilted my head in the direction of City Hall at the end of the street. "Why don't you take her in there and tell the person at the front desk what they make you do? They can put her someplace safe and you'll never have to hurt her again."

He dragged an arm across his teary eyes, then inhaled thickly. "*Really?*"

"I'm almost certain, yes."

He looked toward City Hall and took something from his pocket; a small, cheap, plastic toy modeled after a Saturday morning cartoon character. "I got this for her to say I'm sorry. I always get her something after . . . after, and she always . . . *thanks* me. Do you think she'll like it?"

"I'm sure she'll love it."

"They sell these over at the drug store. I could—*hey*, I could maybe tell them I'm taking her out to buy *another* one, then we could go over there."

"That sounds good. Make sure you use the dark brown metal door on the 5th Street side." That would take them down a short set of stairs into the police station.

"I'll remember. You *bet* I will." And he walked away, gripping the toy as if it were a holy talisman. "*Swear to God* I never meant to hurt her. They made me. They *always* make me. Oh, *God* . . ."

I watched until he disappeared around the corner. I bent down to collect my spilled change and my car's horn sounded from behind. After I'd managed to squeeze back into my skin, I turned, still shaking, to see Listen sitting in the passenger seat. He grinned at me and waved.

"I'd forgotten they were out of the coconut cream pie," he said, leaning out the open window. "I took care of the bill. Let's go for a ride."

I gathered up what change I could find and climbed in but didn't start the car.

"Another story, I take it?"

I exhaled. "Jesus, that guy was . . . was—"

"—at the end of his rope, just so you know. I'd share the specifics of his home situation, but it would only make you sad and sick."

"Do you know what's going to happen?"

"Yes. I won't say he and the little girl will both be fine, because the possibility of *that* outcome died a long while ago. But he'll get her out of there tonight and take her through the brown metal door and, eventually, things will be better for both of them. Not great—never great—but *better.* Now believe it or not, I am on something of a schedule, so if you would please start the car and drive out to Moundbuilders Park . . ."

"Why there?"

He huffed and made a strangling gesture with his hands. "Arrrgh!—and when was the last time you heard anyone actually *say* that? Look, do I strike you as being impulsive? No? Do you think I go about willy-nilly? Of course not. Has any of this seemed *unplanned?*"

I started the car and drove away.

"Have you ever seen any paintings or drawings of Jesus?" he asked.

"Of course."

"Can you remember anything specific about them?"

I shrugged. "Beard. Hair. Flowing robes. Eyes."

"But the faces have always been different somehow, haven't they? The hair longer or shorter, the beard fuller, the cheekbones higher or lower, fuller or more drawn, even the hue of the skin has been different—yet somehow you always recognize the face."

"Okay . . . ?"

"Ever wonder how many different versions of that face exist in statues or paintings or sketches?"

"Thousands, I would think."

"Seventy-two, actually. Followers of the Prophet Abdu'l-Bahá believe that everything in nature has 'two and seventy names.' That's almost right. The thing that has always annoyed me about the various religions is that, with rare exceptions, their beliefs are too compartmentalized. *This* is what we believe in, period. I'll tell you a secret: they're all wrong—individually. The problem is none of them can see Belief holistically. If they were all to 'gather at the river,' so to speak, and compare notes, you'd be surprised how quickly people would stop setting off bombs and flying airplanes into skyscrapers. But I digress.

"Everything in nature *does* have seventy-two names. But certain of these things also have seventy-two forms. Like the face of Jesus, for example."

"You're telling me that Christ has been portrayed as having seventy-two faces?"

"No, whiz-kid, I'm telling you that Christ *had* seventy-two faces. Every picture you see is nothing more than a variation on one of them. Faces change over the course of a lifetime, dear boy. All in all, each of us wears seventy-one."

"I thought you just said—"

"—I *know* what I said, I recognized my voice. There is one face we possess that is never worn—at least, not in the sense that the world can see it. The best way I can explain it is to say that it's the face you had before your grandparents were born. *That* is the face I need from you. It exists *here*—" He cupped one of his hands and covered his face from forehead to upper lip. "—in the *Rami Temporalis*."

"In the muscles around the eyes?"

"No, *those* are part of the *Rami Zygomatici,* an area controlled by the *Temporalis,* which is a much larger and influential group in the temporo-facial division of—oh, for goodness' sake! Are you in the *mood* for an anatomy lesson? Are you worried that I'm going to pull out a scalpel and cut away? I'm not a graduate of the Ed Gein School of Cosmetology, so put that notion out of your head this instant."

I stopped at a red light on 21st Street. "Then I guess I don't understand what you mean at all."

"Perhaps we need to expedite things a bit. Turn left."

The light changed and I made the turn. Even though the entrance to the park should have been a good six miles farther, here we were. I pulled into the parking area and we climbed out.

"I have some luggage in your trunk," said Listen. "If you wouldn't mind . . . ?"

It was a large, bulky square thing that reminded me of a salesman's sample case. I lifted it out of the trunk and damn near snapped my spine. "What's in here, the population of a small Third-World nation?"

"*Is* a tad on the heavy side, isn't it? Sorry." Listen took the case from me and dangled it from one hand as if it weighed no more than a tennis racket. "Do you have a favorite spot here?"

"You already know the answer."

"Of course you're right. I just wanted to see if you'd lie to me again like you did about having your picture taken."

"How did you know that?"

"I do my homework, dear boy. You'll be turning forty-two in July, and since the day of your birth you've been photographed exactly one-hundred-and-nine times, counting your employee identifications and driver's licences. By the time they're your age, the average person has been photographed close to a thousand times, be it individually or as part of a group. But not you. One-hundred-and-nine times, that's it."

"It's over there."

"What is?"

"My favorite spot."

"Ah, yes, the picnic area near the footbridge. Where Penny Duffy kissed you when both of you were in the eighth grade."

I took a seat at the picnic table while Listen walked up to the footbridge and took in the entire park.

"Know anything about 'places of power'?" he said.

"Like Stonehenge?"

"Exactly. Stonehenge is a perfect example. The Irazu volcano in Costa Rica, the Ruins of Copan in Honduras, Cerne Abas Giant, and Bodh Gaya where Buddha achieved enlightenment are a few others. Places where the forces of the Universe are intensely focused and can be harnessed by the faithful."

"Don't go all New-Age on me, okay?"

"Don't make me ill. There are well over a thousand such spots, but believe it or not, only seventy-two are *genuinely* significant. Only seventy-two are filled with such power that you can feel the Earth thrum like some excited child who's filled to bursting with a secret their heart can no longer contain. This park—" He made a sweeping gesture with his arm. "—is one of those seventy-two places. The Indian Burial mounds here are so potent they're scary."

"Is that why we're here?"

"Yes. What needs to be done, needs to be done in a

place of power. Such are the ways of ritual." He joined me at the table. "I have to tell you certain things to aid you in making your decision. Whatever happens, know that Amy's and Tommy's future health and happiness are safe."

He reached down to flip the first of four latches on the case. "The first time a stranger approached you with a story, you were seven years old. It was an elderly woman who was in tears because she'd lost a cameo her late husband had gotten for her overseas during World War One. You sat there on your bike and listened to her and then you said—do you remember this?"

I nodded. "She said she always wore it so she could feel him near. She talked about how he'd loved her home-made strawberry preserves, how she still made a batch every year to give as Christmas presents. This was three weeks before Christmas. I asked her if she'd already made her preserves and she said yes. I knew right away that the cameo's clasp had come loose from the necklace. It had fallen into one of the preserve jars. I didn't tell her that, though."

"No, but you *did* ask the right questions so she could figure it out. Do you know what would have happened if that woman hadn't approached you? She would have taken her own life New Year's Eve. This was a danger-ously depressed gal, Joel, one who'd been the focus of her childrens' worry since the death of her husband. You saved her life that day."

"*No . . .*"

"Oh, yes. And since that day, because you have 'one of those faces,' people keep coming up to you, don't they? Asking for directions, spare change, if you know a good restaurant . . . or to tell you things. *Rami Temporalis,* the face beneath the flesh. That is what draws them to you. They recognize it in you just as you can recognize the face of Jesus or Shakespeare, because regardless of how many variations there might be, the face beneath the flesh—the First Face, the one you had before your grandparents were born—remains unchanged." He opened the case and laid it flat. From one end to the other it was at least four feet wide and three across, perhaps two feet deep.

Something wasn't right. I'd seen this thing closed, had tried to lift it, and though it weighed a ton there was nothing to suggest it would be this wide, long, or deep when opened.

Then he opened it again. Two sections into four, each covered by a square of black material.

"Since your encounter with Cameo Lady, you've lost track of how many people have approached you. But I haven't. Do you know what you are, Joel? You're a safety valve. People see your face and know you'll be sympathetic, so they have no qualms about unloading their woes on you. Do you think it helps them?"

"I have no idea."

"Hm." He removed a small notebook from his vest. Flipping it open to the first page, he began reading aloud. "Over the course of the thirty-four years since Cameo Lady, your listening to others has prevented forty-three rapes, one-hundred-and-twelve suicides, sixty-seven episodes of child abuse, thirty-three divorces, ninety-eight murders, and so many cases of spousal abuse I ran out of room to record them all." He tossed the notebook to me. "Look it over later if you'd like. The point is that all the time you've secretly felt was wasted while you listened has actually made a difference. If I asked how many people were affected by you today, you'd say . . . ?"

"Two. Sandy's friend and the guy outside the Sparta."

He shook his head. "*Five,* Joel." He held up his hand, fingers spread apart. "Five. And one of them—*not* the fellow outside the restaurant, by the way—would have already snapped and be torturing a child nearly to death right now if it weren't for the ninety seconds they spent talking to you." He went back to the case. Four sections became eight. Eight became twelve. Twelve became sixteen, each section attached by hinges to those above, below, and on either side. Already something that should have only taken up maybe six square feet covered at least fifty. Had he been unfolding some massive quilt I wouldn't have felt like the world was disintegrating around me. But this thing was making confetti out of the basic laws of physics. I was standing in the middle of a live-action Escher painting.

Sixteen sections became twenty-four. Twenty-four became thirty-two. Every compartment covered in black, creating a square, bottomless dark pit.

"What are you?" I asked.

Thirty-two sections quickly became forty-eight. "*What,* is it? Not *who.* You catch on fast. Yes, I was being surly. Apologies."

"Are you going to answer the question or should I just wait for a postcard?"

Forty-eight sections were now sixty-four. "Consider me a reconstructive surgeon. My area of expertise is, of course, the face. One in particular." With a final flurry of hands and flipping, the sixty-four sections became seventy-two.

"There," he said, standing back and admiring the massive obsidian square which lay where the ground and grass used to be. "Whew! Sometimes this really wears me out."

"What the hell is it?"

"Funny you should mention Hell. I had to go there in order to get a few of these—and don't think *that* wasn't a bushel of dreadful fun." He pulled aside one of the black compartment covers and the rest, like slats in Venetian blinds, folded back to reveal what lay underneath. "I don't have all of them yet. Counting yours, I still have eleven to go."

In each filled compartment, nestled in a thick bed of dark felt, was a glass mask. Several were full-face, while others were half or three-quarters, but a majority were of isolated sections: the forehead and nose; cheeks connected by the nose bridge; the lips and chin; temples and eyes; the cheeks alone; and one mask, looking like one of those optical illusion silhouettes you see in Psychology textbooks, was of the forehead, nose, lips, and chin only. No cheeks, no temples, no eyes.

"I *thought* this one would interest you," said Listen. "Not that there's anything especially significant about it for you, but something about its shape I knew you'd find fascinating." He pulled on a pair of the whitest gloves I've ever seen and removed the mask. On closer inspection, as the sunlight danced glissandos over its shape, I saw it wasn't made out of glass but some thin, transparent, seemingly organic material that held the shape and acted as a prism on the light.

"Okay. Time you knew the rest. Have a seat.

"Jesus, Shakespeare, Buddha—all of their faces recognizable even though none were ever photographed. Yes, there's an element of the collective unconscious and the archetype involved, but it's a little more complicated than that. People recognize those faces because somewhere in the back of their minds that's what they *want* them to look like. Jesus should look benevolent and spiritual, Shakespeare intelligent and creative, Buddha wise and all-knowing. Everyone has these characteristics in mind when picturing them, and so they are always present in portraits and sculptures and sketches. Consensual reality, to over-simplify it: 'I believe this is what it looks like, so that is how it appears.'

"The same holds true for the face of God, Joel. But just as the portraits of the Blessed Virgin Mary, Da Vinci, Galileo and the rest change from likeness to likeness, just as any human being's face changes over the course of a lifetime or even a day—your happy face, your leave-me-alone face, your confused face, et cetera—the face of God changes. And it's not supposed to. But He doesn't have the advantage of an archetype buried in people's minds. That's where I come in." He squinted at the mask, blew on it, then used his fingertips to brush away some dust or pollen. "I keep forgetting what dirt magnets these things can be. Where was I?

"Ah, yes: the face of God. Have you ever noticed how the horrors of this world seem to never cease coming at you? Hideous mass murders, bombings, wars breaking out in distant countries, rapes, missing children, mutilated children, men walking into fast-food restaurants and opening fire with automatic weapons . . . the inventory is inexhaustible. There's a reason. Simply put, it's because no one has even the *slightest* idea what God's face looks like. Everyone guesses, and though some of those guesses might have a particular element nailed down, *none* of them comes close to the real thing, because there *isn't* one. That's why there's this gaping hole where that face should exist. So, a while ago, God—Who wouldn't know Vanity if it bit Him in the soft parts—consented to allow me to build a face for Him. Being an overly-curious sort, I naturally had to inquire why He'd never made one for Himself. It turns out that He did, but he gave it away. It was the last thing He did on the Sixth Day. He divided His face into seventy-two sections and scattered them into the Universe."

It took a moment for the full impact of this to hit me. "So you're saying that . . . that *I*—?"

"Possess a missing section of God's face, yes."

I looked at the masks displayed before me. "How did you manage to find *any* of these?"

"It would bore you to death."

"Give me the *Reader's Digest* version."

"Prime numbers. Seventy-one—the number of faces you wear in a lifetime—is a prime number, so I took a shot in the dark and began with that. All the digits of your birthday are prime numbers which add up to the same: 7-13-59. Every genuinely significant event that's occurred in your life has happened when your age was a prime, today included—remember, you're still forty-one. It took me several thousand years to figure this out, but once the equation revealed itself, the rest fell into place. I took the true age of the Universe, divided it by seventy-one, divided that sum by seventy-one, and kept repeating the pattern until I was left with a sum of one. I then divided each of the seventy-one individual sums *by* seventy-one and . . . you're way ahead of me, aren't you?

"There was much more to it—factoring in alterations made to the Earthly calendar for solstices and, of course, that pain-in-the-ass Gregorian business—but in the end I pinpointed seventy-one specific years scattered through all of history, and in each of those years, using the prime number formulae, I pinpointed one person whose life not only fit *exactly* the numerical pattern that had been discovered, but who had been blessed—or cursed, depending of course on your point of view—with 'one of those faces.' That's the short version and believe me, it wasn't as easy as it sounds."

"What happens if I say no?"

"I thank you for your time and go away disappointed. I provided for the possibility that at least nine of you would refuse. I can reconstruct most of His face with what I already have, and guess the rest with a large degree of accuracy. But I'm stubborn, Joel. I am so close to having all of the sections. It's been my life's work and I will not be stopped. I won't resort to Inquisition or Gestapo or Khmer Rogue tactics in order to achieve my goal—even though I *could*." He held up the mask. "So—"

"—you need my decision."

"Not until you know what will happen if you say 'yes.'"

"I assume that people will stop singling me out like they've done my entire life."

His eyes narrowed into slits. "Don't let's be flippant, dear boy. Think about everything you've learned today. *Think.*"

The notebook.

I pulled it from my pocket and looked at the pages. "Oh, no . . ."

"Oh, yes. People will no longer single you out. Your face—which you've always thought was so very nondescript—will become just that. Someone meeting you for the first time won't be able to remember what you look like ten minutes after you've parted ways. You'll be just another faceless face in a sea of faceless faces. Now, being the social butterfly that you are, that's probably not going to bother you too much. However—"

I held up the notebook. "The stories."

"Exactly. Since you will have given me your First Face, those same people who won't be singling you out also won't be telling you their stories. And because they won't be doing that, there are going. To be. Consequences. Do you understand?"

A tight, ugly knot was forming between my chest and throat.

"I understand," I whispered. "Is that all?"

"No. There's one last thing, and it might be the deal-breaker."

He told me.

I listened carefully.

Thought about everything I'd learned.

And said yes.

"Lean back." He placed the first mask on my face. It weighed no more than ether. Then, one by one, he removed each successive mask and layered it on top of the one before until I wore all of them.

Have you ever used one of those sinus-headache masks? The ones that have that icy blue glop inside? That's what it felt like. An overpowering wave of cold spread across my face, seeped into my skull, through my brain, and formed a wall of frost in the back of my head. I shuddered and reached up.

Listen grabbed my arm. "Don't touch it. You'll lose your hand."

Soon it became a pleasant liquid numbness. I sighed and maybe even smiled.

"Feels better now, does it?"

". . . yes . . ."

"Then it's done. Keep your eyes closed, dear boy. When you open them again I'll be gone. It's been a genuine pleasure meeting you, Joel. You're a decent man who still has a lot to offer the world. I fervently hope you'll believe that some day. Now take a deep breath and hold it for a few seconds."

I heard something click a moment later. When I exhaled and opened my eyes, Listen was gone. I touched my face. It felt no different.

Back in my car I adjusted the rear-view mirror and caught a glimpse of myself.

Then wept.

———————

I find it difficult to watch the local news or read *The Ally* these days. Every time I come across a story about a murder, a sexual assault, a beating, suicide, or any one of a thousand commonplace horrors we've grown so accustomed to, I wonder if the person who committed the act might have done otherwise if only they could have found some stranger to listen to their story.

It's not that stories like these never appeared in the paper before, it's just I don't recall there having been so *many* of them.

I don't sleep as well as I used to.

———————

I received a postcard from Listen: *Having a here time—wish you were wonderful! (A joke, dear boy.) Nine*

*to go. I think this turned out rather well. You were still
wearing it, by the way.*

On the other side was the photograph he'd taken of me
in the park that day. I am leaning against the picnic table
with my eyes closed. My face seems to glow in the sunlight which whispers a thousand soft colors of thanks. It
is a peaceful face. A beautiful face. A compelling, kind,
compassionate face.

It belongs to a stranger.

———

The question that keeps nagging me is: *Why?*

Why, in order to know the face of God, must the same
horrors caused by our having *not* known it be perpetuated?

You could argue that these horrors on the local news
and in *The Ally* border on the insignificant when com-
pared to the holistic catalogue of human misery. You
would be right, I suppose. Unless you suspect you're the
cause. And, no, filing it under "Sins of Omission" and
going out for sushi doesn't help much.

I miss being asked to pose for pictures, be them of myself alone or in a group. I miss *not* being asked, just having someone click away. But mostly, I miss having
complete strangers come up to me with their stories. I
didn't think I would, but since that day with Listen I've
come to realize just how much that meant to me.

Like I said, I don't sleep so well anymore.

———

The people I know and work with treat me differently.
So do the members of my family. Nothing major, mind

you, but there's a certain caution in their eyes whenever they're around me.

A few nights ago, after Amy, Tommy, and I had gone to a movie (I see the two of them nearly every day now), we went for a pizza. While waiting for it to be delivered to the table, Tommy begged some quarters to play a video game. He smiled when I handed him the money, then exchanged a "You-Gonna-Ask-Him-Or-Not?" look with his mother before sprinting over to the machines.

I stared at my sister. "What was that about?"

She reached across the table and took hold of my hand. "You know that Tommy and I really enjoy spending time with you, right?"

"Okay . . . ?"

"You've been really wonderful ever since the hospital—"

"—Christ, I was just as relieved as you that it was only migraines."

"Oh, the medicine works wonders, Joel, it really does. It makes the pain go away and Tommy says sometimes it makes him feel all 'shiny.' Isn't that the coolest way to describe it?"

"Yes, but that still doesn't tell me what that look was about."

"Tommy's been worried about you, and so have I. Hell, most everyone in the family has."

"*Because* . . . ?"

"You don't look like yourself. I mean, you *look* like yourself, but there's something . . . I don't know . . . something *missing,* I guess. You look so sad these days."

I squeezed her hand and smiled, though I doubt it registered with her.

"I'm doing okay." Which wasn't exactly a lie, but

wasn't exactly the truth, either; it was just safe. I keep hoping that "safe" will help me sleep.

"You sure?"

"As sure as anyone can be, I guess."

"Then why do you look so sad all the time?"

Would you understand? I thought. *If I were to tell you the story, would you even* believe *me, or would hearing it only add to the burdens you already carry? I wish there were some way you could answer me without my having to say anything, but that's a miracle I can only depend on, not believe in, so I will seek safety from my sins of omission in a kind-of silence.*

"I don't know," I said, then shrugged. "Maybe I've just got one of those faces."

All Hands

JOHN R. PLATT

When we read John Platt's submission, it was late in the evening, and we had spent most of it writing rejection slips. We liked "All Hands," but we were tired, and could no longer trust our judgment. So we put it in our possible file, and figured we would get back to it sooner or later. But something weird happened: the next day, and the days that followed, neither one of us could get the story out of our mind. That could mean only one thing—it was a Borderlands *story.*

7 A.M. The alarm clock rings. Jerry reaches up and hits the snooze button with hands that are not his own.

White curtains on the bedroom window do little to block out the morning sun. In the yellow glow, he examines the new day's gift.

Strong hands today. Calloused. Course hairs on the

knuckles. The fingernails are rough and chipped. He flexes the fingers, feels muscles tense and twist. The skin is a sun-burned red, much darker than the flesh on his wrists.

He likes today's hands. They have character.

He changes his mind about going back to sleep, turns the alarm off, and heads into the shower.

———————

The hands can't type, but his arms know what to do. He extends the pointer fingers and hunts and pecks forty words a minute. Not bad. Still, he remembers the day he wore the hands of a speed typist. He finished early that day and left halfway through the afternoon.

Most of the hands don't have any particular skills. They all look and feel and experience the world around them differently, but for the most part, they do what he needs them to do.

Around noontime, Bob Brady comes by Jerry's cubicle. They go to lunch at the local diner. Jerry is surprised to find the hands holding the silverware European style. He's not used to it. It slows him down while he eats. His food grows cold before he finishes.

"Should've ordered a burger," Bob jokes.

That's Bob. The office comedian.

———————

At home in the evening, Jerry takes advantage of the strong hands to finally hang a shelf in the living room. Proud of his work, he also fixes the leaky kitchen sink and ties up a month's worth of newspaper for recycling before calling it a night.

On his way to bed, he stops and washes the hands as

carefully as he can. Best to leave them in good condition. Good stewardship, that's his motto.

Summer turns to fall, and fall to winter. Hands come and hands go. Jerry buys gloves in bulk, never knowing what size he will need to wear on any given day. Some hands don't mind the cold, but others shiver and twitch no matter how thick the gloves. They obviously come from warmer climates.

The hands come in all shapes and sizes, colors and ages. He buys a dozen different brands of moisturizer and lotion, never sure if he's using the right thing. Some days the hands get dry and chapped. Once he experiences what must be an allergic reaction. He feels a pang of guilt about that, but how much can he do?

The aged hands are infrequent, but he has learned to stock a supply of arthritis medicine, just in case.

He feels most awkward with the female hands. He spends those rare days in his cubicle, trying not to be seen.

One morning, he wakes with a child's hands. Tiny, pink, newborn. He holds them up to the light, and can see the bones through the skin. They lack the strength to turn off the alarm clock, so he wraps the power cord around his ankle and yanks it from the wall socket.

He calls out sick that day. It takes him an hour to figure out a way to dial the phone.

At lunch again with Bob, wearing a black man's hands, he mentions that he feels lucky. It could be worse.

He knows a guy who knows a guy whose cousin wakes up with different feet every morning. Jerry can't imagine what it must be like to have to buy shoes for every foot size. The gloves are bad enough.

"Yeah, but think of the poor sap who's got your hands," Bob jokes.

Jerry gets a distant look on his face. He's wondered about his hands so many times. It's why he takes good care of the hands he has. He hopes someone else is doing the same.

———

Spring. On a business trip to San Jose, a man comes up to Jerry in the tiny airport. Older, distinguished, wearing a suit ten times more expensive than Jerry's, the man holds out his hand as he makes his introductions. As they shake, Jerry feels something . . . familiar. A pull beyond even that of the man's charismatic glow.

The older man smiles. "I hope you're taking good care of them." Without looking at the hands on his wrists, Jerry knows that they belong to the man standing in front of him.

His throat goes dry. "I-I'd give them back to you, if I could," he says in a weak voice. He pulls at the wedding band on the right hand. "I can give this to you . . ."

"Don't bother," the gentleman says. He shows off the tanned, athletic hands he's wearing, and smiles again. "I got divorced last year. Keep it!" And with that, he's off, disappearing into the crowd.

Jerry sighs as he heads toward the security line. He was hoping that if he had the older man's hands, the other man would have had his.

He would really like to see them again.

———

He doesn't keep the ring. It would feel too much like theft.

———————

About a month later, Jerry wakes up without benefit of the alarm clock and knows without even opening his eyes that his hands have returned to him. He throws back the covers and holds them up in front of his face. He smiles like a kid at Christmas, flips on the light and turns the hands over and over in front of him.

The nails need trimming, but other than that, they're in pretty good shape. A bit older, a bit wiser, a little black and blue along the side of one thumb. He has a quick memory of the hand getting slammed in a door.

He wonders what other memories they have. None come.

That day, Jerry goes to work but blows off his assignment, sits at his desk and types out poetry all day long. At lunch, he and Bob go to the health club and play a game of basketball. He buys a disposable camera and takes a roll of pictures of his body, back together and whole at long last.

At the office, people who normally shy away from him notice something different, smile at him in the hall. In the break room, he runs into Bonnie from corporate communications, and asks her out for a drink after work. She looks at his hands, then says yes.

That night, he caresses a woman's skin for the first time in years.

He wonders what his hands have seen and felt in the time they've been gone.

They don't tell him any stories, as he loses himself in the moment.

———————

Afterwards, Bonnie dresses in the dark, pecks him on the cheek and disappears.

———————

The next morning, it all begins again.

Faith Will Make You Free

HOLLY NEWSTEIN

Holly Newstein is a new writer who has published her fiction in several anthologies and magazines. Her story which follows is the first thing we'd ever read by her. We were both immediately struck by her ability to tell her tale in a narrative voice that is not only compelling and confident, but also totally believable.

Moze was just another baby-faced kid in the induction center back in '43. Scared and nervous, but willing to go to war for his country. Like all us other guys, he sat on the wooden benches, fidgeting as he waited his turn for his physical. But youth and nerves and patriotism were about all Moze had in common with the rest of us.

He wore a strange black hat, and straying out from under the brim were soft brown curls, shiny as a girl's, ᶜraming his round face. A thin beard covered his chin, and his ankle-length coat of black gabardine might have been fashionable a century or two ago. He kept chewing on his lower lip as he waited, while the rest of us smoked and speculated on the Yankees' prospects this year. I knew the war had changed everything, but until I saw Moze, I didn't realize how much.

There were hundreds of other Jews like me enlisting—Reform or Conservative, ready to go off and fight for our country—for truth, justice and the American Way. We talked of marching triumphantly into Berlin, and of spitting in Der Fuehrer's face. But Moishe Abramowicz was the only Hasidim I ever met in the service. The Hasidim were men of prayer, of peace. They stayed in the synagogues all day and argued abstract points of Talmudic law—when they weren't swaying with joy as they sang the ancient Hebrew prayers. They kept to themselves, in their little sections of Brooklyn—Williamsburg and Crown Heights. They spoke and read Yiddish, a language my parents forbade me to use.

"You're an American. Speak English!" they would say. They never used Yiddish when speaking to us, but later in the kitchen my folks would be arguing about their *meshugganah kinderlach*. Go figure.

We wore *yarmulkes* only on Shabbat and the Holy Days. But once the sun went down on Saturday nights, we went dancing in the jazz clubs in Harlem. We kept kosher at home—but ate cheeseburgers on summer afternoons at Coney Island. We went to Hebrew school and studied Torah, but as soon as it was over, we met at the vacant lot for stickball games. Some of the older guys hung out on the corner at night, smoking Camels and wolf-whistling at girls.

For me, it was all part of being an American Jew from

Rosedale, in the Bronx. You kept your faith, but first and foremost, you were an American. The Hasidim remained proudly unassimilated, Jews who just happened to live in New York, going about their business in their strange black coats and hats just as they had for hundreds of years in hundreds of other lands.

Moze caught my eye and smiled, a nervous, sad smile. I grinned back and extended my hand. He shook it.

Such a simple thing to do, shake hands and be friends. Who knew?

At boot camp I saw Moze come out of the barber's chair clean-shaven, *pais* gone, nothing on his head but inch-high stubble and tears in his eyes. They did allow him to wear his *tallit* under his clothes; sometimes the fringes would show when his shirttail came loose from his pants. Other than that, we soon forgot he was anything more than a regulation GI like the rest of us.

We slept next to each other in the barracks. Moze often cried and moaned in his sleep, but I figured it was home-sickness. A lot of the guys did that.

Our friendship grew closer. We were two people who would never have met in the ordinary world—Jews with nothing in common but Torah. In his eyes, I guess I was a worldly and uneducated heretic. To me, he was exotic. He had studied not only Torah and the Talmud, but also the Kabbalah and mystical Judaic texts.

At night, as we lay in the barracks, we talked and learned about each other. I told him about movies, base-ball and jazz, Rita and Betty, DiMaggio and Sir Duke. He listened to me politely and shook his head at the flashy, Godless *goyishe* world. But then he told me tales from the Zohar, the Book of Radiance. He told me of *Shekinah,* the female side of God, and how we are all part of the mending of the worlds, the drawing forth of the divine. He told me how God created the world from the Hebrew alphabet and the ten *sefirot*—the sacred words. Night after night, he held me spellbound, like a rabbinical Scheherazade.

But there was always about him a sadness, unspoken, yet it clung to him like a fine gray mist.

One night I asked him the question I'd wanted to ask since I'd first seen him.

"Why did you enlist, Moze?"

He looked at me, his brown eyes wide with pain. Then he closed his eyes and sighed. Quickly I added, "You don't have to tell me if you don't want to. It's okay if you don't . . ."

"No, Ben. It's just that I . . . well, it's the dreams."

"Dreams?"

"Yes. Horrible dreams. Every night I see them . . . these prisoners, at least I think they are prisoners. They are being beaten by men with guns. They are crouching naked and defenseless like animals, in their own filth. They are being poisoned and burned. They turn and hold their arms out to me. Burned flesh hanging in black strips from their bodies. Their sightless eyes roll back in their shaven heads. Worst of all are the children . . ." Moze's voice trailed off, and he sighed again, deeply.

"I know that I must go and fight in this war. These dreams have something to do with our people, Ben."

I knew he wasn't talking about our fellow Americans. "Go on," I said.

"I told my father and my rabbi, I must do something about this. They said no. Vengeance is the Lord's, not mine. My father forbade me to fight. But I could not sleep at night. I had to go. Finally, I enlisted—remember, that day I met you," he said. "When I came home and told my family, my father wrapped himself in his *tallit* and began reciting *shiva,* mourning for me as if I were already dead. My mother kissed my eyes, my face, with tears running down her cheeks . . ." His voice shook, and he stopped for a moment. I heard him swallow hard in the darkness. Then, with new strength, he said, "But I am alive, and I will find a way to fight."

I remembered saying farewell to my parents in the swirling hubbub of Penn Station. My father had smiled through his tears as he punched my shoulder.

"Go get 'em, Benjamin," he said. Then he pulled me into a bear hug.

My mother pressed a bag of homemade cookies into my hand.

"Write, son. Write me every day. Promise me . . ."

"All right already, Ma. Geez," but I hugged her, too. And then I had turned and ran onto the train as if I were afraid they would pull me back to them—or that I might let them.

Lying next to Moze in the dark, I wiped my suddenly wet eyes on my arm.

"Do you still have dreams of them? The . . . people?" I asked.

He shuddered and pressed his hands against his eyes.

"Oh yes. Last night I saw a place, a terrible place where men like skeletons lined up, ten and twelve rows deep, behind a barbed wire fence. They were naked, weak and filthy, and covered with lice. Their fingers, more bone than flesh, curled around the rusted wire fence. Their eyes were just empty sockets in their sunken gray faces. Towering flames rose up behind them, licking the night sky. They stood motionless as the flames moved closer and closer. I screamed at them to move, to get away from the fire, but they stared past me into the blackness behind me. Then, as the fire overtook them, they opened their mouths and cried *'Arbeit macht frei'* as one." He blew his breath out in a long sigh.

My mouth was dry. "Do you know what that means?" I whispered. I knew no German words that did not refer to food.

"Work will make you free," he replied with a heavy sigh. "I don't understand it either."

———————

Moze tried hard, but he never seemed to get the hang of being a soldier. The first time he fired his rifle, he dropped it because he was shaking so hard. When we practiced bayonet charges on the straw dummies, he would hesitate. Then Sarge would yell at him, and he would stab half-heartedly and apologize. To a dummy, no less. Grenades, howitzers and ack-ack guns made him shrink into himself like a kicked-around stray mutt. Yet it wasn't like he was scared. For himself he had no fear, and he kept up with the rest of us in every way. It was just that if he was doing something that could kill someone, he could barely bring himself to do it.

"Moze, it's only Krauts and Nips, and you know damn well they'd kill you as soon as look at you," I said.

"Don't you see, Ben? That's the problem. To us they're only Krauts and Nips. To them we're just kikes and Yids."

"And Yankee bastards," I said.

"There is a part of me that wants to kill, but I know that will not help. An eye for an eye, a tooth for a tooth just doesn't make it all right anymore. I think that evil does not stop evil, it just creates more and more. And killing is evil, Ben, no matter who does it."

"But what about the dreams, Moze? You're here because of them. You wanted to come and fight."

"The dreams still come every night, and every morning I wake up crying with the desire to help them. I wish that the Lord would create a Joshua to blow down the walls, or an army of Golem to crush them all."

"A Golem?"

"A *Doppelganger*, a superhuman man. There are stories about them in the mystical texts. You shape them from clay as the Lord did Adam. I have read the secret prayers in the Kabbalah and the *Zohar* that can bring it to life."

"Moze, that's pretty hard to believe—don't you think?"

He looked at me sorrowfully.

"I know it makes no sense, that it's *meshugganah* talk. But I can't help it. I have to believe it, or my soul is forfeit."

After boot camp, we were given a short leave before going overseas. We all went home except for Moze. I told him to come home with me, that my parents wouldn't mind, but he wanted to stay on base. I went home to Rosedale, and my family acted like I was a hero even though all I'd done was survive Basic. It was probably better that Moze didn't come home with me—I was visited by all of my aunts and uncles and cousins, my *bubbe* and *zaydeh,* to see how handsome I looked in my uniform and how brave I was. *Oy vey,* all the questions, the conversations, the noise, the hugs and kisses—and the tears—made me feel funny inside. And they were *my* family.

I was to be posted to the Pacific. So much for my triumphant march on Berlin. Now the enemy was Tojo and his suicide-crazed soldiers and pilots. Moze was shipped off to Europe. In an unusually intelligent move by the Army, Moze was not assigned to the front but worked behind the front lines, in supply and logistics. Me, I was not so lucky.

We wrote back and forth for a while, but as the fighting in Europe got more intense, his letters stopped. I decided it had to be a problem with the mail. I couldn't let myself think about the other reasons why I hadn't heard. But I thought of him often, especially on Shabbat and at night, in the tents and the foxholes, when I longed for a good story to take me away from the heat and the bugs and the fear.

Late in '44, as the Allies tightened the noose around Germany, the existence of the Nazi death camps was finally and dreadfully confirmed. Horrible stories were told of emaciated bodies stacked like so much cordwood by the rows of crematories. Gold extracted from teeth and melted down for jewelry. Hair used to stuff mattresses. Skin tanned to make lampshades. And the gruesome, inhuman experiments on the children. I was sick with anger and revulsion. And I remembered Moze and his dreams.

When I read of how the Soviets liberated Auschwitz and the slogan on the gate—*Arbeit Macht Frei*—I wrote to Moze again, begging him to answer. While I waited for a reply, V-E Day came to Europe. I didn't pay much attention because my war was still on. A couple of weeks later, just before I shipped out to Okinawa, Moze himself arrived in Leyte.

He was changed. He seemed taller and thinner than I remembered, bent as he was under the weight of his pack. There was no more baby-roundness to his face, which was etched with pain. His skin was gray, and his dark eyes were flat and empty. I gasped when I saw how he looked now—and the eyes, the look in them, sent a shudder along my spine. But I was very glad to see my old friend. I was not so glad a few minutes later, when I found out that he was going to the front with me. I was worried about what Moze might do in the face of the Nips' resistance. He already looked shell-shocked, a haunted man.

That night, we talked as we had back in boot camp.

"So, it was all true then? The dreams?"

"Yes, Benjamin. All true and worse. Much worse. Entire *shtetls*, whole villages, just wiped out. Families gone. Worlds gone. My unit was sent to a small camp in Germany, to help feed and clothe the survivors. It was nothing like Auschwitz, but . . . oh, the stench of the place. It got onto your clothes and skin, in your hair and lungs. The smell of shit and puke and death, Ben. The survivors were men and women, more dead than alive. Zombies. They told us that when the SS knew that the Americans were coming, that they would be found, they had all the prisoners dig a big hole in the ground. Then they lined them up with the children, all around the edge, and shot them and threw them into the pit. Then they set the bodies afire before they ran like dogs. The handful still alive were only those who ran and hid, or were too starved and sick to work."

I trembled in the dark, knowing there was worse yet to hear.

"I stood at the edge and looked down into the pit. I looked at the bodies, the burned flesh, the arms and legs twisted and black. Then I ran from the camp, down into the village nearby. I grabbed the first man I saw. A fat German grocer who smelled of sauerkraut. It didn't matter if he was a member of the Nazi party or not. I punched his ugly face. Broke his nose. I screamed 'Didn't you know? Didn't you know that they were murdering people up there? Couldn't you see it? Couldn't you *smell* it?' Ben, the town was less than a mile from the camp. They smelled the ovens and heard the screams even if they were afraid to come and look. But he shrugged and he said it was none of his business what they were doing at the camp." Moze was silent for a few moments. Then he spoke, softly.

"I shot him. Right between his eyes."

I could not speak.

"My C.O. could have had me court-martialed. Instead, he sent me here. Maybe it was because I told him my only friend was in the Tenth Army, and I needed to be with you. Because you understand."

"Understand what?" I asked, my voice thick with tears.

"When we got here and I saw with my own eyes the hate and the horror of what had been done to these wretched souls, whose only crime was to have been born Jew or Romany, I screamed and cried and called God every vile name I could think of. 'You have forsaken me and my people after I devoted my life to you! You let this happen! You are not God!' I wept for the dead—for the piles of starved bodies tossed away like so much garbage or just lying where the SS had shot them before they ran. And I wept for myself, for all the hours spent reading Torah and Kabbalah, for the family I gave up, and for the faith I had so blindly followed."

Moze's voice was almost flat, his eyes cold in the moonlight.

"But I believe, still. I have to have faith, or I am no better than the soulless creatures who wreaked this terrible evil on the world. Ben, you have faith too. That is how you understand. That's why I am here."

His words, said so matter-of-factly, made me angry. By this time I had pretty much given up on God unless I was pinned down by fire, or watching a *kamikaze* plane heading right for one of our ships. I didn't believe in anything but dumb luck anymore, and counted on nothing but myself.

"Faith, schmaith," I said. "I don't believe God gives a damn about us or this war or anything. The age of miracles is long gone."

Moze stared at me. His unblinking eyes held mine until finally I had to look down.

"You'll see," he said coldly.

He rolled himself up in his bedroll and turned his back to me.

———

Places have rhythms, a music of their own. In the synagogue, it's the guttural chant of the Hebrew prayers. In a city like New York, it's the sound of the El, the honk of the cabbies, the click and scuff of feet on the sidewalks, the grinding roar of the buses. Down the shore in Jersey, you have the rolling crash of the surf, the fragmented melodies of a hundred radios tuned to different stations, the screams of the little kids playing in the water, the cries of the gulls.

War has no rhythm. It's either total boredom or total insanity. No middle ground. You can count off the boredom with cigarettes and conversation, but then the world explodes and you find yourself on the express train to hell.

When the first wave of Marines came ashore at Okinawa, there was no resistance. The Nips had vanished. Not until we began pushing inland did we find them. They had built pillboxes into the hills, and fortified caves. They rained bullets and mortar fire down on us, and the only way we could get them out was to take each cave, one by one, with flamethrowers and grenades. It seemed like every man, woman, and child was armed and willing to die for the Emperor.

Moze and I were sent in as reinforcements, replacements for the Marines killed and wounded. When we joined up with a unit pressing on toward Shuri, where the fighting was fierce, we dug in at the bottom of a ridge under a banyan tree. The weather had gotten bad. It rained buckets, and the island was nothing but a sinkhole of mud. I thought the tree might protect us from the rain. I looked over at Moze, resting on his shovel.

He'd barely spoken to me since that first night. I had lived through the hell of Leyte Gulf, with the *kamikaze* attacks, and I figured we had a pretty good chance of dying here on Okinawa.

And I also figured it was a hell of a thing, to come this far to die. As I turned over another shovelful of mud, I decided it was time to make my peace with Moze.

"Moze, I'm sorry about the other night."

He turned and stared at me with those dead, dark eyes.

"It's just that, well, I guess I do believe. A little." I chose my words carefully, trying to be tactful.

Moze kept staring at me, but as I spoke, his eyes began to shine. Then he laughed and clapped me on the back. "I knew you'd come to understand! Wait, Ben, and have some faith. By this time tomorrow, you will be dancing under this tree, laughing with joy."

I grinned at him, but fear clutched my bowels again. Here I was, in a foxhole, facing the desperate and vicious Nips with a crazy man for my buddy. *Oy vey izmeer,* as my Pop used to say.

The shelling that came down on us from high on the ridge that night was heavy. Bullets shredded the leaves of the tree overhead and blasted chips of wood off the trunk and branches. Explosions lit up the perimeter with flashes of blinding white light, and the air was filled with acrid smoke and screams. Moze and I fired our guns at the bunker about halfway up, our designated target. Suddenly Moze stopped firing and leaped from the foxhole.

"What in God's name are you doing?" I shouted. "Get down, Moze. They're going to kill you!"

He paid no attention to me as he ran out into the muddy clearing in front of the foxhole.

"Watch, Ben! I will dance and pray, all the secret prayers from the Kabbalah! I will dance and call out the *Shma,* Yahweh's secret name. I will dance and pray and share the mysteries with you, and then you will dance, too, just as I promised. Finally, this endless killing will stop!"

"Moze, please! For the love of God, get back here before you get killed!"

But he ignored my frantic pleas.

"*Baruch atah Adonai, eloiheynu melech ha'alom,*" he screamed, shaking his fist at the nest of Japs firing down on us. Then he began to chant, swaying back and forth from the waist, praying. His feet churned the mud, splashing a counterpoint to the whine of the bullets, the rat-a-tat of machine guns, the explosions of grenades.

I was beyond terror, waiting every second to see my friend blown apart in front of my eyes. My friend, who apologized to dummies back in boot camp, was committing suicide. Over and over, I yelled at Moze to get back into the foxhole until my voice broke, and I was shrieking like a girl. The Japs were lobbing grenades at us, and all I could do was fire blindly up the hill and watch my friend as he swayed and chanted and danced in circles, lit up in the strobe flashes of gunfire, wreathed in smoke from all the ordnance exploding around us.

I suddenly realized that the bullets *were* hitting Moze. They made a wet, thudding noise as they hit his body, a whistling clang as they ricocheted off his helmet. His dance became a frenzied spinning, his prayers a terrible song. He fell to his knees and stretched his arms to the sky. A bullet carried off two of his fingers; another took off a piece of his chin.

There was nothing but the howling hell of war around us. The world, including me, had gone mad in swirls of smoke and flame and noise and death. Moze was being shot to pieces out there, and he was still dancing. I could only sit in the foxhole and watch and scream.

All at once Moze stood up, sprinted to the foxhole, and

grabbed his rifle. Pointing it at the sky, he let loose round after round. Then he turned on me, brandishing the weapon in my face. I stared back. Half his face was gone, carried away by the Nip slugs, but his eyes burned brightly under his helmet.

"Why aren't you dead?" I whispered. "You should be dead."

I dropped my rifle and crouched down like a dog in the mud at the bottom of the foxhole. Moze scared me more at that moment than I'd ever been scared before—or since. I stared up into the barrel of my friend's rifle, the beckoning finger of Death twitching for me. If the Lord had seen fit for millions of Jews to die in the German death camps, why would He bother with a *meshugganah* Hasidim and his friend? I waited for the white-hot pain that would end my short life.

"Benjamin, where is your faith?" Moze asked in his sad quiet voice. And I heard him so clearly, above all the fury of the battle.

A grenade exploded not ten feet away from us. The force of the blast was stunning when it slammed into me. The banyan tree crashed down on top of the foxhole, and onto my head. I sank down into a deep, gray void.

When I came to, Moze was lying face down in the mud. My friend had lost his family, his sanity, and finally his life. I had been spared by the falling of this shrapnel-scarred banyan tree. Guilt washed over me, and a desire to avenge Moze pushed me out of the foxhole.

Climbing up through the shattered tree, I staggered to my feet, my ears bleeding and my head pounding.

"NO!" I shouted. I raised my rifle and began firing madly, aiming into the flashes from the Nip guns up on the ridge. I kept firing until the clip was empty. Then I pulled a grenade from my belt, took the pin out with my teeth, and threw it toward the pillbox. The noise of the explosion was deafening, the smoke thick and hot. My throat, already raw from yelling, burned as I gasped for air. Finally, after lobbing two or three more grenades, there were no more flashes.

I spun around and faced the lump on the ground that was my friend a moment or two ago. I fell to my knees beside Moze, to embrace him. But my arms encircled nothing but mud. His body was gone. Unbelieving, I felt frantically around in the black muck, trying to find him. My fingers closed on a scrap of paper, but that was all. I clutched it and kept searching, moving in circles, plowing the mud with my hands.

"Medic!" I cried in my broken voice. "Medic!"

I don't know how long I searched for Moze. Bullets whined around me. Grenades exploded fifty feet away, a hail of dirt and metal rattling down on my helmet. I fought off the gray mists that were rolling over me, in a frenzy now to find him, widening my circles in the mud until I passed out again.

Just before my mind went away, I remembered to slip the paper in my pocket.

I finally regained full consciousness a few days later on the hospital ship. I had a bad concussion, ruptured eardrums, and a nasty shrapnel wound in my left leg, but—miraculously—no bullets had hit me.

"Where's Moze?" I asked the nurse.

"Moze who?" she replied, looking at me curiously.

Nobody had ever heard of Moishe Abramowicz. But a lot of people had heard of me. Seems as though I single-handedly took out a company of Nips who were hunkered down on the ridge that night. My unit would have been slaughtered if I hadn't blown their cozy little nest all to hell. I was a hero. *Mazel tov.*

I tried to explain that I wasn't alone, that Moze had been there, but it did no good. I guess they thought I had shellshock or battle fatigue—they call it post-traumatic stress disorder now—and they let me rave on about my imaginary friend.

I received a Purple Heart. I couldn't even look at it. But later I did look at the muddy scrap of paper I found that night. It was the *Shma*—the secret name of God. I put it in the box with the Purple Heart.

———————

A few weeks later, while I was in the hospital in San Francisco, the atomic bombs dropped on Hiroshima and Nagasaki, and Japan was forced to surrender. I saw pictures of the roiling black mushroom cloud reaching up to the skies. I read about this new, unstoppable, terrible weapon that was born to wreak vengeance on the enemy, and remembered Moze talking about evil, how God could end this war with a Joshua.

For a long time after that, I worried about my soul as well as my sanity.

But the Army headshrinkers finally convinced me that I was okay, that Moze on Okinawa was just a glitch in my thinking brought on by stress, and I went home to New York. I went into the family business—men's clothing and haberdashery—and business was good. So I got married to a wonderful, beautiful girl named Maxine, bought a house and made babies, all the American Dream stuff that we fought—and a lot of us died—for. Life went on.

But I couldn't forget Moze. As time went on and my children got older, I began to do some research. I wanted to find out what had really happened to him, and what the muddy scrap of paper meant. I wrote letters to Washington, to other men in Moze's unit—and I began to read the Kabbalah. It took a few years, but I finally pieced the story together.

Moze's unit had indeed been sent to a small camp in Germany, and Moze did go insane and kill a German civilian—and his C.O. sent him back to the States with a Section 8. He died in 1950, in the psych ward at the V.A. Hospital in New York.

Moze had been shipped out in June of '45—two weeks before I met him in Okinawa. One of his buddies wrote and told me that the day before he was shipped out to New York, Moze had done something very strange. He was allowed an hour each day to exercise outdoors before returning to the prison they had made for him out of the camp Kommendant's office. That last hour he spent digging with his fingers in the soft earth near the graves. That night, he escaped—only to be re-captured, standing by the mass graves, alternately laughing and weeping.

He raved and babbled on like a demon, the letter read. *He said he could make the war be over. Then he'd cry and say his soul was four-footed, or something like that. But, he said he had to save somebody else.*

I don't mind telling you that it was a mighty scary thing, seeing Moze like that. He was always such a nice, gentle guy. Wouldn't hardly swat a mosquito.

I remembered Moze's sad eyes, haunted by the dreams that were too horribly true. "I must believe, or my soul is forfeit," he had said. His family, his sanity, his life were indeed forfeit to this war. But he had his faith.

Faith enough to bring forth a Golem. Not enough to save the world, but enough to protect a friend. Enough for me to understand.

N0072-JK1

STUDY OF SYNAPTIC RESPONSE OF THE ORGANISM TO SPONTANEOUS
STIMULATION OF VULNERABILITY ZONES. PHOTOGRAPHIC ANALYSIS.

ADAM CORBIN FUSCO

*Sometimes we encounter a story so disturbing, its
appeal goes way beyond merely liking or disliking it.
The following piece is presented with such dispassion-
ate realism, we could not get it out of our minds. If
you have ever read any of the professional journals of
the "social sciences," you will appreciate Adam Fusco's
razor-edged satire.*

—A study is made of synaptic response focusing on the
laughter vector during spontaneous stimulation of vulnerability zones, popularly known as the Tickle Response. This is to address the question, Why do we
laugh when tickled?

—Each subject, in an isolated room with a chair and monitor, was instructed to remove footwear and to place the right foot through a black screen. Subjects were told they were to be tickled on the sole of the foot by a robotic, metal hand. This was done to render invalid any foreknowledge of human interaction and "play" expectations. In actuality, a researcher donned a metallic glove to perform the stimulation.

—During stimulation, subjects were shown via the monitor three comedic performances along three modalities: an HBO special of a prominent comedian, a Three Stooges short, and cartoon imagery that contained violence. The laughter response with and without visual input was measured and found to be non-cumulative: it did not increase from visualizing comedic performance, nor was it prevented by administration of sympatholytic drugs (e.g. propranolol, phenoxybenzamine). This suggested consistent, though non-concurrent, neural pathways. Subjects did exhibit increased "openness"—that is, greater sustainability—of response during cartoon imagery. Priapic response in males during tickle stimulation of the foot increased twenty-two percent while viewing imagery of a popular cartoon duck, most strongly when said character was subject to explosive force and in particular if the duck's bill was displaced or removed from the head altogether. Orgasmic initiation in females increased by ten percent while viewing imagery of a popular cartoon pig when said character wore spacesuits or ballet tutus (the binding referent). These results are correlative.

—The study, in the absence of cumulative affect, turned to initiating a time curve, where it found an emergent pattern after four hours of stimulation. Stimulation density was consistent, but was paused at three-minute intervals for thirty seconds for recovery of synaptic pathways. Laughter response fell below basal levels after thirty minutes and dropped away altogether after one hour. At two hours, an inversion was noted, and laughter response continued to increase thereafter.

—Photograph H shows a female subject at the four-hour mark of tickle response. Subject presents facial rigor, gritted teeth, and tears of laughter (note Study 10M8/42-2-14 "Spinal Cord Harmonies in Comparison to Violin String"). Response increased over the next three hours, peaking at the seven-hour mark. It remained at this plateau until the fifteenth hour when stimulation was halted due to lack of skin integrity of the foot.

—It has been noted elsewhere that openness to cartoon imagery is consistent with response to human infant and baby animal physical features. This "primal face" response, which elicits nurturing, initiates in the presence of eyes twenty-five percent larger proportionately than those of adults, as well as diminutive limbs, large hands, and protuberant belly; and is consistent whether directed toward puppy, kitten, human infant, or baby chimpanzee, all of which have the same proportional measurements in the facial domain. Cartoon imagery is purposefully rendered with the same proportional measurement to induce the same open response. Said measurement is also found in Nazi propaganda posters and shows a seven percent increase in cartoons made during the Second World War.

—Reaction to the "primal face" as an increase-operant of the laughter response was then taken into consideration. (Note the study conducted by Gelertner and Grimes regarding the homicide of newborns by their mothers shortly after birth, principally by strangulation or abandonment, entitled "Postpartum Depression As Excuse and Removal As Cause: The Murder Response to the Sudden Other"). Subjects who were shown slow-motion videotape of a running cheetah were more "open" at the four-hour emergent mark, which matched response to eye-gouging comedic skits featuring The Three Stooges.

—Photograph K shows a male subject at the five-hour mark of tickle response during a cheetah footage test. The mouth is stretched wide and the tongue laid back in laughter response. The showing of the whites of the eyes is indicative of the onset of free-operant avoidance contingency in an effort to remove from comedic stimulation. The arms are tied behind the back. The foot is clamped at a point above the ankle.

—Reaction to the "primal face" is correlative to reaction to the "laughter response face." Subjects were shown a photograph of a theater audience. They were told the audience was viewing a comedic film and were asked to rate the comedic value of the film on the one to five Tortelli scale based on the audience's facial reaction. Seventy-nine percent of males and seventy-two percent of females rated the comedic value at a four or greater. The fact that the audience was not watching a comedic film at all maintains the consistency of the study. (Note photographic archive of Nazi "Laughter Cabaret," wherein each seat delivered mid-level electrical shock via anal probes during strategic "punchlines.")

—The study sought to develop a cartoon image to instill maximum "openness" to the tickle response by combining cheetah imagery with what is known of prehistoric predatory felines during the pre–Homo sapiens era. These animals employed two killing methodologies after chase and capture of their prey: suffocation and strangulation. The necessity of speed-operant body architecture precluded brute strength for the snapping of the neck (the modern cheetah is on an extinction vector due to its specialized killing modalities). During the time it takes for its prey to succumb, the belly and sides of the victim are open to the free-operant claws of the feline. These remain vulnerability zones today, as do the bottoms of the feet, which were exposed during pursuit.

—The chase model—as seen in a parent chasing an infant, who is exhibiting laughter response whether the intention of the parent is punishment or play—is consistent. When cheetah modalities are taken into consideration, the tickle response, as developed in pre–Homo sapiens, is either a release of tension (the death referent) or a "play" response as practice for avoidance contingencies. Laughter *per se,* however, for the requirement of synaptic explanation, remained non-correlative at this point of the study—though indications of reaction to the Other, as in postpartum murder, were encouraging (one cannot tickle oneself).

—A cartoon character was developed as an amalgam of feline imagery, dubbed "Fluffbucket." It utilized the large eyes and "comic" hands and feet modalities noted above, resembling a pot-bellied leopard with floppy ears and mismatched spots (pattern-recognition referent to inconstant spotting in puppy and kitten pelts).

—Photograph O shows female subject presented with "Fluffbucket" imagery during tickle stimulation at the nine-hour mark. Avoidance contingencies are highly marked. Arms are necessarily bound, and eyelids hooked open while saline solution was administered every fifteen seconds. The teeth are fully exposed. The subject is nude to facilitate access to several vulnerability zones, which were studied utilizing the "mechanical hand" modality.

—The point at which the tickle response was developed in pre–Homo sapiens was concluded to match the vector at which said organisms—prodded by environmental stress factors, notably recession of the forests—came down from the trees to explore the open plains. It was at this point—threatened by feline killing methodology, and in concordance with more frequent locomotion on level ground and the necessity of height for vision—that the organism developed the locking knee joint, which allowed pre–Homo sapiens to walk fully upright, whereas previously mobilization occurred in a crouch position as seen in modern chimpanzees and monkeys. This split the paradigm. It allowed much greater mobility for exploration of the plains, but also incited the chase response in predatory felines.

—Subjects were operated on to remove the kneecap and kneejoint. These were replaced with a non-locking

metallic analog. A running track at a local university
was utilized to further the study.

—Photograph S shows the entire track. At the starting
point is a female subject, in crouch position, in whom
has been installed the non-locking knee joints. The
subject was given a thirty-second head start.

—Photograph T shows in the distance the subject "hob-
bling" in an effort to run, being unfamiliar with
pre–Homo sapiens locomotion modalities.

—Photograph U is taken shortly after the thirty-second
mark. A researcher, dressed in a "Fluffbucket" costume, is running past the starting position. The costume is made from hypo-allergenic synthetic fur.
Anatomical features match the proportions of "Fluffbucket" imagery developed in the lab. Eyes, paws, and
belly are oversized. A "cute" angle to the tail was
added along with "comic" fangs. The ears here are
flopping.

—Photograph V shows the track at the forty-second
mark. The subject's mouth is open in laughter response. The "play" modality has been invoked. It
should be noted that the "Fluffbucket" costume also
functions to render invalid foreknowledge of human
interaction, as with the "mechanical hand" in the lab:
the subject does not know *who* is in the costume.

—Photograph W shows the subject approaching the
curve of the track. "Fluffbucket" has grasped the subject's left foot. Vulnerability vectors rise to the top of
the scale (Achilles Heel referent).

—Photograph X shows continuation of the chase along
the curve of the track. "Fluffbucket" has released the
subject, but is batting her on the side of the body, as

seen in cheetah modalities. The "play" response is again noted.

—Photograph Y shows the subject stumbling. "Fluff-bucket" has grabbed the left side of the subject's blouse.

—Photograph Z. The subject is prone. "Fluffbucket" kneels above the subject, whose facial turgidity indicates laughter.

—Photograph A1. "Fluffbucket" places the mouth of the costume mask over the subject's face, initializing suffocation. The "paws" begin spontaneous stimulation of the subject's belly.

—Photograph A2. The skin of the belly is exposed.

—Photograph A3. Blood has spattered the "Fluffbucket" costume.

—The study concludes that concurrent with the "fight or flight" response, as seen in all predatory exercise, there exists a "fright and delight" initiative that cohabits neural pathways. Openness to the tickle response is concurrent with "primal face" response, whereas inversion of openness is noted in those said to be "non-ticklish." Eighty-seven percent of mothers who commit postpartum murder are described by their families as "non-ticklish." Tickle response testing may become mandatory for military recruits as prerequisite for induction into "special service." The reader is referred to further discussion in the author's paper "The Pleasure of Pain."

—Further study is highly recommended.

Time for Me

BARRY HOFFMAN

There are certain templates in imaginative fiction which have become fixtures, even classics. The "Twilight Zone" story is one of them, and we will fall prey to its deceptively simple constructs when it's as well written and poignant as Barry Hoffman's examination of a life punctuated by "quiet desperation."

"Okay, what do I do today?" James said aloud to himself staring down at a sheet of paper containing just two words. Lists. James had *always* made lists. There had been times he'd had so much to do that without his lists he would have been lost. He'd drawn a line through each chore as it was completed. He seldom got through all items on the list. There were just so many hours in the day. Yet, he felt a sense of satisfaction at all he'd accomplished. Those tasks he hadn't gotten around to would go on the next day's list.

James had been retired for nine months now and he'd recently noted his lists had dwindled to a handful of items. There were bills to pay, to be sure, but not many and only twice a month. There was a food list for shopping. A short list and only once a week. Doctor and dental appointments had filled his lists for several months, yet like a rebuilt car other than a six month checkup his body no longer cried for attention.

"What do I do today?" James asked again, aloud, then sighed. Unlike so many other days, today he knew.

A teacher for forty-five years James had grudgingly retired at sixty-five. He had long ago lost his zeal for the profession, but the daily routine had appealed to him. Kids had changed. Their parents had changed, and not for the better he had told colleagues who nodded in agreement. And during the last years on the job he'd felt like a worker on an assembly line. He was to follow lessons in teacher manuals almost verbatim. The flexibility and creativity that had brought him so much joy was removed. *Teach the test* were now his marching orders. Each school was evaluated by results on State-mandated standardized tests. Any deviation from his lesson plans was frowned upon. Spontaneity was discouraged. *Teach the test.*

His malaise had been building over time. And he had to admit there had been warning signs. In the last two years sometimes he found himself dozing at his desk while his students recited something from memory. He most definitely dozed at weekly faculty meetings. A colleague would poke him in the side when he began to nod off or snore. At first it had been once a meeting. Near the end he'd fallen asleep three, even four times during the hour. Recently he'd begun to forget student's names when they returned from their Christmas or spring break. And his last year he had to admit he was operating on auto pilot, recycling the same lesson plans he'd used the year before.

The proverbial straw that broke the camel's back, though, had been when he'd left a student at the Franklin Institute on a class trip. He had no idea how it happened. Each student had a number. During a trip he'd line his students up no fewer than a dozen times and have them call out their numbers. Yet somehow when his class left the Institute Eddie what-was-his-last-name had been left behind. James wondered what had been worse: his lapse or the fact that none of the other thirty students had noticed Eddie's absence on the twenty minute walk back to school.

There had been no lasting damage, other than to his pride. Eddie, as James had instructed his students before each trip, had found a security guard. He had wandered off, for just a few moments, something having grabbed his attention. The Institute had called the school and the principal himself had driven to the museum to pick Eddie up. He had bought Eddie a slice of pizza and a soda. It had been a great adventure, Eddie had told his parents and the principal.

James had called Eddie's mother that night to make sure the ten-year-old was okay.

"You've had three of my other children, Mr. Hennings," Eddie's mother had told James as he apologized profusely. "It wasn't intentional. Shit happens. Don't worry yourself."

"Still it was an unconscionable lapse—"

"You and your big words, Mr. Hennings," she had interrupted. She was a high school dropout and a waitress at a greasy spoon diner James had visited once. James had to laugh at himself for coming off sounding like a pompous ass. "No harm, no foul, as they say," she'd added. "And Eddie has a wonderful story to tell. *Please* don't blame yourself."

James' principal had been far less understanding. Mr. Scalia came from the CYA school of leadership. Cover your ass and always, *always* find someone else to shoulder the blame. James sat through a forty-five minute berating, only taken aback that Scalia himself hadn't been in touch with Eddie's mother.

"What am I to say to . . ." Scalia stopped and looked down at a folder that contained Eddie's name. Mr. Scalia was a hands off principal when it came to the three hundred students in his charge. He knew the troublemakers. He knew those few who brought glory to the school by winning contests. Eddie was neither. ". . . Mrs. Jankowicz when she comes marching in demanding an explanation?"

"I've already spoken to her," James said, locking eyes with his nemesis. Yes, he knew he was to blame but he had at least had the decency to call the boy's mother and apologize. He couldn't believe the principal hadn't done the same. Where was the man's concern? His compassion? James was tempted to ask the man, but kept his anger in check. Suicidal he wasn't. "She told me Eddie was no worse the wear for the incident and appreciated my call."

Scalia looked at James dumfounded. "You called her?" he asked.

"Of course. I was concerned," James had responded.

"I . . . I still have concerns, Mr. Hennings," the principal went on, no longer making eye contact with James.

He usually addressed his teachers by their first names. When angry it was the more formal Mr. Hennings. Scalia went over a list of mandatory suggestions James was to follow if he took his students on any other trips. James tuned the man out.

The incident, coming two months prior to the end of the school year, preyed on James' mind. *It shouldn't have happened,* he kept telling himself. Hadn't in the previous forty-four years and hundreds of trips. He still had no idea how it had occurred. He replayed the incident over in his mind countless times, knowing the obsession was unhealthy. Each time there was Eddie calling out his number. Obviously, though, Eddie hadn't. There was no way James could again place a child in harm's way. He was slipping. It was his dissatisfaction with the job, he knew, but that was no excuse had Eddie panicked or been irrevocably scarred. It was time to go.

James left as he had entered the profession with a minimum of fanfare. He had precious few friends on the faculty. Only one other teacher was his age, a first grade teacher who publicly belittled her children in the hallway. He had only contempt for her. He had even been tempted to reprimand her in front of her class for her callous disregard for their feelings. Most others whom he had been on speaking terms with had retired in a slow but steady stream the last five or six years.

James had no desire for one of those contrived retirement dinners given those parting at the end of each school year. He himself had avoided them like the plague when colleagues left the profession. He was no hypocrite so he kept his plans to himself. So he submitted his paperwork to the district office and packed what few mementos he cared to leave with. As a final gesture of his disdain for bureaucrats like Principal Scalia, James left a letter of resignation on the man's desk the last day of school. Knowing his principal's poor organizational skills it might be midsummer before Scalia knew James had retired. Hell, he thought with a laugh, it might be two months into the *next* school year before the man was aware James was gone.

The first question James had asked himself was *what would he do?* He tried to make light of his dilemma. He was certain he could make a list of several pages of what he could do to keep himself busy and content. Yet at night, alone in his bed he wondered just what the hell he *would* do. He shivered, uncontrollably, though the nights were warm. He hadn't planned for his retirement. Financially he was secure but what would he do with his day? Summers he had caught up on reading, taken in movies and visited his children and grandchildren, now scattered across the country. And that's what he did his first summer of his retirement.

He and his wife had been divorced thirty years earlier. She had passed away the year before, leaving her fourth husband with a mountain of bills. She had won custody of his three children after she had remarried. She had also moved across the country. James saw his children for two weeks during the summer and every other Christmas. He hardly knew his seven grandchildren. Visits were strained. Everyone was so damned polite. There were many awkward silences. Everyone, himself included, seemed relieved when his visits came to an end.

With the onset of a new school year the thorny question remained. *What would he do?*

His barber suggested a trip to Italy, Greece or the Holy

Land might be in order. But other than visits to his family James had no use for travel. He made a poor tourist. Museums, for the most part, bored him to tears. He was a meat and potatoes guy, most definitely not into exotic cuisine. The two times he had traveled abroad he'd split his time between the trips to the bathroom and craving a good steak or even a lousy McDonald's hamburger. Moreover, he detested airports. Arrive an hour early for a flight that invariably left at least a half hour late, tedious layovers then the interminable wait for baggage. Just the thought exhausted him. No, he wouldn't travel, though money was no obstacle.

A recently retired acquaintance suggested he start a home business. A diversion, he had called it. He himself went to yard sales and sold books and memorabilia on eBay, he told James.

"I'm a jazz buff. There's no better feeling than going through a box of records and finding a Miles Davis on *vinyl*, in mint condition, no less," he told James. "And finagling the price of the *entire* box down to five dollars. The Davis alone I sold for a hundred dollars," he said proudly.

"I couldn't rip someone off like that," James said. "It goes against everything I taught my students over the years."

"I didn't put a gun to the dude's head," his friend had said, sounding irritated. Then he shook his head. "You're missing my point, James. What I'm trying to say is I have something to do that's satisfying. Each yard or estate sale is an adventure. And it's lucrative. Forget about what *I* do. You must have some interests you'd like to explore. Why not start your own business? It beats sitting around the house waiting to die."

James had shrugged. His friend meant well. But James

hadn't left one job to start another. He certainly didn't need the money. Once he'd become a teacher his life had revolved around the profession. He went to the track occasionally with a friend, but he had no great interest in horse racing. And he certainly had nothing in common with the regulars he spotted each time he visited the track. He sometimes wondered if some of them slept at the track. Not only were they always there, but they seemed to be wearing the same clothes.

But his friend had said something that resonated with James, at least as a fantasy. *I didn't put a gun to the dude's head.* There had been times when James had taught that he wanted to put a gun to someone's head. A negligent parent. A teacher who berated her kids. And most assuredly his principal. Yes, there were times when putting a gun to Scalia's head, seeing him pee in his pants as he awaited his demise, made James smile contentedly as he sat as his desk. Maybe he *would* buy a gun and take some lessons at a shooting range. But why? he thought. He'd never do the deed so it would be a waste of time.

One of his children proposed an athletic pursuit. Nothing too strenuous. Maybe tennis. James had been physically active through his forties. He'd played basketball twice a week. The contact, verbal jousting and arguments that almost led to fist fights had been a great outlet for his pent up frustrations. But his knees had begun giving him problems. He'd torn a ligament in his knee when he was forty-five and after a grueling rehab was advised to find a less arduous outlet.

But what was there besides basketball? He detested golf. It was like a walk in the park, *literally*, made even worse by the fact some he knew were so lazy they drove

golf carts. He'd tried swimming, but that, too, bored him.
His knees wouldn't allow jogging, even if he had the
urge. Tennis meant having a partner so he tossed the idea
aside.

Even if he had found a suitable activity, his early
months of retirement saw his body fail him for the first
time. He felt like a car whose warranty had just expired.
He began falling apart, or so it seemed. Odd, he thought.
He'd missed no more than a dozen days in all his years
of teaching. He'd taught when he had bronchitis. He
hadn't missed a day of work when he'd injured his knee.
A few cases of the flu. Only in his final two years did he
take "mental health" days off. Sometimes he just didn't
want to face the children. But he'd never been seriously
ill.

Suddenly he was beset with any number of ailments. A
fall in the snow necessitated a hip replacement. He'd had
a scare when he discovered blood in his stool. He feared
the worst. He'd heard of colleagues who had retired with
great plans only to drop dead or be felled by the "Big C"
after six months. A battery of tests gave him a clean bill
of health. "You have hemorrhoids," his doctor told him.
He hated to admit it but his sudden physical limitations
had shaken him to the core. He was reminded of the commercial for some product that eluded him. An elderly
woman is sprawled on the floor, conscious but unable to
move. "I've fallen and I can't get up," she cried out. There
had been a sense of hopelessness in her voice that James
thought was more than the actress reciting her lines. *He*
lived alone. What if he took a tumble and *couldn't get up*.
For several nights he had dreams of laying on the floor
watching his body waste away. His throat was so parched
that when someone knocked on his door he could utter no

audible sound. A slow painful death. A painfully slow death.

After the third such dream he purchased a device that looked like a watch. Press a button and paramedics were promised to be at his house within ten minutes. He wore the damn contraption, but it made him feel terribly vulnerable. There might come a time he couldn't live alone. The thought came unbidden, but once it had surfaced he couldn't deny its truth. He would never impose on his children and move in with them even if they would take him. And retirement communities were euphemisms for nursing homes. He shuddered at the thought of strangers having to care for him. Some male nurse giving him a sponge bath or wiping up his excrement if he lost control of his bowels. A nursing home. *Never.* Suicide was preferable.

Now, once again, he thought of purchasing a gun, but this time not to shoot his principal in revenge, but to end it all on his terms if life became too intolerable. A bullet in the head was preferable to a male nurse sponging his genitals. He wouldn't even have to go to a target range. Gun to the head. Pull the trigger. The deed done. Let his children clean up the mess so they could sell the house.

He thought the worst had passed and then he suffered from a toothache that wouldn't allow him to sleep. He had put off going to the dentist for . . . well, for years. During more than four decades in the classroom he had no more than three cavities. Now that toothache that wouldn't quit turned out to necessitate a root canal. The dentist had taken a full set of X rays and chided James for his lax dental hygiene. Seven cavities, another root canal and the beginnings of gum disease made visits to the dentist a weekly affair for four months. Brush and floss he'd been told. He had been remiss in the past, but he didn't want to visit the dentist anytime soon again so he followed the man's instructions to the letter.

After the last dentist appointment he had celebrated by purchasing a gun, not that he thought he would use it. There was a gun shop right next to a bakery he often frequented. He thought the two stores next to one another incongruous. Maybe that's why it stood out to James every time he went into the bakery. It was like a church amidst a block of liquor stores and strip clubs. He'd peer into the window of the gun shop. Talk about weapons of mass destruction. There were enough guns in that one shop alone to cause an awful lot of havoc.

So after he'd finished with his dentist, for at least the next six months, he decided to splurge and go to his favorite bakery. Instead he found himself walking into the gun shop. It was almost as if he were having an out of body experience. He was talking to the proprietor about what gun to purchase while a part of him had no desire for such a weapon. But, it was all so fascinating. For someone his age with the desire of self-protection a small firearm would most definitely suffice, he was told. James agreed, but he still wanted to hold a Magnum 357 out of curiosity. Though tempted to walk out and buy a Napoleon or canolli next door he found himself handing his charge card to the gun dealer. There was a seven day waiting period, but with no criminal record and only time on his hands James could be patient. Still, he remained in the store for another half an hour as the store's owner showed him how to handle the gun and to clean it. He almost wanted to point it at the man behind the counter and tell him to go fuck himself with his waiting period, take his gun and walk out. Common sense prevailed and he left and waited. Looking at the bakery, as he left, he found he had no need for pastry.

One of the many ironies of retirement was that now that he *could* sleep until mid-morning, if he wished, his body wouldn't cooperate. He'd risen at 6 a.m. for forty-five years five days a week, often waking groggy and disoriented. Weekends he awoke at ten feeling fully refreshed. Now he found his bladder screaming at him twice a night. He'd stumble into the bathroom at 3 a.m. and then fall into a fitful sleep. He was awakened again at 6 a.m. like clockwork. Try as he might he couldn't fall asleep again.

The question still begged. *What would he do?*

Find a hobby, his daughter had told him often over the phone. He'd tried cooking gourmet meals but he was soon put off by all the preparation for twenty minutes of pleasure. And little that he cooked using six books of supposedly tantalizing menus tasted as good as a greasy pizza he could order from a corner store a few blocks away or a steak or burger he could cook in fifteen minutes. His experiment with gardening was even less successful. Volunteer work? Teaching had been volunteer work for the paltry salary he had drawn. He no longer had the patience nor stamina to work with handicapped children. He had no desire to work with the elderly. And he certainly didn't want to be reminded of his mortality by working with those who were ill.

He found he spent more and more time in his Lazy Boy lounger, one of his few new purchases since his retirement. He decided to catch up on his reading. He had hundreds of novels and biographies he'd purchased and never had time to read. He attacked them with gusto.

After reading several chapters, though, he'd get a headache. His optometrist prescribed new, even thicker glasses than the ones he'd already had. After a month the headaches returned. Worse, his concentration wandered. He found himself reading the same page, *the same paragraph* over again and again. A book that had taken him days to finish just a few years before now took two weeks. And as so much of what he read was instantly forgettable he finally gave up the effort. The daily newspapers, *The Sporting News* and *Newsweek* served his reading needs. He seldom made his way through those without dozing.

He'd awaken in his lounger with a start and he couldn't see his feet for several minutes. *They weren't there.* He could sense them, like an amputee, but they had vanished. Soon, though, they reappeared. Maybe he'd been dreaming that he'd awakened when he hadn't. But it seemed so real. And over the next several weeks it only intensified. He'd awaken—or so he thought—and he couldn't see his feet nor his legs. Another time his feet and arms appeared to have melted away. Once his penis shriveled into nothingness before his eyes. He had to stifle a scream.

Bad as the dreams, hallucinations or whatever-the-hell he was experiencing were, worse was that he had nobody to confide in. His few good friends—precious few—had all died several years before. He couldn't speak to his children. They'd think him crazy and send him to the dreaded nursing home. He feared seeking out a shrink for the same reason.

Each time when he'd finally come to his senses and literally counted his toes and fingers making sure he still had all ten of each, he was again assaulted by the question. *What would he do?*

What he did was pick up his gun. He'd completely forgotten his purchase when he answered one of his infrequent phone calls and was told that he'd received a clean bill of health and his gun was waiting for him. He began to visibly shake as he put the receiver down. Not from fear, but anticipation. He wanted the gun more than he'd wanted anything in his life, not that he had any use for it.

At the gun shop the owner again indulged him, showing him again how to properly load and clean the gun. The proprietor suggested he purchase a lock box. James shook his head. There was nobody who could get hurt in his house. He purchased several boxes of ammunition. He had no idea why. He just felt a surge of power knowing he was fully protected. When he arrived home he put some of the ammunition in every room in his home. He sat in his lounger caressing the gun. Fully loaded, he pointed it at a picture of his ex-wife and made believe he shot her. He then unloaded the gun, just as he'd been shown and pointed the gun at his head. Pulled the trigger and laughed aloud as he thought of the mess he'd make if he hadn't emptied the gun. He imagined a Realtor trying to sell the house. A nice young couple, with the woman expecting, walking into the bedroom and asking what had happened to the former owner. The Realtor, of course, had lied. "He passed away." Suddenly the blood splatter and brain matter appeared on the wall where James had shot himself and the couple fled.

After several hours, however, he put the gun away. Okay, now he had a gun, but he wasn't about to do anything rash. It had been an impulse purchase. But what use did he have for a gun?

He began watching more and more television. With cable there were so many choices he felt like a kid in a candy store. *Biography* on A&E, episodes of *The Twilight Zone* on the Sci Fi Channel and reruns of *The Honeymooners* on any number of cable outlets were just a few of the delicacies he feasted upon. He devoured movies on HBO and Showtime as he didn't want to go to the theater alone. College football, pro football, baseball, college and pro hoops. Sometimes he'd doze during sporting events. He'd be watching the first quarter of a basketball game and awake with a start to find the game well into the third quarter. Most movies disappointed him. Reruns of his old favorites like *Star Trek* now seemed inane and outdated. After his initial burst of enthusiasm he soon gave up the tube.

So what would he do? It was then that a second question surfaced. *What do I have to live for?* He had no answer.

He decided to try to reconnect with his children and grandchildren. That he hadn't been the model father was not his fault. His ex-wife had won custody of the children and he saw them so infrequently after the divorce the bond he'd had with each quickly dissipated.

He called Stephen, his oldest son, who had always been his favorite. Before the divorce he had taken Stephen to see Sixers basketball contests and Phillies baseball games. They'd replay the game on the way home. Stephen had been a fanatical fan. No matter how bad a season the team was having, Stephen looked on the bright side. A prolonged winning streak. Once in the playoffs anything could happen. His son was an eternal optimist.

He called Stephen now and his nine-year-old grand-daughter Carly answered. After a quick hello, she called out to her father. James was sorely disappointed. He'd wanted to ask his granddaughter about school and activities she was involved in, but she hadn't given him the chance.

". . . calling, Dad?"

"What?" James asked. His son was talking to him. His mind had drifted.

"Why are you calling, Dad?" Stephen asked, again. James heard concern in his son's voice.

"Do I need a reason to call?" James asked. "Maybe I just want to shoot the shit with my son. You know talk about the Sixers."

"Dad, I live in New Mexico. I haven't been in Philly in over thirty years."

"You don't keep up with the Sixers?" James asked, perplexed. "You were such a rabid fan."

"I didn't have a job or family then," his son said. "I don't have time for frivolous pursuits."

"Like talking to your old man," James said and instantly regretted the rebuke. Then he was angry at himself. He might not have been the best father in the world, but it hadn't been completely his fault. His wife had taken his kids from him. And now his son wanted to dismiss him. For a fleeting minute he thought of the gun that rested in a drawer on a night table beside his bed.

"I didn't mean that," Stephen said. "Look, is something wrong, Dad?" He sounded impatient to James, like he wanted to end the conversation unless there was some emergency.

"I'm fine, son," James said. "As important as your job and family are you have to make time for yourself."

"Easy for you to say now that you're retired," Stephen said. "Now are you going to tell me what's bothering you?"

I'm lonely James wanted to say, but he held his tongue. "Nothing son. Really, I just called to shoot the breeze."

"I'd like to talk, Dad. I really would, but I have to take Billy to soccer practice, Jason to the orthodontist and Carly has a Girl Scout meeting."

"I didn't mean to impose," James said.

"Look, I gotta go. I'll call you in a few days when it's not so hectic," Stephen said. "Promise. Okay?"

Stephen hung up before James could answer. Moments later James found his gun in his hand. "You've gone too far, Stephen," he said aloud. He pointed the empty gun at a picture of his son and blew his brains out. "You little shit," he shouted. "You don't know what it is to be . . . to be alone. All I wanted was to chat. But, no, you're too busy for your old man. Wonder how busy you'd be if I flew out and stuck this gun in your face?" He was standing now, shouting at the picture of his son, pointing the gun steady just as he'd been instructed. "And that bitch daughter of yours. Didn't you teach her any manners? I'm her grandfather, her fucking grandfather but she doesn't want a thing to do with me." He pointed the gun at a picture of his granddaughter. "Maybe this will convince you to be polite," James said, unaware he was shouting. Slowly he calmed down. Maybe Stephen would call. He'd give his son a chance. Stephen, after all, wasn't a bad kid. Just a little too preoccupied with his own life to worry about his father.

His son hadn't called back. Any number of times James put his hand on the receiver. But he feared catching his son on another of those days when his family responsibilities overwhelmed him. So much for reconnecting with his family. And he felt foolish when he thought he would use his gun on his son or granddaughter. No, *if* he used his gun there were far more deserving targets.

On a whim, while downtown one day for his six month checkup, James returned to his school to visit. Maybe, he thought, he'd volunteer some of his time. He could come in when he wanted and leave when the spirit moved him. Best of all he would no longer have to fear his old pal Mr. Scalia, his former boss. Unfortunately, he felt like an outsider as soon as he stepped in the building. Over the past six months he'd forgotten the names of many teachers on the staff. Hell, in his last years he barely knew the names of a third of those who taught. He was met with stares of indifference or a polite but insincere hello.

Then he bumped into Pat Rutherford, the school counselor. She had also been the school's union representative. While not close the two had talked often about the sorry state of education and the ineffectiveness of their union. He remembered, with a chuckle, how Pat had hounded him for three dollars to pay for a gift when Principal Scalia remarried. James had been adamant. He detested the man. He was no hypocrite. He didn't care if it got back to Scalia that he'd been the only one on the staff not to contribute. If nothing else, James had principles. No, he told Pat half a dozen times. But Pat had finally worn him down. "Forget Scalia. Do it as a favor to me," she implored. Why it was so important to her James had no idea, but he'd relented. Now seeing her he thought she was someone he could relate to.

"Pat, it's good to see you," James said.

"Good to see you . . . James," she said. James had the

impression she'd had to dredge up his name. Had she already forgotten him in six months? "How's retirement treating you?" she asked, with what looked like a forced smile. She looked at her watch. James didn't have to be a rocket scientist to know what was coming next. "I'd love to stay and chat, but I have a meeting to attend," she said. "Maybe some other time. No . . . *definitely* some other time."

Right, James thought. A not too subtle brush off. As Pat walked down the hall James couldn't control himself. "That three dollars I gave you for Scalia's wedding present. Think I could have it back?"

Pat turned and looked at James oddly. "You haven't lost your sense of humor, I see," she said, then made her way down the hall.

I was being serious, James wanted to reply, but thought the better of it. So much for a meaningful conversation with Pat.

He went outside and watched students at recess. Seeing several children taunting and chasing a small, chubby boy with glasses brought back ugly memories he longed to suppress. "Animals," he said aloud, not deserving his time. He left vowing never to return.

At home that night James sat in his lounger and cleaned his gun. Lately he'd taken it out of his drawer several times a week and indulged in fantasies. "Pat," he said aloud, "You *really* should have taken the time to talk with me. But you were too busy." He pointed the gun at the imaginary Pat and ended her life. Then he imagined bumping into Scalia who had heard the commotion. James pointed the gun at Scalia's groin. "I was going to kill you, you son-of-a-bitch, but I think I'll just shoot you in the balls. See how high and mighty you are when you recover. Every time you berate someone their eyes will venture downward, knowing you don't have the balls to carry out your threat . . . *literally*."

What appealed to him most about this scenario was he really wouldn't be held accountable for his actions. Not for long anyway. He was an old man. Life in prison didn't have the same meaning to James as it would to some teen who shot another in a drive-by.

There were days when James put the gun in his pants pocket with the intention of visiting his old school and settling some old scores. But common sense always prevailed. At times, though, just barely.

When the weather broke and it was breezy and balmy without being stifling James walked over to Rittenhouse Park where he had often taken his students on scavenger hunts. It literally took up an entire city block. On three sides were apartment houses and office buildings. On the fourth side was a bank and stores. An oasis in the middle of the city, so out of place, James thought often, but somehow just so right. Mothers chatted while their young children played. Senior citizens sat on benches, some feeding bread to the hordes of pigeons who shared the park. A few homeless men made the grass their bed. The police would occasionally shoo them away, but as they seldom bothered anyone the police just as often ignored their presence.

James sat on a bench taking it all in. He tried to ignore the ever-present question of what he would do with his days. Today he was sitting in a park taking in the sights, sounds and smells he had so often taken for granted. But this was only a temporary respite. He couldn't very well come here daily. Yes, he had something to do *today*, he thought, then sighed. But what about tomorrow?

"Mr. Hennings?" a voice asked tentatively, taking James by surprise. He looked up and saw a teenager who looked vaguely familiar. "Mark Connors," the youth said, when James didn't reply. "I was a student of yours in the sixth grade. I wouldn't expect you to . . ."

"I *do* remember you, Mark," James said, before the boy could finish. "You've grown, of course, but you haven't really changed," he went on. James remembered Mark Connors as introverted with few friends. He still wore thick horn-rimmed eyeglasses. He still had a shock of long brown hair, with bangs that reached past the tips of his glasses. Sometimes James thought Mark hid behind the hair, a blanket obscuring his eyes. "Aren't you supposed to be at school?" he asked.

"I go to the School for the Performing Arts," he said. "They're having a half day. Some teacher's conference at the school."

"You played piano," James said, remembering how Mark helped out the music teacher during lessons. "You were quite good."

Mark blushed. "I didn't think you'd remember. I . . . well, I sort of blended into the background. The piano was my ticket into the School for the Performing Arts. I do my thing, but I'm still pretty much a loner."

While they talked James noticed several people pass them by, giving them odd looks. A young boy with an old man, he imagined them thinking. James must be some kind of pervert. He ignored them.

Mark looked at his watch. "I've got to run some errands for my mother. I wish we could talk longer. There are so few people I can relate to, but I always seemed to be able to talk to you." He paused. "I . . . I get an hour for lunch each day. Tuesdays and Thursdays I have a study hall right after. I don't want to impose, but if you're not busy we could have lunch here Thursday. You probably have other plans but . . ."

"I'd love to," James said. "Same time, same place?" he asked.

"Sure," Mark said, then hustled off.

James looked at his watch. Two hours had passed. He couldn't believe it. It seemed more like half-an-hour. Mark was very much like his son Stephen before the divorce and custody battle. He hadn't known Mark was such a rabid sports fan. They'd talked about everything he'd wanted to talk to his son about. The Sixers, Phillies and Flyers, the city's hockey team. Yes, James *had* had something to do today. He couldn't wait until Thursday.

Thursday, James was waiting when Mark came jogging into the park. James had felt a bit like a fool. He kept telling himself that Mark wouldn't show. Yes, they'd enjoyed one another's company, but Mark surely had had his fill of his former teacher. He'd probably use his lunch hour and study hall to practice the piano. James had bought two hoagies at a Wawa convenience store. The smell was delicious but James refused to give into the temptation to eat before Mark arrived . . . *if* he arrived. He'd just about given up hope when he saw Mark. Glancing at his watch he saw Mark hadn't been late. James's apprehension had gotten the best of him.

James took out one of the hoagies and held it out to Mark. The youth laughed. From a bag of his own Mark took out a hoagie and held it out to James. "I didn't know if you'd bring your own lunch," Mark said. Soon they were both laughing. Then talking. Time flew, just as it had the first time. The only disquieting moment was when two teens, obviously cutting class, looked at the two of them and began laughing. James couldn't make out their words. He wondered if Mark felt uncomfortable, but looking at the boy it didn't seem like he cared at all.

Their time together passed all too quickly. If Mark didn't hustle he'd be late for class, he'd told James, reluctantly getting up. "Next Tuesday?" Mark asked, tentatively.

"I'd love it," James said.

"I'll bring lunch," both of them said at the same time and laughed.

"We'll alternate," James said. "I bring the hoagies next Tuesday. No arguing with your elders," he added when he saw Mark about to protest. Mark nodded, smiled then jogged across the park, turning around and waving as he neared the exit.

Tuesday couldn't come too soon for James. This time as he sat on the bench he was far less apprehensive. Looking at his watch he saw he'd arrived fifteen minutes early. He relaxed. Mark has classes, after all. He *couldn't* arrive whenever he wanted. Mark arrived right on time. James handed him a hoagie and soda. Mark took a bite. His mouth still full he nodded toward James. "Even a bad hoagie—and this isn't half bad—is delicious," he said after he'd swallowed.

James and Mark were discussing the failings of organized religion when a mother and her daughter walked by. The little girl, who couldn't have been older than seven, was holding her mother's hand. She stopped in front of the bench upon which James and Mark were sitting. Her mother gave a slight tug, but the child held her ground. "It's not polite to stare," the mother whispered to her daughter, but James overheard her.

"Why are you talking to yourself, Mister?" the girl said, looking at James.

"Hannah!" the girl's mother said, in a louder voice. "That's enough." This time she tugged a bit harder and the girl went with her mother. She stared back at James several times before being distracted by pigeons her mother allowed her to chase.

James didn't understand. What did the little girl mean? He turned toward Mark and the boy was gone. On the bench where Mark had sat was a wrapped hoagie. My God, James thought. I've been talking to myself. I created a . . . a friend to talk to. "I feel like such a fool," he said, aloud. This time a number of others turned and looked at him oddly. James rose and left the park as quickly as his sixty-five-year-old legs would take him. He couldn't have been more embarrassed if he had peed on himself.

At home he debated with himself long and hard whether he had just been lonely or was going mad? With no one to confide in—not even Mark, he thought bitterly— he chose the former. He vowed, though, never to return to the park again. He took out his gun and for the first time seriously debated ending his life. He loaded a single bullet in the gun. He cursed himself that he hadn't bought a revolver. Russian Roulette. Let the fates determine whether he'd live or die. But, with the gun he'd purchased with the bullet in the chamber, if he fired the outcome was certain. Still, what the hell did he have to live for? And creating an imaginary friend. How could he? Kids, *little kids* invented friends to play with, not grown men. What have I become? James wondered. He held the gun to his temple, his finger on the trigger. Then he started to cry as he lowered the gun. He didn't even have the courage to end his pitiful existence. He cried himself to sleep in his lounger, waking up for his nightly pee at three in the morning. His back ached. He jumped at the sound the gun made when it fell to the floor as he stood up. He'd completely forgotten about the gun. Then he began to laugh hysterically. What if it had gone off? What if, coward that he was he had *accidentally* killed himself? What a hoot he thought and laughed again. When he got into his bed his sleep was fitful, full of images of all who had wronged him. His gun in his hand he shot each in the face, obliterating their features. But like clay, their faces would reassemble and they'd laugh at him for his inadequacy. He couldn't even kill right.

Soon it wasn't what should he do with his life, but what should he do *today*? And the day before when he looked at his list for the first time it was blank. He stared for what must have been twenty minutes at the paper, his hand trembling. "*What do I do today?*" he asked aloud.

The phone rang. It was a solicitation for life insurance. While fully covered he listened to the man's spiel, then politely declined. It had given him something to do, even if for just ten minutes. He hung up and looked at the phone for fifteen minutes willing it to ring again. Surely Sprint or MCI would want his long distance business.

A knock on the door. James padded downstairs in his slippers and bathrobe expecting to be greeted by a pair of Jehovah's Witnesses. They always seemed to travel in pairs he thought. Before his retirement he'd shunned such visitors. Now, though he had no desire to convert, they could at least spice up his day.

He opened the door and saw a package. A UPS driver was on his way back to his tell-tale brown truck. James picked up the box the man had left. Excitement gripped him, which quickly turned to disappointment. Wrong address. He called out to the driver. The man must not have heard him. He got into his truck and drove away.

Later he went outside for a walk. He saw his next door neighbor, Thomas McGinley mowing his lawn. McGinley looked his way. James didn't know his neighbors well at all. He'd kept pretty much to himself. McGinley, also retired, seemed nice enough, though. Maybe a brief conversation. James waved and said hello. McGinley ignored him. James' hand went instinctively to his pocket. He now carried his gun with him. *Ignore me, McGinley? Ignore this!* He imagined taking out his gun and pointing it at his neighbor. How rude would he be then?

James walked two blocks to the mailbox and deposited some bills. On his way back, as he crossed the street, some fool turned the corner to beat a yellow light and almost hit him. James gave the driver the finger, almost hoping the clown would stop so he could at least argue with the stranger. It would be a short argument. James had his equalizer in his pocket. Let the fool vent at him. What would he have to say with a gun stuck in his face? But the driver disregarded him. Everyone's in such a hurry, James thought.

As he reached his home he saw two of his other neighbor's children playing in the driveway they shared with him. He watched them on their Big Wheels. They, too, took no notice of him. No better manners than their parents, James thought. They would grow up to be clones of their parents. Maybe he should end their pitiful existence now, he thought. He shrugged. Maybe he should just take out his gun and shoot himself in the head in front of them. *That* would give them something to think about. Maybe then they'd feel guilty for ignoring him. It would certainly leave a lasting impression on them, he considered with a laugh. He didn't know how long he stood outside looking, but not seeing anything. A car's horn startled him. The sun had gone down. His neighbor's kids were in their house.

That night James stared at his empty list. He wrote down one item.

The next morning at 6 a.m sharp James' bladder provided his wakeup call. After urinating, James felt the stubble on his face. When he taught he shaved daily, even on weekends. He continued to do so for a few months after he retired. Then it was every other day, then every third or fourth day. It had been the same with haircuts. Every two weeks without fail he got a haircut when he taught and for the first few months of his retirement. Then once a month, every six weeks, and now every two months. Actually, he couldn't remember when he'd last had his hair cut. He decided to shave. At least he'd look respectable before completing the one item on his list. *What do I have to live for?* he had asked himself the night before. Nothing . . . had been his response. He still shaved with an old-fashioned straight-edged razor his father had given him. Yes, a quick shave and then he'd cut his throat with the razor. That he could do. *Would* do. He wouldn't use his gun. He'd hesitate and lose his nerve as he'd done before. But after shaving, a quick flick of his wrist. Yes, that he *could* do. He was tired of wondering what to do with his days. He realized the night before that he *had nothing to live for.* At least he'd end his life by his own hand. No being a burden to his children as his health deteriorated. No dreaded nursing home. He wondered for a moment how long it would be before he was missed? A few days? A week? Maybe a month if the stench of his rotting corpse didn't alert his neighbors.

James turned on the water until it was good and hot. A mist clouded the mirror. He wiped it clear with a towel.

He stared into the mirror.

Nothing stared back.

The Growth of Alan Ashley

BILL GAUTHIER

One of the goals of the Borderlands *series is to discover new writers. Although Bill Gauthier tells us he's sold a few pieces to some small press 'zines, we fully intend to claim him as our discovery. If his first appearance in hardcover is any indication of how good this guy is going to be, we know you'll be looking for him in the future. (And by the way, his Mom is really proud of him, too . . .)*

At five-thirty, his alarm clock's radio came on and the radio personality spoke to a caller about world affairs. Alan Ashley's eyes popped open. What day was it? Wednesday. The interview! The morning show began at seven. His segment was supposed to be at 7:30, right after they came back from commercial and local news. Alan's new book had just been released and was already predicted to be the rage this season, every bit as popular as his movie this past summer. He looked forward to speaking with the morning show anchor again.

Alan noticed the growth near his right ear while shaving. A smooth bump that resembled a blister but would not pop. He ignored it, finished getting ready, and left the apartment.

He drove himself to the studio where the morning show was aired. Traffic was bad and he was afraid he'd be late. Alan entered the building and went to the elevator. He blocked out everything around him, though. The morning show was done at ground level so the crowds outside could watch. The elevator stopped on the fourth floor and Alan stepped out.

"We need that report by eleven, Alan," the producer said, too busy to stop and formally greet him.

Report. Must've been talking to the newswoman before Alan arrived and had mixed up *report* with *autographed books.*

Alan sighed and walked toward the green room. It was rather small, considering how popular the morning show was and how many guests were usually on, but Alan didn't complain. He plopped his briefcase down

(When had he picked it up?)

It has a new manuscript for your editor in it.

(Yeah, that's good.)

and flicked on the computer. He looked over the walls of the cubicle—*green room,* he corrected himself—and saw no one. His watch said 7:30 and he sat.

The morning show anchor waited for the signal and began with the intro. A few seconds later, Alan was on, chatting with the anchor. It was amazing that this book, just like his last one, was selling off the shelves. How could he explain it?

"I can't," Alan said, looking at his shoes, fashionably modest. "I just write the best story I can."

The anchor smiled, amazed, and asked about whether the success of the latest movie might have had an influence.

"It's possible, I guess," said Alan. "The thing is, though, I don't really notice. It's as though I'm two people sometimes. One worries about the movies, one about the books."

The morning show anchor reminded Alan that he'd also acted and produced, as well as directed the movie.

"I guess, then, there's more than two—" Alan began to say when movement out of the corner of his eye made him turn.

Gina stood at the opening of the cubicle, a tote bag dangling from her shoulder, her jacket still on. Her eyes were wide as she stared at Alan, a bemused smile on her face.

"Who're you talking to, Alan?" she asked.

His right leg, which had been resting on his left knee, dropped. The thing near his ear itched and Alan scratched at it, his face heating up. He looked at the clock in the corner of his computer monitor. 7:37 AM. He'd expected Roland—the producer—to be here, but no one else usually got here until closer to eight. Especially Gina, who had the cubicle beside his. She continued staring at him, expectantly.

"I was thinking aloud," he said.

Her stare didn't falter. Neither did the bemused smile. "About movies and books?"

"Yes."

"And you write what you can?"

It felt as though his heart, stomach, testicles—*everything*—turned to concrete and fell.

"It looked like you were talking to someone," she said. "Like you were being . . . interviewed."

Alan was on his feet before he realized he was going to stand, and he reached out, hands trembling.

"*Please*," he whispered. "*Please* don't say anything to anyone. Sometimes I—I—"

Gina shook her head and stepped toward her cubicle. The smile was gone, replaced with something else. "Calm down, Alan. I won't say anything."

"My career, my life, would be ruined. Please—"

"I said I wouldn't say anything. I won't."

She disappeared behind a cubicle partition. Alan thought about following her, making sure she wouldn't say anything to anyone, but didn't. Instead, he sat and his thumb went to his mouth to be gnawed.

It was bound to have happened sooner or later. Reality, like a giant monster from an old Japanese monster movie, destroys everything at some point. He'd had to hide these lives for twenty years, since the kids in seventh grade began making fun of him for acting out his stories outside. Something he'd spent his life doing all of a sudden taken from him.

No! a voice in his head demanded. *Stay focused. Roland wants that report by eleven, do it by ten. Go out for lunch. You have a meeting with Scorsese about his new movie.*

Alan tried to push the voice away as he wheeled his chair closer to the computer. He realized his wet, bleeding thumb was no longer in his mouth, but near his ear.

His hand rubbed at the growth. He made a mental note to keep an eye on it.

———————

Though the lunch meeting with Scorsese went very well (the great director wanted *Alan* to play a hitman in his next movie . . . time permitting, of course) Alan's heart sunk as he walked past Gina's cubicle. He stopped and stepped back, looking in. The photographs, art magazine clippings, all personal effects were gone. The back of his neck prickled with the feeling of eyes on him. Alan turned. He barely glimpsed Gina and Francine's heads disappearing behind a partition several cubicles away. Then came the sound of laughter trying to be suppressed.

Alan's eyes went to the floor and he went back to his cubicle. He spent the rest of the afternoon trying to work, though he swore he could feel the eyes of many people looking at him. A disturbance in the Force, perhaps.

Your adoring fans, the voice reassured him.

———————

Alan watched Larry King and Charlie Rose. He watched Letterman and taped Leno. He watched Conan O'Brien and taped Craig Kilborne. Lying in bed after the shows, listening to talk radio, he watched light travel across his ceiling from cars speeding up and down the street. The thing near his ear had gone from itching to burning, but not too bad. It was there but he'd become used to it.

The voices from the radio alarm clock didn't penetrate Alan's mind, not this night. He remembered the look Gina had given him. That smile—no, *smirk*. He remembered that smirk. He'd seen it in school as a boy and then as a teenager. That smirk that people gave to someone who was strange to them, outside their narrow view of the world and how it should be. Someone who didn't fit the "typical" mold. The Phantom of the Opera or Quasimodo or even Carrie White. He swore he'd never see that look again. Yet, here he was, fifteen years after high school, eleven after college, having been looked at like that again. The shell that had been so carefully built around him, that had protected him those long study hall periods and gym classes, that had comforted him after girlfriends had found the notebook with the movie lists and poster designs he'd made and noticed the dates, that shell with its intricate ornamentation had been taken down years ago. He'd realized he'd never meet a woman with his kind of imagination. Never. They'd never truly understand him. That was fine, he could live with that. But now, when he was supposed to be safe, supposed to be okay with himself, that goddamn motherfucking *look*.

Alan sat, tossing his legs off the side of the bed. The growth felt bigger to him but he ignored it as his overactive imagination, hypochondria. It worked both ways, imagination did. The thing that could produce great Art— films, music, literature, paintings, sculptures, and so much more—could also be the genesis of fears, anxieties, paranoia.

The radio personality asked him about the rumors of the new Scorsese movie on the heels of the novel's selling more copies than anyone ever had in one week. Alan opened his mouth, ready to answer and stopped. This wasn't right. For Christ's sake, it wasn't right. He was thirty-two years old and should *know* better. It was purer if he kept the fantasies separate. A movie actor/writer/ producer/director, that was fine. A novelist/screenwriter/and sometimes-maybe-if-they-let-me director was fine. But not together. Sure there were those people who lived those lives, but it was better to separate them.

The growth near his ear burned and itched but it faded as Alan Ashley, novelist, chatted about his new novel. He *was* on a book tour, after all.

Thursday and Friday passed. Both days were hell for Alan. He went to work early, just as he always did, and felt the change in the office as Thursday progressed. There were whispers. People seemed to pass by his cubicle more often than normal, peeking in as they went like people new to cubicle work often did. The voice in his head told him it was because they'd heard his radio interview this morning on their way to work but Alan tried to ignore the voice. Also, the growth was larger.

More of the same on Friday. Alan hoped the weekend would quiet the whispers down. Maybe being away for two days, getting on with their lives, they'd forget about what Gina had seen and reported.

Gina. That lying bitch. She said she wouldn't say anything. That fucking lying cunt. He had the mind to—

To what? the voice asked. *You want to go down in history like Fatty Arbuckle, O.J. Simpson, and Robert Blake?*

Alan calmed himself.

Throughout Friday, it felt as though the growth were on fire. The pain pulsating from it seemed to send a high-pitch buzzing through Alan's head until his brain ached. The afternoon was a waste. Nothing got done. He touched the mouse slightly every time the screensaver came up, but never actually did anything. No reports were written, nothing was analyzed. Yet, he forced himself to stay later than everyone else so he wouldn't have to go through the nightmare he'd gone through Thursday, of standing in an elevator with his coworkers as they smirked, stealing glances at him through the corner of their eyes.

He got home Friday night and crashed on the couch. He watched the *E! True Hollywood Story* marathon. Maybe it was time to end the fantasies. Maybe it was time to grow up and stop living false lives, begin living a real one.

But how do you want to go out? the voice in his head asked. *Who does what?*

The musician was mostly dormant unless a really good song came on the radio, so he would be easy. The writer would be tough right now and so would the actor/producer/director.

Alan stood, took his Springsteen CD, and put it on. He rocked to it, rocked to Aerosmith and Billy Joel. He ended with Elton John and then waved to the audience. By the time he got to the limo, reviewers were hailing this first concert of the tour the best concert he'd ever given. He played and performed as though there were no tomorrow. One reviewer even wrote that they didn't know how he'd be able to make a whole tour with that kind of energy. However, Alan the musician wouldn't need to worry. The private plane he was on went down in Idaho. The famous rock 'n' roll musician, Alan Ashley, was dead at thirty-two.

———

The writer took to drinking. There was no booze in Alan's apartment, he couldn't hold it, but there was plenty of Diet Pepsi. At a benefit, Alan drank. He was supposed to speak that night and he went to the podium. The growth's burning, itching, humming, was almost too much to handle and Alan suspected he felt like a real drunk.

"Thank you for inviting me to speak to you this evening," Alan said, trying hard not to slur his words but knowing they would still come out that way. "I just got word, tonight, that my book has sold more copies in such a short period of time than any other book by any other author. Maybe I celebrated too early. Fuckit."

Alan went on for almost two hours. He babbled about the life he'd created for this fantasy, how he'd run with street gangs and had gotten secret access to all sorts of lifestyles. He talked about the art of writing and the commerce of publishing. He went on until he finally passed out.

Alan lay on the worn carpet, the growth pointing toward the ceiling. It ached. Throbbed. Sent out waves of sound through his head. He pushed himself off the floor, went to the bathroom, and looked in the mirror, staying in character. How had he gotten to his hotel room? What had he said that night?

The growth was bigger. It was no longer smooth but had indentations.

I'm going to have to have that checked out, Alan thought.

You're out of character, the voice in his head told him.

"Fuck you," Alan mumbled. "This is serious."

But he slipped back into the problems of the alcoholic writer. No, not alcoholic. He'd gone on for years saying he didn't drink. He couldn't rewrite that history, all those awards he'd received from MADD and SADD and other organizations for being a good role model. Then what? A one night binge. His first. Only on an extremely bad night.

Alan went to bed. He didn't watch any interview shows. He allowed sleep to take him even though they needed to travel over the painful road the growth was paving.

———————

He awoke to excruciating pain that tore through his head and brought tears to his eyes. In the bathroom he flicked the switch and stared into the mirror. The bump had grown more overnight. The side of his face now looked swollen. Gravity seemed to dissipate. He stared at his new visage, unaware of the physical world around him, his ramming heart the only sound in the world. He needed to get to the emergency room, *now.*

You're fine, the voice in his head said. *It'll go away by Monday. Just give it some time.*

Alan couldn't take his eyes off it. The growth almost took up the whole side of his face. How could he not go to the hospital?

The papers, the voice said. *You made the papers.*

They reported Alan Ashley, best-selling author of numerous novels and stories, had ruined his image by being drunk at a benefit. It wasn't the drunkenness the socialites didn't like, either. Fuck, most of *them* had been drunk. It was the fact he had denounced so many of them for drinking and then had gone up on stage drunk. He ruined the evening when he passed out and fell on the table of *the Vice President of the United States.* The TV reported the event, noting that sales of his books were already dipping and half the bookstores in the country weren't even open yet. His agent called and told him that Oprah didn't want him on the show Monday after all. He called back half an hour later to report that his publisher was dropping him because he grabbed the head honcho's wife's left tit and had asked if he could take a sip.

Shattered by his own momentary stupidity, his weakness, he went into his bedroom and opened a desk drawer. The gun was in the back, just as it had always been. He took it out, looked at it. Then he put it in his mouth, closed his eyes, and squeezed the trigger.

Alan fell back on the bed at the sound of the dry click of plastic on plastic. He lay there, staring at the ceiling, writing the obituary of Alan Ashley, author. He took his own life in the Plaza Hotel in New York. He didn't even write a final note.

After an hour of lying on the bed with the growth throbbing, Alan sat up. The toy gun was still in his hand. He remembered playing cops and robbers with it as a boy. Until he couldn't anymore. Until he'd been harassed for his need to act things out.

The actor, the voice said. *One last time.*

———————

It was a party in L.A. Alan Ashley, who began acting in his teens and had become a screenwriter, producer, and director, wasn't usually found on the party scene. But a mid-morning party couldn't lead to trouble, could it? This was L.A., though. He was with the cream of the crop—this year's Brat Pack, last year's Brat Pack, fuck, the *original* Brat Pack. In the kitchen, Alan Ashley, who'd won awards for being a good role model to kids by not doing drugs or even drinking, decided to give in a little. He tried a drink. Then he snorted some coke. He loved it. By the end of Saturday he was on a binge. Everyone told him to slow down. You're gonna end up like John Belushi, they told him. Or River Pheonix or Chris Farley or Janis Joplin or. . . .

But he didn't stop. He stayed up Saturday night doing lines and drinking and staying in the cloud that seemed to come from the growth on his face. It still ached and throbbed. He paid it no mind. In the early-morning hours of Sunday, Alan Ashley, famed actor, died of a drug overdose. His agent found him in his Malibu home.

Alan Ashley, who'd been born, raised, and lived in Harden, Massachusetts, sat on his couch and stared at the blank TV. On the TV tray in front of him was the paper plate he'd used to snort the Coffee Mate, a rolled-up one dollar bill lying near it. Empty Diet Pepsi cans littered the apartment. The walls were bare. No artwork, no photographs, nothing. Books, vidcos, and DVDs lined shelves or were stacked around the place. His clothes lay strewn about. The apartment cost nine hundred dollars a month. He had trouble paying it. His freezer in the kitchen consisted mainly of frozen entrees. The refrigerator was almost empty except for milk and soda. He owned only a few dishes, hand-me-downs from his parents. The semen stains in his sheets were not from the different women he met on booksignings or press junkets, not actresses or fans, but from himself, by himself.

Alan Ashley, a marketing guy for a firm in Harden. He went to work daily, sat in front of the computer or on the phone analyzing sales and marketing, not really important, not making waves. Usually his coworkers nodded to him, aware of his existence but unaware of *him,* the person. Gina being the only one because she'd had the cubicle near his. Now they were aware of him, but for what? For talking to himself. For living in fantasies.

Alan Ashley looked at his hands. What good were they? What had he ever done with them? Type reports for things he couldn't care less about. Jerk off. Pick his nose. Wipe his ass. Eat. But what had they *done*.

The side of his face ached. He touched it. The indentations on the growing bump were more defined. What the hell was this?

It's me, the voice said.

At that moment, pain exploded from the large growth and Alan cried out. He slid off the couch, onto his knees, and wept.

"That's right," the voice said. "Let it out."

Alan stopped. The pain was still there, still ravaging, but he forgot about it. The voice hadn't sounded internal. It sounded like it was in the same room.

"You wanted me," the voice said. "And I've come."

Alan used the couch and the wobbly TV tray to stand. He stumbled, almost fell, but finally stood. His legs quivered and he didn't know if he could walk, but knew he had to. He had to get to the mirror. He made his way down the small hallway to the bathroom and flicked the switch. That explosion of pain had been the growth opening up. Two new eyes looked at him. A new nose breathed and a new mouth smiled.

"You created me," the face said. "You wanted me long enough and then you try to destroy me. That's fine. I'll just do what you never could because *you* were too weak."

Alan screamed while the face that had grown beside his laughed. When the screams died, Alan realized he couldn't feel his body. That sensation of zero-g had returned. Only now, when he tried to raise his hand to touch the growth, it wouldn't move. When he wanted to run from the bathroom, his feet wouldn't respond.

Alan watched as Sunday became Monday and he quit his job, telling Roland to take his reports and cram them. He watched as he told Gina that she was a lying, backstabbing cunt and should go home and take the bottle of valiums the same way her mom did. He watched, though through a fog, as Tuesday came and he packed a few books, videos, DVDs, and CDs with his clothes. As he took the money out of the bank. As he got in his car and began driving.

Somewhere in Pennsylvania, heading west, Alan saw himself as a growth that was fading on a face. This face knew what it wanted, knew what it would do. Alan watched as the hand that had once been his came up and its fingernail dug into him. He was aware of being pulled off, pain tearing through him, until everything went black.

The Goat

WHITT POND

Whitt Pond is a man of faith. He believed we would publish this story when we told him how much we liked it seven years ago. That you're reading it now is proof that he was not only right but his story has withstood the test of time.

"**C**'mon, Scotty," Josh urged, fighting the steering wheel as the battered pickup bounced along the ungraded North Texas back road. "We're gonna be there in a few minutes. Say it now."

Across the seat, a small skinny boy with straw-colored hair stared unhappily at the floor.

"I can't," he mumbled.

"Try harder!"

No reply came. Josh glanced over at his younger brother. With eyes closed in silent concentration, Scotty was doing "touches," his right hand executing the familiar pattern over and over again. Thumb touch little finger, ring finger, middle finger, index finger, little finger again. As the repetitions increased, he opened his mouth in soundless pain.

"I . . . I *can't*!" Scotty cried finally. "I just *can't*!"

Josh looked away, but the view did nothing to improve his mood. The drought was everywhere. In the churning clouds of hot red-brown dust obscuring his rear view. In the sun-tortured fields with their endless rows of useless, shriveled peanut stubble. And in the solitary weathered houses that now lay empty and neglected.

"Why can't you, dammit?"

"I don't know," Scotty said in a subdued voice, staring down at his lap as he continued his repetitions. "I just can't, that's all." The rest of the trip was spent in silence.

The bouncing suddenly ceased as the truck pulled from the dirt road onto the highway into Morgan. A small official sign from better times stated the population to be 1,258. The real number was much lower now. Nobody wanted to know how much.

Further down the highway, a large and long-faded billboard paid tribute to the town's sole moment of glory, a single-A state football championship of twenty years earlier, never to be repeated.

As the truck slowed for the single traffic light, the hard times in Morgan were immediately evident. The peanut mill that had once provided the majority of jobs now stood like a gray metal mausoleum. Half the stores on the town's main street were boarded up, and the half that remained shimmered with defeat.

The handful of townfolk out on the sidewalk paused to stare at the pickup as it rolled by. Scotty slumped further down in his seat to get out of sight. Josh kept his eyes forward, avoiding the hard, angry faces that turned their way.

The Morgan Baptist Church parking lot was almost empty when they arrived. Scotty bit his lip and stared at the walkway leading to the entrance.

"C'mon," Josh coaxed gently, "it probably won't be that bad." He wondered if the words sounded as phony as they felt.

Pastor Roberts was waiting on the church steps, his hands clasped one atop the other over his belt buckle, the way all preachers seemed to stand when they were being preachers. Three other people were with him, the bright sun bleaching away any sympathy Josh had hoped to find in their hard-lined faces. One of them was his mother.

Josh's stomach tightened at the way she seemed to shrink into herself, physically withdrawing from "this evil world" that she so often railed against. Her bouts of depression had become more frequent and more consuming. This one was the worst.

"Mom, are you sure . . ." he began, but her piercing look stopped him cold. Further words would only bring on the screaming and the fist-shaking. For the hundredth time in the last two years, Josh wished his father was still alive.

"Well, boys," the Pastor said, "why don't we go inside where it's cooler?" He gestured to where the church doors stood open but made no move toward them. Nor did any of the others. They were watching, Josh knew, and waiting.

"Uh, Scotty," Josh said as casually as he could manage, "you forgot to roll up your window. You go do that and then join the rest of us inside."

The small boy's face flashed from puzzlement to surprised relief and he started to run back to the parking lot. But his mother grabbed him before he had gone two steps.

"You'll do what Pastor Roberts says, do you hear me?" his mother hissed, slapping her younger son across the ear as she spun him back toward the doorway.

"Calm yourself, Sister." The pastor guided the shaking woman away with one hand but kept the other firmly on Scotty's shoulder. He then glanced at Josh knowingly. "I think the window can wait until our business here is concluded. Scotty, why don't you go in first?"

Please, God, Josh prayed silently, *please let my brother get through Your doors the normal way. Just this once? Please?*

Gingerly rubbing his ear, Scotty stepped up and stood so that the toes of his sneakers barely touched the bottom of the doorway at exact right angles to the frame. Then he hopped through, landing with both heels touching the inside of the frame. He looked nervously down to see if his feet were still at right angles. After staring for a moment, he hopped back through the doorway and began again.

Josh's heart sank at the dark looks gathering on the adults' faces. It had taken Scotty half an hour to get out of the house this morning. The pressure he was now under could only make it worse.

Finally, on the eighth attempt, Scotty seemed satisfied that he had "done it right," the only explanation he was ever able to give for his strange behavior. Josh quickly followed and found him staring at the floor, trying not to look at any of the framed scriptures hanging on the wall.

The ordeal was repeated at the doors into the auditorium. But before Scotty could manage to get through, his mother grabbed him and pulled him inside.

"No!" Scotty struggled wild-eyed to get back to the doors he had passed through wrong. "Lemme go! Lemme go!"

"You see what he's like?" his mother cried as she dragged Scotty all the way up the aisle. "I can't take any more of this!" She slapped Scotty again, then kept on slapping him as he cried and struggled all the harder. Josh rushed up and pulled her away.

"Mom, stop it. You're hurting him."

"It's not *him*. It's that devil that's in him." She looked over to where the two church deacons were holding Scotty between them. He was crying but no longer resisting. "We've got to get that devil out of him." She stared back at Josh, her gray eyes uncomprehending. "Can't you understand that?"

Josh wanted to say something but before he could find the words Pastor Roberts came up.

"I'm sure Josh understands that, Sister." The preacher led them to a front pew. "You remember Mark, don't you Josh?"

"Yes, Pastor. Mark, chapter one, verses 23 through 27. The man in the synagogue with the unclean spirit."

"And?"

"Mark, chapter five, verses 2 through 19. The man with the legion of unclean spirits that were released into the swine."

"And you believe your Bible, don't you Josh?"

"Yes, Pastor."

"There, you see, Sister?" The Pastor smiled with approval, and his mother seemed comforted. "Josh knows what is right and what is not. Now as for Scotty here . . ."

Pastor Roberts held up a book. Scotty's Bible. Josh wondered how he had gotten ahold of it. Scotty looked down at the floor. The Pastor opened the book and began flipping through it.

"There seem to be a lot of words blacked out here, Scotty. Would you know anything about that?"

Scotty shrugged, refusing to look up.

"From the looks of it," the Pastor continued, "it's really just one word that's been blacked out, isn't it?"

Closing the book, the Pastor resumed his clasped-hands stance. "Say the word, Scotty. Your mother here needs to hear you say it. We *all* need to hear you say it. Say 'Jesus.'"

Scotty flinched and did a quick touch series. Josh hoped the others didn't see it.

"I can't." Scotty's whisper seemed to bounce off the walls.

Reaching down, the Pastor lifted Scotty's face up and clasped it in both hands.

"Yes, you can. Say it with me now." Lifting his own face heavenward, the Pastor closed his eyes and began speaking in sermon cadence. "Praise Jesus."

"Praise . . ." Scotty's mouth stayed open but nothing else came out.

"Everyone," the Pastor commanded without looking, "help our Brother Scotty in his hour of need. Praise Jesus."

A chorus of "Praise Jesus" went up. Josh thought his own voice sounded hollow. He couldn't hear Scotty's.

"Praise Jesus!" the Pastor shouted, as if he were speaking to an entire congregation.

Please, Jesus, Josh prayed even as he voiced the response, *help my brother. Help him say Your name.*

Tears were streaming down Scotty's upturned face and his fingers danced their ritual dance. When the Pastor looked down again, he grabbed the boy's hands in his own, stopping the motion.

"Brother Scotty! Jesus needs to hear you say His name. He needs to hear it now. Praise Jesus!"

"Prai . . . prai . . ." Scotty stammered. Suddenly he tried to twist away, but the Pastor held him fast. Then he threw up.

The smell was sharp and sour and it tugged at Josh's stomach. One of the deacons went for a mop and a bucket. The Pastor was staring at Scotty in astonishment, and even a little fear. Josh wondered about that. He had never seen the Pastor, or any other preacher for that matter, afraid of anything. Taking out his handkerchief, he began cleaning Scotty's face.

"You okay?" he asked in a low voice.

Scotty coughed, trying to answer.

"I tried, Josh. I really did."

"I know you did, Scotty."

"Josh . . ." It was scarcely a whisper. "I'm scared."

"Don't worry. It's gonna be okay." Josh looked up at the faces around them, again seeing the fear in their eyes. "You'll see," he said, to Scotty, to the others, and to himself. "It's gonna be okay."

———————

The Pastor kept Scotty at the church for an all night prayer vigil and sent Josh home. Josh's mother went back to the neighbor's house, where she had been staying for the last three days. Wheezer, a black-and-white dog of unplanned parentage, kept him company. Josh fed Wheezer and then fixed his own dinner. Later, he lay in bed, thinking about his father. After a long while, he finally fell asleep.

Deacon Evans called the next day and told Josh to bring some fresh clothes for Scotty. He sounded tired and distracted.

"How's Scotty doing?" Josh asked.

"Well, it's been a powerful struggle, and it ain't over yet," Evans admitted. Josh could hear him scratching the stubble on his chin. "But don't you worry none. Ever'one in Morgan's prayin' that the Lord'll guide Pastor Roberts' hand in this matter."

When Josh arrived, Deacon Evans was in the back of the church, sitting outside the room where the choir robes were kept. His suit was rumpled and his tie hung loosely around his neck. He nodded at the door but did not follow Josh in.

Scotty was asleep, lying across a couple of folding chairs. When Josh touched him on the shoulder, he awoke with a start, almost falling off the chairs.

"Hey, s'okay," Josh said quickly. "It's just me."

Scotty blinked a couple of times, confused. He looked tired, his face drawn and pale.

"Oh," he finally said, rubbing his eyes. "Is it over? Can I go home now?"

"I don't think so," Josh said, remembering Deacon Evans outside the door. He looked around the room. The windowless walls were bare of any adornment, other than a rack of choir robes pushed up against one wall. "Have you been here all night?"

"Yeah, I guess so."

"What have they been doing?"

Scotty pulled his knees up to his chin, his feet resting on the edge of the chair.

"Well, they pray a lot, asking God to get this devil out of me. And, and . . ." Scotty bit his lip, thinking.

"And what?"

"They keep asking me my name all the time. I kept telling them 'Scotty,' but they just got mad. So I quit telling them that. But I don't know what else to tell them."

"Anything else?" Josh took the clothes out of the paper bag and laid them on one of the chairs.

Flexing his heels, Scotty rocked back and forth on the chair. He stared at the floor for a long time before answering.

"Yeah, they . . . they made me take my clothes off once. They said they were looking for devil's marks. The only thing they found was that spot on my arm, where the skin's a different color. They argued about that a lot."

Josh glanced back at the closed door.

"Scotty," he asked quietly, "why did you mark through all the . . ." He hesitated, then continued. ". . . the Jesuses in your Bible?"

The finger ritual was still there, but slower this time.

"I don't know. It's just that every time I see it, or hear it, I just feel like . . . like somethin' bad's gonna happen. Somethin' real bad."

"Like what?"

"I don't know," Scotty cried, "Just something bad."

"Were you able to say it last night?"

"No." Scotty looked up. "Josh, I'm tired. I wanna go home."

"I know. But . . ."

The room suddenly felt too small, the air too thick. He needed to get out of there. Away from there. Away from all of it.

"Look, it won't be much longer. Just hang in there. God . . ." The word seemed suddenly strange, like he didn't know what it meant anymore. "God'll take care of it. You'll see." He forced himself to smile, and to believe. "It'll be okay."

———————

The barbed wire cut at Josh's work gloves as he pulled the last line tight along the fence. The job done, he got the water jug out of the pickup and drank deeply.

It had been two days since he last saw Scotty. He had gone into town each morning, but both times the Pastor had said it was not the right time to see him. Something about not giving the devil a weakness to exploit.

From where he was, he could see both the farmhouse and the cemetery. As he looked from one to the other, a kaleidoscope of memories rolled over. The family having a barbecue down near the creek. His father grooming Wheezer out on the front porch, carefully picking out the cockleburrs. His mother working on a painting. Scotty off looking for arrowheads in the newly plowed field across the road. His father asking where Scotty had gone.

Josh threw the jug on the seat and climbed in the pickup. The dust blew up behind him all the way into town. He was still wearing his work gloves when he reached the church. Deacon Evans was sitting outside the room.

"I've come to see Scotty."

"Now Josh . . ." Evans stood up, shaking his head. ". . . you know the Pastor said you couldn't . . ."

Josh ignored him and started for the door. When the deacon tried to stop him, Josh shoved past him, causing him to fall over the chair.

Scotty looked bad. Dark gray crescents hung under his eyes, which seemed drawn back in his head. His lips were cracked. The room, bare now except for the chairs, smelled of sweat.

"You're coming home," Josh said. He started to lift his brother up but stopped when Scotty cried out in pain. "What's wrong?"

"My shoulder." The voice was dry and rasping. "My arm got twisted around and it hurts."

"Can you walk?" Josh looked out in the hallway but the deacon was gone. "We gotta get out of here."

Scotty looked up from where he was sitting. He had to swallow a couple of times before he was able to speak.

"No, Josh. I can't. I gotta stay here."

"What?" Josh's heart was beating fast, and the seconds seemed to drag by. "Why??"

"I . . . I wanna be cured. I want this devil out of me." The boy began to sob. "I don't want to hurt anyone anymore."

Josh opened his mouth, but nothing came out. He raised his hands in a helpless gesture, struggling to find the words.

"What are you talking about?" he asked finally. "You've never hurt anyone in your entire life."

"Yes, I have!" Scotty cried. "It's this devil that's in me. I'm the reason it doesn't rain anymore. I'm the reason the peanut mill closed. I'm the reason all those people are getting cancer." He struck his fist weakly on his leg. "It's me. It's me. It's me."

Suddenly there were voices and footsteps coming up the hall. Josh thought frantically but the men reached the room before he could act. A moment later, he was dragged back into the hall and held before Pastor Roberts.

"Brother Josh, you are not to come here again," the Pastor said softly. His face was oddly sympathetic. "I know you are worried about your brother. But the devil is using you as his instrument." He reached out and put his arm on Josh's shoulder. "Scotty needs you to be strong. And that means letting us fight this devil to the finish. We must *all* be strong. Our faith is our only defense. Doubt is the way to destruction."

Josh shook his head in disbelief. The arms holding him drew tighter, but he made no effort to break free.

"Pastor, I don't know what to believe anymore. But Scotty's no more got a devil in him than you do." He looked around at men he had known all his life, men who had been his father's friends. "I know he acts funny, but what has he ever done? To any of you? To anyone? What has he ever done?"

The Pastor gazed at Josh sadly.

"I'm sorry, Brother Josh, but your faith isn't strong enough to resist the devil's tricks. And we can't allow your weakness to stop us from saving your brother."

"There's no devil!" Josh shouted as he was dragged outside. "Do you hear me, Scotty? There's no devil!"

"Hey, kid! Wake up!"

Josh looked up and saw Mr. Brodie bending over him. Brodie had been Morgan's peace officer until the town had to lay him off. Now he was the volunteer peace officer.

"What is it?" Josh asked. He tried to sit up. It was difficult with his hands handcuffed around the support beam. Morgan couldn't afford a jail, so they had used the back room in Higgenbotham's hardware store.

"You're free to go," Brodie said as he unlocked the cuffs.

"What about the charges?"

"Well, there aren't any no more. Pastor's dropped the unlawful entry and Evans's dropped the assault. Like I said, you're free to go."

The usually talkative peace officer seemed subdued, his mind elsewhere. He stared out at the street while Josh got dressed, not saying a word until Josh started out the door.

"I think you oughtta go on home." Brodie spoke without even glancing Josh's way. "I think your mother's gonna need you."

Josh saw the smoke from the trash fire before he reached the house. *Well,* he thought, *at least she's not lying in bed listening to those mournful gospel songs all day.*

She was coming out of the house when he pulled up. Her arms were filled with Scotty's clothes. She didn't look at Josh as she headed toward the trash fire.

"Mom," Josh yelled as he ran to catch up with her. "What are you doing? Mom?"

His mother ignored him as she threw the clothes on the fire. Josh could see other things in the flames. Books. A baseball glove. Shoes. Without waiting, his mother turned away and headed back to the house. Josh followed.

"Your brother's run away. He's not coming back." She was staring straight ahead as she spoke. "I'll need your help with his bed." It was not a request.

"His bed? Mom, what are you doing?"

She turned toward him, and for a moment she was his mother again, in pain and needing comfort. He reached out instinctively but she jerked away and the moment was gone.

"I told you, he's gone and he's not coming back," she screamed, her fist shaking in the air. "Not here. Not ever. Now you get in here and help me with this bed!"

Josh got in the pickup and sped away, his mother's voice fading as her image shrank in the rear-view mirror. It was Saturday, so he headed straight for the Pastor's house.

The Pastor was kneeling by a single rose bush, checking the leaves for cut-worms. It was the only green thing left in a yard of dead grass and withered leaves.

"Where's Scotty?" Josh asked, his tone flat and disrespectful.

The Pastor leaned back but did not look up. He suddenly seemed tired and worn out, as beaten down as the sun-burnt grass he knelt on.

"Your brother ran away, Josh. The devil was too strong." The Pastor looked down at his hands, shaking his head. "I wasn't able to save him. I'm sorry."

"Then where did he go?" Josh looked around angrily. "Nobody here would hide him or help him. Not in this town."

"I don't know where he went. No one does." He reached haltingly for a browning rose leaf but stopped short, dropping his hand. "Go home, Josh," he said softly. "Your mother needs you, more than ever. Go home."

———

Josh sat in the pickup. He had stopped where the road ended at the edge of the creek. The bare hulk of what had once been a bridge lay rusting across the small trickle of water that still managed to flow past. The shadows grew longer as the sun edged toward the horizon.

Scotty wasn't anywhere to be found. Not in town, or on any of the roads leading into town, or in any of the abandoned houses along those roads. Josh ran over the problem again and again, not liking what he was thinking but unable to do anything else.

As the first stars began to twinkle into view, he remembered something, something he'd seen. He sat up, wondering why it seemed important. A moment later another memory came to him, and then he knew why.

He went home first. The house was dark and silent, his mother gone. Off near the edge of the yard, the embers of the trash fire glowed red in the deepening dusk. Josh got what he needed from the workshop behind the house and loaded it into the pickup. Wheezer jumped in on the passenger side and they drove off.

The Selby place, abandoned for years, sat at the end of one of the most remote and least maintained roads around Morgan. But it did have some metal holding pens that people sometimes used, especially when the ownership of the livestock was in question.

Eight large hogs roamed the confines of the nearest pen. He had noticed them on his earlier search of the place. They hadn't seemed important then. He shut off the engine but left the lights on. The snuffling and squealing rose as he walked closer. "And the unclean spirits went out," he quoted softly, "and entered into the swine. . . ."

The ground looked unusually torn up, even for hogs. Two sets of fresh tire tracks led up to the pen. One might have been a truck, but the other had the distinctive third-wheel marks of a back-hoe.

Opening the connecting gate, Josh waited while Wheezer herded the protesting hogs into the neighboring pen. Then he pumped up the Coleman lantern, and soon a bright white-ish light shone over the scene.

He tested the ground with his shovel. The blade went in easily, going much deeper than it would normally have been able to. For a moment, he just stared at the ground, trying to see through it. Then he began to dig.

———

Josh wondered why he was hearing birds. Then he realized that he had fallen asleep. The ground under him was hard, and his sore muscles screamed their abuse when he sat up.

It was morning, and the sun was well on its way to warming things up. Wheezer looked up from where he was lying next to the pickup and then put his head down again. The hogs were shuffling about listlessly, uninterested in anything that did not involve food.

The hole was large and uneven, but it was still just a hole. There was no sign of anything in it. Struggling to ignore the stiffness and pain, Josh picked up the shovel and slid down to begin again.

Josh worked slowly and without thought. Each shovelful was the same as the last, and the hole deepened before him. The sun's light edged lower along the dirt walls as the morning wore on.

Suddenly Wheezer lifted his head up and looked around. His body tensed up and he sneezed. A moment later he sneezed again and was up on his feet. Padding around the hole, he sniffed at the piles of dirt with growing agitation. Then he clambered down and began digging.

Josh's throat ached and his eyes burned. Putting the shovel aside, he knelt down and began using his hands alongside Wheezer. He stopped when he felt something resist, something smooth and rubbery. The toe of a sneaker.

Figuring the distance, Josh moved over a few feet and brushed the dirt away. A thatch of straw-colored hair came up under his hand. He cleared the rest away slowly and carefully.

At first glance, Scotty looked like he was just waking up. But the half-open eyes were glazed over, and bits of dirt still clung to his lashes. His face was tired and gray, except where a large purple bruise crossed the left side. The lips were almost blue.

Scotty's shirt-tail was hanging out, down across his belt. Josh was always having to tuck it in for him. Reaching down, he did it again. A powerful grief welled up inside him and spilled out in hot blinding tears. It took a long time to run dry.

He left Wheezer with Scotty and headed back into town. The streets were deserted. Then he remembered it was Sunday. Stopping in front of the church, he shut the engine off but stayed sitting behind the wheel. Everything was quiet.

He thought about the rifle hanging on the gun rack across the pickup's rear window, but he couldn't bring himself to even reach for it. Leaning his head against the steering wheel, he closed his eyes.

The sound of music drifted out through the open windows. Looking at the church entrance, he thought about going inside. Part of him still wanted to. Everything and everyone he had known was in there, waiting.

"Amazing grace," the voices sang, "how sweet the sound, that saved a wretch like me."

"I once was lost," Josh joined in softly, "but now I am found. Was blind, but now I see."

Reaching down, he started the pickup again. The sound of the engine and the crunch of gravel beneath the tires blurred away the hidden choir, but Josh continued on his own.

"T'was grace that taught my heart to fear, and grace my fear relieved." He held the note long as he turned onto the highway. It was thirty miles to Comanche. There was a state police office there.

"How precious did that grace appear . . ." Out of the corner of his eye, Josh saw Scotty sitting on the seat beside him, singing along. He knew he wasn't there, but he didn't care. He was glad for the company.

". . . the hour I first believed."

Prisoner 392

JON F. MERZ

After reading more than seven hundred submissions and having bought twenty-four stories we figured we were finally done. But the last story remaining to be read demanded that we buy it. It was that good. We're thinking, Kafka; we're thinking Ambrose Bierce; we're thinking Melville. We told you: it's good.

They called it the slit.

And it was the only way Prisoner 392 could see the outside world.

Cut into the iron door of his cell, the six-inch wide by two-inch tall opening looked like a mouth, rusted burs jutting up and down from the unfinished edges like serrated teeth.

The slit giveth; he could see the general population walking in the yard where the sun scorched the fecal brown earth into a fine dust that exploded in the wake of every footstep.

And the slit taketh away; it rubbed salt into the open wound of a life sentence spent in solitary confinement. It teased with tempting glimpses—walking more than eight feet in a straight line, breathing the dust-caked air, feeling a simple breeze, almost feeling . . . free.

Even the slit's position in the door reinforced its cruel purpose. Cut exactly four feet from the ground, an average-sized man would have little choice but to stoop in order to peer through. Soon, his back muscles would spasm. His quadriceps would burn. His neck would stiffen.

But still, he would look.

He'd been called Jakob once. He'd been called other names before that. Before the murders. Before the trials. Before everything.

Now he was simply Prisoner 392.

They'd stripped him of his name as easily as they'd stripped his clothes when the transport steamer had finally docked in Belize. Jakob was grateful to have merely survived the journey. Storms had pounded the vessel mercilessly enroute. In the vast hold, three hundred prisoners waded through a viscous muck of urine, feces, vomit, sweat, and blood. The few times the sun managed to pierce the heavy gray clouds that had been the ship's albatross throughout, it had baked the cargo hold until a cloying mist issued up from the bacterial swill.

Fifty men died crossing the ocean.

Those with the constitution it took to withstand the hellish trip spent the time discussing the impossibilities of escape. Marauding cats the color of night prowled the jungles outside the prison. Heathen tribes that still feasted on human flesh hunted like silent ghosts. Venomous asps slithered through the underbrush. And famished sharks filled the waterways hoping for a tasty morsel in the guise of a foolish convict.

Jakob only smiled. Let the rest of these fools suffer a lifetime away from the fruits of civilized society. He would be going home.

Soon enough.

Tumbling down the rickety wooden gangway toward an equally unstable dock, Jakob got his first glimpse of Belize. It looked like a brothel built onto the ocean. Whores draped themselves over railings of the closest buildings taunting the men with quick glimpses of bare breast or plump buttock. Jakob found himself unable to look without feeling a surge of adrenaline bloat his bloodstream.

Other rogues clotted the streets. Traders in wide-brimmed hats offered up exotic animal skins, revolvers dangling like Christmas ornaments from their hips. Vagabonds loitered by the docks, their clothes ragged and their futures uncertain.

But the children drew his eyes most.

They ran barefoot begging food and money from any-one they could. Their lean legs powered their quest for nutrition. Their eyes gleamed bright with hope. A thin sheen of salty sweat basted their tanned lithe bodies.

Jakob licked his lips. Oh, but he could give them such salvation as they never knew existed. Such delicious de-lights could he perpetrate upon their innocent souls. And such heinous pleasure would he derive from their screams and pleas for mercy.

The sharp clang of an iron bell—a single toll—fell over the raucous chatter that had assaulted his ears.

And silence dropped like a guillotine blade on a soft fleshy neck.

Everyone in the town watched them march off the dock. Jakob looked around. What did they know? What was this place? He felt like a lamb being led to the slaughter.

Armed guards herded them like cattle, ready to shoot at the slightest provocation. The trip hadn't been easy for them either.

Two miles from the docks, down the winding dirt road lined with thorny bushes and spindly trees bearing no fruit, Jakob caught sight of the prison itself.

At first glance, the line from Poe's poem jumped into his head.

Up Babylon-like walls, he thought. Appropriate given the imposing height of the sun-baked fortifications. Jakob almost smirked. Poe had gotten it right. But this wasn't the *City in the Sea.*

They passed through the main gate—a spiked portcullis held aloft by twin hemp ropes the width of a fist. The chief of the guards turned then and barked out a single command.

"Stop!"

The cloud of dust that had followed the human caravan from the docks settled on their shaved heads and shoulders. Under the blazing sun, they waited.

Two more men died in the sizzling inferno.

The chief of guards bellowed out a list of numbers. Roll call. Prisoners answered in time to their numbers. One by one they were led off to various cellblocks to be deloused and issued their camp garments.

Jakob stood under the blazing sun wondering when his number would be called. He had to close his eyes to keep the brilliant yellow from burning his eyes. The heat hung on him, an oppressive yoke he longed to throw off. Sweat cascaded down his back, soaking through the red and white striped threadbare shirt he wore. With every breath the air grew heavier, bloated with a humidity perfumed by oleander and lilacs. He felt woozy. His thoughts swam through molasses.

He felt the gazes of other inmates—the veterans already serving their sentences here—rove over his moldy, putrid body. Were they singling him out for pleasure or pain? Would they seek some torrid release later that night, dreaming about Jakob? Or would they hope for a chance at him during the communal shower sessions?

Dreams are all you'll have, he thought. For Jakob knew one certainty about his sentence beyond his inevitable escape.

"Prisoner 392!" The chief of guards barked out his number.

He wavered.

"Prisoner 392!"

Jakob shuffled forward and fell. The chief ordered two other inmates to pick him up. He could barely stand, but finally managed to hold his head up.

The chief glared.

"Prisoner 392," he said. "Solitary."

With that Jakob felt himself dragged to the cell. At least it was out of the direct sun, he reasoned stumbling into it. The door slammed shut; the iron impacted the doorjamb with a solid clang like the bell back in the town. He leaned against the cool rough walls and then drank from the clay water pitcher that had been shoved rudely through the opening at the base of the door.

He sucked down what must have been almost a gallon of the stagnant brew before he heard a pounding against his door. He frowned and slid the container back out. Someone grabbed it and the opening slammed shut.

Jakob turned his attention back to the cell. He paced it out and found it measured eight feet by eight feet. Only eight feet? The injustice of the situation annoyed him. How would he exercise? How would he keep himself in good condition for his eventual dash for freedom?

His gaze shifted to a 12-inch diameter hole in the rear right corner. What was this? His toilet? There was no seat. There was no . . . he groaned with the realization that he would have to squat and clean himself with his hand. Disgusting!

And what of his slumber? He pressed down on the bed only to discover it was a crude cement base covered with a thin straw mattress, sheet, and single blanket. A burlap sack stuffed with dried grass would act as his pillow.

Surely the warden would have to be informed. No man could be expected to live out his sentence with dignity in such dreadful conditions.

He thought of the children in the town. Lord Byron's poetry danced in his mind.

A rose with all its sweetest leaves yet folded . . .

He sighed and glanced skyward.

Bars?

Steel bars roofed his cell. Worse, he could hear guards walking patrols on a walkway that ran atop the cells, able to peer in and instantly ascertain what was going on below.

No privacy, either? But how on earth would he . . . ?

A guard appeared overhead.

"Strip!"

Jakob complied. A torrent of water rained down. The guard tossed a bar of soap.

"Wash!"

Jakob scrubbed himself. He wondered vaguely if the guard was enjoying the show. He risked a glimpse up and saw the guard talking to another. Jakob felt a small measure of relief.

Another deluge rinsed him and Jakob watched the soapy residue slide off and stream toward the toilet hole. He considered this and reasoned the floor of his cell must have been built at a slight grade to enable drainage.

A towel plopped onto his head. "Be quick, Prisoner 392."

He dried himself. New clothes fell through the bars. "Get dressed and push the old rags through the food gate."

He did. The guard disappeared.

Jakob lay on his bed, feeling the coarse straw bite into his back. The pillow offered little comfort. In Paris, he would have dined on figs and dates while reclining on sofas with the softest pillows. He would have drifted off to his deviant dreams while his houseboy plucked the strings of a harp. And now, he had none of it.

But despite that, he soon fell asleep.

—————

Oil lamps burned all the time so the guards could keep watch. Jakob covered his eyes with one arm until pins and needles stabbed at every nerve. Then he switched arms.

Breakfast, watery rice porridge, arrived at six o'clock.

A lunch of rice and vegetables came around noon. And dinner, which normally included fish or chicken, was served promptly at six. On particularly hot days, a jug of water would appear up to four times a day. Jakob couldn't argue with the idea that the prison staff did seem to want to keep their inmates alive. He felt lucky about that.

But he also figured that by keeping them alive, the prison exacted the full toll of their punishments. Living wasn't much of a life at all.

Not any more.

———

On the third day, he moved to the slit in the door.

Men wandered around just twenty feet from his cell. Further punishment, he decided. Solitary inmates weren't allowed to speak. Any infractions resulted in a plate being placed over the slit. No more views of the outside world.

And yet, the temptation to call out to a passing inmate bore down on him with such ferocity that Jakob wondered if he'd be able to hold out.

He must!

One prisoner drew his attention more than the others. He stayed alone, a bookish man wearing thick spectacles. His slender limbs reminded Jakob of the arachnids belonging to the Phalangida order. He smiled as the Latin popped into his head. All of that knowledge he'd acquired so long ago seemed to belong to a different man.

His eyes refocused on the small man. Eventually, he could see the faded number on his back. "53."

How long had he been here that his number had faded so? What crimes had he committed that he now called this pit of hell home? Did he dream of escape the way Jakob did?

He fell asleep thinking about 53.

And dreamed about being free. He dreamed about escape, about getting out of the cramped cell. He dreamed about climbing over the wall, about fleeing the prison and finding his way back to his home.

He had work to do, after all. More cities to visit. More bodies to gut. More organs to feast upon. More children to . . . liberate.

He woke up drenched in sweat, gasping for breath, and aware of the pulsing in his loins.

The reality of where he was crashed down on him and for the first time since he'd been caught, he allowed himself to weep until he fell back asleep.

———

Through the slit the next day, he saw 53 again. The little man shuffled across the flat ground, shoulders hunched and hands shoved deep into his pockets. Every few steps, he would glance about, almost as if he expected someone to attack him. Jakob suspected 53 suffered mentally. Had the neurotic delusions of his mind pushed him over the edge? Were they the spring from which his criminal career had jetted itself out upon the world?

Jakob slumped back away from the slit and allowed the muscle aches to bleed out of his back and thighs. He closed his eyes and saw his own torrid past dredged up and played out across the screen of his mind.

But instead of shrinking from the horror of his past, Jakob smiled.

And embraced his true self.

He'd been a doctor once. Originally from Russia, he had traveled all over the continent, touring the largest cities. But he never stayed long. Just enough to slake the peculiar dementia that possessed his soul.

He'd enjoyed his life until Paris.

Who would have thought the gendarme would find him in such a compromising position?

Open wide, young sir. That's it. Now just hold still while I slide this . . .

Surely the fates had intervened that time. God's own bizarre sense of humor, he supposed.

Regardless, he was here now.

But he wanted to be back there.

The realization that he needed to escape set his heart hammering inside his cavernous chest. Adrenaline punched him in the bowels. Excitement gave him goosebumps. Blood surged south, thickening his veins.

The plan seemed fantastic.

And yet . . . it could work.

Perhaps.

———————

Jakob wondered if his vocal chords would function once he escaped. Even now it felt like a fuzzy fungus had begun growing at the back of his throat. He tried to assure himself he'd be able to speak any of the five languages he knew—once he got out of there.

The slit in the door became Jakob's microscope. Prisoner 53 became his laboratory specimen mounted on the slide of desire driven by necessity. Every day, Jakob subjected the little man to the most intense scrutiny he could focus through the tiny peephole.

He began with the obvious.

From watching his stride, Jakob decided 53 had injured his hip at some point since he shifted more weight to his right side and dragged his left foot a bit. It hardly registered.

But Jakob noticed.

Prisoner 53 inhaled roughly ten times each minute. Jakob concluded the little man was reasonably fit, despite his mousy manner.

His shoulders hunched up and rode forward of his head. Jakob had once seen a bare-knuckle fighter who punched with a similar head position. But 53 wasn't a fighter.

While Jakob studied him, 53 suddenly stopped.

Turned.

And seemed to stare right at Jakob.

Did he just wink at me?

Jakob smiled. How delightful. A friend of all things and here of all places. Surely this would be truly worthy of note.

The physical qualities of 53 noted and organized inside his head, Jakob began practicing. Walking posed the most difficulty. He kept bumping into the damned walls. Eight feet! Who had designed this cell? Why so little space? Wasn't it enough to rob a man of his freedom without forcing him to live within such pitiful dimensions? A heat rose within him. Jakob punched the wall and felt a flap of skin tear away from his left hand. Bright red smeared the grayish white surface. Jakob licked his wound and felt a rush of saliva at the first coppery taste.

Jakob sighed. Perhaps what mattered most weren't the physical characteristics at all, but rather the inner workings of 53's mind. The things he could readily observe merely served as a gateway to the inner being.

What Jakob wanted most of all.

———————

At night, the demons came. The faces of his past, brightly painted with red streaks and pinkish hues, screamed and laughed at him. They pointed with long fingers. They taunted with shrieks and howls. They chided his physical inadequacies.

What can you do with that?

I have fingers longer than you!

Go away you terrible ugly fool!

"NO!"

Jakob woke screaming and had to clamp a hand across his mouth for fear that the guards should hear him. More than ever, now he needed the slit.

He heard footsteps overhead and risked a look up. A guard frowned at him.

Would he report Jakob? Would they punish him? Would they take away his only view of the outside world? The only chance he had of escape?

The guard merely shook his head and walked away.

Jakob slept no more that night.

———————

"Rusilov. That's Russian, is it not?"

Jakob stood with his face to the wall. Behind him, the warden waited in the doorway of his cell. The chief of guards stood nearby. The visit had surprised Jakob.

He said nothing.

"You may talk, Prisoner 392. And I would like a response to my question."

The cultured voice bit into Jakob's brain, its edge as slight yet precise as a scalpel. The inflection seemed clear: the warden would be civil if Jakob behaved. But the civility would end at any sign of disrespect.

"I was Russian. Yes sir."

"Was?"

Jakob shrugged. "Now I am simply Prisoner 392."

The warden chuckled. "Indeed. Turn around and face me."

Jakob did and almost blanched at the sight of the bloated dwarf seated in a wicker wheelchair. What sort of fetal abnormality had produced such a specimen as this, with his tufted curly black hair poking out of his pink scalp and his lopsided eyes set lower than the bridge of his hawk-like nose? Jakob tried to remain unfazed.

The warden smiled; was he enjoying Jakob's discomfort? "One of my guards informs me you had a rough night last. Is that true?"

"A nightmare, sir. Nothing more."

The warden leaned back drumming his stubby fingers on the arms of his chair. "Perhaps an omen for you." He smiled again. "Do you believe in an afterlife?"

"Do you mean God?"

"There is no God," snapped the warden. "A truly benevolent deity would never have stirred the ovarian cauldron that eventually gushed me out." He frowned. "I mean, do you think there's another place your soul travels to when your body dies?"

"I don't know."

The warden smiled. "Your file says you took pleasure dismembering children. That you . . . availed yourself of their virgin orifices. And then you hacked them into little pieces. It says that you even dined on their body parts."

Jakob said nothing.

"You're a beast, Prisoner 392. I am also a beast. But we are different. You are a beast of mind and spirit. But I am merely a beast of the flesh. Horrible to gaze upon, but most would agree I am not a monster."

"Sir?"

"The true monsters in our world are not born of the seed of man and egg of woman. They are spawned in the forge of a diseased mind." He fixed Jakob with another gaze. "Do you believe this is hell, Prisoner 392?"

"You said as much, sir."

"But do you believe it?"

Jakob looked up at the warden and for the first time saw the gleam in his eyes. The skin around his mouth stretched taut against his brown teeth. He was enjoying this.

"I think it is, sir. Yes."

The warden nodded. "Do yourself a favor, 392. Don't try to escape from my house. We have had several attempts over the years. None of them lived to get past the guards."

"I'm not trying to escape, sir."

The warden looked at Jakob hard. "Good. Good." He nodded at the chief. "Perhaps this one is not like the others after all."

"One way to tell, sir," answered the chief.

The warden smiled once more. "Indeed." Both men backed out of the cell and the heavy iron door slammed shut—another toll of the bell.

Jakob stood absolutely still for a long time afterward.

The slit called out to him. It demanded his presence. And Jakob complied.

He peered through the opening and found his target—locked his eyes on 53's back and again studied the man.

He absorbed as much as he could. Would it be enough? Would it enable him to escape? He'd lied to the warden, of course. But had he fooled him? Jakob shuddered, recalling the puffy distorted face that had seemed to know every thought that passed through Jakob's head.

Did 53 just wave at me?

Jakob snapped his attention back to the little man. Was there a gleam in 53's eyes? Did he know Jakob was studying him? Surely he couldn't realize Jakob's purpose.

Could he?

He had to escape. To stay here meant death. But Jakob doubted that it would end there. Perhaps the warden really was the caretaker of hell. And if Jakob died here, might his soul not also be in mortal danger?

No, he had to go ahead with his plan.

And so, as he stooped at the slit in the door, he began matching his own inhalations and exhalations to those of 53. He watched as 53 walked slower now. Jakob allowed his own mind to expand, to fuse across the distance with that of 53. A mental link of sorts.

If only . . .

Jakob focused his thoughts. He saw the command he wanted 53 to carry out. He formed the words in his head.

He exhaled and sent them out into the mental ether.

But 53 merely continued walking as if nothing in the world mattered more.

Jakob tried ten times more before slumping away from the door.

Exhausted.

———————

Something was missing.

A key ingredient that would enable him to make the connection and force 53 to do his bidding. But what?

He studied 53 again. But this time, his attention was drawn to a steady undulating creak that came from somewhere on his right.

The warden rolled into view, his rickety wheelchair the source of the sound. His misshapen figure reminded Jakob of the flightless marine birds he'd read about explorers discovering in the Southern Hemisphere. The warden's stubby arms seemed as useless as the faulty wings evolution had gifted those birds with.

But surely they were not as ugly to gaze upon.

Why was the warden in the yard?

Jakob watched in amazement as the warden directed his chair toward 53. And then stopped. Jakob could see the warden's mouth move.

What is he saying?

Prisoner 53 responded. Jakob watched him smile and nod his head.

Smile?

Who smiled here?

What cause for mirth or gaiety could there ever be in such a horrendous place as this?

The warden wheeled himself away, the creak-creak-creak that echoed across the yard a hellish metronome marking an eternity yet to be served.

Jakob stared at 53.

Studying.

Had he chosen correctly? 53 was the guinea pig, after all. Jakob felt no real compunction about trying to force his will on him. After all, he'd forced plenty more physical things on his victims in the past.

His mouth swam in saliva as the vivid memories surged back into his head.

Soon, he thought. Soon, he must get free.

———————

The sun shone even brighter the next day and Jakob sweltered in the confines of his tiny cell. A shimmering haze boiled up out of the ground in front of Jakob's cell door. The air inside his cell felt sticky; it was almost too painful to breathe.

His mind and body couldn't take much more.

Back at the slit, he saw 53 shuffling around the yard. Without a care in the world, Jakob thought.

53 stopped and looked at Jakob again.

His mouth moved.

What had he said?

A clap of thunder broke over the prison and Jakob saw the dark clouds coming from the east.

From the sea—the sweet ocean that would be Jakob's path to salvation.

A whistle sounded in the yard. Prisoners filed past Jakob's door, hurrying to get inside before the rain fell.

Then 53 drew close.

Closer.

And Jakob heard him.

"I can help you."

Surprise clogged Jakob's mind. He couldn't find his own voice. 53's cut him off before he could try.

"The rainy season is coming. When it storms, I'll be here at nightfall. And together we will leave this place."

Then he vanished inside.

Jakob rocked back.

Stunned.

But strangely . . . hopeful.

Had it worked? Had Jakob's plan to somehow control 53's mind succeeded? Or had 53 simply been waiting for the right time to get out of here? Perhaps 53's plan required something he didn't have.

A friend.

Jakob smiled.

Let the rains come.

———————

He dreaded the night. Despite the light from the overhead oil lamps, a heavy darkness enveloped his mind. He floated through their faces. He tasted their coppery blood. He swam through a sea of intestines, livers, and kidneys, all slick and run together like melted ice cream.

He vomited and ejaculated almost simultaneously; he woke covered in his own filth and semen.

"392!"

He looked up, knowing he had undigested bits of dinner stuck to his face. The guard frowned and directed a water hose down on him. "Wash yourself. And be quick about it."

Jakob scrubbed himself clean. The water vanished. The vomit, feces, and spurted seed disappeared as well.

But when he closed his eyes, the darkness returned.

And with it, the demons.

———————

Another cracked scalding day dawned outside Jakob's cell.

This heat!

Jakob wanted to claw his way through the iron door. He wanted to tunnel down into the depths of the cool, dark earth. He wanted to hide under his bed. If he could just get away from this damned heat!

But he could go nowhere.

The stagnant water in the clay pitcher tasted like dirt. Grit swam in his mouth with each gulp.

He paced in his cell.

Two steps.

Turn.

Two steps.

Turn.

It was too hot to stand. Jakob squatted in his cell, thinking a layer of cooler air might be close to the ground.

Maybe lower.

He lay on the floor.

It was still hot.

And he could go no further.

Jakob went back to the door. He wanted to shout. He wanted to call out to 53, "Hey! When will the storms come? When can we escape? Friend?"

But 53 only glanced his way once.

The smile he gave Jakob didn't make the heat or his tiny cell any easier to endure.

———

Jakob spent the rest of the day peering through the slit at the lifeless brown exercise yard. He stared at the hard-packed earth, longing to feel it beneath his feet. He listened to the birds chirping beyond the walls, safe in their trees. And he watched the sun's rays fade as evening came on.

He tried to sleep. But closing his eyes for even a minute brought the demons. They shrieked louder. They bullied. Poked. Prodded. Slapped. Smacked.

Are you crying?

Oh, you poor little boy.

You poor little baby.

Jakob screamed.

Just go away!

He shot up.

Had he screamed? Or only imagined it?

He looked up.

Waiting.

But the guards never came over.

He leaned back.

I must get out of here!

———————

Sometime later, after exhaustion had finally dragged Jakob down into the depths of a dreamless purgatory, the rains fell.

Soft at first, the showers soon turned to sheets.

Lightning flashed.

Thunder cracked.

And Jakob woke.

Was it time?

Was this the moment?

Would it be tonight?

He swung his legs over the side of his cement bed and crept to his door. He huddled against the iron, longing to feel the cool rain touch his skin. He could taste the moisture staining the humid air. He could inhale its clean scent.

But still, he couldn't touch it.

And he didn't dare risk sticking his hand through the slit. The burs would have sliced his hand open.

Then he heard it. A slight sound out of harmony with the rest of nature's discordant symphony.

53?

Is that you?

A set of eyes appeared at the slit.

A whisper tickled Jakob's ear. "392. It's time."

Jakob heard the key slide into the lock, fit the tumblers, and then turn. A dull thunk and the door swung open.

53 stood there. "Be quick!"

Jakob looked up at the top of his cell one last time. The guards weren't around.

Now!

He followed 53 into the downpour. The cold rain stung his skin as it washed the sweat off his body and out of a thousands little nicks and cuts that Jakob hadn't even had time to catalog.

They ducked beside a wall. 53 put his mouth close to Jakob's ear.

"Follow me. There's a section of the wall that we can break through."

Break through? But the walls were made of cement. Surely 53 couldn't be serious.

But the little man sped them along the exercise yard toward a place Jakob hadn't been able to see from his hot box. And as they approached, Jakob spotted little flecks of concrete on the muddy ground. Was the wall crumbling?

53 pointed at the wall and then looked overhead.

Lightning flashed.

And then as the thunder boomed, 53 kicked the wall.

Chunks of cement broke off.

But 53 wasn't a strong man. His legs hadn't been conditioned by squatting in front of the slit all day long.

Jakob pushed him away and waited.

Flash.

Boom.

Crumble.

A two-foot section of concrete fell out of the wall. Jakob grinned. Then he let all the anger well up within him. The heat. The cell. The warden. The demons. All of it.

Flash.

Boom. Jakob's kick exploded into the wall. The final piece of wall crumbled. A hole three feet in diameter beckoned.

Go

53 slid through the gap. Jakob took a final look at the prison yard, thankful that the hurricane-like wind and rain had kept the guards inside, and then sank into the mud and clawed his way through the squishy goo.

He emerged on the other side of the wall.

53 looked at him, his mouth a runny mess of rain, spit, and smile. He wiped his glasses.

"We're free!"

Jakob nodded. "How did you get the key to my cell?"

"A hobby of mine, actually. I was the best safecracker around. That's why I'm here." He grinned. "Or was here. It's simple enough to fashion a key out of the spare metal laying around the prison. General population prisoners actually enjoyed a few more privileges than you."

"But why help me?"

"The rest of these fools are destined to rot. Let them. I saw you the first day. Something different about you, mate. You had the look."

"The look."

"A gleam in the eye. I knew you were the one."

Jakob smiled and held out his hand. "To my new friend."

53 grasped Jakob's slippery skin.

Jakob squeezed 53's hand and pumped it. On the second pump he jerked 53 toward him, hit him in the nose with a left backfist, then looped his left arm around 53's neck, squeezed, and jerked up.

The wind drowned out the sound of 53's neck breaking.

Jakob let the little man's body slide into the oozing ground and stared at him for a moment.

"If only I had more time to properly seal our friendship." He spat a mouthful of water. "But I'm in a bit of a rush."

Jakob turned toward the main road. How much of the night did he have left? He had to reach the town and board a ship while it was still dark if he was to make good on his escape.

More wind assailed him. Walking grew difficult. Rain pounded his face and his back. The ground sucked at his feet.

But still Jakob trudged on. Only two miles, after all.

He could see the lights of the town.

And then he reached the outskirts—how long had it taken him to slog through the mud and grime? Exhaustion overwhelmed him. But joy lifted his spirits—to be free and to have killed on the same night! Perhaps a drink to celebrate . . .

But how could he in his prison rags?

No. Time for celebrating later. He had to be smart.

Find a ship.

One leaving as soon as the storm abated.

He skirted the docks. But only one ship lolled in the harbor surf: a tramp steamer with a huge cargo hold.

Perfect.

The bell tolled, knocked about in the howling winds.

No gangplank led to the ship. Jakob had to shimmy up one of the ropes and slink over the side. He felt his feet touch the deck and he celebrated another big step.

Further away from the prison.

He opened the closest bulkhead and peered into the darkness. There didn't appear to be anyone on board. Probably they were all drinking in the bars. And later on they'd squander their money on cheap thrills with painted ladies.

Good for them.

Jakob slid down the steep steps into the bowels of the ship. He finally found the entrance to the cargo hold and entered.

He'd expected it to be cool down here, but the ship must have baked in the sun all day. The cargo hold felt hot and sticky.

He tucked himself in among splintery wooden crates. They contained nothing. Jakob frowned. He'd hoped to find some fruit. Perhaps they'd load some before the ship weighed anchor.

Jakob smiled.

He'd done it. What they claimed couldn't be done.

And thanks to his recently-departed accomplice, Jakob was a free man. Soon, he'd be back in Europe. Soon, he'd be back living in luxury.

"Would you care for another fig, sir?"

Jakob tasted the fruit and chewed slowly. He nodded. "Please."

"Are you comfortable, sir? We can bring more pillows."

Jakob nodded. "One can never have enough pillows."

"And is the fanning to your liking, sir?"

"A little bit faster, please. The heat in here is quite bothersome."

He woke up drenched in sweat. How long had he been out for? He had no way of knowing. No way of penetrating the darkness down here. Was the sun up? Were they already at sea? He hadn't heard any shouts or yells that would have announced a prison search party.

The heat.

Jakob's mouth felt dry. Sticky. His throat felt thick. Sweat ran down his body.

He needed air. Just a bit. Sea air was supposed to be good for the constitution, wasn't it? Maybe just a quick peek topside to ascertain what time it was. Perhaps even a quick forage for some water and food. Then he'd come right back down and not show himself until they were well out to sea.

Perhaps there'd even be time for Jakob to indulge himself on a few of the crew. He smiled. He'd enjoy that.

Oh, yes.

He crawled toward the door.

Stretched his right hand out to the handle.

And screamed as something lanced his flesh.

Sudden light.

Sunlight.

Heat.

Sticky.

Jakob looked at his arm. Blood trickled down it in jagged lines.

What—?

His hand.

Stuck

On the rusted bur teeth of . . .

The *slit*.

In his door.

In his cell.

Jakob screamed.

And didn't care much who heard him.

The Food Processor

MICHAEL CANFIELD

This is one of the strangest stories we encountered. It qualifies as a fitting tale for Borderlands *because it has that quality we love—when you read it, you will not forget it. Regarding what it might be, or not be about . . . well, let's just say we saw it as kind of a creation-myth for the 21st Century.*

Though the boys' birthdays occurred weeks apart, Mother combined their gift to please Father.

"You may choose your present this year, boys," said she. "Something to fulfill your destiny, perhaps." The boys were born to change the world.

"A cement mixer," said the oldest, James.

"A hammer and nails, and wood," said Charles, two years and two weeks younger. "We want to make things."

Mother pushed her tongue against the inside of her

mouth. "You could choose a gift that would make Father happy."

The boys lowered their eyes.

They lived in a basement, down below the kitchen where Father made soups, casseroles and souffles much demanded by hungry people in the city. Every year Father bought the latest blenders, electric mixers and grinders. He ordered the best ingredients in the world. Father wanted the boys to join him in the big kitchen one day, when ready, but they feared that day. The kitchen boiled, and steam leaked out the vents cut in the door above the basement stairs. Blenders and mixers raged and whined into the night.

"I think Father would be pleased if you asked for an industrial food processor," said Mother.

James knew Mother could not hear their birthday wishes. Love and allegiance to Father overwhelmed her senses. Charles bounced in place. He dreamed of things to build with.

James said, "If a food processor is what you think we should have, Mother, that is what we want."

Charles' puffy cheeks reddened; his lips trembled. James caught his eyes and encouraged him to be brave.

The birthday party came and Mother dressed the boys in party hats. Cooks from Father's kitchen brought down special dishes, in stainless steel mixing bowls, for the meal. Poultries, and young calf and foal so tender the meats fell off the bones to liquefy in their own juices. Pastas so drenched in butters and unclarified oils the brothers could not discern the noodles' shapes. The brothers had eaten so many rich, creamy, dishes in their lives they could no longer tell foods apart.

They emptied each bowl tasting nothing.

When they finished one, the white-coated cook who'd brought it took it back and climbed the left side of the stairway back to the kitchen. More cooks brought fresh dishes down the right side. The meal could not end until dishes stopped coming and the boys had finished everything.

From her rocker in the corner, Mother looked on, pleased. Next to her rested the tall box containing the boys' gift.

After many courses, the boys lagged in their eating, forcing the cooks to wait for empty bowls to return. A voice blasted from within the steam-filled kitchen above.

"Where are my cooks!" cried Father.

The cooks hunched and shook. Mother called up in her gentle voice. "The boys relish the dishes so much, Husband, they are not emptying each bowl as it is brought, but savoring their meal," she said.

Even though no one could withstand Father's will, she protected them as best she could.

"Never mind the bowls," cried Father. "I have dishes for my sons to eat. How can they ever join me in the kitchen if they do not eat what I make?"

The cooks left the bowls on the floor, and the table, and scrambled back up the stairs to carry more.

After the party, the boys lay on the woven rug amid empty bowls. James' belly rose and fell.

Bowls lay stacked in mountains. The cooks had not returned for them; Father would need his cooks later to prepare the next day's orders and he'd sent them to bed for a few hours.

James drifted, gut splitting. Charles whimpered in agony.

The creak of Mother's rocker stopped; she rose and

clapped her hands. "Boys," she said. "Have your forgotten your present?"

James struggled to sit up. His pants button popped off, which eased discomfort. Charles leaned up. He looked at James with hope in his eyes. Perhaps Mother had relented and given them something to build with after all.

Mother stood up. She heaved. She pushed the present, which was bigger than they three combined, toward the middle of the room. She hid a smile, pulling down the corners of her mouth.

Charles tried to rush forward, but managed only to lumber. The box equaled his height. He tugged at the ribbon around it.

James helped him, lifting one side of the box lid, letting Charles try the other. When his young brother stood tip-toe, arms outstretched, James removed the lid.

Charles peeked over the edge. Stainless steel, the food processor shone in the room's dim light. They pulled the box apart to see the gift. Charles made little fists, without crying or showing Mother any sign of disappointment.

He made James proud.

The food processor consisted of a large spout that led into a steel tank that would hold many gallons. Circular blades of different widths and angles fitted the tank. Mother told them they'd received the largest, most powerful, food processor in the world. Besides the electrical power cord, the machine sported an oil-burning motor Father had attached. Father did not like electricity, which was not organic. Not earthy. He insisted his appliances be powered by the grease from his oven traps, or the extractions from his ingredients. Mother said she and Father had decided to give the boys the first one ever made, because they loved them so much and expected them to change the world as Father had. Even Father did not have this machine yet.

She leaned down for a peck on the cheek from each boy. Together the boys lifted the food processor, and carried it to a corner. Mother told them to clear away the bowls from the party and set them at the top of the stairs for the cooks to take in the morning.

She went to bed.

Too tired to work, Charles yawned. "I wish we could blink our eyes and make this mess disappear."

James thought a bit. "Maybe we can," he said. "Let's see what happens if we put a bowl in the food processor."

"We can't!" said Charles. "Father wouldn't like it."

"With so many, he'll never miss a few. Let's see it work."

Charles backed away, but stood transfixed as James set up the machine.

James started the engine and moved the lever at the base to the highest setting: liquefy. It made a shrill whir. This would not wake Mother, who slept through loud equipment noises coming from the kitchen every night.

James dropped a bowl down the spout; a short ripping sound interrupted the steady hum. He stopped the machine and opened the trap at the tank's base. Inside, he found a thin layer of liquid steel, enough to dampen a fingertip. "It works," he said.

He closed the trap and turned the motor on again. He gathered more bowls and this time Charles helped him, eager to feed the machine himself.

The blades responded with a tink for each bowl fed in.

When the final one disappeared down the spout, James smiled. He told Charles to help him shove the food processor into the corner again for the night. The tank was heavy with broth, the brothers couldn't move it.

"How are we going to get that liquid out?" said Charles.

James peered into the tank. It brimmed with steel soup. He dipped his finger, licked it. "We'll drink it," he said.

"I'm too full," said Charles.

"It's only a few more gallons."

James removed the cover. He leaned into the tank. He gulped the liquid. Steel coated his insides. The more he drank the more he wanted. He climbed into the tank to drink more easily.

Charles pulled over Mother's rocking chair to stand on and climbed into the tank himself.

Finished, they stood tall, strong. James and Charles climbed out to get other things for the food processor. They broke up the table that had been set out for their birthday dinner and fed the pieces through the spout. They drank the wood soup.

They shoved every loose thing down the spout: furniture, woven rugs; they went to their bedroom, brought out the beds, and ground them up.

Charles picked up Mother's rocking chair. He lifted it overhead, ready to crush it to splinters.

"No!" shouted James.

"Nothing's left," said Charles.

"There's plenty upstairs."

"Yes, but we're not supposed to go up there."

"We'll have a peek. Maybe Father's gone. Or sleeping."

Charles shivered.

Neither had ever seen Father in the flesh.

"Let's go as far as the door," said James.

They lifted the food processor without effort now, and carried it to the foot of the steps. James climbed the stairs. He bent down to the vents and listened for pots clanging, food sizzling, or Father's booming voice. Silence.

He tried the door: locked and too solid for him to pull it open, even with the strength gained from the bowls and furniture they'd drunk. He descended.

"Help me turn the food-processor on its side." Charles helped, but backed away afterward.

James aligned the spout with the bottom step. He held on to its base and told Charles to do the same.

"I don't want to," he said. "We're not allowed."

"Let me worry about that."

The boys held on fast. James started the motor. Again, he moved the lever to liquefy.

The machine swallowed the stairs, driving upward.

It reached the top, crashed through the door. The boys held tight.

The food processor kept going, into the kitchen, sucking up pots and pans and implements in its path. James managed to reach the lever. The machine whirred to a stop.

He stood up. It had cut a swath deep into the stacks and stacks of pots, pans, and implements that filled the kitchen. They righted the food processor. James opened the cover to drink the tank's fresh contents.

"Where's father?" said Charles.

James lifted his head. He turned. He stepped through a curtain of mixing spoons and butcher's knives. Past it, he peered deep into the kitchen.

Prone, on a long chopping table, lay Father, as big and round as ten cooks: chef's hat awry, white clothes stained with the grease of dishes he'd made James and Charles eat that night. The table held the remains of a hundred ingredients: skins, feet, guts. Father awoke, sat up, scratched a neck boil.

James backed away. He fell against the utensils curtain. Father jumped up.

"Son James! Why are you here without permission?"

"To use our birthday present, Father."

Father lumbered forward, through the pot and pan curtain. Charles hid himself under a stock pot. Father bent down to lift the food processor's lid. James braced himself.

He looked into the contents of the food processor: the soup of staircase, and pots and pans that had been in the machine's feeding path. He took a ladle from the curtain and dipped in into the soup. He brought the ladle up. He sipped. He swallowed. His eyes widened. "What have you done!"

Father spat out the soup.

James ran.

Father chased him. James pumped his legs and arms. The steel and wood he'd taken fueled him, but he lost ground. Father's long strides closed the distance.

James led him to the basement door. He crouched at the threshold. Father stepped off into the darkness. His magnificent bulk fell. A cry escaped. Not Father's.

James peered down into the darkness. He could see little, only black shapes in the gloom below. Father moved, drawing up his body. He bent up, then stood. He lifted the limp mass that he had fallen on. Mother. An enraged cry escaped his lips. Liquid gurgled within his throat, and deep down in his chest. If he spoke words, James could not understand them. Father dragged Mother's broken body with him and, wrecked from his fall, stumbled in dizzy circles within the basement-prison. James shivered in fear that Father would look up and see him, but he could not make himself run away.

Father spat, clearing the liquid from his throat. "Boys! Where are my boys? What's become of my family?"

He raised Mother, tiny, a tiny spare-rib in contrast to Father's beef-flank arm, dangling her. He brought his free hand up to his own jaw and worked it open, stretching the skin around his mouth, widening the mouth's gape.

He stretched it into a maw, an eating machine. James leaped back. He could see Father intended to consume her, to take back in that better part of himself.

The food processor lay right where they had left it upon using it to crash into the kitchen. James put his shoulder against the processor and pushed. It would go faster with Charles' help, but Charles was still hiding, and it would not do for him to see what happened to Mother. James' legs ached, his shoulder ground against the cold steel. The processor moved. A quarter inch, half an inch at a time, until it tottered on the precipice. James peered around it. Father raised Mother over his maw, his face was only teeth and eyes glistened by the food processor's sheen. James pushed.

The food processor tumbled through darkness. It hit Father and Mother and clanged in the hollow of the basement. There was silence.

James realized he was standing on the power plug. The power cord stretched down to the basement, tensed to its limit.

Careful not to move his foot, he stretched himself over to the pot Charles hid under. James lifted it.

"We can't go back now," said James. "We'll stay

above. Help me pull the machine back up. It fell," he said, protecting his brother.

Together, they pulled it back up. James did not allow Charles to look down into the basement. The brothers were hungry and fed one implement after another into the food processor, stopping to drink each time the tank filled, making room for more. At dawn they started on the fixtures, then the ceiling, then the great kitchen's walls. Finally, they exposed the outside world of rock, tree, and road that they had known only from books Mother read them.

Charles told James he wanted to go below and find Mother.

"This is not the time," said James. "We have to change the world." He picked up a piece of earth and fed it into the machine.

The boys found the landscape nourishing and pushed the food processor forward. Bit by bit, they ate a path to the city.

Story Time with the Bluefield Strangler

JOHN FARRIS

As much as we like to publish the work of new talents, it's just as much fun to be able to present the work of acknowledged masters in this field. John Farris, the author of such classics as When Michael Calls, The Fury, *and* All Heads Turn When the Hunt Goes By *surprised us with the following story.*

Six-year-old Alison was on the candy-striped swing set in the side yard of the big white house on the hill. Turning her head at the sound of tires on the gravel drive. Daddy's home. Alison holds Dolly in the crook of one arm, holds the swing chain with her other hand. Alison has many dolls that Daddy and Mommy have given her but Dolly was the first and will always be special, in spite of wear and tear.

Alison turns her head when Daddy calls. He comes across the bright green lawn of the white house on the hill smiling at her. Daddy smiles a lot. He doesn't frown. One hand is behind his back. Of course he has a present for her. He brings home something every day. There is one huge tree on the lawn at the top of the hill (Alison sometimes forgets that). The leaves of the tree are dark green. They shade the swing set and play area where she spends her day. Every day. Because it never rains in the daytime on the hill with the big white house.

Daddy sets his briefcase down. Some days he wears a blue suit to work, some days it's brown. His shoes are always black and shiny. One day Daddy had a mustache but Alison decided she didn't like it so Daddy doesn't wear it any more.

"Here's my girl!" Daddy says, crouching and waiting for her to run into his arms. It's what he says every afternoon when he comes home.

("Where does your daddy work?" Lorraine asks Alison, and after a few moments Alison says, "In a office," as if it isn't important to her. "Do you know what kind of work he does?" Lorraine asks then. Alison shakes her head with a hint of displeasure. Lorraine smiles, and doesn't ask more questions.)

Alison reaches around Daddy trying to find out what he has for her. Daddy laughs and teases for the few seconds Alison will put up with it. Then he offers her the present. It's tissue-wrapped, and tied with a pink ribbon. Alison allows Daddy to hold Dolly, which is a special privilege on the occasion of gift-bringing, while she unwraps her present.

It's a glass jar in the form of a girl with pigtails. Like Alison herself. And it's filled with candy. Red candies.

Daddy shows Alison how to open the jar. The glass girl's head twists off.

Mommy comes out to the back steps of the porch and waves. "Hey, you two." Mommy wears her blue apron. Mommy is beautiful. She is so blonde her hair looks silver in the sunlight. She wears it in a bun on the back of her head. Alison calls back as she always does, "Daddy's home!" (as if Mommy can't see that for herself), "and he brought me a present." (As if Mommy couldn't guess.) They love Alison *so much*.

Mommy calls out, "Just one of those before supper, Alison!"

"Just one," Daddy repeats to Alison, and she nods obediently. Daddy picks up his briefcase and walks across the lawn as if he has forgotten that he has Dolly in one hand. Alison runs after him and tugs Dolly away from him. Privilege revoked. She hugs Dolly and the glass girl against her breast and watches Daddy give Mommy a big hug. They love each other, a whole lot. Alison watches them and smiles. But then she looks up from the porch, way way up, to the third floor of the big white house, and *he's* up there in one of the rooms looking out the window. Alison can't smile any more. She takes a deep breath. Big Boy is home. The day is spoiled.

("Why haven't you said anything to Daddy and Mommy about Big Boy?" Lorraine asks, after an unusually long, glum silence on Alison's part. Sometimes Alison isn't willing to talk about Big Boy. Today she shifts Dolly from the crook of one arm to another, picks at a flaking lower lip while she slides down until almost horizontal in the big leather chair in Lorraine's office. Staring at her feet straight out in front of her. Her shoes are red slip-on Keds sneakers. "Because they'd be scared," Alison says finally.)

After dinner. After her bath. Mommy undoes her pigtails and brushes her hair smooth down over her shoulders while Alison reads to both of them from her storybook. Daddy comes upstairs to Alison's room with cookies and milk. Then it's lights out and time for sleep. Mommy forgets and shuts the bedroom door all the way. Alison calls her back. The door is left open a few inches. Mommy and Daddy go down the hall to their own bedroom. Alison lies awake with Dolly on her breast and waits for Big Boy.

("How long has Big Boy been in the house?" Lorraine asks. Alison fidgets. "A long time. It's his house." Lorraine nods. "You mean Big Boy was there before you and Daddy and Mommy moved in." Alison mimics Lorraine's sage nod. She fiddles with her box of crayons. The lid remains closed. Alison hasn't drawn anything today. Not in the mood. "Only nobody knew about him," Lorraine says. "So does that mean he hides during the day?" Alison nods again. She opens the Crayola box and pulls an orange crayon half out and looks at it with one eye squinched shut. "Do you know where?" Lorraine continues. Now Alison shrugs. "Oh, in the walls." "So he lives in the walls." "Yes," Alison says, turning around so that she is on her knees in the big leather chair with her back to Lorraine. Well-traveled Dolly continues to stare at Lorraine with a single button eye. The other eye is missing. Dolly has yellow yarn curls around a sewn-on face.)

Tell me a story, Big Boy says. It's always the first thing he says to Alison on those nights when he comes out of the walls. The second thing is, *Or I'll go down the hall to their room and hurt them.*

Alison holds herself rigid beneath the covers so that he can't see her shudder. She looks at his shadow on the section of wall between the windows with the shades half pulled down on the tree of night and stars so bright beyond the hill where the big white house is. She doesn't look at Big Boy's face very often, even when he comes to stand at the foot of her bed, lean against one of the bedposts with folded arms. One hand tucked into an armpit, the other, the hand with the missing finger, on his elbow. Big Boy's hair is dark, short, mussed-looking. He's only fifteen, but already he has a man's shoulders and strength.

Alison clears her throat.

There was a beautiful butterfly, Alison begins, a thrum of desperation in her heart, *who—who lived in a glass jar shaped like a little Dutch girl with pigtails.*

(Bluefield detective sergeant Ed Lewinski says to Lorraine, over coffee in the cafeteria of the children's hospital, "I did a global on the street name 'Big Boy.' Nothing turned up. No wants, no arrest record, juvenile or adult." Lorraine sips her coffee. "What about the missing finger? That's an interesting detail, even for an imaginative six-year-old." But Lewinski shakes his head. He's having a doughnut with his coffee. The doughnut's stale. After two bites he shoves the plate away. "Maybe that wasn't just the kid's imagination, Doc. She could've seen someone on staff here at the Med who has a missing finger. That could be a traumatic thing, for a kid who may have been traumatized already." "*May* have been?" Lorraine says with a wry smile. "Traumatized? Oh, yes, deeply. Alison is quite a challenge, Ed." Lewinski nods sympathetically. "Three months, but nobody's come forward. Kids get abandoned all the time; we have to assume that's what happened to Alison." Lorraine doesn't disagree. "How long before Family Services takes over?" he asks. Lorraine says firmly, "She's not emotionally prepared to go into a foster home. Alison shows no willingness to interact with other children here. Abandonment can crush a child. In Alison's case her psychic refuge, her protection, is a vivid imagination. Betrayed by her real mother and/or father, she's blanked them from her mind and created new ones—parents who adore her and never, never, would do such a terrible thing to her." Lewinski thinks this over. "I understand her need to invent new parents. But what's all this about 'Big Boy'? How does he fit into her, what d'ya call it, psychological schematic?" Lorraine checks her watch, says, "Let you know when I know, Ed. I have a couple of ideas I want to explore." They walk out of the cafeteria together. "Do something different with your hair this weekend, Doc?" "I cut it. Two weeks ago. Some detective you are." Lewinski has a fair face that blushes easily. "Seeing our girl this afternoon? Sorry I couldn't turn up 'Big Boy' for real; might've been some help to you. Bad for Alison, but a break for us cops." Lorraine, already on her way to the elevators, turns and stares at him. Lewinski laughs. "I mean, Bluefield doesn't need another teenage strangler, no matter what his name is.")

Three a.m.

The low drone of a siren in the night. Alison wakes up on her back looking at the flush of ambulance light on the ceiling of the small room. Dolly in the crook of a thin arm. Alison knowing instantly that she's in the Wrong Place, where they keep the crazy children. She must get back to the White House on the Hill, to her beautiful room with wallpaper and the white cases filled with dolls and books that Daddy made for her in his workshop. But something bad has happened. Out There. On a lonely street. With trees to hide behind, shadows. The red light swirling on her ceiling, a crackle of radio voices too distant to be understood distracts her; she can't leave the Wrong Place.

Alison trembles.

And becomes aware of someone standing in a corner opposite the iron bed in this bleak room that smells like medicines, stale peepee.

Oh no!

"Wake you up?" Big Boy says.

"What are you doing h-here? You're never sposed to be here."

"Tell me about it," Big Boy says; and he moves a couple of steps, to where the light from the single window with its chicken wire glass and shabby shade bathes his face in a hellfire glow. "But if you're here, then I have to be here, don't I?"

"No! I don't know. Just go away."

Big Boy, grinning. Closer.

"Don't you want to know what I did tonight? Out There?"

Alison flinches, cold from terror. "No, no, no! Not Mommy and Daddy!"

"Whoa. I'll never hurt them. Not as long as you tell me stories."

"But I'm in the Wrong Place!"

"So what?"

"I can't think of any stories here, it—it isn't pretty and smells like peepee!"

"Oh." He sighs, a big show of regret. "That's too bad, Alison. I really wanted to hear a story tonight." Big Boy shrugs, on his way to the door.

"W-where're you going?"

"The only other place I can go," Big Boy says with a glance over his shoulder.

"Oh no *please* don't!"

Big Boy hesitates at the door.

"It'll be dark for a few more hours. I'll find another pretty head to twist off."

"No no no wait!"

"Alison. It's what I like to do."

"Tell you—tell you a story if you don't!"

That sly Big Boy grin. "But you said you couldn't think of a story. Because you're in the Wrong Place."

"I'll try, I'll really try!"

Big Boy considers her appeal, then nods.

"Know you will, Alison. Because the one thing you don't want is for me to twist Mommy and Daddy's heads off. Because without Mommy and Daddy to go to, where would you be? You'll just have to stay with the Crazy Children forever. *And nobody loves you here.*"

"I'll . . . try . . ."

"Okay, okay, Alison. Don't cry any more. Tell you what. I'll help you out." Big Boy sits on the side of the bed with her. "Let me put my thinking cap on, now. Umm-hmmm. Hey, I know! I've got a swell idea for a story. Want me to start? Then you can pitch in."

"Oh—kay."

"It's a story about . . . Dolly, and how she got lost." And before Alison can react, tighten her grip on one-eyed Dolly, Big Boy has mischievously snatched her away with the hand that has the missing finger. He holds Dolly high in the air, letting her swing by a stuffed lanky leg, delightedly watching Alison's mouth open and close in horror.

("His name was Walter Banks," Ed Lewinski says to

Lorraine. They've stopped at a Wendy's for burgers after the movie. "I heard about him from an old-timer at the jail; the case file went into dead storage twenty years ago. I thought old Ed was just yarning, so I looked up Banks in the Tribune's morgue. Sure 'nuff. Between 1943 and 1945 Banks may have murdered as many as eight women in Bluefield. Same m.o. every time. He broke their necks. He was all of sixteen when he started his career as a serial killer. Eighteen when he disappeared, and the stranglings stopped, about the same time as World War Two ended." Lorraine adds ketchup to her double with cheese, takes a bite, stares thoughtfully at Lewinski until he smilingly waves a hand through her line of concentration. "Sorry," Lorraine says.

(Ed says, "Your eyes turn a different color when you do that." Lorraine nods but she's already out of focus again, thinking. "Is there a photo of Walter Banks in the Trib's file?" "From his high school yearbook. I copied it for you." "I don't suppose you know where the Banks kid lived." Lewinski takes an envelope from his inside jacket pocket and lays it on the table. "Two-oh-four Columbine Street. The house is still there, but it's badly run-down." Lorraine gives him a questioning look. "I drove by this afternoon and took some pictures. Two-oh-four Columbine is occupied, but they all look like slackers and drifters. Take better care of their Harleys than they do their own selves." He shakes his head before Lorraine can ask. "Yeah, Doc, I showed the present occupants Alison's picture. They didn't know her. But like I said: drifters.")

Six-year-old Alison on the candy-striped swing set in the side yard of the big white house on the hill. Drawing tablet in her lap, crayons in a pocket of her apron, blue like the one Mommy always wears. Alison has been drawing furiously all afternoon: bears, dragons, space-ships. But now Mommy calls from the steps of the back porch: "it's time to go shopping."

("Alison? How about some lemonade now?" A few minutes before the close of their hour together, during which Alison has been deeply involved with her artwork and uncommunicative, she sighs and closes her drawing tablet, careful not to let Lorraine see what she was work-ing on—that's a special intimate privilege when things are going well between them, but not today—and re-places all of her crayons in the box. She looks at the pitcher on Lorraine's desk. There's nothing Alison likes more than lemonade when she's thirsty. Lorraine pours a cupful for each of them. "Alison, I wonder if you'd mind looking at a couple of pictures for me?" Alison nods, sip-ping. Lorraine places one of Ed Lewinski's shots of two-oh-four Columbine Street on the edge of her desk. Alison leans forward in her chair, needing to crane a little to see. She doesn't touch the digital photo. Studies it with no change of expression. "Is that where *you* live, Lorraine?" "No. I thought you might—" "I'm glad. Because it isn't pretty." Alison's nose wrinkling. "I wouldn't live there." There is a hint of something in the girl's face that gives Lorraine a reason to press on. "But have you ever been to this house?" "NO," Alison says, with a show of revulsion to close the subject. "It looks like it has rats." Lorraine smiles and withdraws the photo of two-oh-four Columbine Street. "Could be." She replaces it with a murky copy of Walter Banks' old yearbook photo. "Do you know this boy?" Alison stares at the likeness of Wal-ter Banks for almost ten seconds before blinking, twice. Then she sits back in the deep leather chair and closes her eyes. "Alison?" "I have to go home now," Alison says. A small hand twitches in her lap. There is a sighing in her throat, a windy plaintive sound. "I have to . . . help Mommy bake the cake. Because today is . . . Daddy's birthday.")

And what a wonderful party they have, in the big white house on the hill! Surprises galore for Daddy after his special birthday dinner. And the cake, oh, oh, she can't count how many candles blazing in thick swirls of icing. Alison did most of the frosting herself.

With tears in his eyes, Daddy gathers Mommy and Alison into his arms and kisses them both. He loves them so much. Alison knows that they are the happiest family that ever lived. If Lorraine could be there she would see that, and never ask another question. But there are barriers Lorraine cannot cross. Alison won't permit that. And this has made Lorraine jealous. Alison is fearful of her jealousy, afraid of what she might do. Because somehow she has found out. She knows.

"She knows who you are," Alison tells Big Boy later, after everyone is in bed. Alison treated to a cool breeze from the open windows, nightingale's trill, treasure-house of stars.

Big Boy is silent for quite a long time. Silence making Alison nervous. She plays with the yarn curls of Dolly's stuffed and sewn head.

"So what?" Big Boy says at last.

"Well . . . I thought . . ."

Big Boy, arms folded, waits. Alison arranges the yarn curls this way and that.

"What?"

"You might want to . . . do something about Lorraine."

Unexpectedly he grins. "Having Bad Thoughts, Alison?"

Alison thrusts Dolly away, face down, in a tangle of curls. A seam, twice re-stitched, is popping again where Dolly's head joins her neck. Alison looks at it, face filled with dread. No, she doesn't think Bad Thoughts in the big white house under the stars, because . . . because otherwise what good is it to be there at all? Shuddering, she recalls one of the smudgy photographs Lorraine showed her. That shabby brick bungalow with its mildew and greasy kitchen smells. It's what Lorraine wants her to go back to, instead of to her real home, Mommy and Daddy's clean, airy house. The place where instead of stars shining into her bedroom there were the eyes of prowling rats. She wants Alison to go back to *that*. Lorraine is not her friend any more, if she ever was. Alison's heart beats furiously at the thought, she feels a flush of outrage in her cheeks. No *never!* And rising blood forces a flood of tears.

"She wants to . . . send me back to that stinking ol' place! And if I have to go . . . you'll have to go back there too!"

Alison grabs a corner of bed sheet to wipe her streaming eyes. Big Boy sits beside her.

"There's some snot on your upper lip," he says.

Alison wipes it away, glaring at him.

"Well . . . what can you do?"

But Big Boy shakes his head.

"It's only what you can do that matters, Alison."

(Lorraine gets up slowly from her side of the bed so as not to wake Ed Lewinski, who is sleeping on his stomach. She bends to kiss a naked shoulder, then pulls on a nightshirt from her chest of drawers before walking downstairs to the kitchen of her garden condo to get something to drink. Mouth parched from all the kissing and those other things she did with him, after more years than she cares to remember, new meaning to *going all the way;* around the moon and back with sweet Eddie Lew. Carton of tomato juice on the top shelf in the fridge. She pours a glass, adds a squeeze from the fat plastic lime juice container, adds Tabasco: Virgin Mary. Leans against the sink smiling to herself as she sips, probably could use a shower but relishes the smell of her lover on her still-tingling body.

The phone. It's the hospital. *Damn!*

By the time Lorraine walks into Alison's room in the children's wing Alison has been sedated and is half asleep.

"Must've been a nightmare," the charge nurse says. "She woke up hysterical, and what a time we had with her. She wet the bed."

Alison's head moves on the pillow. Her face is nearly colorless except for the small cherry bow of her mouth.

"Rats and bugs. Fights . . . all the time. She hurts me."

Lorraine looks sharply at her. "How are you doing, Sweetie?"

Alison can open her milky eyes only part way. "Headache."

Lorraine holds her hand. "Can you tell me what you were dreaming about?"

"Nuh."

"That's okay. We'll talk about it later. You rest now."

Instead of closing her eyes and subsiding into her sedative cocoon, Alison trembles.

"Where's Dolly?"

"Oh," Lorraine says, noting that Dolly isn't in her usual place in the crook of Alison's arm, "I don't see her."

In spite of the rockabye sedative more hysteria threatens.

"Dolly!"

Lorraine glances at the charge nurse, who shrugs. Alison begins to wail. Lorraine has a quick look around the spartan room but Dolly isn't lurking anywhere. Then she remembers: Alison wet the bed, so the sheets would've been changed . . . she questions the nurse, who nods. Possible. Dolly could've left the room in a wad of soiled sheets. Lorraine moves swiftly to Alison's side.

"I think I know where Dolly's gone. She's not lost. I'll bring her to you." She holds the girl close.

"P-promise?"

"Just give me a few minutes."

Lorraine takes the elevator to the second basement level.

Dead quiet down there, no working in the laundry at one-thirty in the morning. The machinery of the elevator seems unnaturally loud to her ears in the silence of the cavernous basement. Corridors criss-crossing beneath the entire hospital complex. The concrete walls are painted gray and pale green. Yellow ceiling bulbs in wire baskets. Signs point to different areas. Crematory, Electrical, Maintenance, Storage.

Laundry.

The metal door, twenty feet from the elevator, is closed. Lorraine pushes it open.

There's a windowless outer room with a couple of tables, chairs, vending machines for the laundry workers. The room would be full dark except for the illuminated facades of the machines. By their glow she sees, inside the laundry itself, a Dumpster-size canvas hamper on wheels that sits beneath the drop chute. And there's a dim light deep inside the shadowy room. She hears a lone clothes dryer thumping dully as it makes its rounds.

Lorraine draws a breath that burns her throat, eases around the canteen tables into the laundry. The big room has glass block windows on one wall, above the pipe complex that grids the ceiling. The one light is behind pebbled glass in an office door eighty feet away; not enough light to cast her shadow. She tries a wall switch inside the door but nothing much happens to the fluorescent fixtures overhead: a cloudy flickering in two or three of the five-foot tubes.

She draws another breath and begins to search the hamper, pulling out sheets one at a time, shaking them. There are sheets recently peed on, all right, but no Dolly.

"I think I have what you're looking for," he says.

Lorraine turns with a jolt that has her skin sparking.

"Who's there?"

She hears a phlegmy chuckle, then the quavering voice again.

"It's only me. Did I scare you?"

"Did you—? Hell, yes," Lorraine says, shaking her head in annoyance. She is unable to tell where his voice is coming from. Next she hears a dry reedy sucking sound, like someone pulling on a straw to get the last drops from a container of soda or fruit juice. That gets on her nerves fast. "Who are you?"

"Oh—I work nights around here. Just washed my old sneakers, now I'm waiting for them to come out of the dryer."

"What did you mean, you have what I'm looking for? How would you know why—"

She sees him then, shadowy, as he rises from a stool behind a long sorting table; his head, in silhouette against the glass of the office door, looks shaggy. "I believe you come down here for her doll. Throwed out by mistake, was it?"

"Yes. But—"

"Come and get it, then," he says, chuckling, his amusement causing him to wheeze at the end.

"No. Bring it to me," Lorraine says. And adds, "Please."

"All right. All right." Sounding a little cross. The stool legs scrape on the concrete floor. He comes toward Lorraine, slowly, soundlessly. His sneakers clunking around in the dryer. "How's little Missy doing? She calm down some from her bad dreams?"

"Were you upstairs earlier? In the children's wing?"

"That I was. That I was."

"I see. But how did you know Alison's doll was missing?"

"Oh, I know things. I know lots of things. Been here almost all my life."

"Do I know you? What's your name?"

At the instant she asks, the fluorescent lighting flares overhead with the violence of lightning, the laundry is garishly illuminated, and he is closer than she thought, white-haired, stooped, unkempt head thrust forward of his shoulders as he shuffles toward her. Alison's Dolly offered in his right hand. Chuckling fit to kill, is Walter Banks. The thumping of old sneakers round and round the dryer tub is like an echo of the accelerated tempo of Lorraine's heart. She stares in hammering fright at the missing finger on the veiny hand that grips the doll.

"Oh Jesus—!"

The door is only a few feet away. He is old now, and slow and obviously not strong, she can get away easily; Lorraine turns but—

There is no room for her to run.

Because Alison is standing in the doorway in her nightie, arms folded, looking up at her, rigid in her purpose, baleful.

"Oh Alison! But—you can't do this!"

Alison shakes her head slowly, unyielding. Then Lorraine feels the hand with the missing digit on her shoulder. She glances at it. Not an old man's juiceless spidery spotted claw—the skin is smooth, unblemished, his hand large, strong; strong enough to grind her bones. Even with a finger gone.

"Alison—God—it's wrong—listen to me!"

Alison in a quiet kind of huff shuts the door in her face and is gone.

Big Boy bears down and Lorraine screams. He pulls her slowly around to face him. He smiles fondly at Lorraine.

"You don't want to go yet," he says. "It's story time."

Answering the Call

BRIAN FREEMAN

Brian Freeman originally sent us a story that was not quite right; but he was willing to take it through three revisions. When it still wasn't quite right we felt compelled to ask for a fourth draft. He complied by sending us a completely different story, which was so original and creepy, it hit the mark on its first attempt. There's probably a lesson here, but we're not sure what it is.

The young man must be lonely.

There is something unflinchingly terrible about the look in his eyes, about the way his body slumps over the heavy, black answering machine that is perched on his lap. He sits on a barstool in the middle of a nearly empty room, naked except for his white underwear and a gold watch. He's sweating profusely from every pore. A single tear hovers on the edge of his pale, trembling lips. He has dark hair and narrow fingers with fingernails chewed to the quick.

The dark wood floor groans when he shifts his weight. The walls are white. There are no windows, only a door to the hallway and a door to the walk-in closet. The ceiling is white with crown molding. A single lamp next to the barstool glows with a yellowed light, but the corners of the room remain dark. An extension cord snakes across the floor, powering the lamp and the old, boxy answering machine.

He pushes the large button that was once marked AN-NOUNCEMENT but now only says OUNCE. The tape crackles, there is a beep, and a woman's voice speaks: "You've reached the Smith Family, we can't come to the phone right now, but if you leave a message, we'll get right back to you."

This is the voice of the dead. The sound has deteriorated a bit with age, but when the young man plays this tape, the dead woman lives on, just for a moment. The recording crackles, there is a second beep, and the woman is dead once again.

The young man plays the tape one last time, then checks his watch and sighs. He pushes himself off the barstool and puts the answering machine in the closet. He must get dressed. He wouldn't want to be late for work.

And the dead woman will still be here when he returns.

———

This is a nice enough neighborhood, and the young man feels immediately at home. The day is cold and blustery. Fallen leaves are blown about in the wind, thrown from yard to yard, into the air, and out onto the black pavement of the road. There are dozens of tall trees lining this street, and the houses are old, refined, made of stone, surrounded by large multi-acre properties. The young man parks his van a block away from 1804 Equess Court. He puts on his black gloves, removes the key from the ignition, and steps out into the street. There are still several cars along the curb in front of his destination, and he walks slowly.

An icy fall breeze cuts into the young man, yet he refuses to shiver. He blinks the cold away, determined to take the day one step at a time—the same way he handles every day. One step at a time. Hedges and cast iron fences line the properties in this neighborhood, but the gate to 1804 is open. He walks to the front door, which is large and made of heavy wood painted white. He hammers the golden knocker with a quick, heavy slap.

"Hello, ma'am, I'm Mr. Smith. I'm from the Funeral Home," he tells the older woman who answers the door. She wears a black dress, the darkness a stark contrast to her weathered skin. She has been crying. Of course. They usually cry.

"Oh, yes, they said you'd be here," she replies, her voice distant, as if she doesn't even really understand what she's saying. The young man suspects that just might be the case. She carefully opens the door the rest of the way, allowing her visitor to come inside. "Do you need anything?"

"No ma'am," he replies. "I'm here to help you. Please know that you have my most sincere sympathy for your loss."

She only nods.

———

Twenty minutes later, the woman and her family have left for the funeral.

The young man sits in the large kitchen on a high stool at the marble island in the center of the room. He sits with the telephone.

His job is to answer any calls the family or even the deceased—it's amazing how many calls people make to the dead without realizing the person is gone from this world—might receive during the funeral, and his presence is meant to deter thieves who might have seen the obituary in the newspaper and decided this would be a good time for a break-in.

It's a more common occurrence than you would expect.

So the Funeral Home hires people to housesit, and one of the responsibilities of the job is to answer the phone and the door, accepting flowers, condolences, and generally letting the world know someone is watching the place.

But the phone is not ringing.

The young man thinks, *Maybe this isn't going to be one of the bad ones.* His job is not fun. Often someone will call for the Deceased, and he has the unpleasant responsibility to tell them that their friend or associate is dead. Sometimes angry callers are thrilled to discover the Deceased is gone and they feel the need to tell someone. Those often get nasty. Sometimes distraught relatives who couldn't make the funeral need someone to talk to, and the young man becomes a grief counselor. Every now and then he'll get a hang-up, which could be any of the above, or possibly a crook checking to see if anyone's home.

And all too often, the dead call, and he has to handle them. That's the most important part of his job.

Someone rings the doorbell at the front door, and the young man makes his way to the three story foyer with the marble floor, crystal chandelier, vases on pedestals, and dozens of recently delivered flower arrangements. The house is very beautiful and very cold.

He answers the door and accepts more flowers from a teenager whose flesh is bursting with pimples. As the delivery boy walks back to his van, the housesitter scours the neighborhood to make sure there isn't anyone watching the house who shouldn't be. He sees no one.

After he closes the front door and bolts it, the young man carefully proceeds up the curved staircase. It's time to do what he really came here to do. His real job.

The carpet on the stairs is plush. The chandelier is even more beautiful as he gets closer to it.

He continues to the third floor where there is a long hallway. It's nice here. Paintings line the walls. European art. Probably old. Probably original.

At the end of the hallway is an oak door that looks nothing like the other doors in the house.

The young man picks the lock and steps inside.

A chill rips into his spine. Something is wrong here. That's his first reaction. The chill is from a gut instinct, and maybe also because the room is very, very cold, as if the A/C has been running non-stop for days. The floors are polished wood, there is a wide mahogany desk across from the door, and the walls are lined with bookshelves covered in leather-bound books.

There are no windows.

This isn't right, the young man thinks. He's done this many times, dealt with the worst of the worst, and he's never felt this way before.

He wants to flee the house, leaving the family to deal

with their own dirty laundry, but he can't. He has a job to do.

He's sweating.

Even with the coldness of the air, he can feel the perspiration forming on his brow.

There's an enormous chair behind the desk, and the young man goes to sit, just as he always does. This is where he'll wait for any calls. The desk is neatly organized, with stacks of papers sorted into bins, a calendar, and a phone with a built-in answering machine and multiple lines.

Just as the young man sits in the chair, he realizes this was a mistake. Coming here is going to cost him his life. The owner of this leather chair was almost certainly the most evil person the young man has ever encountered. He's dealt with people who committed terrible acts before, done terrible deeds, but nothing like this.

Invisible arms shove him back into the chair when he tries to stand, and the coldness that started in his spine spreads to his arms and legs, chilling his blood. His brain begins to throb. He feels a dagger shoving its way through his skull and into his brain ever so slowly. The pain is simple and precise and extraordinary.

He wants to run from the office, to run all the way home, but he realizes he had his chance and let it slip away.

A horrible screaming pierces his mind, making him throw his head back, open his mouth wide and scream, too.

The phone begins to ring.

Not any of the family's lines, but the private line to the office. This is the call he's been waiting for.

His arms are paralyzed, but he must answer the phone.

If he doesn't, he'll probably die, and the family who lives here will never be safe. No one will ever be safe in this place.

With a burst of strength from deep within, he breaks free and grabs the phone. The invisible hands fight for control of it. His gloves and sleeves shred instantly, like the seams have been yanked in a million directions. He can see the blueness on his pale flesh where fingers are wrapping around his bony arm, trying to stop him from answering the call. The gold watch on his wrist is ripped away—sent flying across the room.

He screams, focuses all of his energy and talent and knowledge, and he breaks free yet again. He gets the phone to his ear and pushes the RECORD ANNOUNCEMENT button on the base at the same time.

There is a roar like a thundering train in a tunnel as images rocket past the young man's eyes and sear into the soft tissues of his brain, where the cold ice pick sensation only grows worse.

He sees: a woman in 1930s attire being tied to a bed and raped, a woman he knows is the mother of the Deceased; children being rounded up in a gray and ugly WWII concentration camp, those children as they are led into a room where they are told their parents are waiting, those children as they suffocate when the poison gas collapses their lungs; a little girl in Argentina in the 1950s sitting on the lap of the Deceased, smiling and laughing and playing with a yellow flower, the little girl laying bloody and dead and raped in an alley; a group of hippies hanging by their necks in a barn in Iowa in the 1960s; a security guard and three bank tellers dead in a vault with bullets between their eyes in Chicago in the 1970s; the Deceased and his young bride in Hollywood in the 1980s on their wedding night, when he ties her to a bed and reenacts what he did to his mother fifty years earlier, the young bride's "accidental" slip and fall in the shower later on; the Deceased's rise as a respectable businessman and high price consultant in Silicon Valley in the 1990s; finally the Deceased's discovery of a woman named Marge, a woman whom he loved and who knew his dozens of terrible secrets and didn't care, the woman who answered the door, the woman whom the Deceased now wants to finish off, the reason he's calling today.

The young man tries to open his mouth, feels the fingers of a dead man push between his lips, grabbing his tongue. The fingers are cold and dead and slimy, and they pinch and they pull.

The young man gags, expelling the putrid fingers from his mouth, and he screams into the phone as those cold hands wrap around his throat and begin to squeeze: "Blessed be the people who dwell within this residence and may they be free of your furious spirit when they stand in darkness, when they sleep within these walls that I bless in the name of Jesus, the Holy Son, and may they be free of your residual presence for as long as they live, and you shall be banished to the tape in this Earthly machine as your mortal frame is interned to the ground forever and ever in the name of our Lord!"

The hands drop from his burning throat, the icy dagger withdraws from his brain, and the room begins to warm, ever so slightly.

———————

Much later, the young man is sitting in his home. He sits on the stool in the room that is almost empty except for the lamp on the floor, and he holds the new answering machine on his lap.

He is so very pale, and so very sweaty, and so tired beyond human knowledge, but he's finished his job yet again. There will be burns all over his body from the hands and fingers of the Deceased, but he doesn't bother to look. It goes with the territory.

The woman named Marge and all others who live in that house are going to be safe from the dead.

At least until Marge dies. He has a bad feeling about her.

The young man sits and he presses the PLAY ANNOUNCEMENT button.

The room's walls hear a thick German voice say: "You've reached the private line of Mister VonMueller, please leave a message and I'll get back to you as soon as possible."

The young man hears a screaming shriek: "I'LL KILL YOU, HURENSOHN, YOU LITTLE MUTHAFUCKER, YOU LITTLE STÜCK SCHEIßE, VERDAMMTE SCHEIßE, IF YOU DON'T LEAVE THIS PLACE NOW AND I MEAN RIGHT NOW . . ."

The recording goes on like that for almost seven minutes—the young man had no idea it had taken him that long to say the words he needed to say after he answered the phone, but he also knows that time works funny when he's doing his job—and eventually the words of the Deceased turn into all German profanities and then they become the language only the dead understands and then finally there is the young man's chant and nothing else.

He scoots off the stool in the middle of the empty room, walks to the closet door, and opens it. He turns on the light and steps inside.

The closet extends for as far as his eyes will allow him to see—hundreds of yards, maybe thousands, maybe more—and he walks until he reaches the place where the millions of answering machines lining both sides of the closet from floor to ceiling are barely stacked waist high.

He adds this one to the collection.

He knows he isn't the only person in the world who has this job. He occasionally sees other people here, entering and exiting from any of the hundreds of doors that line the hallway, but he never talks to them. Doing so is forbidden, a violation of the most sacred laws of the universe, and that's one of the reasons why the young man is lonely as hell. He wishes he knew his true purpose. He wishes he wasn't so alone all the time.

Yet maybe there's another call to answer in life. He suspects there's more for him to do with his days than listen to the voices of the dead. The dead are dead, after all. They shouldn't have any bearing on our lives.

They shouldn't have so much control over *his* life.

Someday the young man hopes to move on, too. To be free of this terrible job and this wounded flesh.

Someday very soon.

Smooth Operator

DOMINICK CANCILLA

Rich Chizmar, and his Cemetery Dance Publications, *has been nurturing the career of Dominick Cancilla. However, if we had been able to get this volume into print when originally scheduled, we could have laid claim to yet another new writer. The story which follows is a clear indication of the talent we recognized all those years ago.*

For the eighth fruitless day in a row, Clarissa sat on a bench in the open-air mall and waited for Charles, her one true love. Through dark lenses she stared across the promenade toward the Surfside Café, a popular eatery with both indoor and patio seating. It was a casual but romantic place, the kind of place where a man, holding a woman's hand in his own across the table, could speak the words which would make her every wish come true.

Charles wanted to meet Clarissa there for just that purpose—she knew it without him even having to tell her. His every thought, his every word, his every motion was an open book to her, such was the depth of their love.

Clarissa wore the yellow flower-print sun dress he had bought for her, just as she had each day prior, and plain white gloves. Very elegant. Although the summer sun was still high in the sky, she found a scarf necessary to warm her head and he had been kind enough, thoughtful enough, to provide her with one.

She wondered where he was.

Every few minutes Clarissa glanced up and down the promenade, looking for his handsome face, his familiar smile. It was not like Charles to be late.

The hours passed slowly.

Ten o'clock.

Eleven.

Eleven thirty.

With nervous fingers Clarissa twisted her beautiful new silver and diamond ring through the thin fabric of her ill-fitting gloves. It was not an engagement ring—at least not yet—but more of a pre-engagement gift, a symbol of their undying love, and Clarissa was more than satisfied with that for the time being. Keeping the diamond in slow orbit about her finger brought Clarissa great comfort, even though the skin beneath the ring was slowly being rubbed raw.

Noon.

One o'clock.

Clarissa was not sure that Charles would be meeting her for lunch, just as she had not been sure if a champagne brunch had been his intention. By half past one she felt confident that it was a romantic dinner that he had in mind.

Two o'clock.

Three.

Children played in the water of the fountain between Clarissa and the restaurant, and she caught herself wondering how her own children would one day look. She searched for her and Charles' features in their smiling faces.

Three thirty.

By four she began to worry.

It was silly to begin fretting about such an odd hour, of course. Too late for lunch, too early for dinner and all that. Why would he show up at such an inconvenient time? No reason. Still, Clarissa didn't move from her seat—just in case.

Five.

The sun hung low, staring into Clarissa's eyes. Deep in her heart she knew that he was not going to show up, and she knew where to lay the blame.

Oh, on the first day she had been surprised that he stood her up. She had run home crying when the restaurant closed its doors at eleven, cursing him beneath her breath, paying no attention when cars screeched at her fleeing form. But when she'd gotten home the reason for his disdain had been all too clear, staring out at her from the bathroom mirror. Red, puffy, tear-swollen eyes. Nose running. And hair.

Hanging down her forehead to touch her eyebrows, hanging down her back in a stream of red to brush across her hips. Hair.

It had repulsed him.

Not bothering to get the scissors, Clarissa had used a

razor blade—left so long ago by a fickle lover—to saw off every strand that reached below her shoulders. It had been difficult work, arduous, painful as the threads tugged at her scalp. But the result was more than satisfying. Clarissa had left the ends uneven, giving her a wild, devil-may-care look that she knew would excite Charles.

———————

The next morning she'd returned to her place at the mall puffed up with confidence and anticipation. And once again he had passed her by. It had been a Sunday, and she could picture him in her mind's eye laughing at her, chastising her for thinking that what she had done would be enough to please him.

Clarissa knew that he was with another woman. Rutting, fucking, screwing, all the time taunting Clarissa, letting her know that it could have been her instead. Clarissa couldn't see the other woman, who she was. Probably a prostitute, a stranger, a co-worker. Maybe his wife.

That night, Clarissa worked on her eyebrows, thinning them, and plucked the unsightly hair from her nose with a pair of tweezers. It wasn't enough.

———————

The soft hairs above her lip and on the rim of her ears drove him away the next day, forcing her to endure a thousand stings as she plucked them gone. She removed the last of her eyebrows for good measure.

———————

Clarissa had not spent long on the bench the day after that. She had been distracting herself from the monotony of waiting by flipping through his wallet, and that was when she realized what was *really* keeping Charles from coming to meet her as he had intended.

The wallet was much as it had been when Charles left it on the seat of the bus for her to find—pictures (minus the one of his wife which Clarissa had "lost"), a driver's license, someone's address scribbled on the back of a receipt, a lottery ticket. The only real difference was that most of the cash was gone. And, of course, the credit cards had stopped working after the second day, but that wasn't a difference you could see. With a flush of embarrassment, Clarissa remembered the clerk in the shoe store telling her that the card had been refused. Charles hadn't bought her anything else after that, and she was forced to come to meet him each day with silk stockings that led the eye down to a grungy old pair of sandals.

But of all the wallet's contents, it had been the pictures that gave Clarissa the clue she needed to unravel the mystery. One of the photos was a picture of a baby lying in a crib, newborn, hands in tiny fists. The other was a snap of Charles holding the child, looking down at it with an expression of infinite love. That was what had tipped Clarissa off.

Soft, round, smooth—Charles loved the baby. Loved it. Loved it.

She'd been back home before noon.

On the bathroom floor, her bare bottom against the cold tile, Clarissa had sat with tweezers in hand looking at herself in the full-length mirror on the back of the door. And as she looked, she groomed. She started with her face, wincing at the sight of her eyelids distorting as each lash was tugged away, watching the pale skin of her scalp emerge as her hairline receded.

Clarissa worked her way down. Across her shoulders, down her arms, the hairs that ringed her nipples, the soft down on her belly—nothing escaped her notice. Her arms were aching almost beyond the point where they would obey her direction long before she had finished with her back, but she didn't let the discomfort sway her. By the time she reached her inner thighs and her pubic mound, Clarissa was numb beyond feeling, and that, at least, seemed a blessing. She hoped that Charles would appreciate the effort.

It was after midnight when Clarissa finally cleared the last tuft of hair from the last toe. She stood, stiff, sore, and looked at herself in the mirror. Her hands roamed across her body. It was bare, smooth as a baby's skin, soft as silk. With a whisk broom, she gathered the mass of hair into a large zip-lock storage bag and hid it at the bottom of her canvas purse, in case she had been wrong about Charles and needed to put herself back together in a hurry later.

In the morning, Clarissa found that the more sensitive parts of her skin were peppered with red welts, like angry goose bumps. After a cool shower, she rubbed them with lotion, closing her eyes and imagining Charles' hands, enjoying the sensual slipperiness. A healthy splash of perfume on her dress to counteract the effects of four days in the sun, and Clarissa was ready to face the world. She headed for the mall.

By closing time, Charles had still not shown up.

Being abandoned a fifth time made Clarissa more

despondent and confused than angry. She had done everything right, hadn't she? How much more could she do?

Sitting at home staring into darkness, her hand had touched her leg and shown her the answer. Stubble.

When her alarm rang at four, Clarissa got up and bee-lined to the bathroom. Plucking the short hairs, making herself perfect, proved more difficult than she had thought it would be, and Clarissa did not make it to her spot on the promenade until almost ten. To make up for her tardiness, she wore no underwear and accented her legs by splitting her sun dress to the thigh.

Clarissa was careful about how she sat, crossing her ankles, folding her hands. She was a vision, a goddess, exuding sex and desirability. She caught every eye, aroused every man's base instincts. The thrill of being the center of attention was an aphrodisiac—invisible to those around her. Clarissa clenched her legs together and rhyth-mically flexed her thighs, bringing herself repeatedly to climax.

But when night enshrouded her and the crowds thinned, Clarissa found herself alone.

It was when she saw the body of a dead pigeon laying at the base of a tree no more than a hundred feet from her that Clarissa realized Charles was beginning to doubt his love for her.

Clarissa hardly slept that night, tossing and turning, every touch of the sheets renewing her desire for his soft caress. When she closed her eyes, she could feel his dreams calling to her through the ether.

Charles' dreams were confused, filled with conflicting

visions of herself and an aging, hairy thing that could only be his wife. Although the bond of love between Charles and Clarissa was strong, it could not compete with the whining and wheedling of his wife, or the inhuman lustings of her genital maw. Clarissa woke up repeatedly, screaming.

In her heart, Clarissa had believed that true love would win out, that Charles would break away from the thing he had married and come to her, but he had not. She was at a loss to figure out what she should do.

———

Clarissa repeated her morning ritual daily, always hoping that her physical perfection would call Charles away from his marital prison, draw him to her.

It had been ten days since Clarissa had seen her love. She had counted every hour, was counting them still as she stared into the setting sun, watching the restaurant where she had been so sure that he would say the secret words and put magic into the ring on her finger.

Six o'clock passed, and Clarissa felt her resolve crumble. She began to cry.

Why is he doing this to me? she asked herself. Why have I been abandoned? She cursed out loud, drawing stares.

But the calm, cool voice of Charles still lived within Clarissa. It spoke to her of the spark of love and how it needed to be fanned. It asked what she had done to deserve him when he had done so much for her. Beauty was skin deep and nothing more, after all.

The voice asked for a sign, a token of devotion.

At the sound of the voice Clarissa's anger bred a giggle, and then a joyous laugh. She leapt from the bench and ran down the promenade. A telephone; she had to find a telephone.

It didn't take long for Clarissa to phone a cab. While she was waiting for it to arrive, she found her lover's number in the phone book and called his house. The thrill of Charles answering stole her words for a moment, but she found them soon enough. Disguising her voice, she told him that she had found his wallet, asked if he wanted it back. Although he explained that the credit cards had been canceled and that he had already arranged for a new driver's license, he said that he would come pick it up for the sentimental value of the remaining contents. Clarissa gave him a fictitious address in Brentwood and hung up after he said that he'd be there in an hour.

The last of the money which Charles had left for her bought Clarissa a ride to the address on his driver's license.

Charles' house was like something out of a dream. Yellow with white trim, a two-car garage, a perfectly trimmed box hedge under the large front window. The front walk was illuminated by a streetlight, showing Clarissa the way to the door. Almost as if he knew that she was coming, Charles had left a key for Clarissa in the dirt next to the porch, hidden within a box that was fashioned to look like a rock. It took Clarissa only a few moments to locate.

The house was dark inside, and Clarissa made her way through the rooms with care and respect. In every room in the front of the house, Clarissa could feel Charles' presence. The fireplace, the chair by the reading lamp, the shelves of books, the dining room table, all had his aura about him. Only the kitchen was dominated by the stench of his wife.

The hallway proved to be another matter entirely.

All along the hall's walls, barely visible in the shadowy light, were framed photographs of Charles and the wife. Wedding photos, party photos, group shots with the extended family. Clarissa was repulsed by them, by the stain of the other woman that they smeared on the image of her intended.

There was a picture of Charles coming out of a hospital, walking next to a nurse who was pushing the wife in a wheelchair. The wife held a newborn baby.

Clarissa wondered if Charles had been fucking the nurse and knew that he probably had. He was that kind of man. Clarissa was willing to forgive him for such indiscretions— such was her love for him. Could the woman holding the child say the same? She thought not.

Something clicked in Clarissa's mind and she made note of the fact that the woman, the wife, was in a wheelchair in every picture. How pretentious! As if every day were the day of the birth of her child. How selfish! The woman was horrible, thoughtless. Charles deserved more. Much more. Charles deserved perfection.

The photos faded into darkness as they got farther and farther from the dim light that filtered in through the front window, but Clarissa could feel them even when they were swallowed by blackness. Her illness at being in their presence was equaled only by the gut-wrenching shock she received when a voice from the darkness beyond an open door whispered, "Charlie?"

It meant nothing to Clarissa that the wife was at home— Clarissa was not here to see *her*—and she wouldn't let the woman become the center of attention by answering her call. In fact, it was all Clarissa could do not to laugh at the woman's ignorant usage of the diminutive "Charlie." Instead of letting herself be distracted, Clarissa went right ahead with her plan.

What she intended to do was leave the engagement-ring-to-be on Charles' pillow. That would be the sign of her love that he needed. It would tell him that Clarissa would only wear his gift if he put it on her finger himself. What could be more clear? More romantic?

The ring didn't come off easily because Clarissa's finger was a bit swollen, but she'd managed to get it off with the help of some tools she found on a workbench in the garage and the flame of a burner in the kitchen. Clarissa reveled in the scent of Charles which covered every inch of the workbench and breathed only through her mouth while in the kitchen.

With the aid of a few other tools, Clarissa cleared off the bed and placed her present on the pillow. She took the hair from the bag in her purse and spread it around the room, banishing the wife's spoor and replacing it with her own. When Charles returned, he would walk into a sanctuary, a temple of their love.

The baby was another problem altogether. In the confines of its crib next to the bed, the child was never quiet for long, even when Clarissa tried to feed it. She was tempted to take it from the room but decided against the idea. Charles loved the baby dearly and, in any case, it would one day be *their* child.

In the end, the room was perfect but Clarissa's gloves were ruined. That, she supposed, was what she got for doing heavy work in dainty clothing. In any case, the way that the empty ring finger drooped made them look too silly to wear, and they were tainted with the smell of her burnt flesh.

Clarissa took the gloves off and stuffed them in her

purse as she left the house, noting with dismay that, to add insult to injury, she'd broken one of her long, lovely nails while packing the wife into the garage refrigerator.

Because she knew that Charles would be home soon, Clarissa hurried down the street. It took her three hours to walk home, but the night air did her a world of good.

———————

The next morning, Clarissa stayed at home. She groomed herself as before, more out of habit now than necessity, and placed herself next to the telephone, waiting for Charles to call.

He didn't.

Noon passed, but Clarissa knew that he was just stalling, trying to find the words he would use when she answered his ring. It was so like him.

As the afternoon wore on, Clarissa turned on the television to distract herself. There was a game show, then Oprah, then news. The news talked about scandals and taxes and war and controls, then it talked about Charles. Clarissa almost shrieked when his picture flashed into view to the left of the newscaster's head. She turned up the volume.

"—his wife and at least one other woman last night. The police report that they were responding to a neighbor's 911 call just before nine o'clock when they found him kneeling on the blood-stained floor of his garage screaming hysterically. Only a few feet away stood the open door of the refrigerator in which a dismembered body was found. Upon searching the house, police found a pair of severed breasts which had been left in the baby's—"

Clarissa was stunned. She couldn't believe that

Charles could have done such a thing. Still, it *was* on television, and where there's smoke . . .

"—time being, little David has been taken into custody by his grandparents in Santa Monica. Although Mr. Orman claims to have no knowledge of how—"

The sight of their baby, flesh of Charles' flesh, being handled by cold, uncaring strangers made Clarissa's skin crawl. None of them had Charles' look of love in their eyes.

"—unverifiable alibi. Police are making no comment at this time, but News Extra sources report that the only fingerprints police found on the murder weapons were those of Mr. Orman. Because of the special circumstances involved, the district attorney is expected to request the death penalty. In other news, federal agents—"

With a touch of a button on the remote, Clarissa silenced the television.

Well, *that* certainly explained why Charles hadn't called, she thought to herself as the weight of grim understanding settled on her.

For a while Clarissa felt angry, betrayed. All the time he was supposed to be coming to see her and get his wallet, Charles had been doing these things with another woman. She had to admit that betrayal hurt more than she ever could have imagined. Still, deep inside she knew that she would not be able to stay mad at her man for long.

Charles was the one great love in Clarissa's life. She could forgive him anything. If he were destined to spend time behind bars away from her, then she would learn to be patient. Just look at how well she had done over the last few days!

That afternoon, she looked up Charles' parents and

brought her child home. She would show it a mother's love, use baths and powders and tweezers to keep it clean and pure. Clarissa would teach her child about its father, loving and concerned although far, far away. And when Charles was finally freed to return to his true home, he would find them waiting for him—arms open, smiles wide, and skin very, very smooth.

Father Bob and Bobby

WHITLEY STRIEBER

We think Whitley Strieber is a great short story writer as evidenced by his career-spanning Evenings With Demons *published by Borderlands Press. "Father Bob and Bobby" is his most recent journey into the darkest regions of a tortured soul. A Strieber story never shies away from what is truly terrifying.*

The church stank of dead incense and the thick perfume of old women. The school reeked of floorwax and the tang of overheated children. The walls of the rectory were infused with cigar stench, and the portraits of pastors that lined the staircase were stained yellow by years of nicotine laden smoke.

He hated it all. No, loathed.

He loathed the church, the school, the rectory and, above all, their smells. He loathed with the infamous zeal of the convert. For he once had been a lover of all these things, even the damned cigars, which he had smoked because his pastor and his bishop smoked them. He'd been thrilled when he administered the sacraments, felt a quiet warmth at being called father, gratitude that the people brought him their problems. He'd coached basketball and soccer, taught Catechism, visited the sick and polished off ten masses a week. He was a priest in a hurry, scurrying after the needs of his faithful.

Now he despised the mere sight of the damned cross on the wall above his iron bedstead, saw the grandeur of Archbishop Potter as the destructive affectation of a dried up old queen, and the love affairs and hate affairs that smoldered among the old men of the cloth who surrounded him as the death rattle of an institution of the human imagination at its most perverse.

If some character named Jesus died on a cross in first century Palestine, he'd stayed dead. The sacraments had all been invented later to infuse the organization with power. They were meaningless.

Still, he wanted to confess his fall from faith. He wanted to beg the Palestinian to help him and to find solace in the weathered Holy Office that had been at his bedside or in his pocket for nearly fifty years. He wanted to hear the angels singing. He wanted the love of God that burned in him, exploding like a little supernova into the unseen world, to be not just in his damn head!

He kept to his duties because he had nothing of his own and when you left the church it cut the cord completely. He'd seen plenty of other guys, better than him in every way, fall and keep falling, past foundation work, past insurance sales, past pumping gas, until there was nothing left for them to do but live in the wind.

Don't set that bum on fire, boys, he gave you your first holy communion. Don't set that bum on fire, boys, he heard your desperate confessions and set your souls free to sin again.

Oh, what the hell, burn him, boys, burn the old fool!

He feared the street and he feared prison, and both were now shadows in his life—oh, the life of any priest, really. The thought of being behind bars made the stink of his own fear rise off him and mix with the incense that haunted the nave from the Mercurio funeral two days ago. He'd come in to check that the lights were out, but now he found himself pausing before the altar, mesmerized by the glow of the sacral candle. He'd consecrated the hosts in the tabernacle this morning, so the Blessed Sacrament was here, so the candle was lit.

"Jesus," he whispered. Listen to the acoustics! Oh, yes, the wondrous St. Mary Martyr acoustics, famous all over this side of town. Maria Gennaro once said that this was a wonderful place to sing, and she tried out for the Met in New York City.

"Jesus!" Listen to the echo! Oh, yes, the famous St. Mary Martyr echo, famous all over—

"JESUS!" The word went whonggg off into the flickering, candle-stunk dark. "Jesus loves you Jesus hates you Jesus isn't sure!"

He thought to take out his dick. He could. He was all alone. It was his frigging church. Then he thought, 'this is madness. I'm actually going mad.' Immediately there washed over him a gigantic regret, that his madness must be this stupid, this religious, this awkward and pitiful.

"Confetior Deo omnipotenti, Beatæ Mariæ semper Virgini, Beato Michaeli Archangelo, Beato Joanni Baptistæ, Sanctis Apostolis Petro et Paulo—I have given this thing my life blood and I will not feel the need to confess! I will not!"

He shouted at the stone, the marble, the candles, the wood, the little pile of bleached, sterile wafers in the tabernacle, in their golden chalice there in the dark. "What can I have been thinking, to have given my life—my whole damn life—to pieces of bread?"

Kneeling there as he was, he would have appeared the very picture of devotion, but who was watching him knew his weakness, had heard everything, and knew, now, exactly how to execute his plan.

A few moments later, Father Bob went striding across the sanctuary and into the sacristy . . . and into a great darkness.

The door made a puffy slam. Father Bob's footsteps clattered away into silence. A moment later the air conditioning went off, followed by the faint boom of ductwork suddenly empty of air pressure.

Then it was silent here in St. Mary Martyr. It was truly, beautifully silent. At first, the church appeared empty, so empty that a mouse that had been waiting to eat crumbs off the altar began to move out into view.

It stopped, though, when something like a sigh whispered through the silence. An instant later, it saw movement back among the pews. It ran.

Quickly, a figure passed down the aisle, making the votive candles lit by the old and the desperate flicker uncertainly. A few moments later another door, this one small and at the rear of the church, opened. A figure slipped out, hesitated for a moment, then went out into the night.

This figure, tall, bent against the wind, clutching the

collars of a thin raincoat, crossed beneath the streetlight and went on off down Morris street, a shadow beneath the tossing trees.

Mrs. McKorkle came during the day, and it was good to have her bustle in this mausoleum of a rectory, the moaning of the Electrolux, the clatter of dishes being put away, the small humming under her breath of popular standards from fifty years ago. At five she would make him his dinner. At five thirty, he would sit in the front room with a cigar watching Dan Rather, and then at six go to the kitchen and take his food out of the warm oven. He would eat in the dining room at a table that had once troughed six priests.

Father Martin Berg had enjoyed the sort of invincible faith that you would have thought would have carried him through to eternity. But it had not carried him through. He'd lost it all in an afternoon, for no particular reason, and gone and joined Catholic Life as an agent, and called on the parish with a sheepish, awful grin on his face. They bought nothing from him.

He'd fought back by using his considerable organizational skills. He had cards printed and tacked them up on bookstore and coffee house bulletin boards. He'd even rented an office, bought a couple of suits from the Salvation Army, the works. A handsome man, he looked like he might once have been corporate poster boy, circa about 1955.

Unfortunately, he couldn't write a million dollar policy for fifty cents on a cancerous octogenarian with an artificial heart and kidneys. Or so he'd said when he'd come up the back walk looking for a meal and his old bed, just for the night.

He had wept at this table. He'd died at fifty-six. Fallen under a bus.

So many hopeful, blustery Irishmen had sat across from him at this table that they had blurred together in his mind into a single mournful presence, as heavy on his memory as Mrs. McKorkle's scones were in his gut. Then there had been Father Lupe Zaragona, with his beloved Mount Blanc pen his father had given him, and Father Robbins, the evangelist of homosexuality, who had blown his brains out—and into—the boiler, shutting it down for two very cold weeks in December of 1997. And that inevitable dirty old man—what was his damn name?—who got shuttled from parish to parish and diocese to diocese. Bob had discovered by accident that he kept a picture of the child actor Kelly Reno in his wallet.

The phone rang.

He stopped chewing the roast beef flavored string he'd been given. Money problems. Actual starvation, here and there, these days—priests being cheerful about fasting.

It rang again, and kept ringing.

Mr. or Mrs. Dying was dying, perhaps, wanting a little grease for the forehead and the loins and a quidquid delquisti toodle-oo.

He would have answered it, but he knew that it would soon ring again if it was urgent. He got his black death case ready, small and frayed, with its red plush interior with room for the host carrier, the holy oil, and a cross.

The case had been bought from the Paulist Priest Supply back when he'd just been ordained.

A priest! Me! Oh my god o my god o my god. And that night, feeling as if his soul had been transformed into some kind of a crystal set tuned to Christ, he had masturbated four times, each time after going down beside his narrow bed and saying a rosary, then back up and here came Mr. Hand again, groping and punching him up, and bip bap boom until there was nothing left in his crotch bag but rust.

He had been plunged into St. Michaels, then his first turn at St. Mary Martyr when there was a choir the size of an infantry brigade and two hours of confession and six masses, then St. Christopher's under Monsignor Calabrese who had been a hand smeller (whatever sort of fetish that was God literally only knew). You would wake up and there kneeling beside your bed in the duff with an erection like an evil lantern would be the pastor, bent over and smelling, not kissing, your hand. You'd lie there praying for him for yourself for the parish the people the church the pope the saints and sinners while snufff, snufff on and on it went, and finally you would fake a little snore and turn to the wall. Then he'd go to the next boy priest, sniffing his mad way across more damp night skin.

Priests shot through that parish like meteors. He'd died in a fire, that one, smoking in bed so they said and when Detective Reilly Mann had pointed out that he didn't smoke, the Chancellor said as smooth as eelskin, "he'd just taken it up. He was clumsy with it, poor devil." The archbishop called them in and spoke of how it is that tolerance is part of piety. But then he added boys will be boys, and threw them a sumptuous dinner, pot roast and old wine.

The truth is that the inner history of the church—the real history—is a history of sex gone all contorted from compression and disuse and ignorance. Above all, the sexuality of the church is an ignorant one. Not innocent, though, no.

It is the story of the urgent effort of semen to escape from generations of human prisons, made in the name of God by a pope ironically named Innocent, who Father Bob suspected of having been a rough-skinned demon under his fabulous vestments.

And then there was the matter—the awful matter—of the relief of priests by altar boys, a tradition that went back to Roman times, when the local pontifex could neither marry nor be seen with a whore.

It had always been part of the institution, a service performed by somebody whose smoothness echoed that of a woman enough to pass, and whose knowledge of the organ meant that he could be quick and even sometimes splendid.

Before mass in the sacristy with the smart right hand. After mass in the rectory with the clumsy, surprising left.

Part of the institution, of no consequence to anybody, not in a past when child servants had routinely amused guests at dinners by diddling them under the table. No, it was the discovery of childhood itself, and its sanctification in the nineteenth century, that had oh so gradually surrounded the church and its ancient habits, until what was routine became scandalous, the ordinary transmogrified into the horrible. Boys who once would not even have bothered to laugh the matter off now took priestly need to be evil, and the satisfaction of it a guilty and awful sin. They became the hollow-eyed men in the courtrooms, who sent the priests off to a life of frenetic, devastating buggery under prison sheets, their consecrated hands locked in steel.

The phone rang again. Okay, that was it. He had to answer.

"St. Mary Martyr."

"Father?"

"This is Father Randall."

Breathing. He knew the sound of grief. He waited. A gulp, again: "Father?"

It was a child. "Are you in trouble?"

Silence. Then a click, something changing in the telephone system. Then the dial tone.

The moment he hung up, the phone rang again. It was the same caller. He went through the same drill, then dashed into his office to look at the caller ID. He was astonished to find that the number calling was the principal's office over at the school.

He didn't waste an instant. A child was in the school, which meant vandalism, which meant a disaster tomorrow morning, and more students not coming back after Christmas. He remembered when only the best could make it into St. Mary Martyr. The rest must go to General Grant, poor things. Now the dopes and misanthropes went to St. Mary Martyr. The real kids—normal, loud, strong—played for Give Me a G, a Big Big G, Go Grant, Go Grant, Go G-R-A-N-T!

Go Saint Mary Martyr! Hey, we're here! We have balls, too!

Yeah, basketballs with all the bounce dribbled out.

He left the rectory, which looked at night like the haunted house that it was, and hurried along the short street to the school.

The night had turned cold, tangy with autumn smoke, the air as clear as God's own eye. The moon shone down, that parched desert in the sky, that appalled face, and a reef of leaves raced along the sidewalk. Oh, dear God, how beautiful is thine world, that is thine.

You must exist. Sure, life might have arisen out of mud and lightning or whatever, but where did the esthetics come from?

The school building was dark, absolutely dark, a forbidding old hulk that frightened him always, because it was four stories of wood-frame construction that would go up like a Walpurgisnacht bonfire if ever anything in the basement went alight.

He was forever having the fire department over on inspection, the boilermen, the alarm company, the sprinkler company. He threw money at safety, demanded a fire drill every week even though they all, from the fire marshal to Mr. Saenz the alarm man, assured him that it was completely and absolutely safe.

Then he would walk up the creaking linoleum stairs and hold the ancient mahogany banister, and see the children in their prim blue uniforms marching in their trusting line, their faces full of the assurance and hope of childhood, that I may be a car dealer or I a ballerina, and he would get all the checking done again.

Now he fumbled out his fistful of keys and took the long, strange one that fit the elaborate lock that had replaced the old, easy one after Mrs. Kiel had come in and found a pile of defecation on the floor. That discovery had been the beginning of a tour through devastation so unspeakable that it seemed to belong to some other reality. Somebody had urinated in the biology lab drawers, poured the fish out and chewed them up, then spit them against the blackboards. They had ripped the lizards and the snakes in half, and slashed into the ceilings of half the classrooms with what must have been a scimitar. There were spatters of dry semen all over Mrs. Kiel's Virgin Mary Martyr statue.

But the main thing was the shit. He'd never seen so much defecation. How could anybody shit that much? The police had said that it was a gang. They had dusted for prints and found many—surprise, surprise—in a school. In his dreading heart, he wondered if perhaps the whole student body had not participated?

From a distance, a child appears to be a complicated, valid creature, some of them even beautiful, some of them curiously sensual. In fact, the casual, unformed nature of that sensuality—the wriggling movements, the sparking eyes, the moisture of the smile—could make it actually a little arousing . . . sometimes.

But up close, they were fragile things, all soft skin and big eyes and so touchingly eager to be held. He found it almost impossible to believe that those gentle, polite slips had come in here en masse and done this, somehow each escaping from his or her home at an appointed hour.

He unlocked the door. The alarm was full on, its red "armed" light glowing. At once, it began to squeal. He put in the code, turning it off. Then he closed the door and turned it on again. A flip of switches brought light to the hall. No sound, though. He'd expected something—a gasp, the patter of small feet. Nothing came, though, just the contemplative quiet of an academic place in repose.

He moved along the hall. "Hello?"

His voice echoed in the waxed silence. Stopping, he listened. All he could hear was his own breathing. He went upstairs, heading toward Mrs. Kielbasa's office. The door was dark mahogany, and as he put his hand on the knob, he found himself unwilling to turn it.

He was deep in the building, all alone, and he thought perhaps somebody had lured him here. The idea of getting a cop had never entered his mind. He'd been too intent on protecting his beloved school. But now he thought that he'd been a fool. He laughed a little. It wasn't surprising, was it? He could be a damn fool. One of his skills.

Distantly, there was a thud, like a deep underground explosion or a faraway bomb blast. In that second the lights went out. He started to yell, but the words stopped in his suddenly very dry throat. He could see literally not a single thing. The hallway opened onto doors, and all the doors were closed. He might as well have been in a cave.

He flapped his hands around his head, felt for the wall. Then he heard something—a click, very faint. The air moved just a little.

Then he knew that Mrs. Kielbasa's door had been opened. He stepped back once, then again. And suddenly his feet were slipping out from under him. He'd backed all the way to the top of the stairs. He almost overbalanced, but he regained his footing. Had he gone down those stairs, he would now be lying in the landing, broken or dead. He caught his breath. Reaching back, he felt for the top of the banister, then turned and went down.

There was more light in the broad foyer, which opened out to the street in front and the playground behind. He wished to hell that he'd brought his cell phone. Well, whoever was in here, they were going to get a taste of the cops just as soon as he got back to the rectory. Damn bastards and their bastard games, he could've been killed.

He was unlocking the front door when he felt something. There was a sensation between his legs. Before he had a chance to move, his genitals had been gripped. For a moment, it felt like somebody was goosing him from behind and he started to get furious. Then he realized, by the vibration, that it was not a hand.

The vibration spread like fire down his legs and up into his solar plexus. The pleasure was so intense that it actually surprised him. Before he could so much as draw another surprised breath, it became more intense still. He was aware that he'd gotten a tremendous erection.

The vibration deepened, sending gusts of white heat all the way up to his face, flushing him, causing wild, savage desire to burst forth in him. He threw his head back, he cried out, he couldn't do anything else, it felt so good that the deepest part of him, the savage part that sleeps beneath the heart, was awakened and did not cry out or scream, but roared as the apes who spawned us must have roared when they found pleasure.

He was agonized, tormented, exalted. The vibration would lessen and he would bend forward gagging, gasping, trying to ask for respite. Then it would go deep again, touching him in sexual places he didn't even know existed—behind his balls, in his anus, along the rigid shaft—and he would howl again, throwing back his head, every muscle tensing, the spittle flying, the sweat pouring out of him.

It kept on like that, not for seconds but for minutes, until he was screaming and babbling, gushing sweat, his guts churning, his balls aching between bouts of hideous delectation. In his mind's eye he saw women dancing in heavenly light, and he almost went mad with desire, wanting not only the pleasure but the flesh, to kiss, to lick, to enter it. He had never felt himself in a woman but he wanted to now, he had to, oh, God, he had to!

The vibration rose higher and higher and went deeper and deeper. His penis became impossibly rigid, tensing against the fabric of his pants, and it pumped and pumped and pumped and pumped, and he felt all over him hot semen, running down inside his pants, greasing his legs.

Then it stopped. The instrument—and he felt now for certain that it was not a hand, but a cage of stiff wires that caught on the weave of his trousers—was withdrawn. He choked, toppling forward, seeing a flash as his forehead hit the door.

He still had the key in the lock. Gathering what presence of mind remaining to him, he turned it and stumbled out onto the front steps. Somebody came out right behind him, he heard them—heard a buzzing, crackling sound, anyway. It reminded him of the throaty sputtering of a grackle. He whirled around, just in time to glimpse a shape about four feet tall go rushing into the bushes that grew beside the entrance.

"Hey—hey!" He dashed forward and clawed into the bushes, trying to part them. Deep among the branches, he saw a black disappearing gleam.

Silence, but for the night wind and a distant radio. "The song of love is a sad song . . ." a voice crooned. Across the street was an old house. He knew the occupants enough to smile and say hello. They weren't parishioners. He would go there, knock on the door, use their phone.

As he crossed the street, he became aware that his gut was aching down deep, that his penis felt as if it had been sanded, and that he was wobbling on his feet and had semen dripping down his inner thighs. He couldn't be seen, dared not risk something being visible, a wet spot or some such. He bypassed the house and went straight on along the block, past the bulk of St. Mary Martyr with its thick, square steeple with the electronic bell concealed in it, and the black windows reflecting scenes from the life of the Virgin, ending with the martyrdom of her heart at the feet of Jesus's cross.

He reached the rectory, threw himself at the front door, fumbled for his keys and fought with them, finally got the door open. He ran down the deep central hall, past the life-size statue of Mary that stood beside the circular staircase and up the stairs.

He went into his bathroom with its old clawfooted tub and worn porcelain sink. He turned on the light, went to the mirror.

He looked at the apparition in the glass without understanding, staring at the horrible, hollow eyes that stared back, and the skin dripping its curtain of red. His face, his hair—he was soaked with blood. He tore at his collar, ripped it off and tossed it aside, then tore open his shirt.

Blood, blood, blood! He screamed, then immediately stopped. Heaving, gagging, he held onto the sink. Big drops of blood dripped down, spattering against the dim white of the porcelain.

"Oh, God . . . oh, God . . ."

He raised his hands to his face, wiped them through the sheet of blood. There were no cuts, there was no pain . . . but it was—and then it hit him. He was sweating blood. He was.

"I've got something . . . oh, Jesus help me, help your son . . ."

A sound? Was that somebody downstairs, just coming in, that faint creak sounding ominously like the back door when you close it.

Oh, Jesus, Jesus . . . (Yeah, now you pray. Now, you better believe you pray, just like the assholes you've preached against, pray only when you're in trouble.)

He prayed, he prayed hard. He went into the hall—there was a footstep on the stair, that creaker just below the landing, oh, shit.

He ran down to his room and grabbed the phone. He hurt, he was aware of it, his dick hurt like it had been worked in some kind of a steel damn tube for hours. They had used a flashlight tube filled with gauze at the seminary. "Boys, you're going to do it. Keep it private and give your failings to God."

"Check it out."

"What? Who is that?"

Nobody there. Strange voice, a little too soft, a little too hard—a childish, soft voice with a rasp in it. If an animal could talk, maybe that's how it would sound.

He grabbed the phone, a lifeline in a storm, jammed at the buttons.

"911, what is your emergency?"

"This is Father Robert Strickland, St. Mary Martyr. We have an intruder in our rectory."

"Saint Mary Martyr, 153 Oak Avenue?"

"That's the church. Rectory, 157 Oak."

"One Five Seven Oak Avenue?"

A long, rattling cough echoed through the dark. It was an immense sound. "Hurry! Good Christ, hurry!"

"The police are on their way."

He hung up the phone. What the hell had this been? He'd been lured away from the rectory, that was obvious, so whoever this was could get in without being detected. But what had happened at the school?

He was caked with drying blood, his shirt ripped open and his guts aching like he'd been rubbed raw inside. He was on fire, he wanted to scream, but what was worse was that something had been broken open inside him. Something that he had kept tightly locked up for years had been ripped open and the guts of it had fallen out, and those guts were all the joys and the pleasures he'd given up on behalf of the little piece of bread.

Another cough, and then a scraping sound. That voice again: "Help me, Father."

What? That sounded like a kid. Little kid with a voice full of—God, was it age? It was the voice of an ancient child.

He was going to say something. Reply. Yes, he was. His throat felt as if it contained an out of control blowtorch, but he opened his mouth. He spoke. "We can help each other."

A shadow appeared in the doorway. It reached up. It turned on the light.

Standing there was a boy. He was about four feet tall, maybe eleven or a smallish twelve. He wore white shorts and a white T-shirt. His skin was almost as white. On his face there was the suggestion of a smile, the lips partly opened, the teeth just visible behind them. He had one of those ambiguous boy's faces, lovely and soft and yet full of the harder presence of the coming man.

"Father, I need to pee."

What?

"Where did you come from?"

The boy smiled, a little anger in it, a little confusion. Then he came into the room, marched past Bob and entered the bathroom. An instant later, there was the sound of a powerful stream going into the toilet.

Bob stared at the closed door. He felt drained, his body ached, he wanted to sleep. But he had to deal with this situation. There was a child in his rectory in the middle of the night. Once, it wouldn't have meant anything. He'd have called the family or, if there was no family, put the kid up for the night and taken him downtown to Catholic Welfare Services in the morning.

You put a kid up now, you're a kidnapper, a pederast, you're going to be questioned by the police, and so is the kid. Did he put his hands on your body, son? Where on your body? Here, point on this doll where he put his hands. Did he have you open your zipper?

"Have we got any more of that cake?"

"What cake?"

"The Entenmann's chocolate cake Mrs. McCorkle left in the fridge. Hello?" When he smiled, his face looked like something out of the middle ages, some painting of a Satyr. The teeth glistened. "What? Have you had some kind of a stroke? Hello, Bob, it's me. It's Bobby."

As the child came closer, Bob backed away. "Get out," he stammered. "Go home. You have to go home."

"Oh, yeah, like she'd let me in at this hour. You got some kind of a problem, Father? 'Cause you look weird." He reached up and put his cold, wet palms on Bob's cheeks and pushed his lips together. Then he giggled. "Father Fishie!" He patted his cheeks and strolled away. Suddenly he whirled around. "You know I'm scared to go to the frigging kitchen alone! Now, come on! Damn you."

Bob followed him. In the gloom of the long back corridor, his blond head looked like a lantern. Who was he?

Where had he come from? Had he been at the school? Had he . . . done that?

Oh, God, no. But he could have. Look at him, he acted like he owned the place. How did he know about Mrs. McCorkle? How did he know about the cake in the fridge? Dear God, how had this person who had never been in his life before suddenly appeared in it like this?

Something terrible had happened at the school, something that had somehow restitched the world, put it back together in a new way. Who had been in there?

Bob had no sexual interest in children, least of all in boys. Conceivably, he could have been attracted to a girl mature beyond her years, but that was just nature. A boy, no, never. Especially not that one with his gangly, preadolescent limbs and the hardness that was coiled in his vulnerable little boy's eyes. That was a kid who would tell anybody anything, a destroyer.

"You have to leave. Where's your home? What's your phone number?"

"It got disconnected."

"You still have to leave. We have no accommodations for you here."

The boy appeared indifferent to this. He opened the refrigerator, leaned into the yellow light. "I do believe we've eaten the whole thing. Shitabrick. We ate it all at supper."

"I didn't . . . eat the cake. I dislike those cakes, she knows that."

The boy turned around. "Well, I certainly didn't eat an entire cake, not after all that roast beef we stuffed our faces with."

"You—you weren't here. You didn't eat here. You've just appeared!"

The boy put his hands on his hips. "You crazy horn, stop tooting your crazy song. I got enough trouble without you going nuts on me."

"What trouble do you have, son?"

"First off, don't you 'son' me, son. I got a mother won't stop drinkin' and the socials wanna foster me an I got no place to go and, good sire, I have not a penny farthing." He opened his arms. "But I have enough love to fill the whole world."

"Who are you?"

"Oh, manny man, this is so nuts. I am me, Bobby, Roberto, Bobby-Pot, as I was known in the springtime."

He came close and put his arms around Bob and hugged him. Bob looked down at the cowlick that swirled in his hair. The child's arms were strong and he hugged hard, and he pressed his cheek against Bob's chest. Bob could not help but feel compassion toward him, and he said, "How can I help you, son?"

"Our candle went out, for one thing."

"What candle?"

"Oh, you know, when you were in there laughing it up, the candle went out. The mouse noticed."

What in hell?

The boy released him. "Do I have to show you?"

What would this lead to? Bob was fascinated. "Please do."

He marched off toward the side door. Bob followed him. On the way to the church, Bobby murmured a kind of litany, "I died, oops, I just died again, whoa, I got burned, I died, died again, got drowned, got starved, got shot, oops, oops . . ."

"What's that all about?"

"Bobby radio. News to myself. What's happenin' to me all around the world all the time. Bobby radio. Would you kiss me?" He held up his hand like a little prince. "Prove your respect," he said.

Bob took the child's hand and held it, but he had no intention of kissing any part of this youngster or any desire to. He unlocked the church.

"I want this thing kept open, boy! What if somebody wants to come in here and talk to my dad?"

Talk to his "dad," indeed, the blasphemous wretch. Who ever heard of a twelve year old with a Jesus fixation? Poor little abandoned crazy fella.

"All right, now, what's wrong in here, young man?"

"What's wrong is in the ding-dong sanctuary, Bobus."

As the boy marched through the sacristy Bob hurried along behind, he felt, like a prissy old woman. When he straightened his shoulders and concentrated on striding, laughter pealed ahead of him, and it was so bright and so delightful that he laughed, too.

"See," Bobby said, pointing at the sacral candle, which was out.

"You've been in here."

"I live here." He pointed at the tabernacle.

"Son, you mustn't blaspheme."

"Okay."

"You obviously don't live in the tabernacle."

He shrugged. "So anyway, light it."

Bob no longer smoked, so he had to get matches from the sacristy. He took them from the small box beside the tapers where they were kept, and returned. As he did so, he turned on a couple of the sanctuary lights. It took him a moment to realize what he was seeing—a small, dark animal standing there. Its head snapped toward him, he saw yellow, vulpine eyes—and then he saw Bobby.

"Hey, Fath," the boy said, and this time when he smiled his teeth gleamed like pearls behind his damp, heart-shaped lips, and the thought crept into Bob's mind that children could be devastatingly sensual. Then he thought, "I have just seen this child's soul, and this is a very dangerous child."

"Oops, I went in a sewer, oops, my brain got blowed out, uh-oh, that's hot . . ." He shook his head. "I die about sixty times a second nowadays." He stamped his foot. "Honestly!"

"You die when other children die?"

"I die when anybody dies, and I am very busy dying all the time. Especially with the ones who pray-ay-ay, I die inside them like a heart or some damn thing. I'm always, like, stopping. Like the brakes're something."

Bob struck the match and lit the sacral candle.

"Mm, that's nice. That makes it warm in my bedroom. I share, you know. I share with all the cold kids all over the whole world. That's why my daddy wants the candles, so the children will be warm."

As he spoke, he walked toward the altar.

"You should have kissed me when you could," he said, "but you were afraid of yourself. You're going to miss that kiss." And with a flip of his hand, the hand he had raised for kissing, he disappeared right before Bob's eyes. Or rather, he walked into the altar and was gone.

Bob heard somebody cry out, realized that it was he himself, then rushed toward the altar. Fumbling frantically, he unlocked the tabernacle and reached into the dark space with shaking hands. He closed his fingers around the neck of the chalice he had so carelessly thrust in after mass this morning and drew it out of the tabernacle. His hands were almost out of control. His inner voice was babbling so fast he could hardly understand himself. "Miracle," it was saying, "miracle, miracle," and there was within him something that was going to turn into madness of the kind that you did not recover from.

The thought of the infantile whining and posturing he'd done at this altar a few hours ago made the acid of revulsion boil up into his throat. He was a damn priest, it was in his blood, what had he been thinking? The old ladies he so detested—he saw them now as extraordinarily noble souls. He saw their lives as they had been, the follies they were balancing with the rosaries of age.

He drew the lid off the chalice, and remembered how bitter he had felt at giving his life to a little piece of bread. In that instant, a cloud dropped down from above, surrounding him, actually weighing on him like a sheet of iron, crushing him to the floor, to a kneeling crouch with the chalice cradled beneath his chest. The weight was like a great boot on his neck and the chalice began to buckle, the bowl of it twisting toward the floor.

The host—He must not touch the floor, not who was dying all the time with everybody, not somebody that brave, that sacred. He could not reach into the chalice, it was breaking beneath his weight. Forcing his face downward, thrusting with his chin until his mouth and nose were inside the bowl, he gobbled the hosts like a dog.

The weight left so abruptly that he lurched upward, then slipped and fell back. He lay staring upward into gold gleams from the ornate ceiling and the glaring balls of the sanctuary lights. "He's so old," he thought, "and yet he's still a child."

He wondered if Bobby would have been there anyway, even if the hosts had not been consecrated, and what did it mean now that he had eaten them, that he had taken the body and blood within him?

He soon found out what it meant. He was not at all sure what had just happened to him. He'd taken psychology and family counseling courses, and he knew something about psychosis and hallucination. In thinking the thing out, it became clear that there would be one piece of hard evidence that would tell him whether or not this whole, bizarre chain of events had any basis in reality at all.

This was his Caller ID. He went back to the rectory, entered the mahogany foyer and went directly into his office. The small plastic box sat beside the telephone. When he approached it, the screen showed only the date and time. But they were correct. It was working. He pressed the review button. And there it was: a call from the school, just as he remembered it. But the time—it read 4:53 PM, not closer to ten, as it should have. He pressed the button again. There was the call from Bill Crawford about how to use Quickbooks. The readout said 4:19. But hadn't Bill called more like two? Or no—God, when was it? He wasn't certain.

He had an idea. He pulled his cellphone out of his pocket and dialed the rectory. As the phone rang, he watched the call come up on the Caller ID. By his watch it was 11:44 PM. The reading showed 10:44—an hour earlier. So, the call from Bill would have really been at 3:19, and that sounded about right.

The problem was that he had taken no call from the

school this afternoon, not at three or four or any other time.

He decided on a course of action: a major drink was what he needed. Christ wouldn't appear as that lascivious, evil-looking little monster, anyway. And he certainly wouldn't refer to God the Father as "dad." Good Lord, what a stupid fantasy it all had been.

Well, it had passed. He was fine now. He'd been working like the devil on the books. The damn archdiocese had cut its subsidy to pay lawyer bills for Father Richard Jordan, who'd buggered, it seemed, half of the boys in St. Hubertus school, the damned old reprobate. His lunacy was going to cost the Church a cool twenty-five mil, and a lot of that was going to come right out of the Parish Fund. So he had a deficit to deal with, and the local banks were hesitant as hell, understandably. Who wanted to risk having to foreclose on a church? What did you do with it—turn it into a gym? A car dealership?

He went to the sideboard in the dining room and took out the Johnny Walker Black. This was going to be a serious drink, and he intended to use his best. He poured about four fingers of the golden joy juice into a crystal highball glass that was probably fifty years old. Like everything in this wonderful old rectory, it was the very best. A gift, no doubt, from some wealthy and long-forgotten parishioner.

He knocked the entire thing back, then poured another, knocked it back. Better. A little. He was still damn well shaking like a jelly and he was in a very strange mood. The thing was, he wanted that kid. He, him. He was aching for the boy. It wasn't sex, at least, he hoped not. He just wanted to be with him. Bobby. His same name. That little boy had been the most charismatic person he had ever encountered. Dear God, what the kid said was true. He did want to kiss him. He wanted to cherish him, to protect him. Bobby was like the son of all sons, a child who could set the fatherly instincts of even a dry old priest to blazing.

A little fantasy rustled up: Bobby comes back. It turns out his mother is the disaster he implied. Father talks to her—and she asks if Bobby can stay at the rectory. She asks. Father Bob doesn't see why not. So they begin a life together. Bobby excels at St. Mary Martyr. He plays on the baseball team. He loves to fish, which inspires Bob to get his old boat out of the garage and they take fishing trips up to Starlot, the diocesan fishing camp on Lake Binny. Bob gets to watch him grow up, to help him learn, to encourage him when he is struggling, to console him when he is sad, to laugh with him and cry with him over the days of his young life.

Then he felt something down below, something funny. When he realized that he had a huge erection, cold, awful fear went through him. As the scotch came boiling back up like lava, he raced upstairs to his bathroom. Amid the marble and the gleaming brass, he vomited and vomited and vomited, until he thought he would have a stroke.

He sank down on the floor, gazing blankly across the tiles. Dear God, what is happening to me? Please God, help me!

It hadn't been Christ and it hadn't been a psychotic break. It had been a damn demon. He'd glimpsed it in its reality—that second when it had looked like an animal, its face covered with black, gleaming fur, its eyes as blank and terrible as an animal's. But brilliant. Oh, yes, brilliance without the spark of humanity. If there was any better definition of the demonic, he didn't know what it was.

At least he'd eaten the hosts. He hadn't allowed that thing near them, no damn way. And he was not going to become some kind of a pederast and end up on the evening news. He was going to go on being the good priest everybody thought he was, and nobody was ever going to hear or even so much as sense his inner doubts or his loathing for the hierarchy. He would not quit. No.

So, okay, he wasn't going to get drunk, at least. The scotch hadn't had time to enter his bloodstream. He got up from the floor. A glance in the mirror revealed what looked like some sort of a Halloween mask made from his face. The eyes were bulging with terror, the lips were twisted into a grimace, the skin was gray and slack.

He decided to take a shower. As he undressed, he found that his underwear were sticky. It was vile, just vile. He wadded up the briefs and put them on the drain beside the sink. These could not be seen by his house-keeper, for the love of all that was holy. He realized, also, that his anus hurt. It hurt a good deal, in fact. Reaching back, touching it, he jumped forward.

This was no hallucination. Whatever had or had not happened on this night—whatever was real and was not—he had most certainly been penetrated.

"I've been raped," he said. He looked again in the mirror, and now the face was atrocious, almost unrecognizable, streaming with sweat, as gray as death, the eyes like the eyes of a hog that has smelled the blood of hogs. He knew that look, you never forgot it, not if you were brought up on a farm, as he had been.

"Fucking raped!"

He twisted around, trying to use the mirror to see what

it was like down there. He couldn't see much, but his cheeks looked kind of red where he could see. The way it felt, though—he had received an injury there. But when? Had he gone over to the school, after all? Had it happened there? Dear God, what had happened there?

He threw off the rest of his clothes and ran the shower until it was billowing with steam. This goddamn thing— what if somebody had given him a dose of AIDS or something?

He got into the shower. He still felt like absolute hell. Then he was crying. He was crying hard in the middle of the shower, in the nice, private white place that was always a source of enjoyment.

He had been a good priest, damnit. Never in all his priesthood—and never in his youth, if the truth be known—had he experienced sex with another human being. Oh, sure, he'd failed the Lord many times. He sometimes thought he was married to Sally damn Fivefingers. It had been like this since he was a kid. "Bless me Father, for I have sinned. I have masturbated forty times since my last confession." "And when would that be, my son?" "Three days ago." "Dear heaven, boy, are you hurt?"

In all his life, also, he had never had feelings of desire for a man, let alone a boy. When he dreamed of sex, he dreamed about women. Now, he leaned against the wall of the shower and opened his crack and let the stream flow in, let the warm water cleanse him and heal him. But the hurt was deep, it was way too deep.

He didn't want to go to the emergency room, but there was pink blood in the drain water, he could see it. He was experiencing rectal bleeding, and maybe that plus whatever in God's name had happened earlier with the blood that had come out of his pores, perhaps that was why he just felt so awfully weak.

"Oh my God, I need medical attention!" Where would he go? Should he drive to St. Louis? He couldn't go to the hospital here. "Father came in with a torn rectum," they would say. Jesus, the cops would be watching him, then, the way they watched other priests.

"It's all ruined," he screamed.

Then something came out of him—spraying out, he couldn't control it. He hadn't felt it coming. It was just spraying out like a firehose, but it—oh, holy Jesus, help me. "Help me! Help me!"

It was flying around in the air, buzzing around in the shower stall. But what? He batted at them. They were coming out of him, he could feel his bowels emptying steadily.

Bugs were coming out of him, little, speeding bugs that stung like pinpricks when they struck his skin. They smelled like shit. It was like being enveloped in a brown shit-cloud. Oh, my God. My God!

He leaped out of the shower and threw himself to the floor and rolled like a burning man, rolled to the door and then to the stall and back, all the while spewing massive clouds of flies.

Then it stopped. He was crying and screaming, his butt burning, his guts inside burning worse. Drugs. He'd been lured over to the school and drugged hard and deep and it was destroying him, because, you see, a man cannot shit flies, can he? So all these flies that smelled like shit and were crawling all over this damn john, they weren't here, were they?

He came to a sitting position. No, they were not here.

They did not exist. So he could safely ignore them. He drew himself to his feet.

And this time, what he saw in the mirror was not at first recognizable to him. The man he saw in the mirror was a cadaver. He had lost maybe eighty of his two hundred pounds, eighty or ninety. Maybe half. Maybe he'd lost half his weight.

Poland, 1944, people had looked like this. Biafra. Sudan. But not in a prosperous community in middle America, and not a perfectly healthy man of sixty-two, and certainly not in a few minutes. And who the hell had shaved his head? Damn, but look—there was hair all over the floor. The place looked like a barbershop.

He was tired, too. Oh, boy was he tired. In fact, he thought that death itself was maybe not so far from this kind of tired.

"Bob, we gotta go down the hall now."

Who the hell said that? It was like there were people moving around out there, but he couldn't see them. "I got a lotta flies in here," he said. It came out as a shout.

"What's he saying."

"Get him on his feet."

"He shit all over the place."

"Fuck, this is gonna be a hard one. Bob, do you know what's goin' on, here? Hello? Christ, the guy's, like catatonic."

He was going into the light. It wasn't unpleasant, he was sort of drifting—levitating, that's what they called it. Or no, suddenly he was heavy and his underarms hurt. He was being carried!

This was Bobby's doing. "Bobby! Bobby!"

"Sick fuck, Jesus!"

"Shut up. Just—"

Somebody started praying, an old man's voice, but familiar. There was a lot of light. The windows were black, though. He was lying down. Jesus, thank you. "I'm sure ready for this," he said.

"What was that?"

"He's ready for it."

"Yeah, sure. The bastard shit himself in the damn hall."

A woman's voice, sharp, hard, called out, "Are you sorry now, you scum? You scum!"

Jesus Christ help her, she is filled with spleen and hate. Then he saw a hospital attendant. Oh, thank God, somebody had found him, somebody had gotten him to the emergency room.

"I've been raped," he said.

"Ask the good Lord for forgiveness. Ask these poor people for forgiveness. Robert, let their spirits be at peace."

"I? Why? I'm the one who needs help. I've been raped, I've been drugged."

His arm hurt, but when he tried to move it, it wouldn't go anywhere. Then they dimmed the lights. Then they turned them out.

St. Louis Post-Dispatch,
August 8, 2002

ROBERT JAMES MURPHY
EXECUTED

Former Catholic priest Robert James Murphy was executed at midnight tonight for the rape-murder of Robert Kevin Cox, who had been a student at

St. Mary Martyr school when he was drawn into an abusive relationship with Murphy. When the boy threatened to tell his parents about Murphy's activities, the former priest strangled him and hid his body in a hollowed-out area inside the altar at the church. St. Mary Martyr was consolidated into St. Matthew's parish last year, the church was deconsecrated and sold to Pyramid Development as part of the new Crossroads Mall expansion project. Murphy leaves no survivors. He never admitted his crime. He offered no last words. Murphy is the first Catholic priest to be executed in the United States.

A Thing

BARBARA MALENKY

Barbara Malenky's work has appeared in hundreds of venues, but we must admit that she was totally new to us. After subsequently learning of her many previous publications, we were disappointed to realize that we weren't discovering "another great new" writer. At least it proves that past accomplishments don't sway us; but a good story always will.

My stomach hurts but he puts it in anyway and we get to moving with some kinda rhythm just like a rock and roller and for a little while I forget the cancer they told me I got in my guts.

Later the pain sticks me again and I roll over but he's asleep when I want to tell him about it and I watch the shadow folks outside is throwing on the blinds walking by the Hog Walla Motel.

I don't wanna sleep cause of the dreams but I do and I see my daddy Roy waving at me from the gates of the brimstone hotel and he's laughing and showing the same rotten teeth he had when he died.

My fella is gone when I wake up and he's left me a twenty on the dresser under my moisturizing night cream and I put it in my purse cause that will be my lunch for I eat more to keep my weight up.

There ain't nobody on the streets I can complain too so's I walk down to Homer's and climb up on one of them bar stools that's got pink plastic over the seat and a big fat man behind the counter flipping eggs and burgers and bacon like a pizza-maker throwing his dough.

I used to diet cause my body was the kind what gained weight fast and dropped it next to slow as molasses and I was always needing to look pretty but there ain't no use to worry on that anymore and I order two burgers with everything and a malted and a double wedge of chocolate cake that makes my mouth water just looking at it.

A voice says a thing in my right ear and I look at the fella that has come up and took the seat next to me and I see he's no bigger than a kid trying to fill out his britches and I start to ignore him when something makes me look twice.

He's got an old man's face and a dead man's eyes and his lips is caked with spit and a thing what looks like mud and a brown tip of tongue that flicks out like a snake feeling its way to a next meal.

He snatches hold my hand and slips a thing in it and closes his fingers around it and his person is so smelling bad that I have to catch up my breath and fix my eyes on the counter top to keep the vomit from coming out of my dying guts and spewing over Homer's clean floor.

"Yer take him," he whispers barely above the sizzle of my burgers on the grill, "cause I got no more use and yer can feed him until yer gets well enough and then yer pass him on to another near dead."

He lets go my hand and I open my mouth to tell him I don't want nothing from the likes of him but he's gone and disappeared and leaves a thing that jerks like a heartbeat in my palm and when I open my hand it's as small as a tick and black as a coal stone and blank as a sheet with only a tiny hole in its middle like the head of a pin.

I look at it and I reckon it's looking at me and I don't rightly know what to do with it and my burgers and chocolate cake is sitting in front of me with a nice clean fork and a big glass of sweet malted milk and I'm as hungry as I've ever been.

I push my palm against my shirt and rub up and down real hard and scrap it against the counter top and try to bite it off but nothing works cause it has bedded itself into my skin like a chigger and won't let loose.

I eat with one hand and keep the palm open of the other one and watch a thing digging deeper and filling itself with my flesh while I fill up on the flesh of something else and it all becomes clear how the world works.

Human beings are the worst parasites of them all and they get their due like me being eaten by cancer and a thing that looks like a drop of ink cause everything is a parasite on something else.

My burgers are tasting real good with all these thoughts and I'm tasting good cause the dot is gouging out a hole and burrowing deeper and deeper until by the time I'm finished with my malted it's gone invisible and there's a single drop of blood to replace it.

By the time I walk back home my gut cancer's talking

like it's full of green apples from my mama's old orchard trees and I barf a couple of times before I hit the stairwell that'll take me to my apartment on the sixth floor.

I'm so sick I figure the time has come that the doctor told me to expect and I'm supposed to prepare to meet my maker only I don't need to prepare cause I already know where I'm heading due to my life of sin.

The bed sure looks good to me and I decide it's where I want to end a thing so I crawl under the sheets and stretch out as long as I can but the hurt is so bad I have to curl up like a little baby waiting to be born.

Sleep takes me away and I see my daddy Roy again waving and grinning and waiting just like a spider for a thing to happen and I try to run away from him and that's what wakes me up and the sun is shining bright through my window and the air smells clean and cool and the pain in my gut is gone so that I feel like I used to before a thing happened.

As the day goes on I feel better and better until I think I'm sixteen years old again and life is stretched out like a long winding road with sunshine beckoning the way and I clean my apartment and wash my clothes and give some thought to maybe buying a new dress at the Wal Mart store.

And all the time a thing in my palm is growing big as an orange so that I think I maybe should lance it with a razor but I remember what the old man said about getting well and passing it on to another near dead and then I remember the story.

It's one my granny Lottie used to tell me when I was a young'an and it went that because all illness is caused by sin God made a thing to eat it and cleanse the mind and soul but there is only one in the whole universe to be passed around and if you are a chosen one you will get a chance at it and be saved.

The thought comes to me on how a thing is going to pass from me to be given to another near dead and the answer is soon to come for I feel a thing like hot bile moving up my insides through my throat and stopping at the back of my tongue and growing like a rain-fed creek.

I start to shake cause a thing is cutting off my air and when I finally open my mouth it begins to ooze from me like a creature I saw once in a horror movie over my chin and on down my whole body like a snake and across the floor and it's red and green and gray and black sin. It pulls me to the floor with it and I feel so good and clean that I don't even try to scream just roll with it until the floor is covered by a thing and my body is so light and my insides are even lighter as I am reborn and soon go to sleep in the middle of its thick nastiness.

I see my old daddy Roy not grinning and not waving but only being pulled further and further away from my dream until he is as small a thing as possible and my dreams are full of bright sunshine and flowers and a big blue and white bird flying a kite tied to its tail feathers.

One day one night and another day and another night pass and I am between sleep and consciousness hearing the phone ring and the doorbell ring but not moving just resting to gather new strength and a thing grows smaller and thinner digesting my sin and on the third day I wake and find it small as a tick and black as a coal stone and blank as a sheet and I know it's time.

I move about the city streets slowly and watch for just the one and I see him on the fifth day sitting on a park bench so thin and ash colored he blends into the natural wood and I pass him before I see him.

When I circle him a few times I understand a sign is being given by a thing cause I can not move from him for he is the right the chosen the deserving one.

I sit by him but he does not acknowledge my presence just hangs his head far below his chest maybe a few minutes from touching the ground and I take his hand and slips a thing in it and close my fingers around it and I am smelling so bad that I see him catch up his breath and keep his eyes on the ground below to keep from vomiting.

"You take him," I whisper barely above the sound of the wind in the trees, "cause I got no more use and you can feed him until you get well enough and then you pass him on to another near dead." He looks at me and sees a young woman's face with a living woman's eyes and my lips is caked with spit and a thing what looks like mud then looks at his palm while I move away and go back to my apartment to start living again on my second chance.

The Planting

BENTLEY LITTLE

Bentley Little enjoys the unique distinction of appearing in all five volumes of Borderlands. *He has talent for creating the kinds of story we like—original and decidedly odd.*

I planted her panties by moonlight.
I watered them with piss.

The desire came over me suddenly, although where it came from or how I got the knowledge, I could not say. One day she was my neighbor, the nice mom next door, and the next I was climbing over our shared fence into her backyard while she went to pick up her youngest from preschool. The family's laundry was hanging from the line, children's clothes mostly, but her underwear was

pinned behind a row of small jeans, and I carefully in-
spected each of them before picking a pair of pink bikini
briefs. I folded them carefully, crotch-up, then put them
in my pocket and climbed back over the fence.

I was in my front yard setting up the sprinkler when
she came home, and I waved to her and the little boy as
they walked into their house for lunch.

That night, I went into the woods, dug a hole at the
foot of an old oak and planted the panties.

———————

It was a drought year, and the bears were coming
down. Mike Heffernon saw one over on Alta Vista, and
the police had to take one out who sat in the center of
Arbor Circle and refused to budge. People in town were
warned to stay away from uninhabited areas, and the Forest Service not only put fire restrictions on the camp-
grounds but closed them entirely, along with the hiking
trails.

But I still went into the woods on each night that the
moon was out and pissed on the spot where I'd buried her
panties, waiting to see what would grow.

———————

Her name was Anna. Anna Howell. And despite the
fact that she was in her late-thirties/early-forties, at least
ten years older than me, and a mother of three, she was
still the most beautiful woman I had ever seen. Mine was
an objective appreciation, however. I didn't covet her, had
no plans to try and seduce her, no fantasies about having
an affair with her, neither her face nor body entered my
thoughts when I masturbated alone at night.

But I was still compelled to steal her panties and plant

them, and the impulse to water them when the moon was out was always with me, a vague urge that was almost—but not quite—sexual.

Sometimes I thought of her panties when I masturbated, lying crumpled in a ball in the wet dank ground, deteriorating.

And it made me come much faster.

————————

There was a circle of old cabins out past Dripping Springs in one of those pockets of private land in the middle of the national forest. I'd heard that it had once been a resort—or that the onetime owner had tried to make it into a resort—but it had failed and been abandoned long before my time, and now was the type of place that local kids said was haunted. I didn't know if it really was haunted, but it was certainly a spot that bums might make their own or that drug dealers might find desirable: remote, isolated, far from civilization and the prying eyes of others.

Because it was technically on private land, when a late-summer lightning fire started and word came down that the cabins were burning, they called out the volunteer fire department rather than have the Forest Service put it out—which would have been the most logical thing to do. But, as usual, jurisdictional concerns trumped common sense, and shortly after midnight the ten of us were speeding down the control road through mile after mile of oak and juniper and ponderosa pine, between rugged bluffs and rolling hills, in and out of hidden gorges and seasonal stream-carved canyons, until we reached the flat land on the other side of Dripping Springs.

The cabins were gone when we got there, little more than charred piles of ash hemmed in by black and still-burning sections of frame. Luckily, a dirt road circling the perimeter of the old resort had acted as a break and contained the fire somewhat, keeping it from setting the entire forest ablaze. A lone finger stretch of brush on the north end was burning brightly and had created the only real problem we had to face, but we had ten men, two trucks and full pumpers—and even if we ran out of water, we had snake hoses long enough to tap any nearby creek, spring or pond we could find.

We set to work.

It was nearly morning before we finished, the sky in the east brightening enough to turn the trees into silhouettes by the time the last of the flames was extinguished. Blue-white smoke rose from the ashes around us, dimming the sun as the day dawned and we finished repacking the trucks. Through the haze, I saw a building behind the burned brush, a cabin of rough hewn wood that looked more ancient than the old growth trees surrounding it, although I did not understand how that could be possible. Either the cabin had not been there before or else the fire had cleared out the brush that hid it from view because none of us had seen it previously. I stepped closer to get a better look, then immediately stepped back. The facade of the windowless structure bespoke great age, and there was about it an air of dread and unsettled malevolence that shook me more than I was willing to admit.

"God lives there," Andre said, sidling next to me.

I looked at him askance. "What the hell are you talking about?"

"That's always been the rumor. That God lives out

here. That's why there's no graffitti, no beer bottles or syringes or cigarette butts or McDonald's bags. Everyone's always been afraid to come out this way because God is here. And watching."

"You knew about this cabin?"

"Not this cabin exactly. But I knew God's home was in these woods, somewhere near the resort, and when I saw this place, I knew this was it."

"Yeah," Rossi said. "And the Easter Bunny's vacation house is right behind it."

The rest of us laughed, but Andre remained resolute in his conviction, and I had to admit that his somber certitude freaked me out a little. If it had only been the two of us, I would have acceded to his wishes, left the cabin alone and we would have returned to town. But there were others here, and they were curious, so I had to be curious, and I joined the group as we made our way over the still smoldering ashes across the charred dirt to the ancient shack.

It was small, I saw as we approached. Not small as in limited square footage—although it was that, too—but small as in short, as though it had been made for people not as tall as we were. The top of the front door was just about eye level. I reached up and was able to place my hand on the roof.

The door was stuck but unlocked, and after several shoulder shoves, it opened, scraping the dirty wooden floor. I'd been expecting a one-room cabin based on the exterior of the structure, but instead we found ourselves in a narrow hallway that ran the width of the structure. We filed in one by one, Mick and Garcia and Big Bill and Ed Barr flipping on their flashlights, all of us ducking, and it occurred to me that this would be a perfect place for an ambush, that some psycho could be lying in wait just around the corner and take us out one-by-one as we stepped into the next room. There were no cries of shock or pain, however, only the ordinary speech of continued conversation as my stooping fellow firefighters rounded the end of the hallway.

I followed, and once again, I was surprised. The cabin went back far deeper than its exterior facade would indicate, and the long room in which we found ourselves sloped steeply downward from the door, with the ceiling at the entrance barely above five feet and that at the opposite end twelve to fifteen feet high. The room had obviously been dug into the ground at an angle, but there were no windows, the floor was wood as were the walls, and that gave the room the appearance of space that grew as it moved away from us, like the optical illusion of an amusement park haunted shack.

"It's like a fuckin' fun house," Big Bill said, shining his light around.

Andre remained silent.

We clomped down the sloping floor in our heavy boots. There was furniture only on the sides of the room: two twin tables with collections of nearly identical gray rocks arranged on their dusty tops. Though it stretched back far, the room was half the width of the hallway, so there had to be another chamber behind the wall to our left, although no way to enter it from this room. In front of us, however, a closed door was built into the back wall, a construct of solid wood hewn from a single section of tree that had been bolted to the surrounding planks. It had no handle or knob, no visible means by which it might be opened, and there was something both secretive and intriguing about the tightly sealed entrance. It was Ed Barr who said what all of us were thinking: "Let's see what's back there."

"No!" Andre said, and there was fear in his voice.

"This building's obviously abandoned, the area around it's burned to a crisp, let's break down the door and see what's behind it."

"You can't!" Andre shouted.

"Out of the way." Rossi pushed him aside and hefted his ax.

Andre actually started crying, and that, more than anything else, creeped me out. Standing half-underground in an ancient windowless cabin in front of a knobless door watching a grown man the size of a football player sob was just plain unnerving, and at that moment I wanted to get the hell out of there.

The door was tough and it took several swings, but Rossi finally managed to smash a hole through the wood large enough to put his hand and arm through. There was an inside latch, and he used it to open the door. Four flashlights shone into the darkness, and there was sudden silence as we saw what lay in the small dank room beyond.

It was a mummified creature of some sort, a wrinkled shriveled figure that looked like a dried black monkey. The skin of its face had been pulled back from its skull, and it appeared to be grinning, its sharp rotted teeth exposed in a way that made it seem insanely gleeful. It was seated on the floor of the small room, next to a small pile of those gray rocks. Behind it, a rounded section of the wall had been bleached white, as though exposed to harsh sunlight or radiation.

Andre fell to his knees in front of the monkey thing like some primitive tribesman worshipping a stone idol. Rossi dropped his ax and followed suit. I would have laughed, but I could see similar expressions of awe on the faces of the others, and I have to admit that I felt something myself. I thought of Anna Howell's buried panties, and at that moment I wished that I had not stolen them, had not planted them, had not peed on them. I was filled with an emptiness, a sadness, a sense that I had gone off track somewhere, that I had lost something that should have been very important to me. The feeling radiating from the dead creature was one of great sorrow, and its mood affected my own, made me want to get the hell out of there as quickly as possible.

And then . . .

Something changed.

I don't know what it was, if it came from that mummified creature in the middle of the floor, if it came from my fellow firemen or if it was simply a figment of my imagination, but the sadness I felt was suddenly replaced by fear, a cold bone-deep terror that left me rooted in place, filled with the certainty that all of us were doomed, that we would never leave this place but would spend eternity in this tiny room with that hideous black monkey.

To my left, Ed Barr let out a strangled stifled cry. Andre was sobbing, though from religious fervor or despair it was impossible to tell. Garcia's flashlight dimmed, went out. Big Bill's and the others followed suit and moments later we were in darkness, an inky jet so deep and penetrating that I could not tell whether my eyes were open or closed. I stood there, stock still, waiting for the end. Someone cried out. Someone else giggled. There were more noises, more cries, and I felt soft fingers gently stroke my hand and then teeth sink painfully into my right calf.

I have no idea how much time we spent in that place,

but by the time we emerged, the sun was high in the sky. Everyone was disheveled. Big Bill was naked.

We left the mummy there, sealing up the room as best we could with additional branches and mud from a small slough to the side of the shack. That was Andre's idea, and the rest of the brigade went along with it, some more willingly than others. I wanted to burn the fucking place down—whatever that dried black creature was, it did not deserve to exist—but I knew I was a minority of one and kept my feelings to myself. It would be enough just to get away from here and make sure that I never came anywhere near that cabin and its horrid occupant again.

I quit the volunteer fire department a few days after.

So did Rossi.

So did Ed Barr.

And though we saw each other on almost a daily basis, we didn't talk about it, didn't ask each other why, didn't discuss what we'd seen, what had happened in that shack.

A week later, Andre killed himself. Ate his shotgun in the woods.

And we didn't talk about that either.

After that, the panties sprouted. I was standing in front of the oak tree when the moon finally reemerged after a week of cloudy nights, and I saw a pale shoot poking upward through the mulchy dirt, a blue-white almost gelatinous tendril that was clearly growing, aspiring to some greater form.

What would it be, I wondered, when it reached maturity?

I pulled out my pecker and pissed on it.

I saw Anna Howell the next day, waved to her over the fence while she hung her laundry out to dry, tried not to look at the underwear she was pinning on the clothesline. She smiled at me, waved back, said it was a nice day, and if she suspected that I had stolen a pair of her panties she did an amazing job of hiding it.

I slunk back inside and realized that I had some soul searching to do. What exactly did I want from that thing I was growing in the forest? As much as I admired and recognized Anna Howell's beauty, I still did not desire her, and I did not think that I was growing the woman for a sex partner, as a substitute for the real McCoy.

The woman.

I said it to myself for the first time, admitting what I had known subconsciously all along—that I was growing a person from Anna Howell's panties.

A woman.

But why?

That was still not clear to me, though I felt the impulse to continue even more strongly than I had before. My every waking moment seemed consumed with the thought of my secret in the woods, and I got through each boring day only with the knowledge that at night, if there was a moon, I would be able to visit my spot at the foot of the oak where I had buried my neighbor's freshly laundered underwear in the soft and fertile soil.

The next time I saw the sprout, it had a face. Under the moonlight, it had grown to nearly two feet high and now had the vague contours of a woman. Although they were closed, there were eyes, and while there was no nose to speak of, the thing had Kewpie doll lips pursed in an unappealing fashion that needed only color to grant them authenticity. Small nubs halfway down the form looked as though they would eventually differentiate themselves into hands and arms.

It seemed wrong to water the figure at this stage of its growth, so I turned my back and relieved my bladder on a bush, then zipped up and crouched down before the oak tree to look at what I'd wrought. The sight was horrible, a travesty of humanity so fundamentally unnatural that my first impulse should have been to destroy it. But instead I sat on my haunches and examined its emerging form. The figure was small but perfectly in proportion rather than dwarflike, and despite the garish elements of its evolving face, I could tell that it would grow into a beautiful woman. Looking closely, I could see a slight indentation that would become the vaginal cleft, two small humps that would expand into breasts. It was composed of that same transluscent bluish-white material, a slimy looking substance that shone in the moonlight and appeared sticky to the touch. I wanted to reach out and press my finger against the shiny skin to see if it felt the way it looked, but I did not want to jeopardize the form's growth by tainting it with my touch, so I refrained.

The night air was moist and dewy, the ground itself damp, but I wondered if that would be enough to keep the budding woman watered and facilitate her growth. I looked at the nascent crotch, thought about what Anna Howell's own vagina must look like under her panties and found myself thinking that I should masturbate on the figure to provide it with moisture and nutrients.

I stood, pulled down my pants, took my penis in hand and started stroking, my head filled with dark thoughts, my fantasy scenario one of depraved perversity, but at the last minute I pulled away, spurting all over a lushly growing fern rather than onto that blue-white flesh, grunting with animal abandon as I emptied my loins on the hapless plant.

The pursed colorless lips seemed to me to be almost smiling.

I arrived home long after midnight, too wound and wired to sleep, my head filled with ideas I did not want to acknowledge, my body wracked with impulses I dared not act upon. Under a lone lamp in the living room, I read the local paper which had been delivered with the mail that afternoon. On the front page was a photo of Giff McCarty, head ranger for the region. He was wearing a woman's wig and thick mascara, his dark lipstick obvious even through the black-and-white newsprint. FOREST SERVICE OFFICIAL ACCUSED OF MOLESTATION, the banner headline read, and I suddenly understood why we had been called to put out the fire at the old resort. I remembered what had happened inside that shack

God lives there

and saw the madness in the old ranger's eyes, the whorishly rouged cheeks bookending his carefully drawn lips, and I crumpled up the paper and made my way to bed.

———————

In my dream, I was standing at the dirty urinal of an old gas station—Enco, Richfield, Gulf, one of those chains that no longer existed—and next to me, at the adjacent urinal, was a wino, a filthy man with wild gray hair and an unkempt beard wearing a greasy topcoat and smelling of spilled beer and sewer stink. He was nearly a head shorter than me, and when I glanced over at him, he winked. I saw that he was peeing not in the urinal but on the tiled floor between his shoes. From the growing puddle on the chipped stained tile slithered reptilian creatures of every hue and color, horrid creatures with too many legs, small sickening monsters with multiple eyes but no legs at all, formless pulsating slime that inched wormlike toward me.

"The piss of life," the old man said, cackling. "It's the piss of life."

And in the instant before I woke up, I realized that he was God.

I made myself stay away after that.

There was nothing I wanted more than to go out into the woods and continue to care for the budding being I had created, to monitor its growth by moonlight and experience the joy of watching it blossom. But I knew those drives were not mine, I knew they had been imposed on me, and as desperately as I desired to sneak into the forest in the dead of night, I forced myself to remain indoors, trying in vain to fall asleep, fighting the urge to check on the status of the woman I had grown.

Finally, however, I could no longer resist, and exactly two weeks after my last visit, I once again found myself slipping between the trees under the cover of night.

The danger warnings had been heightened over the past week. Two bears had come down into the town, one of them killing a collie, and a mountain lion had mangled a cache of stuffed animals that had inadvertantly been left out on a back porch at night. But I was not thinking rationally as I made my way into the woods. I was not thinking at all. I'd made no conscious decision to return,

I simply found myself walking through the forest to the old oak, the action as involuntary and devoid of thought as taking a breath.

It was gone.

There was a hole at the foot of the tree, a ragged cavity roughly the size of a woman that was lined with old leaves and a twisted net of roots and smelled of raw sewage. I searched around for footprints or a trail of slime or something that would indicate to me in which direction she had headed, but I was not a woodsman or a tracker, and the forest looked the same to me as it always had.

Staring into the white netted roots that formed the womanly contours of the hole, I was reminded of something I'd seen before, a specific sight or image that nagged at the corner of my mind begging to be identified. The roots were clearly of the same substance that had formed the woman, but their bleached quality, as though they'd been exposed to a blast of radiation or a blinding burst of sunlight, reminded me of another scene entirely.

I stepped closer, peered into the bottom of the space and saw a rotted piece of panty held down by several small gray rocks.

It was the rocks that jiggled my memory.

I suddenly knew where I had to go.

I ran through the trees back to my neighborhood, back to my house, then hopped in my old Jeep and sped down the control road through hills and canyons and forest, braking to a dusty stop on the flat land past Dripping Springs where the resort had been.

I got out of the Jeep. The door of the shack was open, and though the moon was temporarily behind a cloud, leaving the woods in darkness, a soft yellowish light spilled from the small rectangular entryway, granting the surrounding brush a disturbing malevolence.

The last time I had been here, it had been with the fire brigade. That had been scary enough. But now I was all alone, and though part of me wanted to turn tail and run, the part of me that had quit the fire department and vowed never to return to this spot, another more instinctual portion of my brain was urging me forward.

I'm out of here, I could imagine Rossi saying. But Rossi was not here. No one else was here. And though I didn't really want to, I walked up to the shack, ducked into the doorway.

There were candles lighting the hallway that ran the width of the structure, even more candles in the long narrow room that sloped down to the chamber containing the mummified monkey thing.

God lives there

Like the doorway to the shack, the entrance to the back chamber was open, as though waiting for me, and I accepted the invitation and stepped inside.

There were no candles here, but the entire room was suffused with a rosy glow that reminded me of those Victorian prostitute's lamps with scarves and stockings thrown over them, although there was no lamp in sight and indeed the illumination did not have an identifiable source.

I stopped just inside the doorway. A naked woman was seated next to the desiccated mummy on a wooden bench that looked older than the earth itself, and there was something about the way she reclined next to the diminutive figure, something about the way her arm was wrapped about its small skeletal shoulder that bespoke intimacy. They're married, I thought, and the second the idea occurred to me, I knew it was true. She was the wife of that thing. She had always been its intended.

The woman's skin was no longer a slimy bluish white. Instead it was the soft peach of a newborn infant, its fresh color emphasized by the mysterious rose lighting of the chamber. She had blonde hair like Anna Howell, and her pubic hair was blond, too. Which made the dried black-ened features of the creature next to her seem that much more grotesque. The face of that monkey and its hideously gleeful rictus had haunted my nightmares, and I looked now upon that dead parchment skin pulled back from those sharp rotted teeth and felt the same fear I had before. The fear was not tempered by the presence of the foolishly grinning woman next to it. If anything, the jux-taposition of the two was even more frightening.

The woman nodded at me, wiggling the fingers of her free hand.

She wasn't a real person, I had to remind myself. She had sprouted from the panties. I had grown her.

As I watched, she spread her legs wide, and from the shadowed cleft between her thighs came flowers, an end-less bouquet that flowed out like water from a spring, a floral fountain that cascaded over the edge of the chair onto the floor in an almost liquid wave, covering the dirt and the small gray rocks so completely that the floor of the chamber was buried beneath a rainbow of color. I smelled the perfume of my mother, my grandmother, my aunts and cousins, my teachers, every girlfriend I had ever had. The scents of all women were tied up in that ol-factory cornucopia, each of the wonderful flowery fra-grances triggering memories of the females in my life, and I was momentarily overwhelmed by a nostalgia that was at once happily welcome and profoundly sad.

The blackened figure had not changed its expression—
it couldn't change its expression—but emotion still em-
anated from its unmoving form, and the feeling I got from
it now was one of gratitude. I had given it a wife, and it
was thankful.

God was no longer alone.

That was crazythinking. I knew this wasn't God. It
wasn't even a god. Yet there was no doubt in my mind
that the emotion washing over me was real, and though
no words were spoken, no thoughts or images transmitted
to me, I suddenly understood that the mummified creature wanted to show its gratitude.

In my mind, I saw Andre falling to his knees in wor-
shipful adoration, and I thought about what had happened
in this room after the lights went out. Once again, I was
filled with that permeating sense of evil and doom.

I knew I should get out of there as quickly as possible,
run out of the shack and back to my Jeep, drive back
home and never even look at the woods again. But I
found myself staring at the flowers still flowing from between the woman's legs, and my mind was soothed by
the emotion spreading outward from her immobile
companion.

God is grateful

I thought about my empty existence, my boring job
and nonexistent lovelife, all of the pointless routines that
made up my usual day.

I considered several possibilities.

Then made a wish.

The feeling imparted to me now from the desiccated
monkey was one of approbation, but when I looked at the
mismatched faces of the couple on the bench I felt colder
than I ever had in my life. The fear was back, stronger

than ever, and I knew instantly and with utter certainty that I had just made a huge mistake, the biggest mistake of my life. My first impulse was to try and take it back, to drop to my knees and beg for another chance, a do-over. But I knew that was not possible.

I thought for a moment, then picked up a flower that smelled like my mother, turned away, and walked out of the chamber, out of the shack, into the darkness, tears streaming down my face.

And as I headed toward the spot where I'd parked the Jeep, I wondered what went through Andre's mind at the second he pulled the trigger.

Infliction

JOHN MCILVEEN

Writer and bookseller John McIlveen lives out his days in a house full of women. Knowing this, it should not surprise you that he's been able to create a story which captures such a striking range of human emotion. However, that does not keep "Infliction" from being a truly disturbing tale.

How do you judge a scar? They are all different.

They are not prejudiced. A ten-pound infant or a ten-ton boulder can scar, or be scarred. In my forty-nine years, I have scarred and been scarred. The knowledge is now more a part of me than my own callous heart.

My oldest one had nearly healed. I had cast off my demon; exorcised from a thirty-year addiction to the bottle. Any bottle, as long as it held the spirit of numbness within.

I walked proudly, with my chin high and my nose in the air, swaggering with the arrogance of a winner, but I wanted to be victor in more than the conquest of alcohol, that merely a battle in the war for my soul.

It has been over seven months since I last surrendered to the drink . . . not so well with the guilt.

I have destroyed my family.

It has been four years since Suzi, my only child, ran away. Two years since my wife Tippi stepped off the Hampton Beach jetty, freely surrendering herself to the icy midnight waters of the Atlantic Ocean.

Tippi . . .

She was a study of smoothness, a classic Japanese beauty. As exquisite as a Monet brushstroke, the way she moved, the way she spoke, the way she loved . . . and the way she died. In one liquid moment, pouring from my life, like mercury, into the Atlantic.

They found her drowned body the following morning, lying on the beach like a gift from the early morning tide. I was at home, unaware; drowning in my own intoxicated death. Too drunk to realize—or care—about her absence from our bed. Unknowing that my only bond to normality was lying not even a mile from where I lay. All her pain and regrets—all her scars—were given up, transposed by water with her last living breath. I attended Tippi's funeral the same way I attended my life, from behind an inebriated gauze curtain. I remember little of the ceremony, but the people with accusation in their eyes will remain with me. Through common respect, while compassionately patting me on the back and emitting a stream of kind words, they tried to hide the blame, but it was like covering an alligator with a bath towel. Regardless of how well they covered it, parts would always show, fully emerging to lash out if I came too near.

Your fault, the alligator would say. *You failed her.*

Tippi, of course, would have seen it as her failure, not mine. That was her way. That was her gift and her curse. I see now that when we met I became her personal venture, her mission of mercy. I know she loved me . . . her passion was pathos.

Suzi's running away was the end for Tippi. She saw it as her final failure; the big push that ultimately and literally drove her over the edge. We knew where Suzi was, though the truth was almost laughable. The idea of a fifteen-year-old girl joining a traveling circus seemed ludicrous, like a plot straight from a child's book or movie. Tippi searched for two years, while I submerged myself deeper in drunkenness. Then Tippi escaped.

I found myself in an empty house. Tippi and Suzi were gone and I was suddenly alone to fend for myself. I was an abandoned infant; everything was new and estranged. I hadn't cooked a meal in over twenty years.

The only child of parents who passed away over a decade earlier, I was left with only two companions, alcohol and guilt. Both ate away at my insides, a violent river eroding the walls of my health and sanity.

———

Bob Lynch was a large but gracious man whose generous heart was his own tormentor. He owned the garage where I had worked since my teens, though a lesser man would have fired me years earlier. He found me, nearly a year and a half after Tippi's funeral, lying on my bedroom floor, holding a bottle like a lost lover. He saw a broken man swimming in a sea of empty bottles and his own waste, drowning, yet clinging to the shards of a shattered life. I had not shown up for work in three days.

Bob signed me into Hawthorne House, a local rehabilitation center, and told them he would pay the bill as long as they did not release me until I was cured. Bob was another love neglected by my weakness. He bestowed the unconditional love of a brother, owing nothing, asking nothing, and getting nothing in return, except a barely adequate mechanic with a life full of troubles.

I signed myself out the next morning with every intention of returning to my comfortable oblivion, nestled between the familiar sheets of guilt and drunkenness. I wanted to drink myself back to the muted memories of a woman who gave me everything. I wanted to return to my gullible drunken form where I could convince myself of happiness and of times that had never existed.

All of that changed with three words. What Tippi could not do with twenty-five years of love and begging, one young woman achieved with three words. Sobriety is a wonderful hearing aid.

I was drawn by the sobs of a teenager who sat in the rehab lobby. She was aged by her addiction, but I figured her between fifteen and eighteen. Her blonde hair was stringy and dirty, and her eyes, sunken and ringed with the mascara of a drug addict. She stared at the floor tolerating the overplayed sympathy from an attendant.

"I don't matter," she said through her tears. Her desperation was a throat clutching smoke that filled the room, seeping through the cracks of soberness in a broken man's armor. The aid tried to convince her otherwise, looking uncomfortable while her eyes scanned the lobby for help. She wore her inexperience like a flamboyant hat.

The girl looked at me, and I saw eyes that I had thought of too seldom in the last four years—in the last nineteen years. In their carved-out depths I read things seldom found in eyes of someone six times her senior. There was pain, rebellion, fear, blame, loneliness, rejection, and beneath it all, unfathomable to me, love. It was illogical. It didn't belong there! It stood singular, a rose in a field of weeds, begging for attention. How could this child still find room for love? For possibly the first time in my adult life, I wanted to cry.

How could I have been so blind? How could I have been so heartless?

Though this girl did not look anything like my Suzi, the connection was there. At that moment I vowed to find her so I could tell her that she now mattered. That I was sorry that fate burdened her with a father who was so narrow—so careless—that he would allow the two finest things in his life to slide through his numbed hands, without even the flattery of an attempted grasp.

I would have given my life, right then, just to feel Suzi in my arms. To kiss her face and hear her say, *I love you Dad. I forgive you.* To embrace my daughter, the only link to Tippi and the remnants of a life that could have been so good, if not for my ignorance. Perhaps there was still a chance for forgiveness through Suzi.

I went home that evening and poured every trace of alcohol down the toilet. I dumped my aftershave, rubbing alcohol and cooking sherry, bidding farewell to my lifelong mistress, and turned my back before she could seduce me again. For two days, I cleaned my home with a vehemence I could not recall ever having. I scrubbed the floors and the walls, behind the refrigerator, stove, washer and dryer. I washed the curtains, sheets and lampshades, and scoured every surface. I wanted to remove any evidence of myself from the house for fear that the ghosts and demons of my past would haunt the next residents and betray my secrets.

The house sold easily after only three weeks on the market, understandably so for such a fine home. A proud manor for which I could claim no credit; I had inherited it. Any personality shown on or within its walls was the works of Tippi or my parents. I was ashamed to accept money for it.

I sold it for $125,000 with furnishings, much to the displeasure of my confounded real estate agent. The house was appraised at $169,000.

Bob Lynch cried when I told him I was leaving, though the revelation didn't really surprise him. Like a parent who loses a rebellious child, there is still love and pity. It still hurts.

I couldn't answer his questions of where I was going, or why. They were answers I didn't have. I simply told him that I had dropped my heart four years ago, and that I needed to find it. I said no when he offered me money.

My search for Suzi was rooted in the shallow and dry dirt of optimism. The prospect of her being with the circus four years later was paper thin, but substantial enough for hope. Perhaps someone would remember the girl I forgot.

Finding the name of the circus was similar to searching for bugs under rocks, you flip one, and then move to another, knowing that eventually it will turn up. I found an ad in the Portsmouth Herald archives from four years earlier, trumpeting the arrival of Dunn & Barlow's Magnificent World Fair.

A traveling circus moves like a butterfly. It flutters erratically on an inconclusive path, leaving little clue of where it's been, and even less of where it's going. Hampton Beach town records showed nothing except a statement for the land that Dunn & Barlow's had leased. Like the butterfly, they arrived, left, and never returned. No information was available beyond that.

———————

Bud Martin has a good memory. He owns The Sand Dollar, a diner located across the boulevard from the Hampton Beach State Park, the land Dunn & Barlow's had rented. Bud's the talkative sort with plenty of nothing to say, and shares his wisdom with the flip of a burger. He serves an abundance of both for your dollar. He recalled the circus, but remembered no names. He said it's better that way. However, he remembered a conversation about a town in Vermont called Woodstock, then spoke of a concert he attended many years ago with the same name.

For more than three months I followed such leads, a man and his Cutlass, tracking baseless clues across the country like a cat chasing a string. I zigzagged across America with my life possessions jammed in the trunk. My conviction and hopefulness died a little more with every dead-end, but in Sarasota, Florida, at 3:00 a.m. in a sleepy cafe, I met a nosy truck driver named Kennedy who overheard my inquiries. He shared a great story with me.

He said that when you live on the road, lonely hour after hour, billboards play a weighty role. They break the monotony of the blacktop, since they are one of very few things in a long-hauler's life that change with any regularity.

Dunn & Barlow's was a name familiar to both the trucker and billboards. Like the truck driver, traveling circuses are nomads, night gypsies that move by the light of the moon. They occasionally cross paths on the dreary road. Kennedy recently saw the name in Pennsylvania, somewhere on Route 80, he said.

Twenty hours later I stood at the edge of a large field in Moon Township, Pennsylvania, staring at the twin yellow peaks of Dunn & Barlow's Magnificent World Fair's main tent. My vision swam in the heat of a treacherous June afternoon, causing the sight to ripple lazily in the golden pasture. My heart yearned to run onto the fairway, calling for Suzi; needing the truth. My heart feared the truth.

I walked tentatively, following the crushed grass of the tire-hammered path. Children dashed excitedly by, reveling in the vow of the big top. I envied their enthusiasm and faith, and their naiveté.

A profusion of smells, sweltering and concentrated, escorted me onto the concourse. Italian sausage, hay, freshly cut wood, animal waste, and new paint merged and hit me with long forgotten memories of days when I too ran with reckless abandon, and little more to worry about than length of wait at the main event.

The bazaar was alive with noise, the screams of excited children, a pitchman's banter, and the mechanical whir of the rides. Over the loudspeakers, the voice of W.C. Fields promised a night of wonders beyond belief and miracles every half-hour. I wandered the park hoping for providence, the hand of an angel to steer me along.

Suzi smiled at me from the photo I held. Her face glowed, a paradox between teenage awkwardness and newfound sexuality. Her eyes sparkled with rebel enthusiasm, but they held a darkness that was barely at bay, a frog in a child's hand struggling for freedom, burrowing for the first opening large enough to allow escape. She had found that hole.

Physically, she was an Americanized version of her mother, a bolder and more solid reproduction. Like her mother's, her hair was black silk, so lustrous it appeared blue. She had the same almond eyes staring deliciously from above high, sharp cheekbones. The only visual difference being that Suzi was six inches taller and twenty-five pounds heavier. She had the body of the All-American girl.

Tippi had carefully chosen the name Suzi, because it and the girl smacked of both Japan and America; you would never be sure without asking.

I showed Suzi to a barker as he bellowed of the terrors in The Devil's Den. Stale air and the smell of dead wood were the only ghosts in that haunted house. He shook his head at the picture and shrugged an apology, then offered me a trip into hell. I told him I'd already been there.

Another yelled of freaks and oddities, of Lucas, the two-headed man, of Belle, the world's fattest woman, of Carla, the human wound, and of Micky, the world's smallest man. He too offered me nothing but a view into *The World of Weirdness*. Madam Zorak had nothing to share, but for five dollars could read my fortune—who knows what it will reveal? I paid her twenty not to.

Well into the night I asked, begged and cried, but received only looks of sorrow and mistrust. Some would ask questions or wish me good luck, but most just wordlessly shook their head.

Nothing could have prepared me for the death of my soul, for the murder of what remained of my heart. I had never experienced such emptiness; an undiluted sense of helplessness, like an astronaut who breaks the umbilical from the ship then drifts too far. I knew at one point in my insignificant life that the possibility of not finding Suzi was the worst thing that could happen. I had never been so wrong.

Suzi, or Carla the human wound, recognized me immediately. The revulsion I felt when I first saw her was indescribable, though I did not recognize her. I had just viewed Belle, the world's fattest woman, and the almost laughable sight of Micky, the world's smallest man, perched comfortably on the meaty pillow of her belly.

I pushed the curtain aside to view the next curiosity. What I saw was a nightmare in flesh. The woman, only distinguishable by the swell of breasts in her dark blue bikini top, rose from her chair as I entered the viewing room. A knowing smile seemed to appear on her ravaged face as she neared the glass.

Gaping scars crossed every viewable surface of her body, parallel furrows bisecting every half-inch. She posed, distending her chest, presenting her legs, arms, and back, as if she were a prize body builder. She ran her fingers down the length of her leg, following the course of the channels in her skin.

Smaller ravines ran from her chin, mouth, nose, and eyes to her ears, which were tattered ribbons of flesh and cartilage. That is when I recognized her . . . Suzi. Those almond-shaped eyes, just like Tippi's, were the only recognizable part of the once beautiful girl.

Her upper lip was split under the nose, giving her mouth a cleft feline appearance, and whatever remained of her lovely oil-black hair, was now a patchwork of stubble and scar tissue.

I watched benumbed as Suzi performed. She modeled with a fervor she probably showed to no other customer. Today's audience was special. Suzi advanced to the Plexiglas wall, her eyes locked with mine, and that smile, that ghastly smile, fixed on her face. Merely inches apart, our faces divided by only half-an-inch of plastic, Suzi licked the glass. Her tongue was divided into three even strips.

I ran from the sideshow, horrified and appalled, trying to escape the incredible blackness that threatened to fold over me. It fluttered at the edge of my consciousness, some horrendous truth, like enormous bat wings that wanted to trap and smother me. I collapsed beside a booth outside, fighting the nausea that coiled like snakes in my stomach.

How could she do that to herself?

Why?

What would make someone do that?

I knelt in the dirt, shaking and sobbing as people walked warily past.

―――――――

"Come with me," someone said. Belle, the world's fattest woman, helped me onto my shaking legs then led me to a Winnebago. I didn't resist; I was too weak.

We entered the trailer and she motioned me to sit at a small table. The inside of the camper was surprisingly clean and smelled of coffee and fried onions. On the counter near the sink, was an open bag of Canada Mints; so commonplace in a world that had just become so alien and foreboding.

"Hello Father," she said, her words ill-formed on the tattered strips of her tongue. She came through a doorway at the far end of the camper, wearing an emerald green housecoat and looking so normal through the dimness of the tight hallway. She carried a bag of cotton balls and a bottle of isopropyl alcohol. She set them on the table and sat across from me.

"Suzi?" I said, feeling sick, saddened and very uneasy.

"Carla, please. Suzi died four years ago." She raised her leg on the bench beside her, freeing it from the housecoat and exposing the web of scars. "Why'd you come here?" she asked, her question whistling, but logical from her tortured mouth.

"Tippi . . . your mother died two years ago," I told her. I was rattled and had a tremendous desire to run, to escape this nightmare and run until I could run no longer.

"Yes, I know. Killed herself." She uncapped the alcohol and poured some into a shallow saucer, then looked at me. "I knew that was coming. We had different ways of escaping you, she was just better at it." Her words confirmed what I had already known, though a small part of me had vainly hoped differently.

She took a single edge razor blade from her robe pocket and unwrapped it. She dipped it in the alcohol, then ran the blade deftly along a rut on her calf, opening a narrow line of blood inside the existing wound. My body contracted in an icy convulsion, and the blackness threatened again. I felt as if I'd just grabbed a live wire.

"Why?" I asked.

"It's a living," she said, then accusingly, "it's a *life*." She dabbed a cotton ball in the alcohol, then ran it along the fresh wound. Her jaw tightened slightly.

"Isn't it odd," she said, displaying the blood-tinged swab, "that the same spirit that cleanses my wounds rotted your soul.

"You're on the wagon now, right?" she asked. "Reformed?"

"I'm trying. It's been a few months."

"A little fucking late, wouldn't you say?"

I was defenseless. I could say nothing. She ran the blade along another wound.

"Why do you do this, Suzi? Carla?"

"They're Novocain. These wounds hurt less than others, but they help take my mind off the bigger and deeper ones." She swabbed at the slice in her leg.

I could sense something bigger than life creeping up on me. Like a stalking cat, it stopped every time I tried to focus on it.

"They're my protection and my savior," she was saying, her distorted voice barely audible above the pulse pounding in my head and in my ears. "My guarantee that no man—no bastard—can ever hurt me again."

Sweat ran down my back, from my brow into my eyes, stinging as it mixed with my tears.

She opened her housecoat, exposing her mutilated breasts. Revulsion and remorse attacked me, a feral beast tearing at my heart. I screamed at the pain.

"What's wrong, *Daddy*?" She spit. "You don't find it attractive anymore, *Daddy*?"

There it was. Like the boy who discovers the forgotten bag of marbles he hid on the top shelf, it all came tumbling down over my head. Sneaking into her room, pushing the chair under the doorknob. Ignoring her terrified eyes and her tears. Hiding from Tippi. Hiding from myself.

Suzi closed her robe, her eyes burning into me. For once she had the upper hand. For once she was the tormentor. I lowered my head to the table and covered my ears, trying to block the truth, hoping it was all an illusion.

"Please leave," she said. "I don't want you here. I don't need you opening old wounds. I do that fine on my own."

What could I say or do? *I'm sorry* would be a colossal insult. It wouldn't amount to a speck of dust in the universe of irreparable harm I caused her. Devastated by self-disgust, I rose without a word and left.

Shortly after, I returned to the camper with two suitcases. One contained several of Tippi's personal items that I hoped Suzi might want; the other contained the cash from the sale of the house.

"These aren't mine," I told her, and slid the two suitcases in. I know that I could never correct what had happened in our lives, and I wasn't going to pretend that the money and Tippi's belongings were a token of such. I stated it as it was. They were not mine. I had done nothing to earn any of it.

Suzi dismissed me with a nod of her head and returned to her handiwork.

I left with nothing, which was truly my own.

Dysfunction

DARREN O. GODFREY

Darren Godfrey's previous appearance in Borderlands 2 *featured one of the scariest little boys in memory. We never imagined he could follow up with a tale
which is actually a sequel to that original story. "Dys-
function" is a hallucinated search for the true source of
our fears.*

Pain; dull, but sharpening.

You don't know what hit you. Careful consideration,
however, suggests it may have been your boyfriend. *Logical, sure, John, John, the Piper's son, slap me around
and away he run . . . again.* No, on second thought, that
isn't right. Not this time, at least. This time he was a
pussycat. God, he even purred.

The vodka, then. *That* was it. Smirnoff knocked you
upside the head.

271

You open your eyes, temporarily forgetting what a terrible mistake doing such a thing can be. White light spears your pupils, rebounds off your frontal brain matter and explodes from the top of your head, leaving behind a massive smoking pain-crater. To the rear, near the base of your brain, cleverly hidden satchel charges detonate.

And you thought you knew what pain was.

You close your eyes.

Retreat.

———

You feel the wrath of Mom like a heat wave as you push up toward the land of the living once again.

"Get up, slut."

Ah, she's in a good mood. Open your eyes, show no pain. "Morning, Mother. Did you sleep well? I sure didn't."

"Just get up and get out. I've got to clean house and you're in my way."

You smile (or grimace, you're not really sure) at the blurred image of the woman who gave birth to you—a white blob of face with a pile of wild red on top of it. You inherited your hair from her and on more than one occasion she has tried to take it back, by the fistful. You wonder, vaguely, if a mother-daughter scuffle is on the agenda for the day. "Well, excuse the hell out of me." You stand, tottering a bit.

"I've run out of excuses for you, young lady."

The smile/grimace has fallen off your face so you tug it back on. "Funny. Funny Mommy. Funny lady."

Another blob of white, this one small but growing fast, enters your peripheral vision. Sudden pain. Close-up view of the fibers in your carpet. Hey, it *does* need vacuuming.

Barbie's House: a pizza & ice cream joint and refuge for the wicked and witless alike.

"My God, what happened to *you*?"

You pull on your second smile of the morning, this one a bit more real, though no less painful. "What you are looking at," you explain to Nancy (your best friend this week), taking a seat opposite her, "is what the proverbial cat dragged in. But before he did that, he dragged me through hell, high water, higher vodka, and Mom-town."

"She hit you?"

"She hit me."

"My God."

Nancy slurps Pepsi while studying the glitter on her fingernails. Her face is almost as blonde as her hair. You can tell she wants to say something—*I'm sorry? Congratulations? Happy birthday?*—but is afraid to.

"What is it?" you ask.

"Huh?"

"What's the bug up your ass?"

"Um. Nothing." Head shaking, eyes now squinting. "I was just . . ."

"You was just what?"

"I was wondering if you were going to John's party tonight?" Eyes darting everywhere, landing on everything in Barbie's but you. A star-spangled nail parts her lips, nestles into a crack between her front teeth.

"I don't know," you say, "Probably not, I'm feeling exquisitely shitty right now. Why? You want him all to yourself? That it? You want to fuck him?"

Eyes wide now, so blue and blameworthy. *"What?"* Fingernail, exit stage left. *"No*—what . . . what makes you say *that?"*

"It's what you've wanted, isn't it? To fuck my sorry excuse for a boyfriend? Go right ahead, but suck his dick first. He expects it."

And she's off in a sparkly peroxided huff.

Okay, so she wasn't the *best* best friend you've ever had.

Barbie's House faces the street. So do you. You watch the bright, colorful cars drift by out there, idiotically wondering who's in them, where they're going, if any of them would mind an extra passenger.

Bye, Mom, nice right cross, need to work on the timing, though. Bye John, take it easy on the new girl, she bruises easily, I'll bet. Let's go, driver, it's the skinny pedal.

The big, yellow face of a school bus looms into view, swells, quickly fills the window with its big, fat grille. It hisses. Its side door squeals hideously and regurgitates a mass of screaming children out into the parking lot.

"Hey, you gonna order somethin'?"

A waitress. Her pink plastic visor says, YOU'RE IN BARBIE'S HOUSE, pink plastic name tag says, HI I'M TAMMY, pink plastic expression says, I'M AN IDIOT, TELL ME WHAT TO DO.

"Bring me an iced tea, easy on the ice, heavy on the Bacardi."

She makes a snorting noise. "I *wish*," she says, and goes away.

The clot of children ooze into the building and start

laughing, shouting, eating, and dropping quarters into vidiot machines. The waitress brings your pale and powerless beverage. Her expression has been altered, you notice, obviously changed by the child-tide. It says, KILL ME NOW.

Two adults with expressions remarkably similar to that of the waitress round up the children, lead them back outside. The school bus eats its own vomit like a sick dog. Exit, stage right.

"Excuse me." A voice, soft and tiny. You turn toward it.

The little girl's hair is black. Her huge brown eyes peer at you over your elbow, which, you realize, is already cocked and ready to . . . so easy it would be to . . .

Jesus, you wonder, *where the hell did THAT come from? Ease up, girl.*

"Excuse me," the girl repeats, "can I sit with you?"

You scan for parents, guardians, leaders of field trips. When your gaze returns to the girl, she has already parked herself across from you. She's looking at you with questions in her eyes and you wonder if one of them might be, "Are you going to John's party tonight?" but no, this girl is tiny and ignorant, the stage just previous to that of your set, Nancy's set, the big-titted ignorant set.

"How old are you?" she asks.

"Too damn old for my own good. You?"

"Seven. I think."

"You *think*?"

Her eyes move from your face to your tea. "Is that good?"

"Yeah. Want one?"

She nods her little head. "Yeah. Want one."

———

The girl attaches herself to the straw and begins to suck, her already narrow face pulling in on itself. Her dark eyebrows angle down in apparent concentration while her delicate hands grip the sides of the sweating paper cup. You notice a small strip of shiny black material is peeking from under the right sleeve of her light blue dress.

You ask: "Were you with the other kids on the bus? The field trip, or whatever it was?"

Her head moves slowly, side to side, her mouth tugging at the straw.

"Then who did you come here with?"

Again, the head-shake, slowly, the straw making funny push-in, pull-out plastic sounds against the cup's lid. The corners of her small mouth move up in a grin.

"Are your parents here?"

She pulls her mouth away from the straw, breaking the seal. Her face seems to re-inflate. "I don't know."

You blink at her. "Okay. Let's start from scratch, shall we? What's your name?"

"Marisa."

"Marisa what?"

The grin widens. "Marisa Meadows," she says.

"Marisa Meadows. Is that your real name?"

"Of course."

"Okay, Marisa Meadows, where are you from? Around here?"

She sucks tea again until it gurgles. "Can I have some more of this?"

"Only if you answer my questions. Where are you from?"

"A far away place."

"Oh? How far away? Mars?"

The girl nods.

"I see. And what are you doing here, Marisa Meadows the Martian?"

"I'm . . . on a field trip."

"So you *were* with the bus. What school do you go to?"

"No school."

"Must be nice. What's the black band for? Someone die?"

Staring in silence for a long while, brown eyes never blinking, she reminds you of a mannequin. Finally, she opens her little mouth and asks: "Do you suck on guys' thingies?"

———————

You're outa there. Up the street, hang a left, four-block scurry to your house. *Holy fucking Jesus, where do they pick this stuff up?* you wonder, shoes slapping pavement, *Do you suck on guys' thingies?* one-two, one-two, left-right, left-right, *suck on,* pale echo of your steps from behind you, *guys' thingies,* smaller, daintier.

You stop.

"Wait, please," says the girl. You turn to her. Somehow her hair seems even darker in the sunlight; eyes, dark holes punched into the afternoon's brightness.

"What is it with you, huh? What do you want from me?"

She holds her small hands out to you, tiny palms up, but does not speak. Again, you see the shiny blackness of a band or ribbon peeking out from her sleeve. The corners of her mouth are turned downward, readying for a cry.

"Oh, shit."

You pick her up, not believing the lightness of her. It's as if she were hollow. Her arms wrap around you, her face tucks under your chin. "There's nobody here," she says, "nobody but you."

———————

Question is: Will Mom buy the lie?

"*Babysitting?* That's bullshit, pure and smelly."

Hm. Guess not. Her face looks more than doubtful, it looks downright painful.

"You've never babysat a day in your life, have you? Who the hell would be stupid enough to trust you with their child? Who?"

Time for more stink: "Marisa's mother, that's who."

"Marisa's mother? What the hell's going on here?"

You urge the little girl out from behind your legs and into the baleful gaze of Mom. "It's only for a couple hours, all right? I'll walk her home later and . . ." and you didn't even know the rest yourself. Mom wasn't the only one you were bullshitting here.

"Marisa?" Mom glowers at the girl. "Tell me the truth. Did your mother really ask this tramp to baby-sit you?"

The little head nods.

"And this is all right with you, as well?"

"Uh-huh. I like her. I want to be like her."

Mom's eyes roll up in her head, "Oh, Christ forbid."

"Mother . . ."

"Don't 'Mother' me, young lady. You are the most irresponsible, untrustworthy little tramp I know, and you expect me to believe that someone's *mother* is willing to let you care for her *child? You?*"

"Thanks, Mom. You're confidence in me is positively inspiring."

A shake of her head, a flip of her hand. "Doesn't matter," she says. She ties a scarf over her fiery pile of hair, picks up her purse. "Please don't trash my house, stay out of things that don't belong to you; best, really, not to move a muscle till I get back."

"Where are you going?"

"Papers, young lady. Papers to sign, property to handle, *et cetera, et cetera.* That man is shrewd, but so are we." And then she is gone with a slam of the door.

"We" would, of course, be Mom and her lawyer. No question, as well, who "that man" is.

"Your mother doesn't like you very much, does she?" asks Marisa.

Dry swallow, it hurts your throat. "Ah, she's a pussycat. It's not what she does that's so bad, it's what . . ."

Quizzical stare from the girl. You answer it with a question: "What difference does it make?"

A wild man with no hair and a guitar the color of mud wags his glistening head from side to side and whines into a microphone. This makes Marisa giggle.

You ask: "Do you have MTV at your home?"

You watch the back of her head move side to side.

"Do you have television at all?"

One thin shoulder lifts in a shrug.

"What does that mean? You don't know, or you don't remember?"

"It means . . . it doesn't matter." She turns around, her eyes now on yours. "It means . . . what difference does it make?"

"I . . ." It's your turn to shrug. "I just want to know who you are. I want to help you, y'know?"

Now her head nods, a smile tugging at one corner of her mouth. "I want to help you help me. Where's your bathroom?"

This is too fucking weird, you tell yourself. *Much too fucking weird.* This was not how your day was supposed to go—you're not exactly sure how it *was* supposed to go, but it wasn't supposed to go like *this.* How are you going to get this girl, this plastic child, back to where she belongs . . . wherever the fuck that is?

Videos and commercials (hard to tell the difference between the two) drone on, proving themselves to be no help to you at all.

What the hell is going on in there?

Another video. Another commercial.

What if—

Was that a moan? A groan? Was that a *gasp*? You're up and in a flash you're at the bathroom door. "Marisa? You all right?"

Another gasp, and something like a cough.

"Marisa?"

Another cough, but this one becomes a word, "I . . ." followed by another gasp, ". . . am growing . . . up."

You turn the doorknob, relieved to find no resistance, and push.

Your relief instantly evaporates.

Marisa's clothes are piled on the rug at the center of the floor. Black shoes, white socks, frilly blue dress, light blue panties. The cabinet beneath the sink is open, allowing a clear view of a blow dryer, a curling iron, a bag of Mom's old hair curlers, and an open box of Tampax tampons.

The girl sits on the toilet, wearing only the black band around her arm. Her small legs are spread. Tears run down her face. She is attempting to insert a tampon into herself.

"See?" she says, "Aren't I growing up fast?"

A modicum of normalcy has been reestablished. The girl is dressed and seated on the living room floor. You sit before her. "Tell me where you live, Marisa, because you are going home right now."

"Well . . ."

"That's deep. Now tell me where you live."

"You are the only one."

"Whatever. What's your address?"

"There's nobody else."

"I don't care. Tell me where you live or I'll take you to the cops and let them deal with you."

Marisa's mouth hangs open, her dark eyes wide. Then, strangely, she grins her plastic grin. "I live here."

"What do you mean by that? What do you mean 'here'?"

She rests a thin, pale finger on your chest. "Here."

"Look." You're up and pacing. "I don't need this shit, okay?"

"Okay." Her finger follows you.

"I don't need *any* of this weird shit, all right?"

"All right."

"What I need is to be *alone*, understand?"

"Understand."

"Stop that! Stop pointing that fucking finger at me! Stop talking like that! Just stop everything!"

She says, "I'm sorry," and she is so sweet, and so terrible, and so cute, and so small, and so . . .

And so you hit her.

———————

Your hand throbs. It feels as if you've just backhanded a wall.

Marisa glares at you, left cheek aglow, but does not cry. You'd hit her hard enough to knock her sprawling on her weird little ass, yet she stands. Not crying.

"Are you okay?" you ask in a whisper.

No movement.

"Marisa, are you okay?"

"What difference does it make?"

Now *you* are ready to cry. "It makes a difference . . . I didn't mean to do that, it just . . . just . . ."

"It's okay."

"No. It isn't."

As if in an extremely delayed reaction, the girl is suddenly on the floor, her body thrashing, her head and heels thumping the living room carpet. Her mouth is open, making *ca! ca!* sounds.

You drop to her side, not knowing what to do, where to do it. "Stop, Marisa, Jesus, stop! Please, calm down!" On and on she goes, where she'll stop, nobody knows. Then you think: *911.* They'll know what to do.

In the kitchen, white plastic receiver in hand, you punch numbers, realizing even as you do it, you're punching 8-1-1. "*Shit!*" Hit the cut-off, dial again. This time you get it right.

Click in the phone ear, suddenly nothing in the other.

Ring in the phone ear, still nothing in the other.

Did she stop? Is she all right?

A tinnified voice says, "Nine-one-one, what is your emergency?"

No thumping from the living room, no noise at all. Was this a joke? Payback?

"What is your emergency, please?"

"Umm . . . um, I'm sorry. This number was dialed on accident. Really, I'm sorry."

Receiver back in its cradle, all is silent.

"Marisa?"

You move slowly into the living room to find no one at all on the floor. No one on the furniture. The room, as you once heard in a funny movie, was full of empty people.

"Hey, Marisa? You still here?"

A noise, muffled. In the corner, behind the end table. A small pile of home decorating magazines. Move them aside. A heater vent. Another noise: a thump.

She's downstairs.

In your room.

How the fuck did she get by you? Doesn't matter. You're back through the kitchen and down the back stairs in a matter of seconds. At your bedroom door. Considering your earlier surprise, you think twice before opening this door.

Are there such things as seven-year-old escaped mental patients? Is Channel Six News running a Special Report right this second warning the public: "The local center for children with diseased minds reported an escape just hours ago. Be on the lookout for Marisa "Mutant Doll" Meadows. She is considered to have arms, and . . ."

Fuck it. She's just a kid.

Turn the doorknob, push the door open.

Before you became your mother's worst nightmare, some years ago, you were her dream-girl. Doing all the things Mom never had the talent, patience, or time for: dancing, gymnastics, tennis, drama. Fifth Grade: a school play (*Mother Goose is on the Loose,* you were Little Polly Flinders), receiving a big round of applause at the curtain. Sixth Grade: spelling bee champion.

Seventh Grade, it was softball. You had your own special bat, shiny aluminum. You never threw it away.

Now Marisa has it.

And she appears to be masturbating with it.

The expression on her face is not one of pain or pleasure. Not surprise or shock. Her face looks dead. Her thin body bucks much the same as it did upstairs, only now her arms aren't flying, they are rigid, her hands tightly gripping the bat at the taper, pulling the knobbed end into herself, her legs apart and shuddering.

Again, the only thing she wears is the black band.

You open your mouth.

Nothing comes out.

When Marisa, thrashing, seems to grow larger in your vision, you realize it is because you are moving toward her, kneeling. You grab hold of the bat, feel its thrumming (*God, her muscles must be spring steel*), and then the notion of an approaching freight train occurs to you, your hand on the rail, its bright cyclopean headlight growing, swelling . . .

(. . . thrumming, growing, twitching . . . spurting, oh, your hand, the mess . . .

. . . a sweet doll, that's daddy's sweet doll . . .

. . . can I stop now, Daddy? Can I stop? . . . is that? . . .)

"ENOUGH!" you scream, yank the bat from the girl, the girl who is screaming, too, loud and high and without words, so you provide them, "MY DADDY! MY DADDY! MY DADDY!" hands sliding down the bat, "WHY, DADDY, WHY?!", still some friction tape there, after all these years, all these years, "DADDY DID IT! DADDY DID IT!" and now you're swinging the bat, high arc, scraping the ceiling, "WHY? WHY? WHY?" then low, plunging into the sweet doll's face. The face folds. You swing again. There is blood.

Again.

———————

Pain: dull in your arms, sharp in your mouth. You bit your tongue, it seems. There's blood in your mouth. You open your eyes and see blood on your pillow. On your hands, your arms.

This is real.

Little Marisa Meadows, on the floor, and didn't you think her a mutant before? a mutant doll? Yes, well she's mutated now, all right, mutated into hamburger, though some parts are still recognizable. A foot. A finger. A pair of lips with glistening dark hair stuck to them.

The lips move.

You lean in, listening.

"B-br . . . break it," the pulpy thing says, "Break it . . . now . . ."

Break what? What haven't you already broken? And why would she—

Then you understand. The black band. Glossy and still intact, around a soft mound of flesh that was once an arm.

"Break it . . . can die . . ."

This can't be real.

Please, God, if You're there, may I wake up again and find Mom standing over me again, hands on her hips, pissed off and ready to wail, and we can start this day over again, okay? okay? okay?

With thumb and forefinger, you grasp the narrow band. You pull.

A high whine rises from the bloody mess of Marisa, material stretches, tissue stretches, pain s t r e t c h e s *snap!*

―――――――――

Pain: none. Nil.

You feel nothing at all as you awaken yet again, rise toward the land of the living, and the dead, for the third time today. Eyes find the mess. Still there. Marisa. Still dead.

This is still real.

Go away little girl, go and play with someone else, won't you please?

Over onto your back, you see tiny drops of drying blood on the ceiling, and you begin to feel now, pain, though not as bad as before, and pressure . . .

. . . light pressure on your right bicep, and you know what it is without looking. The band. Yours now, all yours. Good for you.

The sound of a motor approaching, idling. Off. A door slams, and, after a moment, a door opens. Mom's home. Good for her.

You slide two fingers under the band.

Mom calls out to you.

You make a decision.

The Thing Too Hideous to Describe

DAVID J. SCHOW

Every once in a while we'll both decide we like a story enough to include in this series; but discover we like it for totally different reasons. Dave Schow's story is a great example of this—while one of us found it to be a subtle, inverted parody of the dear, old Fifties monster movies, the other loved its ability to pin down and lay bare the best and worst aspects of our humanity.

... slapped a pseudopod across the SNOOZE button on Its alarm clock. It liked to be half-awake when midnight actually clicked over, so Its alarm was habitually set to 11:59 P.M. The blue glow of the numerals pleased It, reminded It of some of the biogenous hues It could produce in Its tentacled extremities when satisfied or amused, so It had appropriated the device during some pre-dawn wander or other, from one of the townies who had been imbued in sufficient fear to abandon her bedroom in the middle of the night.

Its carapace was running red—glowing softly, from worry, taken to bed and slept on. It was not as young as It used to be (what on Earth was?); slithering to the sink was becoming a chore. It tried not to make the grunts and huffs the elderly use to punctuate every movement. It yawned wide instead, freeing a few flying insects who had invested sleeptime (Its own, not theirs) in the determined consumption of tartar flecks from Its back molars. The little monsters never drowned, they never suffocated, they were a nuisance, they were pestilent, riddled with germs, yet perfectly suited to their scavenging purpose.

Salve, for the burns. The Thing applied an herbal poultice to the gelid patches of still-healing flesh, repellantly smooth and tender to the touch, like a bubo swollen with dead antibodies. Fire had purged detail from Its cratered brown exodermis, the way a child might use an eraser to obliterate portions of a photograph of the Moon's natural topography. It had lost a sucker from the tip of one of Its retractile protrusions. The wounds would scab thickly, then re-armor. They always did. Last night's close call had been nothing new.

Outside, the tarn beckoned. The Thing always felt better after a wake-up rinse and a bit of a roil in the sludge. It furled its feelers for the downhill roll, eyestalks whipping around and causing a rollercoaster sort of dizziness. It flattened Itself to a glistening membrane on the surface of the brackish water, soaking up some lunar rays, and letting the tidal influences provide inspiration. When It rolled out, nearly all the water sluiced free. Its skin was not absorbent.

It was time to go find some teenagers.

———————

Maysville was one of those antique, rural Kentucky bergs that rolled up the sidewalks promptly at dusk, and whose church steeple still constituted its highest structural elevation. The bell tower therein had been tolling the hour, and half hour, for more than fifty years without breakdown or incident. The church itself—alabaster, roofed in green shingles—glowered over the town square, where rustic benches and litter baskets were emplaced with the precision of chess pieces. The manicured, triangular greensward it faced was a sort of local picnic spot for those unimaginative enough to venture into the woods. It was near the business district at the intersection of Main and Center Streets, where local merchants closed shop promptly at five in the afternoon.

At quitting time, the locals did familial rituals, talking ceaselessly about food or the weather, sitting on porches in rockers or swinging loveseats on creaking chains. Then they started drinking—most alarmingly, at a watering hole whose neon sign proclaimed it as BAR. If you telephoned the place, the proprietor, a burly ex-boxer with a buzzing, dysfunctional voice and only the vaguest grasp of the world beyond his batwing doors, would answer "Tommy's." The Thing had never called Tommy's; the Thing had no use for telephones, although It recognized that when one human or another grabbed one, it usually meant trouble.

Generally, the residents of Maysville kept to their homes (the better to service the exponential care and feeding of town gossip) and, at night, banded into drunken groups to hunt down the Thing once and for all. Maysville needed a monster, apparently, to rationalize its hidebound prejudices, its oddball religion, its social dynamic, and to unify the townsfolk against some common enemy . . . mostly so they did not tear each other apart.

The Thing Too Hideous to Describe did not know of any monsters in the vicinity; that was one of the reasons It had chosen the area for Its semi-retirement. No werewolves or incubi, no demonic apparitions or defrocked Indian burial tracts. No real estate hauntings, no unspeakable, lowering molochs, and practically no children possessed by devils, although sometimes the Thing was not so sure. The kids here had inherited their progenitors' sense of superstitious paranoia and hidebound, inbred fear, and frequently they *acted* monstrously, but the Thing was capable of appreciating the difference. No real monsters . . .

. . . unless you counted the townsfolk, who got incredibly intolerant when they got liquored up at Tommy's. The formula was always the same: they complained, and drank, and groused, and drank, and started stamping their feet, while drinking some more, and before you could say *boo,* you had a gang of violent alcoholics storming up your nether port—drunk, deluded, waving torches and pointy farm implements, screaming with bloodlust in a democracy of madness and mob unreason.

There were already plenty of frightening things in the world, thought the Thing. Circus clowns, for example. Cartoonists and writers—creatures who invented the kind of lurid pulp that could inflame the basest frenzies of unthinking, potentially dangerous crowds. Such artisans of corruption sat in their high places, and distorted form, and made a mockery of all life, and did not care that their exploitative claptrap sank fear into the souls of the ignorant. The Thing had once seen a photograph of one of their minor gods. The portrait depicted some gloomy Gus, all hangdog and horrific and mostly hairless, his eyes broadcasting doom and cosmic apocalypse, hinting at a near-blasphemous tunnel vision that hated all it saw, and saw only that which could kindle the otherworldly passions resident in the fetid lobes of the man's dark and hateful brain.

The Thing Too Hideous to Describe spooked a couple of smooching high-schoolers, about a block from the town square, against a fence, behind some trees near the cemetery, where these nascent fornicators had assumed they might swap fluids and DNA unnoticed. It was a transient thrill. The humans emitted high, squealing noises and took clumsy flight, colliding with trees and each other in their haste to escape. That buoyed the spirits of the Thing only momentarily. Now the offspring would hurriedly report an extravagant exaggeration of what they had seen, amplifying the disgust factor in order to hide their own guilt in the shadow of the more sensational. Then the local authorities, the town leaders, and their parents would all use *that* as an excuse to partake of more abundantly-available booze, and soon enough the whole process would culminate in smoking torches and riot behavior.

The mob would never cross the tarn, however—none of them would ever be that brave. There were too many hazards not governed by hysteria: bloodsuckers, quickmud, venomous reptiles; no streetlights or convenience markets. Beyond that, a treacherous maze of rocks and switchbacks, where precipitous heights waited to plummet the curious to broken-boned death on sharp rocks, or the lack of geographical benchmarks threatened starvation within a labyrinth. No, the mob would never manage to seek out the lair of the Thing Too Hideous to Describe, because indigenous legend had it that once you went in, you never came out.

Yet upon its return for lunch break, the Thing Too Hideous to Describe saw light. Human light, the artificial light of a battery-operated beam. Once, a group of besmocked know-it-alls in helicopters had buzzed unnervingly close, convinced that the Thing might be some sort of alien invader from another planet. They had given up and retreated to the safety of their grandiose theorizing. They always gave up, when it came to actually learning something. It was more profitable to fall back on whatever make-believe they were selling unwary consumers, this week.

Whomever had chanced upon the Thing's home did not look like a scientist, nor did he appear to be a representative of the military. He looked like a clerk. He was wearing a bulky down jacket and hiking boots. He wore spectacles and had a hairless face (the way humans scraped off their pelts had always made the Thing a bit queasy). It was comical to watch him feel around the edges of the nondescript cave that led down to the Thing's home. He did not appear repulsed by the slime coating the ingress. He sniffed it, from the tips of his gloves. His flashlight beam strayed wild again, as he consulted a big metal notebook he held crooked into one arm.

The Thing Too Hideous to Describe held steady and watched, as this Outsider—for that was definitely what the man was, not from around here—stiffened, the way humans always did when they felt there was some creepy lurker, monitoring them. Now would be an excellent opportunity to pull the old stalk-and-scare, making the guy look toward the most likely source of monsterishness, then drop tentacles down on him, from above. But before the Thing could indulge Itself, the flashlight ray crossed Its big, ebony orbs, causing a stab of pain like a migraine. Before the Thing could rally, the man-creature in the bulky coat spoke to It.

"Oh! Hi there . . . sorry, I hope I'm not intruding or anything . . ."

This struck the Thing as very odd. Usually, they ran away by now, or started shooting. Instead, this manling checked his book again—*a book! Another damned book! Oh, cursed item!* thought the Thing, steeling for the worst. But this did not appear to be a *book*-book, of the sort It reviled. No, it was a ring-binder sort of affair, its pages containing not hated text, and certainly not the most loathsome print of all, *fiction,* but graphs and charts.

And the man-creature was walking toward It, the tone of voice spewing from his mouth-hole not scared at all, but apologetic.

"Sorry to bother you, like I said, but my name is Steve Brackeen. I was going to leave you a note. Um . . . is this a bad time? I was hoping maybe we could talk a little . . ."

Worse, as the man-creature came closer to the Thing, his aura read decidedly cool, not a nimbus of red-hot fright or hatred. He pulled off one glove to expose his hand, that simian tool depending grotesquely from the end of his arm with its upsettingly snake-like five digits, pink and hairless. No slime.

It had been ages since the Thing Too Hideous to Describe had risked vocal contact with a human, and Its works seemed rusty. A lot of bug-infested mucus glopped out of Its face, plus bits of a turkey club sandwich It had enjoyed two days ago, but the man-creature broadcast no distress at this.

"I'm—I'm not a census taker or anything like that. I came here to talk to you, actually, if—if you think you could spare—"

He was flashing a laminated card that featured an inaccurate photograph of him, and his name, spelled out in modern English.

The Thing Too Hideous to Describe did not wish to shake hands with the man-creature, primarily because It disliked that sort of actual physical contact, but also because It had nothing a human could reasonably call a hand.

"Like I said, my name is—"

The Thing was perplexed. This was most assuredly outside the normal playbook. What could It do? It invited the guy inside.

———

"I'm a little grubby," said the man-creature named Steve. "You'll have to excuse that. This is a lot better than stomping all over Europe, lemme tell you." He spread a disposable paper towel over the glistening hump of rock near the Thing's firepit, then sat down, extending his booted leg appendages to compensate for the elevation of the rock. "Nice place. The fire is nice, too."

The Thing Too Hideous to Describe had to pause to ponder the word, one It had almost never heard. *Nice?*

"You know—homey. Anyway, I've been working on this big doctoral thesis. That's what all this hoodoo in the notebook is about. I've been documenting the weird crowd behavior of group insanity in small, isolated towns and villages, you know—the kind of places the world always seems to pass by? And some of the stuff I found out is pretty upsetting. Like in the Black Forest—rampant alcoholism, leading to berserk, antisocial group action. Apparently a lot of those villagers have nothing better to do with their time than invent wild stories about their betters, and use those stories to justify blowing up every castle in a hundred-mile radius. No, sir or madame, your hamlet is not being victimized by one of your own retarded halfwits . . . it must be a *vampire!* That's the way these kooks think. No, your cemeteries aren't being vandalized by teen punks or necrophiles . . . it must be that mean old professor up on the hill, who has more money and pedigree than you could ever imagine, why, he must be *stitching all those corpses together to make a big stupid monster,* yeah, that *must* be it!"

The Thing Too Hideous to Describe was forced to concur. Humans almost never behaved logically, or compassionately. They did bray a lot about tolerance, which exercise for their vocal cords was probably more economical than actual practice.

"I mean, you've seen some of those movies, right?" said the Steve-creature. "Who really makes out, every time the besotted Burgomeister decides, you know, to blow up another dam? Local contractors, funeral directors, hardware stores, the makers of pitchforks and rope, gun dealers and the distributors of ammunition, hell . . . monsters are great for their economy. They all get shitfaced at the inn until they're fizzed enough to see monsters, then they start grabbing for the dynamite. And who do you think gets first crack at developing the destroyed real estate? I mean, *where's the real problem,* here?"

The Thing Too Hideous to Describe had to nod in agreement, at that one.

"I guess the fundamental question is: what are these imbeciles smoking . . . and where can I get some?" The Steve-creature cracked a smile that bisected his misshapen round face into a leer, showing teeth. "Did you hear about the lunatics running the asylum over in Mapleton, USA? They think they're plagued by some mummy guy who crawls out of a bog every quarter-century or so to pick on the descendants of some heat-stroked, hallucinating Egyptologist who drank himself into a coronary before the Second World War! I mean, accounts vary, but the story stays the same: These people refuse to accept responsibility for their own lives. Nah, we were all abject failures in life because we were *cursed by monsters,* not because we're all so inebriated all the time we can barely tie our shoes!"

The Steve-creature flipped open his notebook. The Thing Too Hideous to Describe leaned forward to peruse the data in better light.

"See here? No matter how many times they wipe out these supposed monsters, those monsters always come back, even if they're, you know, utterly purged from the planet. See? It allows for the maintenance of a consistent level of mass psychosis. Pretty soon, your toilet doesn't flush, and voila—it must be the Mad Doktor's fault, or some monster that conveniently runs contrary to whatever religious derangement governs the town. Not only does it maintain the status quo and help the local economy, but it severely limits the employment opportunities for bona fide monsters. Look at this graph—see? Monster jobs and mean income level, down every year. I'm thinking of presenting some of my findings to Affirmative Action."

The Thing Too Hideous to Describe flipped to another page of facts and figures, using one of Its secondary pseudopods, the stumpy, more articulate ones. Yes, the bald information in black and white certainly seemed conclusive enough.

The Steve-creature reached into his shoulder bag. *Here it comes,* thought the Thing. *It's a trap. He's going to whip out a weapon and try to bushwhack me. Or worse, this has all been a setup, and he's going to try to sell me something.*

No, it was merely a little tape recorder.

"I just want to get some of your thoughts," said Steve. "Your angle on the whole phenomenon, and maybe ask you a few questions about your relationship with the population of Maysville, if that's not too intrusive or presumptuous of me. You'll be speaking on behalf of a very broad monster demographic—what you say may affect hundreds of others in the same position as yourself."

The Thing's eyes blinked in incomprehension, fluttering at the ends of their stalks. Not only had It not anticipated company, but there was nothing around that could qualify as refreshment, especially for this iron-blooded, bipedal air-breather. It sighed, making a congested, bubbly sound. It really needed to work on Its hosting skills.

———————

Ominously pleasant, this talk in the dark. An exchange of ideas, seductive in its invitation . . . and almost promising some manner of betrayal as the final course. But I can smell human lies, the way I can sense deceit hidden beneath their too-thin, fragile skins. This one is compas-

sionate and educated. If they were all like this one, never would I have to salve burns from the night before. If they were all like this one, the structure of our universe would not exist. I kind of like him.

*But holy Peter, is he ugly! That jackstraw corpus, with its gangly, meatless limbs. Only two eyes, both the limpid color of poison. The rictus mouth with its nasty, square teeth. The absolute **wrongness** of his geometry brands him as an abomination, something the sane gaze instinctually rejects from view. I think that, were our stations reversed, I might derive pleasure from his extinction. I hope not, for that would make us both, as races, equally uncivilized.*

———

Commotion, in the calm of night. The Thing Too Hideous to Describe was accustomed to such uproar, but this night, It was not the catalyst.

The Thing scuttled up a high tree in the woods and spread his pods out, spider-like, for stability. From here, Its vision, tuned to nonhuman frequencies, could perfectly make out, from this distance, the church steeple and town square. The *sounds* were familiar—inebriated raving, the crackle of firebrands, the hyperactive jostle of sweaty bodies lusting for a kill. All the trappings of a conventional Maysville monster hunt, with their preferred monster as absentee.

A large phone-pole crucifix jutted from a pyre of smashed furniture, the kindling provided by the rent bodies of those few books in town that had not been banned or burned already. Spiked to the pole, his wrists and throat engirded by barbed wire, was the Steve-creature, the human who had called himself Brackeen. The good-folk of Maysville pelted him with rotten fruit and broken glass, from the bottles they had drained. His shredded notebook was utilized to ignite the fire. The lynch chaos of Maysville's drunken residents would not be denied.

He had been found out. He had ventured into the town to do interviews and take notes, and the innkeeper had poked into his guest's luggage, or, more likely, someone had just peered over his shoulder at an opportune moment. He had been damned by his own research. Maysville, ever on the lookout for mutants, would obliterate any aberration . . . especially when they could find no other one to torment.

The Steve-creature hollered protest, at first. Then screamed curses. Then, merely screamed, before he fell silent and continued to cook. His unholy book was consumed by righteous fire. His head sagged and his hair vanished in a puff of greasy smoke.

The Thing Too Hideous to Describe averted Its gaze, with something like pity. They were not all alike, these humans. The Steve-creature had resembled those executing him (hell, they all looked alike anyway), but in no way was he the same as them.

With a measure of melancholy, the Thing Too Hideous to Describe slithered down from the tree and trundled wearily homeward. Tomorrow night, It really should sortie into town, to do what It did best, but It knew the task would come without verve or enthusiasm.

The human conceit of vengeance, however, might be adapted to fruitful use, on some other midnight, soon to come.

Slipknot

BRETT ALEXANDER SAVORY

There's a theory that madness is actually a code written into our genetic structure. Editor and writer Brett Savory has taken this notion through several, bizarre and shocking exponents to suggest that such a gene may also enjoy its own twisted sentience as well.

Slipknot spoke: *You can't kill me, 'cause I'm already inside you.*

Shadows dripped. Silhouettes of emotions stretched themselves languidly against the pitch background of Edward Curtis' dreamscape. They wrapped themselves in his psyche, dispelled myth, eschewed logic, creating a template for their work.

Once the canvas was created, the medium was selected. It was always the same: guilt. It sucked the black

from the darkest part of his heart and vomited its core between his flashing synapses. *Guilt.*

You can't fucking kill me . . .

"I do not want to kill you," Edward whispered in his
sleep.

Like ink from the tip of a quill, the shadows dribbled
through his thoughts, blanketing them, suffusing them
with their intent. Then the deep recesses of shadow-forms
pulled away from Edward's mind en masse. He inhaled
sharply. The cloaking pools of black left him exposed,
shivering, cold sweat beading on his forehead, an image
behind his eyelids of a half-drunk bottle of red wine sitting on an old oak table, the crimson liquid swimming in
and out of focus, making him nauseous.

Edward opened his eyes and the bottle continued to
float in his vision for a few seconds before dissipating,
droplets splashing across his ceiling, dripping onto his
bed.

Like shadows.

"Aw, Grampa!" the boy wailed, "ya can't stop there!"

The bottle between the boy and his grandfather shimmered in the flickering shadows thrown by the fireplace
behind the old man. The boy slammed his little fist on the
oak table in frustration. "Come on! Tell the rest! No fair!"

Grampa chuckled, jowls jiggling, bright red cheeks
plumping with the motion, like a Butterball on Thanks-
giving Day. "No more, my boy. You're getting scared, and
besides, it's bedtime for wee little chumblies like you."

Chumbly.

That's what Gramps always called little Eddie. The old
man had made up the story many years ago about a bear

that wore fuzzy pants and had a wobbly oven and a farting toaster. Pretty bizarre, Eddie thought. He didn't much care for the story of Chumbly Bear, but he liked the name for some reason. It had a nice ring when Grandpa said it.

"But you stopped at the best *paaart!*" Eddie whined, stretching out the last word like toffee.

Grampa chuckled again, shaking the table ever-so-slightly with his big belly as it rubbed up against the old oak. "There *is* no best part of a Chumbly story, Eddie." He leaned forward slowly, chair creaking beneath his weight, eyes dancing. "It's *all* the best part."

Something in the wine bottle moved.

Eyes flying wide open, an electric bolt shot up Eddie's spine. "What was *that!?*" The boy jumped out of his chair and stood behind it, staring, jaw agape, at the bottle.

Grampa sat back in his chair, and looked at the bottle. His eyes glazed over a little, scaring young Eddie. "Gramps? Gramps, are you okay?"

Grampa snapped out of it, his eyes lighting on Eddie's, dancing again. "Yes, boy, yes, just fine, just . . . fine," he said, studying the bottle as though it were some curiosity he'd found at an antique shop. "It's just that . . ." He trailed off again, this time grinning a little as if remembering the punch line of a favorite joke. Eddie came around the chair and sat back down, slowly, never taking his eyes off the bottle.

"What, Grampa? What is it? What's . . ." He raised an arm and pointed at the bottle. ". . . inside?"

Grampa's grin widened. He cleared his throat. "Why, it's the bear, son."

A chill crept up Eddie's spine. He mouthed the words along with Grampa as he spoke them:

"Chumbly Bear," Gramps said, the smile failing to

touch his eyes now, a haunted look replacing it as he re-membered the events of over forty years past. "But I thought he was long gone, the old bugger." He tried to laugh a little then, but the sound caught in his throat.

Eddie frowned. "But Chumbly's just a dumb old story bear. How can . . . *that* be him?"

The thing in the bottle spun around slowly at the boy's words, the glint from the firelight dancing into the crimson waves, washing vague drafts of fear through the boy, stabs of memory through the old man. The indiscernible shape bobbed in sync with the rise and fall of the tips of the flames from the fire hypnotically, mesmerizing.

"Don't know, Eddie," Gramps whispered, barely opening his mouth. "I hoped by telling stories about him, it'd keep him away for good."

Gramps fell back into silence.

Eddie wanted to ask Gramps what he was talking about. When had he seen the bear before? It didn't even *look* like a bear, so how did he know it was Chumbly? Why did he not want the bear to come back? What had happened?

The thing inside the bottle spun around a few more times, then disappeared in a glint of firelight and a ripple of wine.

———————

Edward brushed his teeth in the bathroom mirror and thought about his dream.

You can't kill me, 'cause I'm already inside you.

Memories of Gramps and his childhood, listening to the old man tell his Chumbly Bear stories by the fireplace, flitted through his mind like a broken, too-bright strobe light, the images uneven, unnatural.

Wine and shadows, he thought. *Something dancing in*

the bottle. Something I can't kill. But I do not want to kill it. I don't know how I know that, but I do.

Slipknot hunkered down in Edward's mind and listened. Just . . . listened. Being the bear had been fun, sure. But being Slipknot was *oh* so much better. In every way. It did not want to lose that. Not now. Not after all this time.

Edward leaned over, spit into the sink, rinsed, stood back up . . . and caught a flicker in the upper right-hand corner of the mirror. Something black. Churning. Twisting. *Mulching.*

Dancing.

Slipknot could not resist a titter.

More memories surfaced—these ones like old, forgotten pictures in a photo album, like the dregs of a long-cold cup of coffee sliding down the throat.

Edward grimaced.

Gramps had shot himself in the face with a double-barrelled shotgun two months after that last Chumbly story when he'd been scared by the return of the bear . . . or whatever the hell it was . . . moving around in the wine bottle. Both parents gone before he was old enough to walk— father killed in a car accident, mother run off with another man—he'd been given over to his grandfather, so little Eddie had been the one to find poor Gramps, brains smeared all over the fireplace and oak table, blood splashes streaking across the wine bottle and ceiling, dripping. Dripping like the shadows sometimes dripped in his dreams.

A voice from the bottle, a swirling in the boy's ears, weaving a tapestry of shadows across thought, whispered gently in his ear as he gazed down at Gramps' cooling corpse: *You can't kill me . . .*

Edward had screamed then, and run out of the house shouting for help.

But that was over twenty years ago.

The flickering thing in the high corner of the mirror spread itself out and pulsed in time with Edward's heartbeat. Edward stared, transfixed. The toothbrush dropped from his limp fingers. Then he heard the voice again, this time so close to his ear he imagined he could feel the slight rush of air as the sentence formed, each word like a crumbling tombstone half-in, half-out of the shadow of a tree, caught between this world and the next: *I'm inside you.*

Then the walls dissolved in Edward's vision, and he was no longer in his bathroom . . .

"Shoot the boy," the man said.

Philip Curtis flinched. "I can't, Smithy, he's my only son." The gun wavered, came down by the man's side. "How do you expect me to—"

"Shoot him or I'll shoot you both." Cold fact.

"But Smithy, there's gotta be—"

"No, there ain't nothin' else you can do," Smithy interrupted, raising both arms, gun in each hand, and pointed them at Philip and his son. "You got yourself into this, now you gotta do what you can to get out. And if you're thinkin' you can squeeze off a shot in my direction before I kill you both . . . well, if I was you, I'd stop thinkin' like that, Phil. It ain't gonna happen. You know it ain't. Now FUCKING shoot him. I'm countin' to five.

"One."

Sweat popped out on Philip's forehead. His son, James Curtis—just married, new father—shook his head back and forth, eyes glued to the guns in Smithy's hands, one part of him praying Smithy would pull the triggers and just end it all, the other part praying his father would raise his own pistol and at least try to save their lives.

"Two."

"Look, Smithy, I'm sorry, alright!? We gotta be able to work this out. Why are you doing this? Why do you have to—"

"Three."

Philip Curtis started to cry. James' insides clenched tight as a drum, heart lurching in his throat. Philip raised the gun to his son's face.

"Dad, what are you DOING? Shoot HIM! At least TRY, for God's sake!"

"Four." Smithy smiled, waited a beat, took a breath, and moved the muscles in his face that would form the word "five."

Edward, tears glistening in his eyes, fell over in his bathroom, bashing the side of his face against the tub and curling up into a ball. He cupped his hands over his ears and squeezed his eyes shut, mouthed the word along with James.

"Five."

Smithy only got half the word out before Philip's bullet ripped through James' skull, spraying thick clumps of brain and blood against the nearby trees.

James crumpled.

Philip dropped the gun, fell to his knees, head in hands, sobbing.

Smithy turned around, silent, and made his way through the forest, back to his car.

Edward opened his eyes, the fluorescent light of the bathroom too bright, blinding. He said one word, the sound dropping like stone from between his dry, cracked lips: "Dad."

Slipknot waited until Edward had gone to bed before slipping out again from behind the bathroom mirror.

It would rend this one like it had the last, and the one before that, and on down through history. Sometimes it wished it wasn't restricted to just one family, that it could fuck with others, turn their lives inside out, torment them in whatever ways caught its fancy that generation. But rules were rules, and these were rules of the universe, so there was no one to appeal to.

Smithy had been a long-time friend of the Curtises, and was Slipknot's first and only human host. In its true form—the form it was in now, that of shadow—it was not as limited as when it was the bear or the human. It had forgotten the other forms it'd assumed/created over the many, many years with the Curtises, but it knew, and never allowed itself to lose sight of the fact that they were all, essentially, human creations.

Guilt took all forms, and Slipknot's was only to portray them. Though, in its boredom of late, Slipknot had deigned to help things along their way a little. After all, as there was no one to appeal to about the rules, it stood to reason that there was no one to answer to, either.

Edward often dreamed about his guilt, and Slipknot fed off it, intertwined it with the rest of the family's, splashed it across the ceiling and let it drip down. Slipknot increased the tentative connection with Edward as he slept, and listened hard . . . Edward was dreaming of it again.

And Slipknot was hungry.

———————

In the dream, Edward was taking his twelve-year-old son, Stephen, to a hockey game for his twelfth birthday.

"Woo-hoo! Go Canucks!" Stephen shouted, his little boy's voice lost in the roar of the crowd.

The noise was driving spikes into Edward's brain. The pounding headache/near-migraine was threading through his skull, chipping bits off, and by Christ he wished Stephen would just watch the game and shut the fuck up.

"Dad, did you see Ohlund rip that shot through Hasek!? Holy cats! What a blast he's got! Incredible! Dad, did ya see it!? Dad?"

Edward gritted his teeth, more cracks in his head. The Canucks had scored on the Buffalo Sabres and this Vancouver crowd was going nuts—a jackhammer at the base of his skull. He'd never had a headache this bad in his life. He'd taken aspirin for it before they'd left for the game, but—

"Ha-HO!" Stephen leaped out of his seat with the rest of the capacity crowd and started clapping and hollering. The Canucks had popped another one in. "Dad, Bertuzzi roofed one! Did ya see it!? Wow!"

Shut the fuck up, he thought. *Just SHUT UP. Yes, I fucking saw it.* Edward leaned forward in his seat with his head in his hands, rubbing his temples.

"You okay, Dad?"

"Leave me alone, Stephen," Edward said, eyes shut, a tear slipping down his cheek from the pain. "Just . . . watch the game and let me be for a bit, okay?"

"But what's wrong?" Stephen shouted over the noise of the crowd.

I knew the little shit wouldn't shut his trap. He can't just fucking leave me alone, can he? He has to know what's wrong. He has to shout the question right in my goddamned ear. Has to—

"Dad, can you hear me!? Are you alright!?"

Edward knew he was close to snapping. Teetering on the brink. One more word and he knew—

"Dad, is it your head? Is it—"

Slipknot pushed just then . . . only a little bit, but he pushed. Just enough.

Edward swung around in his seat, lifted his son up to his face by the arms. Stephen dangled like a broken puppet, eyes wide, suddenly terrified. "Yes, Stephen, my FUCKING head is killing me, you little bastard!" The words came from his mouth, but he had no idea where the thoughts that had formed them came from. "My head is pounding like hell, and your constant shouting and bellowing in my fucking ear isn't exactly helping, AL-RIGHT!?"

"B-B-But . . . Dad, I—"

Slipknot shoved a bit more and grinned as the words tumbled from Edward's mouth. "You were an accident, anyway, Stephen," Edward said, and dropped his son back into his seat, utter disdain on his face.

The Canucks came close again, hitting a post, and the drill probed deeper into Edward's mind, stirring Slipknot up even more.

A big, fat Sabres fan—a Mike Peca jersey pasted to his sweaty back—leaned over in his seat one aisle up from theirs and threatened Edward, telling him to lay off the kid. Edward ignored him.

Stephen's face had gone slack at the word 'accident,' but Edward simply could not stop. "We didn't want you. No one wants you. You were an accident. Just a fucking stupid accident."

Edward felt something release from inside him. The headache started to fade, slowly, in increments. Waves of nausea passed over him and he fell clumsily into his seat. He started to cry.

The Canucks slammed their third straight goal through Hasek and the crowd erupted. Stephen remained seated, staring at nothing, wishing he were dead.

Edward woke from the dream, sweating, head pounding. His sheets were soaked through. Breath coming in raspy, choking gulps, he looked up to the ceiling and saw the shadows stretching themselves along the ceiling again, pulsing in time with his breathing. He had only ever seen this in dream before, but now it was real. Dripping onto his sheets. Slithering between the folds of his crumpled quilt. The hushed whisper, *I'm inside you,* slinking through his mind like a back-alley whore. *You can't kill me 'cause I'm already inside you.*

The shadows seeped under the covers and into Edward's pores. Flitting images and vague feelings of broken promises and forgotten dreams: the back of dad's head splashed across trees, the dull thump of his body hitting the leafy ground; Chumbly twisting in his red wine prison; Gramps with his brains splattered all over the oak table and mantelpiece; Edward's wife leaving him after two years of marriage, lurid scenes of the infidelity that had caused it; Stephen at the hockey game, the flat, stone look of worthlessness, of being loved by no one.

"I do not want to kill you," Edward mumbled, dream becoming reality, the words untrue, but practiced, ingrained nonetheless. Guilt tightened, became a machine, thrust forward, immutable. Parts of it became a hard, cold stone in his chest. Other parts swam through his veins, burning, congealing, solidifying. Frozen Pompeii, an ashen statue of grief and guilt.

Then Slipknot told Edward his name.

"Slipknot," Edward whispered, the beginning sibilant like a razor deep and hard across his tongue, the word itself a poisonous miasma drifting through his psyche, ripping out memories like talons tearing at clumps of soil.

When the pain had subsided and only a dull throb remained, Edward slept, and dreamed about Stephen.

Stephen walked through the front door of his house to see his father standing in the hall, a gun pointed at his son's head. He dropped his overnight bag on the floor and tried to think of something to say.

Edward felt the knot tighten. He was sweating from everywhere a human being can sweat from, his entire body drenched, the exposed parts—arms, hands, face—glistening. His whole frame trembled, but his gun hand was steady. He could feel Slipknot racing around inside him, shooting random images of betrayal, regret, and loss through his mind. With each image, each impression, the trigger bent back that much further.

In his son's face, he saw Gramps, saw his father, saw himself . . . and squeezed a little more.

He tried to say he was sorry, that Stephen *wasn't* an accident, that he'd wanted him, loved him, still loved him, would always love him. But Slipknot pulled tighter, securing itself against the accumulated guilt/betrayal of the centuries before him. More images seared synapses, burned grooves through rational thought. Images two, three hundred years old of people Edward did not know, but knew were his blood. Their faces sliced through his will, their deeds crushing it to dust.

The hammer of the gun cocked back slowly as the pressure on the trigger increased. Shades of gray wrapped in shadows in the shape of tears rolled down Edward's cheeks.

Slipknot smiled, and waited patiently for the back of the boy's head to open up all over the screen door.

Finally, Stephen found words. Words he had no right saying. Words he didn't understand, and had no idea from where they'd come. "Pull the slipknot, Dad." His eyes were locked with his father's, somehow, perhaps through the song of their blood, sharing the visions. "*Pull it.*"

Some rules are universal, and with no one to appeal to, they sometimes change on their own, or bend to the will of one stronger.

"Pull it. Pull the knot."

Edward flinched at the words—

you can't fucking kill me

—shook more violently yet, his gun hand finally becoming affected. The disease within him screamed—

I'm already inside you

—pressed harder at Edward, but Edward understood his son's words, and he let it all go.

He just *let*.

It.

Go.

Stephen watched his father raise the gun to his own head, the hand holding the weapon now steady again. Something flickered momentarily beneath the skin of Edward's face, something black and seething, something trying like mad to get out.

Stephen Curtis closed his eyes.

Magic Numbers

GENE O'NEILL

Gene O'Neill's stories have appeared in a wide range of genre magazines from SF to crime fiction. The story which follows does not easily fall into any such neat category . . . which is exactly the way we like it.

TODAY, THE NUMBER IS SEVEN.

Despite common belief, late night sounds are not really muffled in heavy fog, quite the opposite: A siren shrieks sharply in the distance, a dog howls mournfully, nearby music is crystal clear, and a car roars by on Jefferson Street, its tires making sticking sounds on the wet pavement. Forgetting about the fog creatures, you stop, cock your head, and enjoy the night sounds, watching trails of mist swirl about your legs, which reminds you of a neighbor's gray kitten that arches its back, puffs up, and rubs against your ankles.

You almost expect to hear—

Instead of the anticipated purr, you hear a gasp of surprise as three figures materialize out of the fog like black phantoms, their faces momentarily startled by your sudden appearance. Then quickly their expressions turn blank; and for a moment they stare at you in dead silence.

Your heart thumps rapidly and you begin to hyperventilate.

But thinking quickly, you extend all five fingers in the left pocket of your coat; and in the right pocket, you extend two fingers, the tips pressed down into the stolen silk panties at the bottom. The number seven restores your courage, your breathing and heartbeat quickly returning to normal.

"Whatcha doin' here, man?" the short, stocky one on the left asks in a deep voice thick with menace. He's wearing a Raider's windbreaker, the collar pulled up against the misty chill, his hostile black eyes peering at you directly.

For a moment your legs weaken, lose tone, but you repeat the number in your head: Seven, seven, seven.

"Yeah, white boy, whatcha doin' here 'cross Jeff'son?" the big guy in the middle says slowly, his speech softer, less measured, but the sentence full of implied threat. There is a sharp meanness to his features. And he is indeed huge, his shoulders wide, his white football jersey bearing the black number 66; but there is easily enough chest for another 6, which makes you shudder.

The guy on the right is wiry, his partially hooded gaze making him appear sleepy, except his speech is hyper and jumpy. "M-m-may-b-b—" He stamps his foot, which breaks the stutter, "Maybe this white boy t-t-that Lil Bo Peep dude, Leroy."

Oh, no, you think, closing your eyes for a second, hoping one of the fog creatures will swoop down and swallow them up. Seven, seven, seven.

You blink, but they are still there.

"Yeah, whatta 'bout that, boy?" the big guy, Leroy, asks. "You awful funny-lookin'. Now, you ain't that dude from the newspaper, one been sneakin' and prowlin' 'round over here, scarin' all of the women-folks, is you?"

"This little sucker him, alright," the one on the left butts in, before you can think of any answer.

"How you know, Sidney?" Leroy asks, challenging the husky guy's statement.

" 'Cuz, my lady friend, Clorinda, she done tole me what the muthafucka look like, man." He glances at you disparagingly, then nods his head. "Dude ripped off some of her stuff when he peepin' in her backyard last week, but her dog, Spike, he starts barkin', and she see him 'fore he do his Carl Lewis outta there, you know what I'm sayin'?"

Cautiously, you push the panties deeper into your right jacket pocket with the extended two fingers, hoping they won't think to search you.

"T-t-t-t—"

Leroy turns to his left and snaps sharply, "Spit it out, Replay." Then he reaches out and puts his arm gently around the thin guy's shoulder. "C'mon, man."

"This is the dude, L-L-Leroy," he says, almost flawlessly with his friend's arm around his shoulder.

But Leroy lets the arm slide away.

"F-Fits the paper's d-d-d—"

"Description," the one on the left fills in impatiently. "Yeah, Replay's right, Leroy. Just like Clorinda say. Real short . . . kinda lop-sided, you know, with a little-dude body, big-dude head. This here Lil Bo Peep!"

Despite the seven fingers extended in your pockets, your bowels feel loose.

"O-kay," Leroy says, stretching the word into sentence-length with the finality of a court judgment. He withdraws his hand from his pants pocket and flicks his wrist, the light glinting off the opened straight razor. "Let's carve us up a Lil Bo Peep turkey." He grins evilly, taking a step toward you. Then he stops, turning left, "What kinda meat you like, Replay?"

"I-I likes w-w-w-white—"

Even though you are protected by the aura of the day's number, you feel a strong surge of panic that enervates your legs; and as Leroy waits for Replay to finish the joke, you suck in a breath and dart away as fast as you can, leaving the trio of blacks standing in the fog.

You cross Jefferson Street heading west, and even though you can not see the goals, you know you are on one of the basketball courts of Olympic Park, the boundary separating black and white housing, because your feet slap against sticky blacktop, the sound rebounding in the mist, giving your location away.

The three must be able to hear it, too.

And you realize they will follow.

You weave erratically as you run across the grass beyond the courts, whispering and scattering sevens in your wake, hoping to attract at least one fog creature to cover your escape.

At last, ahead in the mist, the glowing orange streetlights of Franklin Avenue appear like blurry Japanese lanterns. You are finally back in the white business district, but too far from home. You must find somewhere close to hide and catch your breath.

Crossing the street, you spot the red neon of the Leaning Tower of Pizza blinking in the mist. You slow as you reach the sidewalk, debating the wisdom of seeking sanctuary in the restaurant. Looking through the window under the neon sign, you see no one in any of the booths, only a pair of tired young men leaning on the order counter, their dirty, striped-red aprons and wrinkled, chef hats looking anything but gay this time of night.

You shake your head and trot by, ignoring the closed Starbrite Videos next door, gazing ahead to the bright green, orange, and red sign glaring like a beacon in the mist: 7-Eleven.

You cry out with relief, almost stumbling into the convenience store.

But you come to a sudden stop in the doorway and glance back toward your unseen pursuers, realizing that you will be trapped in any store if the blacks catch you inside. So you take seven more steps up the street and pause at the mouth of the dark alley running between the 7-Eleven and a boarded-up storefront.

Suddenly, her voice speaks in your head.

Robert, this way, Robert.

It's the Lady of the Numbers!

And she seems to be directing you up the alley.

You move cautiously, the light here off the street very dim, only one shaded bulb over a side entrance to the 7-Eleven about halfway up the alley, doing little more than casting shadows, scary shadows.

Here, Robert, back here.

The voice leads you to the end of the alley, behind a Dumpster. You peer warily around the container piled high with refuse.

Nothing.

Only a brick wall, its graffiti obscured by heavy shadows, the smell of urine strong in your nostrils. Yuck.

Then, you hear footsteps coming to a halt at the mouth of the alley. Quickly you squeeze back behind the Dumpster, ignoring the smelly mess, trying to conceal yourself.

After a moment you peer back around the Dumpster, out toward the street, and even though you cannot see them in the fog, you know who has cornered you in the alley.

The Black Phantoms.

"L-L-Le—" a voice stutters in the mist, confirming your suspicion.

"Shhhh."

You are trapped.

No, the voice interrupts in your head. *No, you are not caught.*

It is her, the voice so soft and gentle, comforting.

Look, here, turn around.

You turn and the shadows along the brick wall seem to stir, to take on depth.

Still, you cannot really see anything, but you sense movement, and some of the shadows are almost shimmering, like heat waves off asphalt.

Here, Robert. It is a cloak, a very special cloak. Turn, slip it on, and pull the cowl over your head.

You turn and feel something slipped over your shoulders. And you shiver, but remember to reach back and pull the hood up over your head.

Good. Be still. No one can see you now, Robert. You are cloaked in shadows.

The footsteps approach warily.

The three must be carefully searching along both sides of the alley.

After a lifetime, you hear breathing just beyond the front side of the Dumpster, and you recognize Sidney's voice. "Leroy, that lil sucker jus' ain't back here, man. Dude disappeared, you know what I'm sayin'?"

"Yeah, well, he gotta be here, some place." You hear things being thrown angrily about. Then, after another eternity or so, Leroy finally admits with a sigh, "You right, Sidney. C'mon, Replay, let's get on back 'cross the playground, 'fore the Man come 'long 'n' bust our raggedy ass."

"I-I-I hears ya, m-m-m—"

"Jus' move, Replay."

You wait, squatting in place behind the Dumpster with aching legs, until the footsteps fade away into the misty night. Then you stand and stretch; and the wonderful cloak is lifted off your shoulders, taken back into the wall.

TODAY, THE NUMBER IS TWO.

It is early, and you are laying on your bed, listening to a tape by The Cure, Robert Smith singing the second song, "Siamese Twins," the part about the girl's face in the window. You listen with your eyes closed, the crotch of your pants tight.

Suddenly you are disturbed by a knocking on your door.

"Bobby?"

Your mother breaks the mood, knocking again, before she jams her head in the door.

"You sure you don't want to go to the Beaumont's?" she asks, her voice hopeful you will change your mind. "Donna says Mary Ann would love to see you again."

You almost laugh. Mary Ann is a cow, a fat cow. She would love to see anyone again, even someone ugly like you.

But you answer back, your anger under control, "No thank you, Mother." Then you add the old clincher, "I have a big assignment in English to finish tonight, you know."

She nods, disappointment heavy on her face. "All right . . ." But she hesitates a moment, then adds in a tentative voice, "I just thought it might be . . . oh, natural for a seventeen-year-old boy to be interested in seeing a teenage girl."

You almost laugh at the irony. You are very interested in seeing women—small, attractive, young women. "Have a good time, Mother."

She nods. "Oh, don't forget your medicine."

"I won't, Mother."

She waves goodbye and reluctantly shuts the door. Actually it's ironic she is so concerned about your welfare, now. For years, when you were little and she had all the boyfriends, she denied your existence. She would bring them home, the men, eventually taking them to her room; and you would watch from the shadows of the hall through the open door, repelled but fascinated by the laughing, giggling, sight and sound of their sweaty coupling. So many of them, so much love for strangers, so little for you. Then the steady stream of men slowed down as your mother grew fatter, aged; and she began to turn to you for attention.

And eventually you responded, letting her closer, except you never let her know about your real life: The creatures in the fog, the Lady's voice in your head, the importance of the numbers, your night walks, and so on.

No, you knew better. Those were all your little secrets, and you were sharing them with no one.

You have no intention of taking the terrible medicine from the talking doctor either. If you do, you won't be able to hear the Lady's voice; and of course, you must know each day's number.

For an hour or so, you listen to The Cure tape; then you fluff-up two extra pillows that have been hidden under your bed, and you stuff them beneath your bedcovers. Finally, you slip out the bedroom window into another misty night.

Carefully, you move down the alley near the 7-Eleven until you reach the Dumpster that still hasn't been emptied. You edge back in the narrow space, feeling the brick wall.

Lady, you think, concentrating.

The shadows deepen, like yesterday. Then:

Hello, Robert. You have come back.

Yes, I need the cloak, again.

For a long while nothing happens, and you are afraid that you may have overstepped a boundary. You shudder. Maybe the Lady is angry.

But eventually she speaks again in your head. *All right, but you must be very careful and return it before daylight chases the shadows away.*

I understand.

You feel there is more, some kind of admonition or warning if you do not come back before daylight; but you are too excited to ask, for again you sense something in the shadows, something blacker than night.

Turn around.

You feel the touch of the cloak draped over your shoulders.

Of course it is better than the darkest, starless night, better than the thickest fog. For with the cloak of shadows you are completely invisible. You can roam anywhere at night and see everything with complete impunity.

You drift across the playground, pause and watch a couple embracing on one of the park benches, the man clutching at the woman's breast; and for a moment your mind drifts back, you are watching your mother, again.

Abruptly, the young man stands, and leads the woman away, back around behind the restrooms. For a moment or two you debate whether you want to follow. But no. Tonight, you have something much better, more exciting planned than watching these two.

Yes, indeed!

You walk down Jefferson Street boldly, right in the middle of the black section, passing a group of boys, another couple, and a drunk and his dog staggering out from Yo Mama's, the bar on the corner near Addison. You almost giggle to yourself, as the mutt follows you a step or two, sniffing the air near your leg; then it offers a tentative growl.

"C'mon, Mr. Nixon," the drunk says, his words slurred. "Wha's the matta wif ya?" He stops and stares down at the dumb animal, which is still looking in your direction and whining. "Ya actin' lak ya seen a ghost, boy. C'mon, now. We late foh suppah."

———————

You climb over the white picket fence and go around back of the one-story frame residence on the corner of Jefferson and Lamont.

Only once before, on a very foggy night, have you worked up the nerve to prowl this yard, because it is so well lit by the streetlights and the backyard so visible from passersby on either street. You walk cautiously up to the back of the house and listen carefully at the frosted window of what you know to be the bathroom.

Water splattering.

Someone is in the shower.

You pull the garbage can quietly in place and climb up on it. The top window, which is frosted too, is cracked about two inches. But stretching up on your tiptoes on the can you are able to peer down inside.

Oh, what luck!

It is her.

The girl.

Kris!

Your thoughts drift back in time.

The number that day had been five, when you first saw her in your fifth period Trig class at school. She had moved here from overseas in January—the fifth month of school—her father in the Air Force. From that first glimpse you were smitten. Kris was a black pixie, no taller than you. And her unusual eyes, almond shaped and glittering like emeralds.

But you have never been able to even speak to her, because Henry Johnson, the school's star basketball player, is always with her outside of class. Although once you thought she looked your way and smiled at you.

He is six foot two.

They look ridiculous together.

As you peer down into the tiny bathroom, Kris is just stepping out of the shower, and her nakedness takes your breath away. Your heart thumps in your chest, your mouth drier than a cotton swab.

She is exquisite, only the barest hint of curves contouring her boyish shape, tiny breasts but the aureoles dark, almost purple against her coffee-colored skin, the nipples pronounced in the cool air as she rubs them dry. Your gaze moves slowly down to the dark triangle, almost velvet-like in texture. You watch for another few minutes as she slips on a nightgown and bathrobe. Then she turns, smiles almost knowingly, and peers directly at the slightly opened window with her sparkling eyes.

You duck down out of sight, holding your breath, until you realize it is too dark out here for her to have seen you. When you ease back up and peek back through the slot, she is gone. You blink twice, hoping the number two will draw her back to the bathroom for some forgotten thing.

But she doesn't return, today's number not strong enough.

After another minute of watching, you finally give up and climb down, moving the garbage can back to its original location.

Then you retrace your steps back to the alley by the 7-Eleven, back to the wall, returning the cloak of shadows.

TODAY THE NUMBER IS ONE.

It is very late, the moon shining brightly, illuminating everything; but you are drawn back to the house on Jefferson and Lamont, the cloak of shadows with its cowl shielding your presence even in this almost daylight brilliance. You vault the picket fence easily and circle the house quietly. It is dark, everyone apparently in bed. You stop at her bedroom and suck in a breath, trying to calm your racing heart.

The window is open, the blind up halfway.

You blink, thinking you must be dreaming. It's like an invitation.

Then, holding your breath, you peer in, and freeze, for in the moonlight you can see Kris clearly. She is lying on her side on her bed, staring directly at you. You blink.

No. Her eyes are squeezed shut. It was only your imagination.

You reach up and test the window. It slides up easily and quietly. With a slight effort you pull yourself up and over the sill, dropping to the floor in her room. Crouched, you watch for any movement. But she remains asleep, a kind of coy smile on her face. She must be dreaming. You rise. Then, on tiptoes, you move noiselessly to her side.

Her chest rises and falls so gently, her face so serene.

Suddenly, she stirs, moaning, lifting up her arms.

She has heard you!

An icicle of dread stabs into your chest; you hold your breath, and will your heart to stop beating. One, one, one.

No, she has not heard you.

On her side now, Kris smiles—something in her dream?

You kneel, only a foot or so away from the sleeping pixie; and you gaze into her face, the features so elegantly crafted. Your chest is about to burst.

On impulse you try to lean down and kiss her lips.

But you have forgotten the cloak, its cowl preventing any contact.

Frowning with frustration, you stand up, glance about, and listen to the house creaking in the night, the moonlight still streaming through the window and spotlighting Kris's loveliness.

You debate with yourself for a moment, questioning the wisdom of shedding the cloak. Should I?

You wait, hoping the Lady of the Numbers will advise you. But there is nothing but the creaking sounds of the house.

Finally, you decide, shedding the cloak, letting it slide to the floor at your feet. Then you just stand there a moment, watching her breathe rhythmically. So lovely, so beautiful. Quietly, you slip from the rest of your clothes, letting them slide to your feet into the pile of blackness on the floor.

It is time we are one, Kris.

You take one step forward and trip over the cloak and pile of clothes, falling and reaching out toward the nightstand to catch yourself. But you only slam to the floor, knocking over the nightstand with a loud shattering of glass.

You leap back to your feet, glancing nervously at the closed bedroom door.

Somewhere nearby in the house, a masculine voice shouts, "Kris, baby, what is it? Are you all right?"

She is awake now, sitting up, with the bed sheets pulled up around her, looking surprisingly calm, a strange mix of exasperation and anger on her face.

Confused, but operating with animal instinct, you scurry to the window and jump through, running as your feet hit the ground. Vision tunnels, panic clutching at your thudding heart, but you keep moving. Run, run, run . . . one, one, one, repeats like words from a song in your head.

The cool air suddenly reminds you that you are completely naked, vulnerable out here in the bright moonlight. Oh, no. You have forgotten the cloak, left it behind in Kris's room. The wonderful cloak of shadows. But you cannot go back now; so you continue running across the playground, two black men watching awestruck as you fly by—a lopsided, nude sprinter.

Then, miraculously, you find yourself on Franklin Avenue, some of the lights off now, a few businesses closed; and, luck still holding, you pass no one very close, until you reach the 7-Eleven.

As you thunder by the store entrance you almost knock over a guy coming out with a bag, who shouts at you angrily, "Hey, what the fuck's the matter with you, kid?"

You dart up the alley.

Sirens whine nearby, the shrill sound rasping at your nerve ends, for you know the police are coming for you; and they will cage you like a mad dog.

You must get away, you think, gasping for breath in the dark alley, which is thankfully shielded from the moonlight.

You scamper to the dead end, and squeeze in behind the Dumpster.

Lady, oh, Lady—?

But there is no answer, only a dirty, smelly wall in the shadows. *Oh, please, please, help me.*

Still, no movement in the shadows, no answer.

You squint, hold back the tears. Maybe there is no Lady, no numbers, no Land of Shadows.

Could that be?

The sirens whine shrilly, but they are off in the distance now, and seem to be moving away from you and the alley.

Could the talking doctor be right? you ask yourself.

Maybe you are nothing more than a weird little man, sitting naked in an alley, all alone. No numbers, no Lady, nothing.

A footstep crunches nearby.

You bite your lip, steel yourself, and peek around the Dumpster; then you gasp aloud.

There, just beyond the light, hovering in the air, are two orbs, glittering like green fire in the dim alley.

A fog creature!

"No," you whisper hoarsely, trying to convince yourself, "it's a clear night. No fog, no fog creature."

Your logical denial quickly disappears from consciousness, like a dream the next morning, and you begin to panic as the green ovals slowly move closer, closer . . . stopping only a few feet away from the Dumpster.

You begin to hyperventilate.

A giggle.

And a face appears in the alley dimness, like an apparition, but a familiar face.

It is Kris!

She is smiling and giggling at you.

Still confused, you blurt out a question, "What—?"

The question breaks off, as more of her body becomes visible.

And it eventually dawns on you, the whole thing clear.

She is slipping the cloak from her shoulders—the special cloak of shadows. She had been wearing it, the cowl shielding her face, only her beautiful green eyes visible as she followed you here and down the alley.

Puzzled, you whisper, "I don't understand, Kris?"

She slips from the rest of the cloak, and only then do you realize that she, too, is completely nude. She steps forward, her arms beckoning, her eyes burning expectantly, and she replies, "Today, the number is one."

You take her hand and slip back behind the Dumpster, facing the brick wall. The shadows deepen, part slightly, and now you see the Lady of the Numbers—tiny, elegant, and so pale, as if carved from alabaster. *Robert . . . and Kris. You are ready to come to me? No, not yet. You must shed your otherness.* And her pale hand reaches out from the shadowed wall, something glittering in the dimness.

A straight razor. *Drain the otherness, Robert.*

You understand, taking the shiny instrument in your free hand. With a frightened expression on her face, Kris tries to jerk away; but you tighten the grip on her hand, smile calmly, and tug her closer . . .

As you grow colder the otherness runs from your hands joining the crimson pool at Kris's feet.

Then the Lady speaks again, but her voice is only a gentle whisper. *Come, my children.* Weakly clutching Kris's hand, you stumble forward into the icy Land of Shadows, into the Lady's arms.

You, Kris, and the Lady are now one.

Head Music

LON PRATER

"Head Music" was one of the very first submissions we read for this volume. Its cover letter mentioned Lon Prater had written it while serving on a Naval vessel. We liked the story very much, but because of our patriotism, we couldn't be sure if our approval stemmed from the quality of the writing, or because its author was out there protecting us. However, we eventually came to realize our judgment had not been clouded; this story is weird and wonderful.

At 1:02 A.M., Diego snapped awake. The haunting, tuneless music was in his head again. Mournful tones rose and fell, reverberating between his temples. Throughout his eighteen years he had heard it: an occasional faint and inviting whisper that tugged at his innards. Now the deep, echoing hornsong was louder, more insistent; it had control of his body.

Barechested and shoeless, he burst through the flaking screen door. The cool autumn night welcomed him with a clammy marsh-salt embrace.

A squeal and a slam: the flimsy wood frame swung shut behind him. The keys to his father's work truck jangled in one hand.

On the horizon, a prowler moon crouched fat and yellow behind a low fence of backlit clouds. His naked back pressed against the chilled vinyl seat. Diego shivered. He was glad that he slept in sweatpants.

His bare feet, wet with dew and grass clippings, pumped the gas pedal and pressed in the clutch. He watched—calmly, serenely—as his right hand twisted the key. The stubborn engine roared in protest.

The truck lurched onto the empty road, headlights darkened. Diego was completely out of control: a passenger within the truck as well as within his own body.

The rusty old heap hurtled down the empty blacktop, landscaping tools clattering madly in the bed. Diego was content. He rode the ebb and swell of a forlorn internal music; he was not afraid.

———————

The beach was part of a state park and nature preserve. Red and white signs threatened after-hours trespassers with fines and jail time. The penalties were even steeper for those foolish enough to bring animals, glass, or vehicles out onto the sand.

The music changed when the renegade truck bounced over the benighted dunes. The plaintive wailing receded;

a cacophony of lesser tones gained in strength. He realized with a start that his body was his own again.

Diego squinted through the dirty windshield. A curtain of dense gray clouds blocked most of the moon's reflected light. This far from town the stars shone with rare brilliance. Their light was mirrored in the phosphorescent foam and sparkle of the cresting waves. Wet sand glimmered at the water's edge.

A shadowed hump lay in the blackness, just yards from the lapping waves. Leaning closer, Diego flipped on the headlights.

The head music erupted into skull-splitting shrieks. His hand shot out automatically, killing the lights. It stifled the blood-curdling screeches as well—but it was too late. He had already glimpsed that unearthly mass hulking on the beach.

Diego wiped the sudden cold sweat from his face and took several calming breaths. Steeling himself, he opened the door and stepped trembling onto the sand.

He shivered. The night had grown mute and windless. Even the tuneless music had faded to a soft mewling; his brain was full of newborn kittens.

Sand and bits of dune grass scrunched beneath him as he approached the creature. It had the length and girth of a small killer whale, but that was where the resemblance ended.

Diego walked around it, unable to fathom what he was seeing. It had slick, warty gray-green skin, flecked all over with lambent orange jewel-like scales. There were no eyes to speak of. Either end of its tube-like body presented a fleshy pucker surrounded by a forest of supple whips and barbed tendrils. Near the center of its girth there were three great vein-lined fans pressed close against its body. Diego suspected a fourth lay unseen beneath it.

The creature stank of window cleaner.

Whatever it was, it had called him here to this beach with its hornsong. The same sounds he had heard over the years, only stronger.

A lonely cry sang inside him. He was engulfed in waterlogged sadness; it drowned out the soft whining chorus completely, but only for a moment. He felt a strange kinship with this thing, one that he could not explain.

Ancient intuition clawed its way into his awareness. The creature—no, she—was stranded, beached here in the alien air. Unable to return to the murky depths, she knew she was dying.

Tears scorched his eyes. He rushed her, vainly throwing his weight into an attempt to roll the immense cylinder of her body back into the sea.

As reward, Diego's bare chest, arms, and back were scored with tiny nicks from the scattered orange scales. His torso was smeared with a gritty, viscous film that made the open cuts swell and burn like bee stings. He cried out in frustration, looking around for a way to save this bizarre and wondrous creature.

His eyes came to rest on the abandoned truck. He strode toward it, aware of but ignoring the piteous lament in his head. A search of the truck revealed a lawnmower and gas can, hand tools and pruning shears, shovels and rakes, a wheelbarrow and some clear bags—but nothing that would help him return this behemoth safely to the sea.

Despair filled him like freshly poured concrete. He returned to her side. The inky waves were almost washing up against one puckered end.

The kitten-like mewling started up again in earnest. He put a hand on her, careful not to let the sharp orange speckles cut him. On some primitive level he felt the squirming fluted mass of life within her.

It could have been her brains as easily as it was her young. It didn't matter to Diego; he *knew* that they needed to come out of her.

———————

He gulped, approaching her ocean-side sphincter again. The dank smell of salt and rotting seaweed mixed with her ammonia odor, an unsettling combination. He carefully pushed the waving tendrils away from the opening. This would not be easy.

Diego plunged his arm into the unearthly creature, straining to keep down his gorge. His heart beat fast and loud in his ears. Something skittered across his foot and he jumped: a tiny crab.

His arm was buried to the shoulder. The keening in his head was louder, more frantic. He grasped the end of a slippery fat hose and pulled. It came out with a slurping noise and a geyser of foul liquid.

He dropped the greasy pus-thing and vomited all over it. It writhed there as if celebrating the glorious emptying of Diego's stomach. Then, like a slow but enormous blond worm, it inched its way into the waves.

The mother-thing's song was all but gone now; the chaotic internal cries of her young continued to gnaw desperately at him.

He jabbed an arm into her again, feeling nothing but the pain of his burning cuts and the squish of her organs. He removed his arm and went to the opposite end. This time it was easier. Diego eased two of the worm-things from the orifice, each over six feet long. He deposited them gingerly into the lapping water.

They were motionless. Diego could suddenly smell their corruption, even over the ammonia and beach scents. *Stillborn. As were the others rotting within the duneside womb.*

He had saved one of the disgusting things. Wasn't that enough? The wailing chorus of those still in the seaside womb begged for release. One day, they could grow into creatures as beautiful and alien as the one dying here before him. But not if he left them inside her to die.

He went to the back of the truck and returned with the pruning shears. Sticking the bottom blade into the sphincter at the water's edge, he crossed himself, preparing for what he had to do.

Diego squeezed the rubber coated handles together with all his might. The blades weren't as sharp as he had hoped. They did not so much cut as chew slits into her, widening the puckered hole. She did not bleed, at least not so he could tell it, but the ammonia smell nearly made him pass out. What kept him awake was the failing tones of her pain—her fear—echoing within his head.

He finished carving a second slit out of the rough, rubbery flesh. He was sure that he would be able to do what was required. Nonetheless, he was thankful that his stomach was already empty. Diego took one last look around.

The moon had escaped from the clouds, leaning closer now to cast a pallid eye on the boy and the primeval sea thing on the beach. His father's truck stood lonely watch from atop the dunes.

Diego pulled off his sweatpants and boxer shorts, leaving them in a heap on the sand. He grunted, drawing in one last breath before he burrowed naked and unflinching into the womb of the beast.

Coarse slimy tissue like pus-soaked leprous scabs pressed all around him. He was waist deep in her, and clawing his way closer to the maggoty nest of her tender young. The vapors were rank, infectious. Every one of the cuts on his body screamed as they were filled with her vile inner fluids. Diego gagged on bile, worming himself farther into her.

He could feel the wind kick up, tickling his feet and ankles. Every other part of him was embalmed in the gelatinous tract to her inner organs.

Diego heard her wordless voice again, softer but richer, a soft ululating lullaby. From within her the music embraced him, made him a part of her. She sang to him of the deep black ocean floor, of submarine cityscapes chiseled from stone and shell: wonders never touched by the sun's warmth. He rode harpoon-fast currents through majestic salt-water caverns. He gazed upon a great and terrible species beyond man's imagination. She crooned to him of an age long past—and yet to come; those who had once reigned would awaken. They would sweep the planet clean of humanity, sloughing man's frail advances from its face like dead skin.

His stinging hands dug into a torn membrane, ripping it farther. Diego reached into the howling coils of her knotted young, dragging them back with him through her awful stickiness in one armful. He collapsed to the sand. The writhing blond creatures squirmed free of each other, and of him, before crawling blindly into the waves.

Finally, the last one slipped beneath the surface, leaving Diego with only the moon and the gorgeous stinking carcass for company. He felt grief wash over him even as he saw the tide drawing his pants and his vomit out to sea.

Scientists would come in the morning, and reporters. They'd take their pictures and measurements, scratching their chins in wonder and speaking earnestly of evolution and the coelacanth. They would cut her up in their laboratories, trying to unravel the secret of her genes. In time, someone would realize the horrible truth; they would warn the world of man's short leash.

Diego rose, his nude body sticky with foul juices and pockmarked by swollen cuts. He dug in his toes, resolutely kicking wet sand across the beach. Not if he could help it.

He made one last trip to his father's truck, rummaging in the cab first before grabbing the metal can from the bed.

With remorse like he had never felt before, Diego splattered gasoline all over the she-carcass and her rotting stillborn young. He stood there feeling the loss of the music for a long time before he set fire to a wad of napkins and papers. Mouthing a silent and unintelligible prayer, he threw the flaming papers upon her.

She went up in a quick blue whoosh that in other cases might have made Diego jump. Instead, he danced a frenzied ring around her until he collapsed, dazed and giddy from the fumes. He was naked to the moon and sand and wind. Diego stared into the stars, making dirge noises not sounded upon the earth in millennia.

———————

The pyre burned itself out about an hour before dawn. Diego sat watching the last smoking embers. She had no bones; the flame left nothing behind but a sprinkling of orange scales. He poked at the blackened sand with the shovel before turning the scorched sand over and over upon itself, hiding even this evidence from the advancing waves.

He was sweating, coated with sand and sticky filth. When Diego was certain that no man would be able to find out about her kind or their eventual return, he swam as far and as deep into the frigid black sea as he could.

The last thing he heard was the music of an underwater orchestra. It reminded him of home.

Around It Still the Sumac Grows

TOM PICCIRILLI

A recurring theme in American popular culture is the absolute, living hell that four years of high school can often be. In the next story, Colorado writer Tom Piccirilli employs his trademark lean prose to take the reader on a journey to a time and place which may seem frighteningly familiar to many of you . . . and then, maybe not.

Somehow, you never made peace with ordinary, familiar dread.

The many everyday weaknesses continue to prod at your conscience. How you can't hit a curve ball and flubbed every lay up shot. How you can't hammer a nail in straight or spackle a hole properly. Your father's toolbox is a well of shame and remorse. You're nearly forty and have never figured out how to change a tire.

There are things you can't let slide anymore. Life is a desperate undertaking now, and it doesn't allow for naiveté once you've turned twelve. After that you're just inept and absurd.

It's the working of the world. You can't sit back and enjoy the day while there are kids nearby. Not in the park, and definitely not on school grounds. This is the modern age. Security guards buck up and give you the killer glare as if daring you to make a play for one of the children. Jesus, you're not doing anything except sitting here. Everybody wants an easy excuse for murder. You can imagine them hauling one of the teenage girls off the bus and waving her at you like bait. Here, you want to try for it? Come on, come get some candy. With the safety off, hands at their gun belts.

The lunacy of ninth grade never leaves. Overwhelming delight, guilt, duty, the bitter embrace of adulthood. It's set the tone for the rest of your life, and you judge everything based on what you knew at that time. No cars have the same muscle or style as a '79 Mustang. No laughter as ugly as that of Mr. Vulatore, sophomore biology. No dog as friendly or smart as Hercules, who followed you to the bus stop every morning until your father backed over him. Twice. No smile as perfect as Linda Abutti's, with her eyes crinkling at the corners, the grin igniting every nerve ending in your pudgy, pale, underdeveloped flesh.

Maybe you've committed a crime by surviving this long, and that's why you feel the need to return to the scene over and over. Or perhaps the crime has been perpetuated against you, and it's grown too hazy to understand anymore. Did somebody tug on your tinkle in the boys' shower room? Did you get your nose shoved down into dog shit at recess? One tiny torture is as good as another.

Anyway, you're here, and you've got to get back in, take a look around.

You are fairly certain that you left your soul in the utilities closet of seventh period study hall.

Busloads of kids are arriving, and the noise is much louder than you remember. Near deafening, ear-splitting. Christ, you drop your forehead to the steering wheel and hug your arms over your ears. So much talking, the blaring of ghastly music, and boys skateboarding in the lot, grinding down the curbs and sidewalks. Sparks splash and skitter. One bad oil leak under any of the cars and the whole lot will go up in an inferno. The skaters fall and tumble with a stuntman's coordination, boards scudding wildly and spinning on until they weakly bump into a tire.

Girls are screaming, yelling about homework, make-up, cheerleading. The guys answer with their own love calls, screeches and caterwauls. It gets your pulse ticking harshly in your neck, all this action. You've lived in a lonely room for too long, reading books you can't remember.

Kids are smoking, necking, eating the last remnants of their breakfasts, and piercing each other with freshly sharpened pencils. You didn't think things would change so much, but maybe it's just you who's forgotten. You aren't old but you feel old. No, you are old. A glance in the rearview mirror confirms your fears. Look at all that pink scalp showing through. The crows feet wrinkles and channels writhing across your face.

So, it's like that. You used to keep count of your dead former classmates until the number broke fifty, then you quit. Drug deals gone bad, a murdered gas station attendant, two drownings, with so many others going to AIDS and cancer. Don't people live to the average age of 72 anymore? You look down at your wrist and see your blood still hammering, and you wonder when it's going to quit and whether you'll have any warning at all. What do you do with the last fifteen seconds of your life?

Whenever you missed the bus your mother would drop you off right out front, give you a kiss that got the tough kids rolling. You'd walk away in shame with the fuckers shoving at your back, knocking your books away. Kid games that skewered. And you'd turn to watch your mother's car drive off, abandoning you to the nexus of dismay and insanity. The snotty laughter.

Even your hatred is cliché. You, like everybody, can blame the smallest drama for your inability to cope. A failed math test and you can't form a solid relationship with a woman. A missed foul shot and you've never earned over twenty-one grand a year. A redhead turns you down for a prom date and for the rest of your life you whine about your incapacity to look a luscious lady in the eye without blushing.

No strangers are allowed on school property, but you're no stranger. You ease up to the security booth—they've actually got the black and white semaphore arm now that comes down in front of your car hood. The symbolism can't be overlooked. This is a toll booth, and you've got to pay just as heavy a price to get back in as you paid to get out in the first place.

The security guard is short and hairy, with the lines of a perpetual scowl seared into his features. It takes a few seconds but you finally recognize him: Vinny D'Angelis.

A year or two older than you, he used to steal your lunch box and liked to smear your glasses with his plump greasy thumbs. You heard he got one of his professors pregnant while he was failing at the community college. The kind of thing that should've been a disgrace but must've just made him feel proud when he had a beer with the boys. The professor left in the midst of a media blitz, had the kid, and moved back in with her parents. Sometimes your life moved backwards like you were on a conveyor belt.

The dead are always nearby, ready to dive. Teachers move toward the front doors like a SWAT team: edgy, wary, and checking every angle for danger, but still somehow in control. They look up to see what might be falling down on them from the sky. Somebody's throwing red viscera against the clouds.

You recognize at least three gray countenances. Without quite realizing it, you begin to tug at the front of your receding hair, which started turning silver a couple of years back. At first it was a touch distinguishing, but now it scares the shit out of you. The thatch keeps growing and the damn thing just won't stop.

D'Angelis glowers. His sneer is twenty years older but no more refined than it was the last time you saw it. A part of you very much wants to surge through his little toll gate and smash his face through the Plexiglas window, but you know he thinks exactly the same thing of you. Fate would almost be satisfied with some kind of crazed animal struggle between the two of you, but there's something else waiting inside. You've got to get in, and it has to be now.

They've given D'Angelis a badge that he's kept polished like he was a real cop. He probably practices ninja rolls in there, diving in and out of his little booth when no one's watching. You can tell by his eyes that he's never seen his own kid and is terrified of the day when his child will come find him.

He knows you, of course. He's been waiting for you, and everyone else like you, to return, and prove to him that you've never become any better than him and everybody like him. The circle was never very large to begin with and it only becomes smaller.

You have no plan, but suddenly a lie is on your lips. You've got to get back to your soul. "I'm here for the reunion committee."

Whoever's really on the council should be planning the event and tracking down former classmates, but they aren't. The ten year never happened and the twenty won't either. Nobody cared to begin with. Nobody's left. You see each other on street corners all the time, shielding your eyes and pretending not to recognize one another.

"What reunion?"

"'83."

"Who's the advisor?"

You don't have any idea, but you think about the teacher least likely to ever participate in that sort of thing. He was ancient back then but those are the ones that never die. They just petrify in their seats until they're hard as stone, and then they're used for bricks to build another hallway.

"Mr. Samuelson."

"Room 214."

"Thanks."

You drive on and park in field two, which was always off limits to students. A sixteen year old girl—luscious, mystical, with a whirlwind of raven's hair swirling in the breeze—knocks you aside like you're the transparent middle-aged creature that you are. You're an affront to her existence and she understands this implicitly.

A surge of impotent anger fires through you and the tension momentarily makes you feel strong and effective. It lasts for perhaps four steps. You're on her heels, the hair snapping into your face like a bullwhip. You almost welcome its painful touch, hoping it will leave scars.

She wheels and spits, "The fuck are you? The fuck are you doing? You fuckin' chasing me?"

"No."

"Good."

"Sure."

She wears her derision like a tiara. Another man would've broken her will to him. Or made a friend. Or acted paternal and offered sage advice. She walks to the front doors and you notice that, alongside the ivy growing against the harsh brick face, there's poison sumac in the same place it's always been.

The school is venomous. You used to try to stay away from the shrubs, but somehow you still wound up with their yellowish plant oil streaked along the tops of your forearms. You recall being covered with rashes and having your mother swathe you with ineffective, over-the-counter hydrocortisone creams. The redness and swelling would soon be followed by blisters and severe itching. Within a few days the blisters became crusted and scaly. The girls would grimace and cut a wide path. Even the lunch ladies would cringe.

The mauled and mutilated live in the walls. At least six of your classmates vanished during your high school years. Some claimed the families moved away, but you can feel those others moving alongside you now, alive but somewhere else.

They never really got away from the school, and yet in some fashion they did. They never turned in their last homework assignments, never did their final laps around the gym. In a way, they graduated with bizarre honors.

The fat kid with the kettle drum disappeared on stage during the Christmas concert. One minute he's banging along to Brahms' "Wiegenlied," and the next his wide ass just isn't there anymore. You were playing second trumpet, staring out of the corner of your eye when you watched him go. Nobody else seemed to notice. Later, they said he died of leukemia. Died of Hodgkin's. Told everybody he got brain damage from the crash out on Route 287, where Bobby Hale flipped his van and hit a tree. Four others dead, one paralyzed, and two walked away with bruises and plenty of psychological damage. One survivor tried suicide six months later claiming rats lived in her belly.

Maybe they were right. But the skin of that drum just couldn't take the goddamn pounding anymore.

So now you're walking past the science labs where you cut open worms, frogs, a piglet, a cow's eye, and the starving Portuguese orphans who came on the black truck that backed right up to the gym doors. Hustled them out, while the lunch ladies and substitute teachers squawked into megaphones, "Não toque nas paredes limpas. Nós estaremos alimentando-lhe muito peixe logo."

Don't touch the clean walls. We will be feeding you much fish shortly.

You see all the brown faces with bad teeth breaking into hideous grins.

"A festa de St. Peter começará dentro da hora. Coloque

nas tabelas e tenha uma sesta até que esteja hora de comer."

The Feast of St. Peter will begin within the hour. Lay down on the tables and have a nap until it is time to eat.

You're in front of your old locker, wondering if the combination will still work. If the pages you cut from newspapers and magazines are still taped up inside. You touch the cold metal and a sob breaks inside your chest.

"You all right?" someone asks.

Christ, you nearly leap through the top of your own skull. You turn and stare. She could be any of the girls who refused to go out with you back then when it mattered most. She smiles warmly and it sends an electrical thrill knifing through your guts. No more than fifteen, has a studious appearance to her—glasses, ponytail, a skirt and tie as if she was at private school, which she's not. It throws you for a second. She gives a melancholy grin and asks, "You lost?"

"Sorry. This your locker?"

"Yeah."

"Used to be mine about twenty years back. I was reminiscing a little."

"About a locker?"

"More or less."

"Okay," she acquiesces, still waiting. You want to ask her if a fat kid with a kettle drum ever wanders around in the middle of the day. If the eviscerated Portuguese orphans crawl down the halls holding the flaps of their stomachs together with dirty hands crying, "Eu acredito que se encontraram me. Não há muitos peixes aqui."

I believe they have lied to me. There is not much fish here.

She's got poison sumac rashes around her knuckles

and you almost get homesick looking at them. Perhaps you'll meet again another two decades from now, both of you roaming about the school, staring at this same locker while some child stares up into mad, sentimental faces.

"I'm gonna be late for class."

"Oh. Excuse me," you say, flitting aside.

"Thanks a lot."

There's an extra glint in her eye as if she's trying to decide whether to do something or not. She's on the edge but can't quite make up her mind. Maybe bring you up for show and tell. Or give you the name of a good therapist. Or slam you out of your socks with a harrowing lie. Scream rape. Or offer herself up for a cockeyed kick, a power trip, something disgusting to tell her girlfriends about later, get everybody laughing—his belly was so big and white as a sheet. His dick was out and maybe four inches long when I finally got it up, and that took forever. I had to get on top or he would've crushed me, and he came in about ten strokes. He cried afterwards. He wanted to marry me. I locked myself in the bathroom and threw up twice.

She opens the locker and you see that the pages and pictures you taped up are still there, yellowed and grimy. You know they're yours but you can't recognize them any longer. Newspaper clippings, magazine art, headlines. You try to read the words but she grabs a book and shuts the door again. She takes a breath and her ripening breasts thrust forward. You jump back a step as if she's just snapped open a switchblade.

"Hey," she says, "this might sound funny, but—"

"I've got to get going."

"Yeah, well, I was just wondering if—"

You shrink away, wheel about and damn near start scampering off. You've never scampered before and it's sort of fun. You've never even said the word scamper before and now you can't stop. She follows for a few steps, trying to grab you by the elbow. You shirk away before she can touch you.

"Stop," you tell her. "Scamper, scamper." It's a sound you can't get out of your head, you fuckin' nut. "Scamper."

"But—"

"I wouldn't cry afterwards."

"Hey, listen, you're—"

You turn a corner, rushing past kids walking in groups, in pairs, everyone with somebody. "I wouldn't want to marry you!"

A skinny boy arched like a vulture gets in your way and you plow straight into him. He's probably a hundred twenty pounds in his white suede sneakers and he lifts off as if from a launching pad. His long hair flails around his ears, little peach fuzz chin curling in flight. He's got some serious elevation, goes up and flies backwards at least ten feet before he hits the wall outside the cafeteria hard. The doors rock open. You can clearly hear his arm snap in two. He glares at the protruding bone and then glances at you, then back to the jagged jutting ulna and then back to you. The pain won't hit him for another minute. A fat kid with a kettle drum says, "Holy shit, man."

You run.

What room is it? What was the number? The utilities closet of seventh period study hall. 306? 308? You lunge into 306 and see shadows writhing in the corner—two teachers screwing around, or two students making out, somebody giving head to the dead, or the smelly orphans still slinking around trying to get their internal organs back.

Eu estarei escrevendo ao congressista local imediatamente. A remoção de meus intestines é certamente uma ação immoral e ilegal. Eu procurarei os danos.

I will be writing to the local congressman immediately. The removal of my intestines is surely an immoral and illegal action. I shall seek damages.

There are shouts and the angry clamor of footsteps. They're probably carrying torches, they've got you surrounded. There will be tear gas soon. Those high-tech laser beam gunsights scrawling over your chest. You slip into the empty classroom next door.

Oh yes.

Here it is, this is it. You give a satisfied grunt and cut loose with your father's chortle.

See. Your tortured soul has been in the corner all this time, curled in the agony of common trauma. It glances up as you enter, pale and shaky. It lets out a pained bleat as you reach down. Tears well and dribble. It jitters happily and struggles forward to meet you. You touch and the cool swims up through your spine.

The security guard puts his .45 to your temple, and you give him a slow and knowing grin, a hip wink that says it all. Of course, it's D'Angelis. Your face is reflected in his shining badge and you can hardly believe you're the same person you were twenty minutes ago, twenty years ago. There was a time you would've begged him, or any other maniac, to pull the trigger and get it over with in one quick solution. But already that existence is drifting away. You're here to stay.

He nods and holsters the pistol, and both of you walk down the hall eyeing all the little girls.

Your soul is restless and fidgety with strange and ugly needs. You touch the poison on your way out the front door and it warms you.

Things are getting better already.

Annabell

L. LYNN YOUNG

Extremely well written fiction has the ability to be complex while appearing to be quite simple. When we read "Annabell," we were first impressed by its quiet, but unsettling narrative style. L. Lynn Young has created a story which continues to haunt us with its elemental sadness.

"A strange looking duckling with gray feathers that should have been yellow gazed at a worried mother."

The Ugly Duckling, Hans Christian Andersen

Mommy, *may I go now?*

I look at my youngest child, that last of four daughters. The one whose hair is fine and limp, whose nose is misshapen, whose mouth crooks to the right. Whose ears protrude comically. She, the one I named Annabell, is a difficult child, an unfortunate born into an even more unfortunate world. God forgive me, but I sometimes feel that it would've been best had she never been born at all.

She is tiny, Annabell. Three years old, but you'd never know it. My second daughter, Christine, who is nine-going-on-ten, refers to her as "Thumbelina." Christine is pretty, as is Margaret, my first, and Madison, my third. They know Annabell is real; they made her real.

We are often stopped when we're all out in public together. We are accosted, really. My husband and I must endure the flaming compliments of strangers who interrupt us as we shop, appreciate museums, play in the park. It's as if we were a walking freak show.

You see, my husband is also pretty. We are clones, a living, breathing representation of some Hitleresque ideal, an anomaly. People we do not know, whom we do not want to know, feel comfortable, as if it is their right to stroke the silken curls of my children and bore their beady eyes deep like rogue geneticists digging for the secrets of our blessed DNA. They browse, those strangers, and they take, as if by touching and breathing in our very auras, they too may become just as lovely.

"Three daughters, huh?" they always say, even though Annabell is hiding in plain sight, clutching my leg. And they shake their heads in disbelief as if we were the only family in all of human history to have produced such a thing. The men sometimes clap my husband on his shoulder and utter variations of, "Boy, have you got trouble," and my stomach tightens against their leering implications, the imagined accusations that exist only in my own consciousness.

"Four. We have four daughters," I always add as I pry

Annabell from my leg and push her forward for their inspection, the end result of my whole life.

She is met with bewildered looks, a scratching of heads, nervous smiles. They leave in a hurry, but not before giving another pat to my husband's drooping shoulder, a gentle, sympathetic pat.

Annabell is invisible. She is my favorite.

Mommy, may I?

I am so beautiful, I get out of traffic tickets. Doormen waive the admission fee. The guy at the deli sneaks an extra quarter pound of ham to my order. I can drink straight from the bottle and make it look sexy. My neighbor's eight-year-old boy fell in love with me. I stopped giving him so many hugs after I realized that he was starting to cling a bit too tightly, his bony chest pressing a bit too much against my bosom. I can drink from the bottle and deceive everybody. Sometimes being beautiful is sad.

Like when ugly voodoo-eyed girls shunned me because of my long blonde hair. In order to get a similar effect, they had to resort to fantasy, humid bath towels and thick rubber bands squeezing tight across their foreheads. Like when my only friend, K.B., tried to seduce me while we were hunting for crawfish. Like when I was about to catch the biggest one I had ever seen, but K.B. grabbed my arm and spun me to his wet, wormy mouth. I lost the biggest crawfish I had ever seen, then I went home and cut off my hair.

Mommy?

Beauty is not good when One is also submissive. A disciplined tongue locked behind naturally plump, pink lips is a sure sign of conceit. Because One must walk head up, eyes straight ahead, ears closed to the horny catcalls and jealous condemnation, One will surely be pegged as stuck up. Or even worse, a cold-blooded killer.

Stories will be built around and around, tall and lonely like a gigantic tower, and One will not be able to descend to freedom due to the fact that One has chopped her only means of escape into short butchy spikes way before it is fashionable.

No one wants to eat lunch with a killer, even if that killer has been exonerated.

One may have to go through Senior year with a funny walk because when everybody stares and scrutinizes everything One does, One becomes so self-conscious, even the mere act of putting one foot in front of the other is excruciatingly difficult. Senior year may bring back horrible memories, such as how hard eating an ice cream cone can be. But only if One's perverted stepfather is present, especially if said stepfather is indulging in some Mexican comfort instead of a triple scoop, his dangerous eyes following One's tongue, eyes full of silent anticipation. One's ugly mother might turn and stare reproachfully, so it is important not to lick in too provocative a manner. One may realize that it is not possible, so the ice cream will invariably melt under Mother's hot stare and gather in between One's fingers, over One's hand. One must never lap at the mess because that would be pornographic. The only solution is to throw the ice cream cone away.

One will eventually come to the conclusion that all ugly women hate as much as all men want. Ugly women will spit foul words and try to kill One's beauty with their hatred, their evil poisons. They will try to make One disappear.

One will finally snap and stab One's ugly mother in the head, the face. Many, many times.

I know these things because I am One.

Mommy, please?

Yesterday I took Annabell and her sisters to the zoo. This is an extremely rare event because I identify with the animals too much. I always cry in the monkey house.

There was a clown there, walking about and miming to the visitors, occasionally squeezing his asthmatic bagpipes as if it were a loaf of bread. The clown wore a bulbous red nose and black eyes, his pate a wrinkle of plastic with loose, familiar wisps of silver that hung to his tartan shoulders. A Scottish fool. Ugly.

My oldest, Margaret, pointed and screeched to no one in particular, "Look! Annabell's twin!"

So then I slapped her. Hard. I took my hand and struck my sweet Margaret across her perfect face. It was an evil, evil thing to do, I know. I don't believe in corporal punishment as the scars on my legs prevent me from being anything other than lenient. But I left my mark upon her cheek, a vivid reminder, my show of pity. I am a protective mother bear, oh yes. And the world should know.

Margaret, perhaps because she was in shock, did not cry. It was Annabell who cried.

The clown clopped over to us then, flapped his happy rubber shoes, balloons bobbing. The scowl that rolled under his fake forehead could not be disguised, and his charcoaled eyes belied the lipstick grin. He offered a balloon to each of my daughters with silent graciousness, his wrists twirling before each presentation as if he were bestowing upon them life's greatest gift.

Giving my best Avon Lady smile, I thanked the clown and clapped my hands like an idiot. I wanted to show him how nice I am, how adult; how I'm not a cruel, weak-willed, self-absorbed thing-of-a-woman who would ever mean to do her children harm. I never meant to harm anyone. Really, Mr. Clown, it was all an accident.

He just looked into my eyes, and for one long, Louisiana second, the aural assaults and manufactured aromas of bastardized Africa dissipated. Gone were the cotton candy elephants and cheeseburgery lion, the unnatural melange of children, baboons and hyena, and all I could see, hear and smell were memories, as if Mr. Clown's eyes had become twin portals pulling me simultaneously into the past, the future. I saw myself in his eyes, my ego stuffed in a bottle, floating like a fetus and dying of shame. I saw myself two years younger— younger but frighteningly crone-like—my face hideous with ancient murderous intent; I saw my ugly little Annabell, blue in her crib, silent at last, free from an inevitable life of hatred, a lock of my hair caught in her tiny fist.

And then he turned on his slick, shiny heel, almost tripping over the ridiculous shoes, and walked away.

My girls had started toward the monkey house, hand in hand, a chain of skipping forgiveness, balloons cringing against gusts of crisp Canadian air, and I walked behind them, watching, feeling something wrong, something besides the eerie experience of ruined illusion; of having peeked into my true self. No, it was more, and it wasn't the ear tweak of motherly failure, the guilt of lost control.

It nagged at me, this something, until I noticed Annabell's balloon, a balloon she was happy as hell to have—a perfectly fine balloon, its string wound tight to her wrist. She kept looking up, smile huge and crooked, the wind parting the silvery threads of her hair and accentuating its thinness. She didn't acknowledge, nor did she care, that her sisters each had the brightest of the clown's bunch: electric purple for Christine, shocking pink for Madison; Margaret's was the brightest of all, a swirling confection of Key-lime green and mid-day yellow, clouds of sunset pink and heartbeat red. It was the universe suspended there, creation itself just waiting to burst.

Annabell's was white. Like surrender.

Mommy?

Annabell is wearing one of her play tiaras, the one with aurora borealis crystals rimming the peak and seed pearls shaped like a star. It sets lopsided on her head, and her eyes are the calm, dark, mysterious blue of India, her lashes sweeping and dense, the color of Egyptian sand. She has become the places she will visit, the places I will never go.

Yes, Annabell, you may go now.

One of Those Weeks

BEV VINCENT

Since we believe we're really clever, it's no surprise we really like stories that owe their success to being clever as well. Bev Vincent has captured the mordant sense of humor and tongue-in-cheek style reminiscent of the masterful short story writer, Robert Sheckley.

MARCH 23

On Tuesday morning, Jeff Adams started having trouble keeping his shoelaces tied. This included the laces on his sneakers, his dress shoes and even his moccasin slippers, where a strand of leather threaded around their circumference and tied—under normal circumstances—in a neat bow on the vamp. He tried every trick he knew, including double knotting, but a few seconds after he tied them the laces worked loose and dangled limply to the ground.

He considered applying glue, but that defeated the purpose of laces, didn't it? Jeff wasn't particularly fussy about his appearance but untied shoelaces annoyed him, either his own or someone else's. He often approached total strangers whose laces were untied to warn them against tripping.

March 24

On Wednesday, his toothbrush stopped working. Toothpaste no longer stuck to the bristles; it immediately slid off into the sink. Jeff was a twice-a-day brusher, morning and evening, without fail. Watching perfectly good daubs of toothpaste fall into the sink—the paste had no trouble sticking to the porcelain, he noted grimly—irritated him.

Even water didn't cling to the nylon fibers. He dragged the dry brush across his teeth but he could tell they weren't being cleaned. If pressed, he couldn't have explained how he knew this, but he did.

He stood in front of the bathroom sink, faucet running cold water, three perfectly good blobs of toothpaste smeared near the drain, wearing his green terrycloth nightgown and yellow leather moccasins—laces dangling—and stared in the mirror. The brush tasted stale. He gargled mouthwash to freshen his breath then put a strip of toothpaste on his index finger and rubbed at his front teeth. This helped, but the process felt incomplete. He didn't sleep well that night.

March 25

On Thursday afternoon, Judy, his girlfriend of sixteen months, didn't recognize him when he phoned immediately after he got home from work. They often went out at least once during the week and spent most of their weekends together. Jeff had been working up the courage to ask her to move in with him. He planned to invite her to dinner and drop some subtle hints and maybe ask her that night, if she seemed interested.

"Hi, honey. You wouldn't believe the odd things that have been happening to me these past few days. Want to meet at the Thai Pepper in an hour?"

"Who is this?"

Jeff blinked at the telephone receiver. "It's me. Jeff."

"Jeff who?"

"Ha, ha. Very funny." April Fools' Day wasn't until next week and Judy wasn't much for practical jokes, but he'd give her credit for this one, even if it was slightly lame.

"I'm serious. Who is this?"

Jeff stared at the handset again before replacing it in its cradle. When he showed up at her apartment door half an hour later, a dozen roses in his hand as an apology for whatever he'd done wrong, Judy regarded him like he'd arrived from a foreign planet.

"You don't know me?" he said, affixing a strained smile to his face in the hopes that this might make him more familiar to her. He certainly knew her. He opened his mouth to tell her about the mole on her back just above her waist but changed his mind. His teeth met with an audible click.

"You must have the wrong apartment," his girlfriend said. She wrinkled her nose in confusion, a gesture Jeff once found endearing. "I didn't ask anyone to fix me up with a blind date."

"I'm not blind," Jeff said to the solid wood door that

materialized between them. He considered ringing the doorbell again, but why bother? He trudged downstairs to the front door, almost tripping on his shoelaces twice. Judy's familiar scent—he had purchased that brand of perfume for her on a trip to Paris several months ago and she'd worn it ever since—followed him partway down, then dissipated like a phantom. Visions of the long, enjoyable hours he and Judy had spent in that apartment resisted his efforts to banish them.

He sat behind the wheel of his car for half an hour. When he had no more tears to wipe from his eyes, he turned the ignition key.

On the way home, he stopped at a shoe store and bought a pair of brown loafers. He was about to throw his old shoes into a garbage bin in the parking lot when he saw a homeless man sitting on a bench across the street.

"Here. These don't work any more, but you can have them."

"Don't work?"

"Cost eighty bucks and now they don't work."

The grizzled man kicked off a pair of decrepit sneakers and tried on the brown suede shoes. "These're nice. Real nice." He looked up at Jeff, a furrow in his brow. "What's the catch?"

Jeff gazed at the shoelaces. The man had tied clumsy loops with weather-beaten fingers, but they stayed tied. After several long seconds staring at the man's feet, Jeff looked up and shrugged.

"You got me, partner. I don't know."

The man pulled his khaki lapels together and skulked off in his new shoes, apparently afraid that Jeff would change his mind. He abandoned his old sneakers beneath the bench. Jeff considered throwing them in the garbage but couldn't make himself touch them.

In his apartment, he searched for pictures of him with Judy, but they were all gone, including the one that once adorned the coffee table. It had been taken during their first trip together, a long weekend in Cancun. A dehydrated potted plant sat on the table instead, surrounded by an array of dead leaves.

The photo he always carried in his wallet no longer occupied its celluloid pocket. In its place was a well-worn frequent flier card for an airline he didn't recognize.

The scrapbook in which he'd kept her letters and e-mails was missing from the drawer next to his bed. Her e-mail account rejected his letters. "Address unknown," the bounced message informed him.

MARCH 26

Jeff got lost on his way to work on Friday morning. He drove around for nearly an hour, looking for his office building but he couldn't figure out where it was. All the streets looked familiar but when he got to a certain point he couldn't decide which way to turn. He tried approaching from several different directions but the result was always the same. The building's location had been erased from his memory. He could picture it in his mind—he just couldn't find it.

He pulled into the parking lot of a strip mall at shortly after ten and called in sick on a pay phone. He couldn't bring himself to ask the receptionist for directions. She sounded puzzled, but took his message without question.

The nearby coffee shop looked inviting, so he went in and ordered a large cappuccino. After the first taste he realized he didn't like coffee any more so he went back to his apartment and watched soap operas for the rest of the day, skipping lunch.

By the end of the afternoon, hunger crept into his awareness. He locked his apartment door and took the elevator to the basement. In the garage, a red Camaro occupied his usual parking spot. Jeff looked around in confusion, but his blue Corolla was nowhere to be found. His car key was missing from his key ring, too.

He contemplated filing a stolen vehicle report, but he couldn't find any proof he'd ever owned a car. The firebox in his bedroom closet where he stored important documents no longer contained his vehicle title. The file in the cabinet where he kept insurance papers and auto repair statements was missing.

He walked to a Mexican restaurant three blocks away and drank four large margaritas with salt while munching on bowl after bowl of chips and salsa. Some game was playing on the TV over the bar, but he didn't recognize either of the teams. He watched anyway, cheering silently for the players dressed in orange.

He didn't feel even slightly drunk when he walked home after the game ended (the orange team lost, which saddened him for no apparent reason), but he woke up with a crashing hangover the next morning.

MARCH 27

That Saturday he stayed locked in his apartment. Without a car he couldn't go very far, and he was afraid that if he did go out he mightn't be able to find his way back home. He picked up a paperback mystery from his shelves he was certain he'd read before, but the character names were unfamiliar and after the third chapter the story went in a completely different direction from what he remembered.

He would have watched television, but he couldn't figure out how to work the remote control. None of the buttons, which were arranged in an odd elliptical pattern, were labeled. The only one that did anything when he pushed it rang his doorbell.

MARCH 28

Late Sunday morning, the telephone awakened him. He had a pleasant conversation with his father, who had died the previous Christmas. Jeff had a clear memory of standing at the hospital bedside when his father took his last gasping breath, but the man on the other end of the line was definitely the same person he'd spoken to by phone most Sunday mornings since he'd moved away from home ten years ago.

"How's Mom doing?" he asked.

"Pretty much the same," his father replied, which was no answer at all but Jeff didn't inquire further. "When are you coming to visit again, son?"

"Soon," Jeff said. "I'm having car problems right now, but once I have that straightened out I'll make plans to fly over."

"That's good. We'll look forward to seeing you."

They talked for several minutes more about the usual topics from the past and then they hung up.

Jeff redialed the number a few minutes later, but it rang at least twenty times without being answered. When he tried again, the phone didn't even ring. He listened to staticky silence, going over things he might have said given this chance to speak to his father again.

After a lunch of raw carrots and popcorn, Jeff turned on his computer, planning to print out a map so he could find his way to work on Monday. When it finished booting up, the only icon on the desktop was for Space Invaders, a game he hadn't played since high school. His Internet software was gone, as was everything else on the computer.

By the end of the evening, he'd gotten pretty good at Space Invaders and had advanced to the forty-third level on two separate occasions before running out of ships.

MARCH 29

The newspaper, which Jeff found on his doormat on Monday morning even though he didn't subscribe, featured a bold headline: No News Today. The front page was blank below the fold. Comics filled the inside two pages. A full-page advertisement on the back said:

WANTED
NEWS
Please call 555-1823

Jeff read the comics. That was what he always turned to first when he bought the newspaper anyway. Some of the strips he recognized but at least half of them were unfamiliar. Some of the jokes he didn't get, which he hated. He read and reread the problematic strips, searching the panels for subtle clues to the punch line. As he read, he flexed his right hand, which ached from playing Space Invaders.

No one answered at his office when he tried to call in sick again. Around noon, he strolled downstairs to check his mailbox. It was full of letters addressed to someone named Walter. Jeff's first impulse was to drop them into the out-going mail slot, but he took them back to his living room. They made for interesting reading and helped him pass the afternoon, especially now that his computer had vanished.

Jeff lay in bed that Monday night, idly wondering what the next day would bring. Or take away. He didn't miss going to work five mornings a week, but he did miss his computer and Judy. At least the comic section still ran in the newspaper—even if he didn't understand all the jokes—and maybe he'd get some more interesting mail for Walter. His loafers had solved that annoying shoelaces problem and he'd grown accustomed to using his finger in place of his toothbrush.

MARCH 30

Tuesday morning the outer wall of Jeff's apartment vanished. Window and all. The first thing he saw after waking up was a pigeon perched at the foot of his bed. He felt an unfamiliar breeze and then became aware of vast space. From his prone position he could see only sky, though a nagging voice in the back of his mind suggested that he should have been able to see at least the apartment building next door.

He climbed out of bed naked, disturbing the pigeon from its perch, and strolled to the edge of his bedroom. His former wall had once held a small window and a framed print of a painting by Camille Pissarro: *Entrance to the Village of Voisins*. Jeff stared through the gaping nothingness that now occupied one full wall of the room.

A gentle breeze rolled in, tousling his hair and hardening his nipples.

Outside his apartment building, in this direction at least, there was absolutely nothing but blue as far as the eye could see. No buildings, no people, no clouds, no sun, no sound. Jeff craned his head around the edge of his bedroom wall but vertigo overcame him, forcing him back into the room.

Still naked, he wandered into the living room and found that the outside wall had vanished there, too. Similarly in the bathroom. Jeff had a hard time peeing in front of all that wide-open space, even though no one could see him. He ran the tap for a few seconds to get his own flow started and then he was okay.

The absence of a wall and the disconcerting nothingness beyond (*Entrance to Village Infinity?*) made it hard for Jeff to enjoy the book he was reading. It was the same one he'd started on Saturday but all the character names had changed and instead of being set in Edinburgh the action now took place in Reykjavik. Iceland was a country Jeff had always intended to visit because he'd read somewhere that it was so much like the moon's surface astronauts had trained there back in the 60s. Some people even believed that the astronauts hadn't really gone to the moon, but had staged the whole thing in Iceland. Jeff didn't subscribe to that theory.

Shortly after noon, Jeff opened his apartment door on the way to the lobby to see if Walter had gotten any mail. As he was about to step out into the corridor, he realized that everything had disappeared in that direction, too. Whatever was responsible for stealing his external reality had been kind-hearted enough to leave him a door he could lock against intruders, though.

He imagined that his apartment would suffer a considerable crosswind if two opposing walls went missing. As it was, he had to shoo pigeons out twice that afternoon. He never saw them fly in—he never saw anything beyond the endless blue interface that began where his outer wall used to exist—but the pigeons materialized in his living room all the same. When he chased them into flight they flitted around the room in momentary confusion, looking for an escape route. Both of them eventually darted into the blue neverland and immediately vanished.

Jeff spent the afternoon reading about a hardboiled cop who drank heavily and patrolled the mean streets of Reykjavik. That afternoon, he reread the book, which now featured a spinster amateur detective who solved cases from her cozy living room in New Delhi.

No one had phoned him since his father's call on Sunday. He dialed the airline number he found on the back of the frequent flier card in his wallet, the card that occupied the slot that used to hold a picture of him with Judy, and booked a flight to visit his parents. He hadn't figured out how he was going to get to the airport, but that was a detail he'd handle when the time came. The airline refused his credit card but seemed satisfied when he read them his YMCA membership number instead.

MARCH 31

The slight breeze had transformed into a moderately healthy gale by Wednesday morning. Jeff's bedcovers rippled under their assault. He snapped on his bedside lamp but the light only penetrated a perimeter of a few feet. Beyond its sixty watt glow, nothing. Even the pigeons had abandoned him.

Fortunately, he'd brought his book in from the living room the night before. He started from the dog-eared page about a third of the way through, reading about a tough but sensitive ex-cop who ran a private detective agency out of the basement of his house in Gdansk, which he shared with a golden retriever. Jeff occasionally allowed his gaze to drift from the pages to take in his surroundings, but one time when he looked away too long he had to start the book over again because the Polish P.I. was now a former child psychologist who assisted the police with their inquiries in Montevideo. Just when Jeff was sure he'd figured out whodunit, too.

He found a couple of chocolate bars in his nightstand and stopped reading long enough to eat them. For a moment he considered saving one for later, but at the rate things were going—going away—he didn't think it mattered. He tossed the crumpled wrappers into the darkness surrounding his bed. The steady breeze caught them and carried them away without a sound.

Turning back to the book, he discovered that the main character was a burglar who ran a used bookstore as a cover for his clandestine activities in the streets of Nicosia. Jeff Adams shook his head, leafed back a few pages and started the chapter over.

Fatigue overtook him shortly before midnight. He dog-eared the paperback, rested it carefully on the nightstand and turned out the light.

APRIL 1

APRIL 2

Adam Jeffries woke up on Friday morning. He sat up, slipped his feet into his moccasins and tied the laces.

Nice and tight.

Stationary Bike

STEPHEN KING

This is one of those stories that should make a lot of English professors salivate. It would allow them to use phrases like "fraught with symbolism," "trenchant metaphors," and "penetrating subtext." We just took it for what it was—one hell of a ride.

I. METABOLIC WORKMEN

A week after the physical he had put off for a year (he'd actually been putting it off for three years, as his wife would have pointed out if she had still been alive), Richard Sifkitz was invited by Dr. Brady to view and discuss the results. Since the patient could detect nothing overtly ominous in his doctor's voice, he went willingly enough.

The results were rendered as numeric values of a sheet of paper headed METROPOLITAN HOSPITAL, New

York City. All the test-names and numbers were in black except for one line. This one line was rendered in red, and Sifkitz was not very surprised to see that it was marked CHOLESTEROL. The number, which really stood out in that red ink (as was undoubtedly the intention), read 226.

Sifkitz started to enquire if that was a bad number, then asked himself if he wanted to start off this interview by asking something stupid. It would not have been printed in red, he reasoned, if it had been a good number. The rest of them were undoubtedly good numbers, or at least acceptable numbers, which was why they were printed in black. But he wasn't here to discuss them. Doctors were busy men, disinclined to waste time in head-patting. So instead of something stupid, he asked how bad a number two-twenty-six was.

Dr. Brady leaned back in his chair and laced his fingers together on his damnably skinny chest. "To tell you the truth," he said, "it's not a bad number at all." He raised a finger. "Considering what you eat, that is."

"I know I weigh too much," Sifkitz said humbly. "I've been meaning to do something about it." In fact, he had been meaning to do no such thing.

"To tell you more of the truth," Dr. Brady went on, "your weight is not so bad, either. Again, considering what you eat. And now I want you to listen closely, because this is a conversation I only have with my patients once. My male patients, that is; when it comes to weight, my female patients would talk my ear off, if I let them. Are you ready?"

"Yes," Sifkitz said, attempting to lace his fingers across his own chest and discovering he could not do it. What he discovered—or rediscovered, more properly put—was that he had a pretty good set of breasts. Not, so far as he was aware, part of the standard equipment for men in their late thirties. He gave up his attempt to lace and folded, instead. In his lap. The sooner the lecture was begun, the sooner it would be done.

"You're six feet tall and thirty-eight years old," Dr. Brady said. "Your weight should be about a hundred and ninety, and your cholesterol should be just about the same. Once upon a time, back in the seventies, you could get away with a cholesterol reading of two-forty, but of course back in the seventies, you could still smoke in the waiting rooms at hospitals." He shook his head. "No, the correlation between high cholesterol and heart disease was simply too clear. The two-forty number consequently went by the boards.

"You are the sort of man who has been blessed with a good metabolism. Not a great one, mind you, but good? Yes. How many times do you eat at McDonalds or Wendy's, Richard? Twice a week?"

"Maybe once," Sifkitz said. He thought the average week actually brought four to six fast-food meals with it. Not counting the occasional weekend trip to Arby's.

Dr. Brady raised a hand as if to say Have it your way . . . which was, now that Sifkitz thought of it, the Burger King motto.

"Well, you're certainly eating somewhere, as the scales tell us. You weighed in on the day of your physical at two-twenty-three . . . once again, and not coinciden- tally, very close to your cholesterol number."

He smiled a little at Sifkitz's wince, but at least it was not a smile devoid of sympathy.

"Here is what has happened so far in your adult life," Brady said. "In it, you have continued to eat as you did when you were a teenager, and to this point your body—

thanks to that good-if-not-extraordinary metabolism—
has pretty much kept up with you. It helps at this point to
think of the metabolic process as a work-crew. Men in
chinos and Doc Martens."

It may help you, Sifkitz thought, it doesn't do a thing
for me. Meanwhile, his eyes kept being drawn back to
that red number, that 226.

"Their job is to grab the stuff you send down the chute
and dispose of it. Some they send on to the various production departments. The rest they burn. If you send them
more than they can deal with, you put on weight. Which
you have been doing, but at a relatively slow pace. But
soon, if you don't make some changes, you're going to
see that pace speed up. There are two reasons. The first is
that your body's production facilities need less fuel than
they used to. The second is that your metabolic crew—
those fellows in the chinos with the tattoos on their
arms—aren't getting any younger. They're not as effi-
cient as they used to be. They're slower when it comes to
separating the stuff to be sent on and the stuff that needs
to be burned. And sometimes they bitch."

"Bitch?" Sifkitz asked.

Dr. Brady, hands still laced across his narrow chest
(the chest of a consumptive, Sifkitz decided—certainly
no breasts there), nodded his equally narrow head. Sifkitz
thought it almost the head of a weasel, sleek and sharp-
eyed. "Yes indeed. They say stuff like, 'Isn't he ever
gonna slow down?' and 'Who does he think we are, the
Marvel Comics superheros?' and 'Cheezis, don't he ever
give it a rest?' And one of them—the malingerer, every
work-crew's got one—probably says, 'What the fuck
does he care about us, anyway? He's on top, ain't he?'

"And sooner or later, they'll do what any bunch of

working joes will do if they're forced to go on too long
and do too much, without so much as a lousy weekend
off, let alone a paid vacation: they'll get sloppy. Start
goofing off and lying down on the job. One day one of
'em won't come in at all, and there'll come another—if
you live long enough—when one of 'em can't come in,
because he'll be lying home dead of a stroke or a heart
attack."

"That's pleasant. Maybe you could take it on the road.
Hit the lecture circuit. Oprah, even."

Dr. Brady unlaced his fingers and leaned forward
across his desk. He looked at Richard Sifkitz, unsmiling.
"You've got a choice to make and my job is to make you
aware of it, that's all. Either you change your habits or
you're going to find yourself in my office ten years from
now with some serious problems—weight pushing three
hundred pounds, maybe, Type Two diabetes, varicose
veins, a stomach ulcer, and a cholesterol number to match
your weight. At this point you can still turn around without crash-diets, tummy-tucks, or a heart attack to get your
attention. Later on doing that'll get harder. Once you're
past forty, it gets harder every year. After forty, Richard,
the weight sticks to your ass like babyshit sticks to a bedroom wall."

"Elegant," Sifkitz said, and burst out laughing. He
couldn't help it.

Brady didn't laugh, but he smiled, at least, and leaned
back in his chair. "There's nothing elegant about where
you're headed. Doctors don't usually talk about it any
more than State Troopers talk about the severed head they
found in a ditch near the car accident, or the blackened
child they found in the closet the day after the Christmas
tree lights caught the house on fire, but we know lots

about the wonderful world of obesity, from women who grow mold in flaps of fat that haven't been washed all the way to the bottom in years to men who go everywhere in a cloud of stench because they haven't been able to wipe themselves properly in a decade or more."

Sifkitz winced and made a waving-away gesture.

"I don't say you're going there, Richard—most people don't, they have a kind of built-in limiter, it seems—but there is some truth to that old saying about so-and-so digging his grave with a fork and spoon. Keep it in mind."

"I will."

"Good. That's the speech. Or sermon. Or whatever it is. I won't tell you to go your way and sin no more, I'll just say 'over to you.' "

Although he had filled in the OCCUPATION blank on his income tax return with the words FREELANCE ARTIST for the last twelve years, Sifkitz did not think of himself as a particularly imaginative man, and he hadn't done a painting (or even a drawing, really) just for himself since the year he graduated from DePaul. He did book jackets, some movie posters, a lot of magazine illustrations, the occasional cover for a trade-show brochure. He'd done one CD cover (for Slobberbone, a group he particularly admired) but would never do another one, he said, because you couldn't see the detail in the finished product without a magnifying glass. That was as close as he had ever come to what is called "artistic temperament."

If asked to name his favorite piece of work, he likely would have looked blank. If pressed, he might have said it was the painting of the young blonde woman running through the grass that he had done for Downy Fabric Softener, but even that would have been a lie, something told just to make the question go away. In truth, he wasn't the kind of artist who had (or needed to have) favorites. It had been a long time since he'd picked up a brush to paint anything other than what someone commissioned him to paint, usually from a detailed ad agency memo or from a photograph (as had been the case with the woman running through the grass, evidently overjoyed that she had finally managed to beat static cling).

But, as surely as inspiration strikes the best of us—the Picassos, the Van Goghs, the Salvatore Dalis—so it must eventually strike the rest of us, if only once or twice in a lifetime. Sifkitz took the crosstown bus home (he'd not owned a car since college), and as he sat looking out the window (the medical report with its one line of red type was folded into his back pocket), he found his eye again and again going to the various work-crews and construction gangs the bus rolled past: guys in hardhats tromping across a building site, some with buckets, some with boards balanced on their shoulders; Con Ed guys half-in and half-out of manholes surrounded by yellow tape stamped with the words WORK AREA; three guys erecting a scaffold in front of a department store display window while a fourth talked on his cell phone.

Little by little he realized a picture was forming in his mind, one which demanded its place in the world. When he was back to the SoHo loft that served as both his home and his studio, he crossed to the littered nest beneath the skylight without even bothering to pick the mail up off the floor. He dropped his jacket on top of it, as a matter of fact.

He paused only long enough to look at a number of blank canvases leaning in the corner, and dismiss them. He took a piece of plain white pressboard instead, and set to work with a charcoal pencil. The phone rang twice over the course of the next hour. He let the answering machine pick up both times.

He worked at this picture off and on—but rather more on than off, especially as time passed and he came to realize how good it was—over the next ten days, moving from the pressboard to a piece of canvas that was four feet long and three feet high when it seemed natural to do so. It was the biggest surface he'd worked on in over a decade.

The picture showed four men—workmen in jeans, poplin jackets, and big old workboots—standing at the side of a country road which had just emerged from a deep stand of forest (this he rendered in shades of dark green and streaks of gray, working in a splashy, speedy, exuberant style). Two of the men had shovels; one had a bucket in each hand; the fourth was in the process of pushing his cap back from his forehead in a gesture that perfectly caught his end-of-the-day weariness and his growing realization that the job would never be done; that there was, in fact, more of the job needing to be done at the end of each day than there had been at the beginning. This fourth guy, wearing a battered old gimme-cap with the word LIPID printed above the bill, was the foreman. He was talking to his wife on his cell phone. Coming home, honey, nah, don't want to go out, not tonight, too tired, want to get an early start in the morning. The guys bitched about that but I brought 'em around. Sifkitz didn't know how he knew all this, but he did. Just as he knew that the man with the buckets was Freddy, and he owned the truck in which the men had come. It was parked just outside the picture on the right; you could see the top of its shadow. One of the shovel guys, Carlos, had a bad back and was seeing a chiropractor.

There was no sign of what job the men had been doing in the picture, that was a little beyond the left side, but you could see how exhausted they were. Sifkitz had always been a detail-man (that green-gray blur of forest was very unlike him), and you could read how weary these men were in every feature of their faces. It was even in the sweat-stains on the collars of their shirts.

Above them, the sky was a queer organic red.

Of course he knew what the picture represented and understood that queer sky perfectly. This was the work-crew of which his doctor had spoken, at the end of their day. In the real world beyond that organic red sky, Richard Sifkitz, their employer, had just eaten his bed-time snack (a left-over piece of cake, maybe, or a care-fully hoarded Krispy Kreme) and laid his head down on his pillow. Which meant they were finally free to go home for the day. And would they eat? Yes, but not as much as he did. They would be too tired to eat much, it was on their faces. Instead of eating a big meal they'd put their feet up, these guys who worked for The Lipid Company, and watch TV for a little while. Maybe fall asleep in front of it and then wake up a couple of hours later, with the regular shows gone and Ron Popeil on, showing his latest invention to an adoring studio audience. And they'd turn it off with the remote and shuffle to bed, shedding clothes as they went without so much as a backward look.

All of this was in the picture, although none of it was in the picture. Sifkitz was not obsessed with it, it did not become his life, but he understood it was something *new* in his life, something good. He had no idea what he could do with such a thing once it was finished, and didn't really care. For the time being he just liked getting up in the morning and looking at it with one eye open as he picked the cloth of his Big Dog boxers out of the crack of his ass. He supposed when it was done, he would have to name it. So far he had considered and rejected 'Quittin' Time,' 'The Boys Call It a Day,' and 'Berkowitz Calls It a Day.' Berkowitz being the boss, the foreman, the one with the Motorola cell phone, the guy in the LIPID cap. None of those names were quite right, and that was okay. He'd know the right name for the picture when it finally occurred to him. It would make a *cling!* sound in his head. In the meantime there was no hurry. He wasn't even sure the picture was the point. While painting it, he had lost fifteen pounds. Maybe that was the point.

Or maybe it wasn't.

II. STATIONARY BIKE

Somewhere—maybe at the end of a Salada tea-bag string—he had read that, for the person who aspires to lose weight, the most effective exercise is pushing back from the table. Sifkitz had no doubt this was true, but as time passed he more and more came to believe that losing weight wasn't his goal. Nor was getting buffed up his goal, although both of those things might be side-effects. He kept thinking of Dr. Brady's metabolic working stiffs, ordinary joes who were really trying their best to do their job but getting no help from him. He could hardly not think of them when he was spending an hour or two every day painting them and their workaday world.

He fantasized quite a lot about them. There was Berkowitz, the foreman, who aspired to have his own construction company someday. Freddy, who owned the truck (a Dodge Ram) and fancied himself a fancy carpenter. Carlos, the one with the bad back. And Whelan, who was actually sort of a goldbrick. These were the guys whose job it was to keep him from having a heart attack or a stroke. They had to clean up the shit that kept bombing down from that queer red sky before it blocked the road into the woods.

A week after he began the painting (and about a week before he would finally decide it was done), Sifkitz went to The Fitness Boys on Twenty-ninth Street, and, after considering both a treadmill and a StairMaster (attractive but too expensive), bought a stationary bike. He paid an extra forty dollars to have it assembled and delivered.

"Use this every day for six months and your cholesterol number's down thirty points," said the salesman, a brawny young fellow in a Fitness Boys T-shirt. "I practically guarentee it."

The basement of the building where Sifkitz lived was a rambling, multi-room affair, dark and shadowy, bellowing with furnace noise and crammed with tenants' possessions in stalls marked with the various apartment numbers. There was an alcove at the far end, however, that was almost magically empty. As if it had been waiting for him all along. Sifkitz had the deliverymen set up his new exercise machine on the concrete floor facing a bare beige wall.

"You gonna bring down a TV?" one of them asked. "Or are you more of the book-reading type?"

"I haven't decided yet," Sifkitz said, although he had.

He rode the stationary bike in front of one bare beige wall for fifteen minutes or so every day until the painting was finished, knowing that fifteen minutes was probably not enough (although certainly better than nothing) but also knowing it was about all he could stand for the time being. Not because he got tired; fifteen minutes wasn't enough to tire him out. It was just boring in the basement. The whine of the wheels combined with the steady roar of the furnace quickly got on his nerves. He was all too aware of what he was doing, which was, basically, going nowhere in a basement under two bare lightbulbs that cast his double shadow on the wall in front of him. He also knew that things would improve once the picture upstairs was done and he could start on the one down here.

It was the same picture but he executed it much more quickly. He could do this because there was no need to put Berkowitz, Carlos, Freddy, and Whelan-the-goldbrick in this one. In this one they were gone for the day and he simply painted the country road on the beige wall, using forced perspective so that when he was mounted on the stationary bike, the track seemed to wind away from him and into that dark green and gray blur of forest. Riding the bike became less boring immediately, but after two or three sessions, he realized that he still wasn't done because what he was doing was still only exercise. He needed to put in the red sky, for one thing, but that was easy, nothing but slop work. He wanted to add more detail to both shoulders of the road "up front," and some litter, as well, but those things were also easy (and fun). The real problem had nothing to do with the picture at all. With either picture. The problem was that he had no goal, and that had always bugged him about exercise that existed for nothing more than its own sake. That kind of workout might tone you up and improve your health, but it was essentially meaningless while it was going on. Existential, even. That kind of workout was only about the next thing, for instance some pretty lady from some magazine's art department coming up to you at a party and asking if you'd lost weight. That wasn't even close to real motivation. He wasn't vain enough (or horny enough) for such possibilities to keep him going over the long haul. He'd eventually get bored, and lapse into his old Krispy Kreme ways. No, he had to decide where the road was, and where it was going. Then he could pretend to ride there. The idea excited him. Maybe it was silly—loony, even—but to Sifkitz that excitement, though mild, felt like the real deal. And he didn't have to tell anyone what he was up to, did he? Absolutely not. He could even get a Rand-McNally Road Atlas and mark his daily progress on one of the maps.

He was not an introspective man by nature, but on his walk back from Barnes & Noble with his new book of roadmaps under his arm, he found himself wondering exactly what had galvanized him so. A moderately high cholesterol number? He doubted it. Dr. Brady's solemn proclamation that he would find this battle much harder to fight once he was post-forty? That might have had something to do with it, but probably not all that much. Was he just ready for a change? That felt like getting warmer.

Trudy had died of a particularly ravenous blood-cancer, and Sifkitz had been with her, in her hospital room, when she passed on. He remembered how deep her last breath had been, how her sad and wasted bosom had heaved upward as she drew it in. As if she had known this was it, this was the one for the ages. He remembered how she'd let it out, and the sound it had made—shaaaah! And how after that her chest had just stayed where it was. In a way

he had lived the last four years in just that sort of breath-
less hiatus. Only now the wind was blowing again, filling
his sails.

Yet there was something else, something even more to
the point: the work-crew Brady had summoned up and
Sifkitz himself had named. There was Berkowitz, Whelan, Carlos, and Freddy. Dr. Brady hadn't cared about
them; for Brady, the metabolic work-crew was just a
metaphor. His job was to make Sifkitz care a little more
about what was going on inside him, that was all, his
metaphor not much different from the mommy who tells
her toddler that "little men" are working to heal the skin
on his scraped knee.

Sifkitz's focus, though . . .

Not on myself at all, he thought, shaking out the key
that opened the lobby door. Never was. I cared about
those guys, stuck doing a never-ending clean-up job. And
the road. Why should they work so hard to keep it clear?
Where did it go?

He decided it went to Herkimer, which was a small
town up by the Canadian border. He found a skinny and
unmarked blue line on the roadmap of upstate New York
that rambled there all the way from Poughkeepsie, which
was south of the state capital. Two, maybe three hundred
miles. He got a more detailed plat map of upstate New
York and thumbtacked the square where this road began
on the wall beside his hasty . . . his hasty what-would-
you-call-it? Mural wasn't right. He settled on "projection."

And that day when he mounted the stationary bike, he
imagined that Poughkeepsie was behind him, not the
stored television from 2-G, the stack of trunks from 3-F,
the tarped dirt-bike from 4-A, but Po'-town. Ahead of

him stretched the country road, just a blue squiggle to Monsieur Rand McNally, but the Old Rhinebeck Road according to the more detailed plat map. He zeroed the odometer on the bike, fixed his eyes firmly on the dirt that started where the concrete floor met the wall, and thought: It's really the road to good health. If you keep that somewhere in the back of your mind, you won't have to wonder if maybe a few of your screws got loose since Trudy died.

But his heart was beating a little too fast (as if he'd already started pedaling), and he felt the way he supposed most people did before setting out on a trip to a new place, where one might encounter new people and even new adventures. There was a can-holder above the stationary bike's rudimentary control panel, and into this he'd slipped a can of Red Bull, which purported to be a power drink. He was wearing an old Oxford shirt over his exercise shorts, because it had a pocket. Into this he'd placed two oatmeal-raisin cookies. Oatmeal and raisins were both supposed to be lipid-scrubbers.

And, speaking of them, The Lipid Company was gone for the day. Oh, they were still on duty in the painting upstairs—the useless, marketless painting that was so unlike him—but down here they'd piled back into Freddy's Dodge had headed back to . . . to . . .

"Back to Poughkeepsie," he said. "They're listening to Kateem on WPDH and drinking beers out of paper bags. Today they . . . what did you do today, boys?"

Put in a couple of culverts, a voice whispered. Spring runoff damn near washed the road out near Priceville. Then we knocked off early.

Good. That was good. He wouldn't have to dismount his bike and walk around the washouts.

Richard Sifkitz fixed his eyes on the wall and began to pedal.

III. ON THE ROAD TO HERKIMER

That was in the fall of 2002, a year after the Twin Towers had fallen into the streets of the Financial District, and life in New York City was returning to a slightly paranoid version of normal . . . except in New York, slightly paranoid was normal.

Richard Sifkitz had never felt saner or happier. His life fell into an orderly four-part harmony. In the morning he worked on whatever assignment was currently paying for his room and board, and there were more of these than ever, it seemed. The economy stank, all the newspapers said so, but for Richard Siftkitz, Freelance Commercial Artist, the economy was good.

He still ate lunch at Dugan's on the next block, but now usually a salad instead of a greasy double cheese-burger, and in the afternoon he worked on a new picture for himself: to begin with, a more detailed version of the projection on the wall of the basement alcove. The picture of Berkowitz and his crew had been set aside and covered with an old piece of sheet. He was done with it. Now he wanted a better image of what served him well enough downstairs, which was the road to Herkimer with the work-crew gone. And why shouldn't they be gone? Wasn't he maintaining the road himself these days? He was, and doing a damned good job. He'd gone back to Brady in late October to have his cholesterol re-tested, and the number this time had been written in black instead of red: 179. Brady had been more than respectful; he'd actually been a little jealous.

"This is better than mine," he said. "You really took it to heart, didn't you?"

"I guess I did," Sifkitz agreed.

"And that potbelly of yours is almost gone. Been working out?"

"As much as I can," Sifkitz agreed, and said no more on the subject. By then his workouts had gotten odd. Some people would consider them odd, anyway.

"Well," said Brady, "if you got it, flaunt it. That's my advice."

Sifkitz smiled at this, but it wasn't advice he took to heart.

His evenings—the fourth part of an Ordinary Sifkitz Day—he spent either watching TV or reading a book, usually sipping a tomato juice or a V-8 instead of a beer, feeling tired but contented. He was going to bed an hour earlier, too, and the extra rest agreed with him.

The heart of his days was part three, from four until six. Those were the two hours he spent on his stationary bike, riding the blue squiggle between Poughkeepsie and Herkimer. On the plat maps, it changed from the Old Rhinebeck Road to the Cascade Falls Road to the Woods Road; for awhile, north of Penniston, it was even the Dump Road. He could remember how, back at the beginning, even fifteen minutes on the stationary bike had seemed like an eternity. Now he sometimes had to force himself to quit after two hours. He finally got an alarm clock and started setting it for six P.M. The thing's aggressive bray was just about enough to . . . well . . .

———

It was just enough to wake him up.

Sifkitz found it hard to believe that he was falling

asleep down in the alcove while riding the stationary bike at a steady fifteen miles per hour, but he didn't like the alternative, which was to think that he had gone a little crazy on the road to Herkimer. Or in his SoHo basement, if you liked that better. That he was having delusions.

One night while channel-surfing, he came across a program about hypnosis on A&E. The fellow being interviewed, a hypnotist who styled himself Joe Saturn, was saying that everyone practiced self-hypnosis every day. We used it to enter a work-oriented frame of mind in the morning; we used it to help us "get into the story" when reading novels or watching movies; we used it to get to sleep at night. This last was the Joe Saturn's favorite example, and he talked at length about the patterns "successful sleepers" followed every night: checking the locks on the doors and windows, maybe, drawing a glass of water, maybe saying a little prayer or indulging in a spot of meditation. He likened these to the passes a hypnotist makes in front of his subject, and to his line of patter—counting back from ten to zero, for instance, or assuring the subject that he or she was "getting very sleepy." Sifkitz seized on this gratefully, deciding on the spot that he was spending his daily two hours on the stationary bike in a state of light to medium hypnosis.

Because, by the third week in front of the wall-projection, he was no longer spending those two hours in the basement alcove. By the third week, he was actually spending them on the road to Herkimer.

He would pedal contentedly enough along the packed dirt track that wound through the forest, smelling the odor of pine, hearing the cries of the crows or the crackle of leaves when he rolled through occasional drifts of them. The stationary bike became the three-speed

Raleigh he'd owned as a twelve-year-old in suburban Manchester, New Hampshire. By no means the only bike he'd had before getting his driver's license at seventeen, but inarguably the best bike. The plastic cup-holder became a clumsily made but effective hand-welded ring of metal jutting over the bike-basket, and instead of Red Bull it contained a can of Lipton iced tea.

On the road to Herkimer, it was always late October and just an hour before sunset. Although he rode two hours (both the alarm clock and the stationary bike's odometer confirmed this each time he finished), the sun never changed its position; it always laid the same long shadows across the dirt road and flickered at him through the trees from the same quadrant of the sky as he traveled along with the manufactured wind of his passage blowing the hair back from his brow.

Sometimes there were signs nailed to trees where other roads crossed the one he was on. CASCADE ROAD, one said. HERKIMER, 120 MI., read another, this one pocked with old bullet-holes. The signs always corresponded to the information on the plat-map currently tacked to the alcove wall. He had already decided that, once he reached Herkimer, he'd push on into the Canadian wilderness without even a stop to buy souvenirs. The road stopped there, but that was no problem; he'd already gotten a book titled Plat Maps of Eastern Canada. He would simply draw his own road on the plats, using a fine blue pencil and putting in lots of squiggles. Squiggles added miles.

He could go all the way to the Arctic Circle, if he wanted to.

One evening, after the alarm went off and startled him out of his trance, he approached the projection and looked at it for several long, considering moments, head cocked to one side. Anyone else would have seen very little; up that close the picture's trick of forced perspective ceased working and to the untrained eye the woodland scene collapsed into nothing but blobs of color—the light brown of the road's surface, the darker brown that was a shallow drift of leaves, the blue- and gray-streaked green of the firs, the bright yellow-white of the westering sun to the far left, perilously close to the door into the furnace-room. Sifkitz, however, still saw the picture perfectly. It was fixed firmly in his mind now and never changed. Unless he was riding, of course, but even then he was aware of an underlying sameness. Which was good. That essential sameness was a kind of touchstone, a way of assuring himself this was still no more than an elaborate mind-game, something plugged into his subconscious that he could unplug whenever he wanted.

He had brought down a box of colors for the occa-sional touch-up, and now, without thinking too much about it, he added several blobs of brown to the road, mixing them with black to make them darker than the drifted leaves. He stepped back, looked at the new addi-tion, and nodded. It was a small change but in its way, perfect.

The following day, as he rode his three-speed Raleigh through the woods (he was less than sixty miles from Herkimer now and only eighty from the Canadian bor-der), he came around a bend and there was a good-sized buck deer standing in the middle of the road, looking at him with startled dark velvet eyes. It flipped up the white flag of its tail, dropped a pile of scat, and was then off into the woods again. Sifkitz saw another flip of its tail and then the deer was gone. He rode on, giving the deer-shit a miss, not wanting it in the treads of his tires.

That night he silenced the alarm and approached the painting on the wall, wiping sweat from his forehead with a bandanna he took from the back pocket of his jeans. He looked at the projection critically, hands on hips. Then, moving with his usual confident speed—he'd been doing this sort of work for almost twenty years, after all—he painted the scat out of the picture, replacing it with a clutch of rusty beer-cans undoubtedly left by some up-state hunter in search of pheasant or turkey.

"You missed those, Berkowitz," he said that night as he sat drinking a beer instead of a V-8 juice. "I'll pick 'em up myself tomorrow, but don't let it happen again."

Except when he went down the next day, there was no need to paint the beer cans out of the picture; they were already gone. For a moment he felt real fright prod his belly like a blunt stick—what had he done, sleepwalked down here in the middle of the night, picked up his trusty can of turp and a brush?—and then put it out of his mind. He mounted the stationary bike and was soon riding his old Raleigh, smelling the clean smells of the forest, rel-ishing the way the wind blew his hair back from his fore-head. And yet wasn't that the day things began to change? The day he sensed he might not be alone on the road to Herkimer? One thing was beyond doubt: it was the day after the disappearing beer cans that he had the really ter-rible dream and then drew the picture of Carlos's garage.

IV. MAN WITH SHOTGUN

It was the most vivid dream he'd had since the age of fourteen, when three or four brilliant wet-dreams had ushered him into physical manhood. It was the most horrible dream ever, hands down, nothing else even close. What made it horrible was the sense of impending doom that ran through it like a red thread. This was true even though the dream had a weird thinness: he knew he was dreaming but could not quite escape it. He felt as if he'd been wrapped in some terrible gauze. He knew his bed was near and he was in it—struggling—but he couldn't quite break through to the Richard Sifkitz who lay there, trembling and sweaty in his Big Dog sleep-shorts.

He saw a pillow and a beige telephone with a crack in the case. Then a hallway filled with pictures that he knew were of his wife and three daughters. Then a kitchen, the microwave oven flashing 4:16P. A bowl of bananas (they filled him with grief and horror) on the Formica counter. A breezeway. And here lay Pepe the dog with his muzzle on his paws, and Pepe did not raise his head but rolled his eyes up to look at him as he passed, revealing a gruesome, blood-threaded crescent of white, and that was when Sifkitz began to weep in the dream, understanding that all was lost. He would weep steadily for the next six hours, like some magical statue.

Now he was in the garage. He could smell oil. He could smell old sweet grass. The LawnBoy stood in the corner like a suburban god. He could see the vise clamped to the worktable, old and dark and flecked with tiny splinters of wood. Next, a closet. His girls' ice-skates were piled on the floor, their laces as white as vanilla ice cream. His tools hung from pegs on the walls, arranged neatly, mostly yard-tools, a bear for working in his yard was

(Carlos. I am Carlos.)

On the top shelf, far out of the girls' reach, was a .410

shotgun, not used for years, nearly forgotten, and a box of shells so dark you could barely read the word Winchester on the side, only you could read it, just enough, and that was when Sifkitz came to understand that he was being carried along in the brain of a potential suicide. He struggled furiously to either stop Carlos or escape him and could do neither, even though he sensed his bed so near, just on the other side of the gauze that wrapped him from head to foot.

Now he was at the vise again, and the .410 was clamped in the vise, and the box of shells was on the work-table beside the vise, and here was a hacksaw, he was hacksawing off the barrel of the shotgun because that would make it easier to do what he had to do, and when he opened the box of shells there were two dozen of them, fat green buggers with brass bottoms, and the sound the gun made when Carlos snapped it closed wasn't cling! but CLACK! and the taste in his mouth was oily and dusty, oily on his tongue and dusty on the insides of his cheeks and his teeth, and his back hurt, it hurt LAMF, that was how they had tagged abandoned buildings (and sometimes ones that weren't abandoned) when he was a teenager and running with the Deacons in Po'-town, stood for LIKE A MOTHERFUCKER, and that was how his back hurt, but now that he was laid off the benefits were gone, Jimmy Berkowitz could no longer afford the bennies and so Carlos Martinez could no longer afford the drugs that made the pain a little less, could no longer afford the chiropractor that made the pain a little less, and the house-payments—ay, caramba, they used to say, joking, but he sure wasn't joking now, ay caramba they were going to lose the house, less than five years from the finish-line but they were going to lose it, si-si, señor, and it was all that fuck Sifkitz's fault, him with his fucking road-maintenance hobby, and the curve of the trigger underneath his finger was like a crescent, like the unspeakable crescent of his dog's peering eye.

That was when Sifkitz woke up, sobbing and shaking, legs still in bed, head out and almost touching the floor, hair hanging. He crawled all the way out of the bedroom and started crawling across the main room to the easel under the skylight. Halfway there he found himself able to walk.

The picture of the empty road was still on the easel, the better and more complete version of the one downstairs on the alcove wall. He flung it away without a second look and set up a piece of two-foot-by-two pressboard in its place. He seized the nearest implement which would make a mark (this happened to be a UniBall Vision Elite pen) and began to draw. He drew for hours, weeping steadily the whole time. At one point (he remembered this only vaguely) he needed to piss and could feel it running hot down his leg. The tears didn't stop until the picture was finished. Then, thankfully dry-eyed at last, he stood back and looked at what he had done.

It was Carlos's garage on an October afternoon. The dog, Pepe, stood in front of it with his ears raised. The dog had been drawn by the sound of the gunshot. There was no sign of Carlos in the picture, but Sifkitz knew exactly where the body lay, on the left, beside the worktable with the vise clamped to the edge. If his wife was home, she would have heard the shot. If she was out—perhaps shopping, more likely at work—it might be another hour or two before she came home and found him.

Beneath the image he had scrawled the words MAN WITH SHOTGUN. He couldn't remember doing this, but it was his printing and the right name for the picture. There was no man visible in it, no shotgun, either, but it was the right title.

Sifkitz went to his couch, sat down on it, and put his head in his hands. His right hand ached fiercely from clutching the unfamiliar, too-small drawing implement. He tried to tell himself he'd just had a bad dream, the picture the result of that dream. That there had never been any Carlos, never any Lipid Company, both of them were figments of his own imagination, drawn from Dr. Brady's careless metaphor.

But dreams faded, and these images—the phone with the crack in its beige case, the microwave, the bowl of bananas, the dog's eye—were as clear as ever. Clearer, even.

One thing was sure, he told himself. He was done with the goddam stationary bike. This was just a little too close to lunacy. If he kept on this way, soon he'd be cutting off his ear and mailing it not to his girlfriend (he didn't have one) but to Dr. Brady, who was surely responsible for this.

"Done with the bike," he said, with his head still in his hands. "Maybe I'll get a membership down at Fitness Boys, something like that, but I'm done with that fucking stationary bike."

Only he didn't get a membership at the Fitness Boys, and after a week without real exercise (he walked, but it wasn't the same—there were too many people on the sidewalks and he longed for the peace of the Herkimer Road), he could no longer stand it. He was behind on his latest project, which was an illustration a la Norman Rockwell for Fritos Corn Chips, and he'd had a call from both his agent and the guy in charge of the Fritos account at the ad agency. This had never happened to him before.

Worse, he wasn't sleeping.

The urgency of the dream had faded a little, and he decided it was only the picture of Carlos's garage, glaring at him from the corner of the room, that kept bringing it back, refreshing the dream the way a squirt of water from a mister may refresh a thirsty plant. He couldn't bring himself to destroy the picture (it was too damned good), but he turned it around so that the image faced nothing but the wall.

That afternoon he rode the elevator down to the basement and remounted the stationary bike. It turned into the old three-speed Raleigh almost as soon as he'd fixed his eyes on the wall-projection, and he resumed his ride north. He tried to tell himself that his sense of being followed was bogus, just something left over from his dream and the frenzied hours at the easel afterward. For a little while this actually did the job even though he knew better. He had reasons to make it do the job. The chief ones were that he was sleeping through the night again and had resumed working on his current assignment.

He finished the painting of the boys sharing a bag of Fritos on an idyllic suburban pitcher's mound, shipped it off by messenger, and the following day a check for ten thousand, two hundred dollars came with a note from Barry Casselman, his agent. You scared me a little, hon, the note said, and Sifkitz thought: You're not the only one. Hon.

Every now and then during the following week it occurred to him that he should tell someone about his adventures under the red sky, and each time he dismissed the idea. He could have told Trudy, but of course if Trudy had been around, things would never have gotten this far in the first place. The idea of telling Barry was laughable; the idea of telling Dr. Brady actually a little frightening. Dr. Brady would be recommending a good psychiatrist before you could say Minnesota Multiphasic.

The night he got the Fritos check, Sifkitz noticed a change in the basement wall-mural. He paused in the act of setting his alarm and approached the projection (can of Red Bull in one hand, reliable little Brookstone desk-clock in the other, oatmeal-raisin cookies tucked away safely in the old shirt pocket). Something was up in there, all right, something was different, but at first he was damned if he could tell what it was. He closed his eyes, counted to five (clearing his mind as he did so, an old trick), then sprang them open again, so wide that he looked like a man burlesquing fright. This time he saw the change at once. The bright yellow marquise shape over by the door to the furnace-room was as gone as the clutch of beer cans. And the color of the sky above the trees was a deeper, darker red. The sun was either down or almost down. On the road to Herkimer, night was coming.

You have to stop this, Sifkitz thought, and then he thought: Tomorrow. Maybe tomorrow.

With that he mounted up and started riding. In the woods around him, he could hear the sound of birds settling down for the night.

V. THE SCREWDRIVER WOULD DO FOR A START

Over the next five or six days, the time Sifkitz spent on the stationary bike (and his childhood three-speed) was both wonderful and terrible. Wonderful because he had never felt better; his body was operating at absolute peak performance levels for a man his age, and he knew it. He supposed that there were pro athletes in better shape than he was, but by thirty-eight they would be approaching the end of their careers, and whatever joy they were able to take in the tuned condition of their bodies would necessarily be tainted by that knowledge. Sifkitz, on the other hand, might go on creating commercial art for another forty years, if he chose to. Hell, another fifty. Five full generations of football players and four of baseball players would come and go while he stood peacefully at his easel, painting book covers, automotive products, and Five New Logos For Diet Pepsi.

Except . . .

Except that wasn't the ending folks familiar with this sort of story would expect, was it? Nor the sort of ending he expected himself.

The sense of being followed grew stronger with every ride, especially after he took down the last of the New York State plat maps and put up the first of the Canadian ones. Using a blue pen (the same one he'd used to create MAN WITH SHOTGUN), he drew an extension of the Herkimer Road on the previously roadless plat, adding lots of squiggles. By now he was pedaling faster, looking over his shoulder often, and finishing his rides covered with sweat, at first too out of breath to dismount the bike and turn off the braying alarm.

That looking-back-over-the-shoulder thing, now—that was interesting. At first when he did it he'd catch a glimpse of the basement alcove, and the doorway leading to the basement's larger rooms with its mazy arrangement of storage stalls. He'd see the Pomona Oranges crate by the door with the Brookstone desk alarm on it, marking off the minutes between four and six. Then a kind of red blur wiped across everything, and when it drained away he was looking at the road behind him, the autumn-bright trees on both sides (only not so bright now, not with twilight starting to thicken), and the darkening red sky overhead. Later, he didn't see the basement at all when he looked back, not even a flash of it. Just the road leading back to Herkimer, and eventually to Poughkeepsie.

He knew perfectly well what he was looking back over his shoulder for: headlights.

The headlights of Freddy's Dodge Ram, if you wanted to get specific about it. Because for Berkowitz and his crew, bewildered resentment had given way to anger. Carlos's suicide was what had tipped them over the edge. They blamed him and they were after him. And when they caught him, they'd—

What? They'd what?

Kill me, he thought, pedaling grimly on into the twilight, every now and then taking a sip from the can of iced tea that would revert to Red Bull once the alarm sounded and the absurd game ended for another evening. No need to be coy about it. They catch up, they'll kill me. I'm in the serious williwags now, not a town on that whole damn plat-map, not so much as a village. I could scream my head off and no one would hear me except Barry the Bear, Debby the Doe, and Rudy the Raccoon. So if I see those headlights (or hear the motor, because Freddy might be running without lights), I would do well to get the hell back to SoHo, alarm or no alarm. I'm crazy to be here in the first place.

But he was having trouble getting back now. When the alarm went off the Raleigh would remain a Raleigh for thirty seconds or more, the road ahead would remain a road instead of reverting to blobs of color on cement, and the alarm itself sounded distant and strangely mellow. He had an idea that eventually he would hear it as the drone of a jet airplane high overhead, an American Airlines 767 out of Kennedy, perhaps, headed over the North Pole to the far side of the world.

He would stop, squeeze his eyes shut, then pop them wide open again. That did the trick, but he had an idea it might not work for long. Then what? A hungry night spent in the woods, looking up at a full moon that looked like a bloodshot eye?

No, they'd catch up to him before then, he reckoned. The question was, did he intend to let that happen? Incredibly, part of him wanted to do just that. Part of him was angry at them. Part of him wanted to confront Berkowitz and the remaining members of his crew, ask them What did you expect me to do, anyway? Just go on the way things were, gobbling Krispy Kreme donuts, spreading road-litter, paying no attention to the washouts when the culverts plugged up and overflowed? Is that what you wanted?

But there was another part of him that knew such a confrontation would be madness. He was in tiptop shape, yes, but you were still talking three against one, and who was to say Mrs. Carlos hadn't loaned the boys her husband's shotgun, told them yeah, go get the bastard, and be sure to tell him the first one's from me and my girls.

Sifkitz had had a friend who'd beaten a bad cocaine addiction in the eighties, and he remembered this fellow saying the first thing you had to do was get it out of the house. You could always buy more, sure, that shit was everywhere now, on every streetcorner, but that was no excuse for keeping it where you could grab it any time your will weakened. So he'd gathered it all up and flushed it down the toilet. And once it was gone, he'd thrown his works out with the trash. That hadn't been the end of his problem, he'd said, but it had been the beginning of the end.

One night he entered the alcove carrying a screwdriver. He had every intention of dismantling the stationary bike, and never mind the fact that he'd set the alarm for six P.M., as he always did, that was just habit. The alarm clock (like the oatmeal-raisin cookies and the nightly can of Red Bull Energy Drink) was part of his works, he supposed; the hypnotic passes he made, the machinery of his dream. And once he was done reducing the bike to unrideable components, he'd put the alarm-clock out with the rest of the trash, just as his friend had done with his crack-pipe. He'd feel a pang, of course—the sturdy little Brookstone certainly wasn't to blame for the idiotic situation into which he'd gotten himself—but he would do it. Cowboy up, they'd told each other as kids; quit whining and just cowboy up.

He saw that the bike was comprised of four main sections, and that he'd also need an adjustable wrench to dismantle the thing completely. That was all right, though; the screwdriver would do for a start. He could use it to take off the pedals. Once that was done he'd borrow the adjustable wrench from the super's toolbox.

He dropped to one knee, slipped the tip of the borrowed tool into the slot of the first screw, and hesitated. He wondered if his friend had smoked one more rock before turning the rest of them down the toilet, just one more rock for old times' sake. He bet the guy had. Being a little stoned had probably stilled the cravings, made the disposal job a little easier. And if he had one more ride, then knelt here to take off the pedals with the endorphins flowing, wouldn't he feel a little less depressed about it? A little less likely to imagine Berkowitz, Freddy, and Whelan retiring to the nearest roadside bar, where they would buy first one pitcher of Rolling Rock and then another, toasting each other and Carlos's memory, congratulating each other on how they had beaten the bastard?

"You're crazy," he murmured to himself, and slipped the tip of the driver back into the notch of the screw. "Do it and be done."

He actually turned the screwdriver once (and it was easy; whoever had put this together in the back room of The Fitness Boys obviously hadn't had his heart in it), but when he did, the oatmeal-raisin cookies shifted a little in his pocket and he thought how good they always tasted when you were riding along. You just took your right hand off the handlebar, dipped it into your pocket, had a couple of bites, then chased it with a swallow of iced tea. It was the perfect combination. It just felt so good to be speeding along, having a little picnic as you went, and those sons of bitches wanted to take it away from him.

A dozen turns of the screw, maybe even less, and the pedal would drop off onto the concrete floor—clunk. Then he could move on to the other one, and then he could move on with his life.

This is not fair, he thought.

One more ride, just for old times' sake, he thought.

And, swinging his leg over the fork and settling his ass (firmer and harder by far than it had been on the day of the red cholesterol number) onto the seat, he thought: This is the way stories like this always go, isn't it? The way they always end, with the poor schmuck saying this is the last time, I'll never do this again.

Absolutely true, he thought, but I'll bet in real life, people get away with it. I bet they get away with it all the time.

Part of him was murmuring that real life had never been like this, what he was doing (and what he was experiencing) bore absolutely no resemblance whatever to real life as he understood it. He pushed the voice away, closed his ears to it.

It was a beautiful evening for a ride in the woods.

VI. NOT QUITE THE ENDING EVERYONE EXPECTED

And still, he got one more chance.

That was the night he heard the revving engine behind him clearly for the first time, and just before the alarm clock went off, the Raleigh he was riding suddenly grew an elongated shadow on the road ahead of him—the sort of shadow that could only have been created by headlights.

Then the alarm did go off, not a bray but a distant purring sound that was almost melodic.

The truck was closing in. He didn't need to turn his head to see it (nor does one ever want to turn and see the frightful fiend that close behind him treads, Sifkitz supposed later that night, lying awake in his bed and still wrapped in the cold-yet-hot sensation of disaster avoided by mere inches or seconds). He could see the shadow, growing longer and darker.

Hurry up, please, gentlemen, it's time, he thought, and squeezed his eyes closed. He could still hear the alarm, but it was still no more than that almost soothing purr, it was certainly no louder; what was louder was the engine, the one inside Freddy's truck. It was almost on him, and suppose they didn't want to waste so much as a New York minute in conversation? Suppose the one currently behind the wheel just mashed the pedal to the metal and ran him down? Turned him into roadkill?

He didn't bother to open his eyes, didn't waste time confirming that it was still the deserted road instead of the basement alcove. Instead he squeezed them even more tightly shut, focused all his attention on the sound of the alarm, and this time turned the polite voice of the barman into an impatient bellow:

HURRY UP PLEASE GENTLEMEN IT'S TIME!

And suddenly, thankfully, it was the sound of the engine that was fading and the sound of the Brookstone alarm that was swelling, taking on its old familiar rough get-up-get-up-get-up bray. And this time when he opened his eyes, he saw the projection of the road instead of the road itself.

But now the sky was black, its organic redness hidden by nightfall. The road was brilliantly lit, the shadow of the bike—a Raleigh—a clear black on the leaf-littered hardpack. He could tell himself he had dismounted the stationary bike and painted those changes while in his nightly trance, but he knew better, and not only because there was no paint on his hands.

This is my last chance, he thought. My last chance to avoid the ending everyone expects in stories like this.

But he was simply too tired, too shaky, to take care of the stationary bike now. He would take care of it tomorrow. Tomorrow morning, in fact, first thing. Right now all he wanted was to get out of this awful place where reality had worn so thin. And with that firmly in mind, Sifkitz staggered to the Pomona crate beside the doorway (rubber-legged, covered with a thin slime of sweat—the smelly kind that comes from fear rather than exertion) and shut the alarm off. Then he went upstairs and lay down on his bed. Some very long time later, sleep came.

The next morning he went down the cellar stairs, es-chewing the elevator and walking firmly, with his head up and his lips pressed tightly together, A Man On A Mission. He went directly to the stationary bike, ignoring the alarm clock on the crate, dropped to one knee, picked up the screwdriver. He slipped it once more into the slot of a screw, one of the four that held the left-hand pedal . . .

. . . and the next thing he knew, he was speeding gid-dily along the road again, with the headlights brightening around him until he felt like a man on a stage that's dark save for one single spotlight. The truck's engine was too loud (something wrong with the muffler or the exhaust system), and it was out of tune, as well. He doubted if old Freddy had bothered with the last maintenance go-round. No, not with house-payments to make, groceries to buy, the kiddies still needing braces, and no weekly paycheck coming in.

He thought: I had my chance. I had my chance last night and I didn't take it.

He thought: Why did I do this? Why, when I knew better?

He thought: Because they made me, somehow. They made me.

He thought: They're going to run me down and I'll die in the woods.

But the truck did not run him down. It hurtled past him on the right instead, left-side wheels rumbling in the leaf-choked ditch, and then it swung across the road in front of him, blocking the way.

Panicked, Sifkitz forgot the first thing his father had taught him when he brought the three-speed home: When you stop, Richie, reverse the pedals. Brake the bike's rear wheel at the same time you squeeze the handbrake that controls the front wheel. Otherwise—

This was otherwise. In his panic he turned both hands into fists, squeezing the handbrake on the left, locking the front wheel. The bike bucked him off and sent him flying at the truck with Lipid Company printed on the driver's side door. He threw his hands out and they struck the top of the truck's bed hard enough to numb them. Then he collapsed in a heap, wondering how many bones were broken.

The doors opened above him and he heard the crackle of leaves as men in workboots got out. He didn't look up. He waited for them to grab him and make him get up, but no one did. The smell of the leaves was like old dry cinnamon. The footsteps passed him on either side, and then the crackle abruptly stopped.

Sifkitz sat up and looked at his hands. The palm of the right one was bleeding and the wrist of the left one was already swelling, but he didn't think it was broken. He looked around and the first thing he saw—red in the glow of the Dodge's taillights—was his Raleigh. It had been beautiful when his Dad brought it home from the bike-shop, but it wasn't beautiful any longer. The front wheel was warped out of true, and the rear tire had come partly off the rim. For the first time he felt something other than fear. This new emotion was anger.

He got shakily to his feet. Beyond the Raleigh, back the way he'd come, was a hole in reality. It was strangely organic, as if he were looking through the hole at the end of some duct in his own body. The edges wavered and bulged and flexed. Beyond it, three men were standing around the stationary bike in the basement alcove, standing in postures he recognized from every work-crew he'd ever seen in his life. These were men with a job to do. They were deciding how to do it.

And suddenly he knew why he'd named them as he had. It was really idiotically simple. The one in the Lipid cap, Berkowitz, was David Berkowitz, the so-called Son of Sam and a New York Post staple the year Sifkitz had come to Manhattan. Freddy was Freddy Albemarle, this kid he'd known in high school—they'd been in the band together, and had become friends for a simple enough reason: they both hated Band, but their parents had insisted. And Whelan? An artist he'd met at a conference somewhere. Michael Whelan? Mitchell Whelan? Sifkitz couldn't quite remember, but he knew the guy specialized in fantasy art, dragons and such. They had spent a night in the hotel bar, telling stories about the comic-horrible world of movie poster-art.

Then there was Carlos, who'd committed suicide in his garage. Why, he had been a version of Carlos Delgado, also known as the Big Cat. For years Sifkitz had followed the fortunes of the Toronto Blue Jays, simply because he didn't want to be like every other American League baseball fan in New York and root for the Yankees. The Cat had been one of Toronto's very few stars.

"I made you all," he said in a voice that was little more than a croak. "I created you out of memories and spare parts." Of course he had. Nor had it been for the first time. The boys on the Norman Rockwell pitcher's mound in the Fritos ad, for instance—the ad agency had, at his request, provided him with photographs of four boys of the correct age, and Sifkitz had simply painted them in. Their mothers had signed the necessary waivers; it had been business as usual.

If they heard him speak, Berkowitz, Freddy, and Whelan gave no sign. They spoke a few words among themselves that Sifkitz could hear but not make out; they seemed to come from a great distance. Whatever they were, they got Whelan moving out of the alcove while Berkowitz knelt by the stationary bike, just as Sifkitz himself had done. Berkowitz picked up the screwdriver and in no time at all the left-hand pedal dropped off onto the concrete—clunk. Sifkitz, still on the deserted road, watched through the queer organic hole as Berkowitz handed the screwdriver to Freddy Albemarle—who, with Richard Sifkitz, had played lousy trumpet in the equally lousy high school band. Somewhere in the Canadian woods an owl hooted, the sound inexpressibly lonely. Freddy went to work unscrewing the other pedal. Whelan, meanwhile, returned with the adjustable wrench in his hand. Sifkitz felt a pang at the sight of it.

Watching them, the thought that went through Sifkitz's mind was: If you want something done right, hire a professional. Certainly Berkowitz and his boys wasted no time. In less than four minutes the stationary bike was nothing but two wheels and three disconnected sections of frame laid on the concrete, and so neatly that the parts looked like one of those diagrams called "exploded schematics."

Berkowitz himself dropped the screws and bolts into the front pockets of his Dickies, where they bulged like handfuls of spare change. He gave Sifkitz a meaningful look as he did this, one that made Sifkitz angry all over again. By the time the work-crew came back through the odd, duct-like hole (dropping their heads as they did so, like men passing through a low doorway), Sifkitz's fists were clenched again, even though doing that made the wrist of the left one throb like hell.

"You know what?" he asked Berkowitz. "I don't think you can hurt me. I don't think you can hurt me, because then what happens to you? You're nothing but a . . . a subcontractor!"

Berkowitz looked at him levelly from beneath the bent bill of his LIPID cap.

"I made you up!" Sifkitz said, and counted them off, poking the index finger out of his right fist and pointing it at each one in turn like the barrel of a gun. "You're the Son of Sam! You're nothing but a grown-up version of this kid I played the horn with at Sisters of Mercy High! You couldn't play E-flat to save your life! And you're a commercial artist specializing in dragons and enchanted maidens!"

The remaining members of the Lipid Company were singularly unimpressed.

"What does that make you?" Berkowitz asked. "Did you ever think of that? Are you going to tell me there might not be a larger world out there someplace? For all you know, you're nothing but a random thought going through some unemployed Certified Public Accountant's head while he sits on the jakes, reading the paper and taking his morning dump."

Sifkitz opened his mouth to say that was ridiculous, but something in Berkowitz's eyes made him shut it again. There was a knowing look in those eyes. Go on, they said. Ask a question. I'll tell you more than you ever wanted to know.

What Sifkitz said instead was, "Who are you to tell me I can't get fit? Do you want me to die at fifty? Jesus Christ, what's wrong with you?"

Freddy said, "I ain't no philosopher, Mac. All I know is that my truck needs a tune-up I can't afford."

"And I've got one kid who needs orthopedic shoes and another one who needs speech therapy," Whelan added.

"The guys working on the Big Dig in Boston have got a saying," Berkowitz said. "'Don't kill the job, let it die on its own.' That's all we're asking, Sifkitz. Let us dip our beaks. Let us earn our living."

"This is crazy," Sifkitz muttered. "Totally—"

"I don't give a shit how you feel about it, you mother-fucker!" Freddy shouted, and Sifkitz realized the man was almost crying. This confrontation was as stressful for them as it was for him. Somehow realizing that was the worst shock of all. "I don't give a shit about you, you ain't nothing, you don't work, you just piddle around and make your little pitchers, but don't you take the bread out of my kids' mouths, you hear? Don't you do it!"

He started forward, hands rolling into fists and coming up in front of his face: an absurd John L. Sullivan boxing pose. Berkowitz put a hand on Freddy's arm and pulled him back.

"Don't be a hardass about it, man," Whelan said. "Live and let live, all right?"

"Let us dip our beaks," Berkowitz repeated, and of course Sifkitz recognized the phrase; he'd read *The God-father* and seen all the movies. Could any of these guys use a word or a slang phrase that wasn't in his own vocabulary? He doubted it. "Let us keep our dignity, man. You think we can go to work drawing pictures, like you?"

He laughed. "Yeah, right. If I draw a cat, I gotta write CAT underneath so people know what it is."

"You killed Carlos," Whelan said, and if there had been accusation in his voice, Sifkitz had an idea he might have been angry all over again. But all he heard was sorrow. "We told him, 'Hold on, man, it'll get better,' but he wasn't strong. He could never, you know, look ahead. He lost all his hope." Whelan paused, looked up at the dark sky. Not far off, Freddy's Dodge rumbled roughly. "He never had much to start with. Some people don't, you know."

Sifkitz turned to Berkowitz. "Let me get this straight. What you want—"

"Just don't kill the job," Berkowitz said. "That's all we want. Let the job die on its own."

Sifkitz thought about it and realized he could probably do as this man was asking. It might even be easy. Some people, if they ate one Krispy Kreme, they had to go on and finish the whole box. If he'd been that type of man, they would have a serious problem here . . . but he wasn't.

"Okay," he said. "Why don't we give it a try." And then an idea struck him. "Do you think I could have a company hat?" He pointed to the one Berkowitz was wearing.

Berkowitz gave a smile. It was brief, but more genuine than the laugh when he'd said he couldn't draw a cat without having to write the word under it. "That could be arranged."

Sifkitz had an idea Berkowitz would stick out his hand then, but Berkowitz didn't. He just gave Sifkitz a final measuring glance from beneath the bill of his cap and then started toward the cab of the truck. The other two followed.

"How long before I decide none of this happened?" Sifkitz asked. "That I took the stationary bike apart myself because I just . . . I don't know . . . just got tired of it?"

Berkowitz paused, hand on the doorhandle, and looked back. "How long do you want it to be?" he asked.

"I don't know," Sifkitz said. "Hey, it's beautiful out here, isn't it?"

"It always was," Berkowitz said. "We always kept it nice." There was an undertone of defensiveness in his voice that Sifkitz chose to ignore. It occurred to him that even a figment of one's imagination could have its pride.

For a few moments they stood there on the road, which Sifkitz had lately come to think of as The Great Trans-Canadian Lost Highway, a pretty grand name for a no-name dirt track through the woods, but also pretty nice. None of them said anything. Somewhere the owl hooted again.

"Indoors, outdoors, it's all the same to us," Berkowitz said. Then he opened the door and swung up behind the wheel.

"Take care of yourself," Freddy said.

"But not too much," Whelan added.

Sifkitz stood there while the truck made an artful three-point turn on the narrow road and started back the way it came. The duct-like opening was gone, but Sifkitz didn't worry about that. He didn't think he'd have any trouble getting back when the time came. Berkowitz made no effort to avoid the Raleigh but ran directly over it, finishing a job that was already finished. There were sproinks and goinks as the spokes in the wheels broke.

The taillights dwindled, then disappeared around a curve. Sifkitz could hear the thump of the motor for quite awhile, but that faded, too.

He sat down on the road, then laid down on his back, cradling his throbbing left wrist against his chest. There were no stars in the sky. He was very tired. Better not go to sleep, he advised himself, something's likely to come out of the woods—a bear, maybe—and eat you. Then he fell asleep anyway.

When he woke up, he was on the cement floor of the alcove. The dismantled pieces of the stationary bike, now screwless and boltless, lay all around him. The Brookstone alarm clock on the crate read 8:43 P.M. One of them had apparently turned off the alarm.

I took this thing apart myself, he thought. That's my story, and if I stick to it I'll believe it soon enough.

He climbed the stairs to the building's lobby and decided he was hungry. He thought maybe he'd go out to Dugan's and get a piece of apple pie. Apple pie wasn't the world's most unhealthy snack, was it? And when he got there, he decided to have it a la mode.

"What the hell," he told the waitress. "You only live once, don't you?"

"Well," she replied, "that's not what the Hindus say, but whatever floats your boat."

Two months later, Sifkitz got a package.

It was waiting for him in the lobby of his building when he got back from having dinner with his agent (Sifkitz had fish and steamed vegetables, but followed it with a crème brûlée). There was no postage on it, no Federal Express, Airbone Express, or UPS logo, no stamps. Just his name, printed in ragged block letters: RICHARD SIFKITZ. That's a man who'd have to print CAT underneath his drawing of one, he thought, and had no idea at all why he'd thought it. He took the box upstairs and used an Exacto knife from his worktable to slice it open. Inside, beneath a big wad of tissue paper, was a brand-new gimme cap, the kind with the plastic adjustable band in back. The tag inside read Made In Bangladesh. Printed above the bill in a dark red that made him think of arterial blood was one word: LIPID.

"What's that?" he asked the empty studio, turning the cap over and over in his hands. "Some kind of blood component, isn't it?"

He tried the hat on. At first it was too small, but when he adjusted the band at the back, the fit was perfect. He looked at it in his bedroom mirror and still didn't quite like it. He took it off, bent the bill into a curve, and tried it again. Now it was almost right. It would look better still when he got out of his going-to-lunch clothes and into a pair of paint-splattered jeans. He'd look like a real working stiff . . . which he was, in spite of what some people might think.

Wearing the LIPID cap while he painted eventually became a habit with him, like allowing himself seconds on days of the week that started with S, and having pie a la mode at Dugan's on Thursday nights. Despite whatever the Hindu philosophy might be, Richard Sifkitz believed you only went around once. That being the case, maybe you should allow yourself a little bit of everything.

ABOUT THE EDITORS

ELIZABETH E. MONTELEONE began her editing "career" with *Borderlands 2* by reading hundreds of unsolicited manuscripts, from which she found her share of stories to include. She did even more work for *Borderlands 3*, but like an idiot, she refused to allow her name on the title page as co-editor because she didn't want "people" to think she hadn't earned it. This changed with *Borderlands 4*, when she finally decided to take some credit, darn it.

THOMAS F. MONTELEONE is completely and totally and utterly in love with the abovementioned editor. He's also written some books and short stories and other stuff.

Together they make a quiet and unassuming couple. They live in New Hampshire with their daughter Olivia, who is, of course, very beautiful and exceedingly accomplished.

ABOUT THE CONTRIBUTORS

GARY A. BRAUNBECK is the author of several short story collections, among them *Things Left Behind; Graveyard People: The Collected Cedar Hill Stories, Vol. 1; Sorties, Cathexes, and Personal Effects; A Little Orange Book Of Odd Stories; From Beneath These Fields Of Blood;* and the science fiction collection *x3*. He lives in Columbus, Ohio and doesn't get invited to many parties, which everyone agrees is for the best.

DOMINICK CANCILLA'S work has appeared in dozens of magazines and anthologies, including *Cemetery Dance* magazine, *Robert Bloch's Psychos,* and *October Dreams.* His first novel, *Revenant Savior,* is available from Cemetery Dance Publications.

MICHAEL CANFIELD'S work also appears in *Mota3: Courage,* edited by Karen Joy Fowler. He's employed full-time in the Northwest, has many close friends and a number of acquaintances.

JOHN FARRIS sold his first novel the summer after he graduated from high school, in 1955. By 1959 he had his first million-seller, at age 23, with *Harrison High—*

which spawned four sequels. (Farris was writing about students planting bombs in high schools in 1962.) You could call him a suspense writer, a blacksmith of iron-clad thrillers. But that would overlook the magical aspect that informs the point of view in most of his work. You could call him a horror novelist, but that's just a launch footing for his mordant sociopolitical observations. He works labyrinthine intrigues better than nearly anyone writing, but to categorize him into a single genre would overlook the fundamental basis of his fiction— the complex characters that he tinkers together from the ground up, and his efforts to realize each book as an entity whole and apart from the preceding book. One-liner descriptives fall short for the simple reason that he is *sui generis.*

BRIAN FREEMAN'S short stories and novellas have appeared in over a dozen publications. He is the editor of *Dueling Minds,* a hardcover limited edition anthology to be published by Endeavor Press. After graduating from Shippensburg University in May 2002, Brian moved to Baltimore to work full-time at Cemetery Dance Publications. He can be found on the web at BrianFreeman.com

ADAM CORBIN FUSCO was an associate with a casting agency in Baltimore for more than ten years. He has worked on such films as *Serial Mom, Avalon, Cry-Baby, Pecker, He Said, She Said,* and the television series "Homicide: Life on the Street." His short fiction has appeared in *The Year's Best Fantasy and Horror: Seventh Annual Collection, Science Fiction Age, The Best of Cemetery Dance, Touch Wood: Narrow Houses 2,* and *Young Blood.*

BILL GAUTHIER started writing in 1990, when he was thirteen, inspired by the first few pages of Stephen King's novel *The Shining*. He made his first sale to a small press magazine in 1998 at twenty-one and has had four more tales published since in small press magazines, twice in Greg F. Gifune's *The Edge, Tales of Suspense,* and in webzines, including the speculative fiction webzine *Ideomancer.* He lives in New Bedford, Massachusetts, where he's a father, a ticket clerk at the local bus station, and a student. And, like every other writer out there, he's working on many projects. His current home on the web is http://www.geocities.com/gauthic2001.

DARREN O. GODFREY spends his weekdays making things go bang that should have gone bang on their own and his weekends and holidays making his head go bang against his writing desk until stories fall out. Darren's fallout has appeared in various anthologies (*Borderlands 2, The Midnighters Club, The Museum of Horrors,* and *Quietly Now: A Tribute to Charles L. Grant*), genre magazines (*Black October, Gorezone, The Scream Factory, Black Petals, Demontia,* and *Aberrations*) as well as a few offbeat publications (*The Art Times, The Goofus Office Gazette,* and *Cracked*). He and his two daughters divide their time between Idaho and California, depending upon their financial needs and the need for sanity.

BARRY HOFFMAN is the author of four dark suspense novels: *Hungry Eyes, Eyes, Eyes of Prey, Born Bad* and *Judas Eyes*. All but *Born Bad* are part of Hoffman's "Eyes" series. *Hungry Eyes* was nominated for both a HWA Stoker and International Horror Guild Award for Best First Novel. Hoffman was also nominated for the

2001 PEN/Newman's Own First Amendment Award, for his fight against censorship of *Born Bad*. He is editor/publisher of *Gauntlet* magazine, the only mass market magazine dealing with censorship and exploring the limits of free expression; and he is the publisher of Gauntlet Press through which he has published signed limited books by Ray Bradbury, Richard Matheson, Poppy Z. Brite, F. Paul Wilson and numerous others. *Gauntlet* won the 1999 HWA Award for Best Small Press and the Ben Franklin Award in 2002 for *Abu and the 7 Marvels*. Hoffman is using his recently-penned Young Adult dark fantasy novel *Curse of the Shamra* in public schools as part of an Authors In Residence Program. He has completed the 4th and 5th book in the "Eyes" series and is currently working on a sequel to his YA novel. He is the father of three who recently relocated to Colorado to spend time with his two-year-old granddaughter.

STEPHEN KING was born in Portland, Maine in 1947, the second son of Donald and Nellie Ruth Pillsbury King. He made his first professional short story sale in 1967 to Startling Mystery Stories. In the fall of 1973, he began teaching high school English classes at Hampden Academy, the public high school in Hampden, Maine. Writing in the evenings and on the weekends, he continued to produce short stories and to work on novels. In the spring of 1973, Doubleday & Co., accepted the novel *Carrie* for publication, providing him the means to leave teaching and write full-time. He has since published over 40 books and has become one of the world's most successful writers. The Board of Directors of the National Book Foundation recently awarded him the 2003 Medal for Distinguished Contribution to American Letters as one of the nation's most popular, imaginative, and well-loved authors. Stephen lives in Maine and Florida with his wife, novelist Tabitha King. They are regular contributors to a number of charities including many libraries and have been honored locally for their philanthropic activities.

BENTLEY LITTLE is a prolific writer who has penned over 11 horror novels, over 100 short stories and nearly 300 articles and essays. His novels include (but are not limited to) *The Mailman, The Store, The Ignored* and his most recent release, *The Association.* His short stories have appeared in such magazines as *Cemetery Dance, Eldritch Tales, The Horror Show, New Blood* and many more. They have also appeared in many anthologies such as *999, Bad News* and *Quick Chills* to name a few. He currently lives in Fullerton, California with his wife Wai Sau and their young son. He divides his time between Southern California and his "writing territory," Arizona.

BARBARA MALENKY, originally from Georgia, currently lives and writes in Texas. Her non-fiction has been published in national crime magazines and anthologies. Her fiction has appeared in over 300 publications, including a six-story chapbook entitled *Human Oddities.* She has received honorable mention for two years in The Year's Best Fantasy and Horror. She has recently completed her first novel and is an active member in the HWA.

JOHN MCILVEEN has a wife named Lisa. He has five daughters and a stepdaughter. He is grossly outnumbered. He purposely leaves the toilet seat up. John works at MIT's Lincoln Laboratory. He lives in Bradford, Massachusetts. He commutes Route 495 daily. John is very tense. John writes in his spare time. He has had more than twenty short stories and numerous poems (when depressed) and articles published, but he hasn't written a novel. John has little spare time.

JON F. MERZ is best known for his hard-boiled Lawson Vampire series from Pinnacle Books (*The Fixer, The Invoker, The Destructor,* and *The Syndicate*). Jon has written full-time for several years. He has written non-fiction articles, monthly columns, short fiction, and his advertising copy has been used by corporations like Polaroid and Red Lobster Restaurants. Jon has several other supernatural and mainstream thrillers coming out soon from major publishers. He operates his website at http://www.zrem.com. When not enjoying life with his wife and son in Boston, Massachusetts, Jon continues to study martial arts—something he has done for the past twenty years.

HOLLY NEWSTEIN is a relative newcomer to horror fiction. She co-authored the novel *Out of The Light* (Xlibris, 2000) with Ralph Bieber, and their short stories have appeared in the anthologies *The Witching Hour, Music Horror Stories Extremes 3: Terror On the High Seas* and the forthcoming *In Laymon's Terms.* She has also collaborated with Glenn Chadbourne on a story entitled "Deep Six," and has appeared solo in *The Best of Horrorfind, Volume 1* and *Twilight Showcase.* Holly lives in southern Maine with the author Rick Hautala. Visit her website at www.darkscribes.com.

GENE O'NEILL lives in the Napa Valley with his wife Kay, a substitute primary grade teacher at St. Helena Elementary School. They have been married for thirty-seven years, their grown children, Gavin and Kay Dee, living in Eugene, Oregon and San Diego. Gene has two degrees (Sac State, U. Of Minn) neither having anything to do with writing (or much of anything else). Gene describes his employment background as "rich, varied, colorful." His brother-in-law, the president of the above plant, describes Gene as more of a "disgruntled ne'er-do-well." After surviving the Clarion Workshop in writing in 1979 Gene has seen over 80 of his stories published. A number of these reprints are now being posted at Fictionwise.com with excellent sales and ratings. Several of his stories have garnered Nebula and Stoker recommendations. Some of these stories have been collected in *Ghosts, Spirits, Computers & World Machines,* released by Prime books in 2001. He has completed two novels, *The Burden of Indigo* and *Shadow of the Dark Angel* that will be published by Prime Books in 2002/2003 along with another collection, *The Grand Struggle* in 2004.

TOM PICCIRILLI is the author of eleven novels, including *The Night Class, A Choir of Ill Children, A Lower Deep, Hexes, The Deceased,* and *Grave Men.* He's published over 130 stories in the mystery, horror, erotica, and science fiction fields. Tom's been a final nominee for the World Fantasy Award and he's a three-time winner of the Bram Stoker Award, given in the categories of Novel, Short Story, and Poetry. Learn more about him at his official website www.mikeoliveri.com/piccirilli

JOHN R. PLATT has published fiction in anthologies like *Horrors: 365 Scary Stories, Crafty Cat Crimes, Bell Book & Beyond* and *100 Menacing Little Murder Stories.*

His first book, the short-story collection *Die Laughing,* was published in 2002. John served three terms as President of the Garden State Horror Writers.

WHITT POND was born in Lubbock, Texas, shortly after a famous UFO sighting, which explains a lot. He has at various times in his life been a Boy Scout, a West Point cadet, an MIT graduate, and a Peace Corps volunteer; and he currently resides in Massachusetts, two blocks from a really good Chinese restaurant. He likes to write horror because "It's easier than screaming all the time."

LON PRATER is an officer serving on active duty in the U.S. Navy. Along with his wife, Angie, and their two daughters, he has lived primarily in Hampton, Virginia, Pearl Harbor, Hawaii, and Athens, Georgia. He enjoys writing speculative fiction and edits the bi-monthly webzine *Neverary.* This story was initially written aboard the USS Nassau during a wartime deployment to the Persian Gulf. It is his first professional sale.

BRETT ALEXANDER SAVORY is a 29-year-old Bram Stoker Award-winning editor. His day job is also as an editor, at Harcourt Canada in Toronto. He is Editor-in-Chief of the *Chiaroscuro/ChiZine,* has had roughly 30 stories published in numerous print and online publications since 1998, and has written two novels, *In and Down* and *The Distance Travelled*—both of which are currently with his agent. In the works are a short-story collaboration with China Miéville, a dark comic-book series with artist Homeros Gilani, and an anthology to benefit the West Memphis Three, which will surface in the fall of 2004 through Arsenal Pulp Press.

WHITLEY STRIEBER is the author of over twenty books, among them *The Hunger, The Wolfen, The Last Vampire* and *Communion.* His website, www.unknowncountry.com is the largest website in the world offering daily news of the edge of science and current events.

DAVID J. SCHOW is a German-born American writer. At once inheritor of the Californian weird tradition of Richard Matheson and Dennis Etchison and leading light of splatterpunk movement, Schow's powerful, sometimes witty, sometimes strangely sentimental stories are collected in *Seeing Red* (1990), *Lost Angels* (1990), *Black Leather Required* (1994), *Crypt Orchids* (1997), *Eye* (2000) and *Zombie Jam Breaks Scissor Cut* (2003). He is author of the novels *The Kill Riff* (1987), *The Shaft* (1990), *Rock Breaks Scissors Cut* (2003) and *Bullets of Rain* (2003). In 2001 he won the International Horror Guild's award for Best Nonfiction for *Wild Hairs* (2000), his collection of essays from *Fangoria* magazine. As editor, he has assembled and annotated Silver Scream (1998), three volumes of *The Lost Bloch* (collecting the pulp novellas of Robert Bloch) and John Farris' *Elvisland* (2003). His screenplays include *The Crow* (1994) and he wrote the definitive book on the eponymous TV series, *The Outer Limits Companion* (hugely revised into an elbaorate second edition in 1998).

BEV VINCENT has been a contributing editor for *Cemetery Dance* magazine since 2001, where he writes News from the Dead Zone and the occasional book review and interview. His book *The Road to the Dark Tower,* the first critical overview of Stephen King's "Dark Tower" series,

will be published by NAL in November 2004. He is a
Ph.D. chemist who works for a high-tech instrumentation
company in a north Houston suburb. In addition to numerous book review appearances in a local newspaper,
he's had short stories in *Cemetery Dance, Shivers 2, All
Hallows* and a number of other magazines and anthologies. He's also a co-author of over thirty peer-reviewed
scientific articles, some containing words longer than this
bio. See his web site: ww.BevVincent.com. Bev lives
with his wife and teenage daughter. Since his daughter
learned to drive recently, he's been writing a lot more
horror.

L. LYNN YOUNG began publishing her work a scant three
years ago, and has since appeared in a wide variety of
small press magazines and anthologies, both print and
web. Look out for "Scarlet's Dolly," forthcoming in the
Wicked Little Girls anthology (Allegra Press), "Jesus,
Mary and Mr. Pyle" in *Scared Naked* magazine, and
"Womb Full of Poppies" in *NFG* magazine.

VISIT WARNER ASPECT ON-LINE!

THE WARNER ASPECT HOMEPAGE
You'll find us at: www.twbookmark.com, then by clicking on Science Fiction and Fantasy.

NEW AND UPCOMING TITLES
Each month we feature our new titles and reader favorites.

AUTHOR INFO
Author bios, bibliographies, and links to personal Web sites.

CONTESTS AND OTHER FUN STUFF
Advance galley giveaways, autographed copies, and more.

THE ASPECT BUZZ
What's new, hot and upcoming from Warner Aspect: awards news, bestsellers, movie tie-in information . . .